CRIMINAL

AGENDA

Words of Acclaim

…A fun and sometimes intense read. I enjoyed this book from page one through the dramatic conclusion. The narrative is tight, the plot compelling. Ms. Glawson's characters are well crafted and realistic. We feel we know them well by the end. I highly recommend this book ….

Ken Thruston, novelist and poet.

My goodness! An exciting new novelist. Welcome to the genre, Ms. Glawson! I found your plot compelling, your characters honest, and your observations of part of the human experience enlightening. I anxiously await your second novel in the series! Four and a half stars!

Karl Dresden, essayist and poet.

CRIMINAL

AGENDA

Book 1 in the
Hometown Wars Series

D.J. Glawson

Nevada Blue
Publishing

Smelterville, Idaho

This book is a work of fiction. Any resemblances to people, places, and/or events are purely coincidental and are used as such. Events and characters depicted are from the author's imagination.

Nevada Blue Publishing
P.O. Box 40
Smelterville, Idaho 83868

To the people who taught me the most. My mother – who was legally blind – and my maternal grandmother. They did their own sewing, canning, baking and home repairs. And showed me you can do anything, if you set your mind to it. I love and miss you both dearly.

Gladys Parker   1906-1973
Clara Taylor Sumpter   1882-1974

Acknowledgements

Thanks go out to everybody who has stood behind me and given me encouragement during this process. There are too many to name. But they include my new found friends at the Silver Valley Writers Group in Wallace, Idaho. My dear friends Sandy Rollins and Sue Kleeberg – who saw the first incarnation of this book. Sandy Hammer – who listened to me prattle about it every time I saw her. And to Ray (Grundy) Ferrell in Pioche, Nevada who showed me many years ago that even adults can have fun.

Special thanks go out to Lt. Robin Heiden and the Salt Lake City Police Departments Public Relations Office for taking the time to answer my questions, and to the Salt Lake City Police Department itself for being the inspiration for some of the characters. Thank you to the great people of Salt Lake City for accepting me thirty some odd years ago. You will always be a special place to me.

1

A lamp threw abstract shadows across the walls. Music blared in the background. Two boys melted something in a spoon then drew it into a syringe injecting it in their arms. Their sighs scared him. He didn't like these boys. Then they laughed, one of them pulling a girl over to him, punching her when she cried. The second boy staggered to a twin bed where a woman was tied and laid down behind her. He looked away from them and noticed the blood where they had beat the girl and the woman. It was dry now, black in the harsh lighting. Empty beer cans and the syringe littered the floor nearby.

Suddenly doors slammed open, men yelled and footsteps pounded toward them. The door to his room flew open and a man in uniform stood bellowing at the boys, his arms locked, a pistol pointing first at one kid then the other. Fear was etched on the boys' faces, their hands raised. One boy dropped a hand to cover himself and the uniform yelled again. The boy jerked his hand up and another uniform joined the first then they started barking orders. The kids complied, allowing themselves to be cuffed. More footsteps and more uniforms rushed into the room, and then

*someone pointed to where he hid. The lid to the toy box flew up
and he screamed.*

James eyes sprang open and he was sitting upright in bed,
pulling huge gasps of air into his lungs, his heart pounding in his
chest, his body drenched in sweat. Then he collapsed back onto
the bed. Would the nightmares ever stop?

He looked at the clock, four p.m. It would be useless trying to
go back to sleep now. James dragged himself out of bed and
started the coffee before he climbed into the shower. Under the
soft spray, he closed his eyes and leaned against the tile, cold and
jarring against his back, his mind replaying that night. His mother
and sister had survived their ordeal, but they had never been the
same. The loop repeated itself and he thought about the trial and
the made up lies afterward, and the way his father had stood
beside his wife and daughter. And the way the cops had stood
behind them, unwavering in their support for the family. The cops
had caught the bad guys in real life, why wasn't it that easy now?

Nine p.m. and James met William at Sambo's on State Street.
Their routine when working graveyard. Either Sambo's or Dee's
on North Temple. A good meal and friendly conversation before
they hit the streets. The quiet before the storm some nights.

A quick scan of the counter and surrounding tables, and he
recognized the usual midday crew trickling in, heading home after
a long day, coffee propping the eyelids open, cigarettes gripped
firmly in their lips. A few men greeted them with a friendly wave
then returned to their conversations.

"Another nightmare?" William asked once they'd ordered.

"You read me too well," James answered. "I can't seem to
shake 'em."

"It'll take time," William replied. "But you'll make it. I still
have mine."

Five and a half hours into their shift they got the call. A couple
had stumbled upon the body of a young girl next to the boat ramp

at the pond in Liberty Park.

James took the information while William flipped on the lights and hit the siren. It had been a long and eventful night already. Payday and the bars were overcrowded, people getting out after a long winter, testosterone and female hormones kicking the alcohol fueled buzz through the roof.

After breaking up innumerable fights, James would be sporting a nice bruise on his shoulder where a woman smacked him with her purse, after he'd pulled her fiancée off of her, and William had a cut on his jaw because a drunk decided tonight was the night he didn't like black guys. They were tired and wanted to go home and relax, but that wasn't going to happen. They didn't get off until seven a.m. By the time they responded to this call, waited for the detectives and the tech crews to finish, they would be pushing the limits of time constraints to complete their reports.

They pulled up and checked the clock on the dash, noting the time. A crowd had gathered by the ramp and a couple pulled away from the knot as they approached, meeting the men half way, explaining what they had found.

'Seventeen going on thirty,' James thought as he looked down at the girl. She was naked except for a tiny pair of underwear tied around her ankles. Her arms were bound in front of her; the expression on her face was peace. As if she'd been asleep during the entire ordeal.

They moved the crowd of spectators back, William peeling away to make the call for detectives, then they set the perimeter so the detectives could work the scene. William chuckled to himself, recognizing a few of the gawkers as earlier partygoers, stumbling their way home, too drunk to drive.

They recognized the lieutenant walking toward them twenty minutes later, rubbing his eyes with his thumb and middle finger, the tech crew just beginning their investigation behind him.

"Lieutenant," William said.

"Officer's," the lieutenant said. "Did anyone tell you anything before the detectives arrived?"

"We talked to the couple who found her," James answered, pointing out a couple on the periphery. "They were doing their normal morning walk when they detoured around the pond. The man said Liberty Park is their usual route, but they were walking earlier today. When they first saw her they thought she was a drunk who'd passed out."

"What time was that?" Lieutenant Ohlmet asked.

"Approximately four-thirty. The woman went home and called the police while her husband waited. We received the call at four thirty-five and arrived at four thirty-eight."

"Have either of you seen her before? Outside any of the known locations on State Street or across from the Salt Palace?"

"No, sir," William answered. "We've seen several girls who looked young, but they all had ID."

"We can start calling in more of the suspicious ones," James said.

"Nope. You're fine," the lieutenant said. "Hold tight."

The lieutenant walked away, William was suddenly aware of James' expression in the strobes of the blues and reds. Pain, discomfort. The same expression James had wore the night he accompanied the chief and Captain Jakes about his wife.

"You okay, James?"

"Yeah, it just seems like such a waste."

William glanced behind them at Lloyd Farmer, the tech directing the crime scene. Like William, Lloyd was a transplant from Louisiana, with skin the color of a chestnut. Lloyd had told him once he wanted something better for his family than losing everything every year to the vagaries of nature. Hurricanes and tornadoes bothered him. William now thought about the chances of Lloyd giving them the dirt on the sly. They weren't detectives, but he and James had questions.

"I want to talk to Lloyd. I'm curious aren't you, partner?"

"Of course."

"Yo, Lloyd," William called. "Got a minute?"

"For you, any time," Lloyd answered.

Lloyd laughed as they approached, understanding why the team graced every recruiting poster and flyer printed. James was six feet, white with coal black hair and vibrant green eyes, William stood six-two was black, but they both had the over top looks and build women went for. They would have made it big in Hollywood.

"How'd you two luck out on this call?"

"Just the way it bounced," William said. "Any ideas? Was she drugged?"

"Why don't you two apply for a detectives spot? You ask too damn many questions."

"I don't think I want to sit behind a desk," William answered.

"You know I can't answer that yet. We just got started, bro."

"I'm not asking if you know for sure. Just what it looks like? You know, kind of a basic idea. We didn't see anything that looked like she'd been choked, and there's no blood. Was she drugged? We're curious."

"It looks that way. I don't think she was killed here, she was dumped. You're right there's nothing indicating strangulation. No entrance or exit wounds, either. No marks at all. I haven't found any track marks or signs that she snorted. There's nothing under a fingernail like she was using one for a spoon. Markings around the eye show signs of asphyxiation which don't jive with the fact that there are no marks on her neck. Is that what you want to know?"

"That's what I wanted to know."

"You still need to put in for a detective slot."

William shrugged. "One more question. How many does this make?"

"This is the first one in two years. There were three or four before."

"So you think this might be the same dude?"

"Maybe."

"Thanks, I'll remember you if I ever go to Vegas and win a jackpot."

"You're blowin' smoke now bro. You'll remember my black ass as quickly as I'll remember yours."

"Hey, Lloyd….."

"I won't remember your white ass, either, Officer Thompson."

"…..you might want to rethink that." James continued as if he hadn't been interrupted, pulling his wallet out and waving a stack of bills. "I went to Wendover and the God's were smiling on me, buddy."

"That ain't right, man!" Lloyd said, his voice taking on the tone of a fake whine. "I never win anything over there!"

William gaped for a second, surprised. "You didn't tell me you won anything," William said. "Maybe I should go with you next time. Do you have to declare that on your taxes?"

"Don't know," James said. "I put a copy of the slip in my safe deposit box, just in case my apartment burns. I figure it can't hurt."

"Officer Harrison, Officer Thompson," someone called.

A glance behind them and Captain Jakes was striding their way. Like the lieutenant he'd worked his way up through the rank and file. A smart, intuitive officer.

"Can you two break away and take a call on Fifth South and Fifth East?"

They turned their portables up; catching the tail end of the call out, James glanced at William.

"Your choice," the captain said. "We have plenty of uniforms here so I'll cut you loose."

"Yes, sir," James answered.

James cleared them from the scene and put them on the new call.

It took less than five minutes to arrive at an apartment complex consisting of two two-story brick buildings and an office. Cliff Roses anchored the buildings corners and Boxwoods, Cactus and Junipers were lined up under the windows, designed to discourage an intruder. Parking near the entrance, they recognized the security panel. Retrofit, but not cheap. They were concerned about their tenants' safety, yet someone had attempted to break in.

James pushed the button for the apartment identifying them as officers' and was buzzed in. They walked the length of the hall checking for any secondary exit that would allow a person easy access, locating one at the far end that opened onto dumpsters. A door opened behind them and a woman waved them down.

As they entered, William's eyes ran along the edge of the frame, checking for signs of forced entry. Inside the apartment, the first thing William noticed was the fit of the blue jeans, and the way her brunette hair swung across her back then he forced his mind back to the reason they were here.

The interior was small and compact with French doors on the far wall. A short hall ran straight ahead, the living room opened off the foyer to the left, a sofa occupying that wall. A chair was positioned with its back to the entry. Both looked worn, but still in decent shape. Across the room next to the French doors was a small console with a television, a stereo occupied the wall to their right. The floors were wood, showing the wear from years of use. A door led into the kitchen on the opposite side of the living area. Nestled in the corner was a battered two drawer file cabinet. Cozy, but convenient.

"Ma'am," William said. "We received a call about a break in."

"He was at the French doors," she said. "That's the down side to a ground floor apartment I guess."

She stepped back and pointed across the room, her eyes locked on William's. Caramel colored eyes that pierced to her soul. Eyes that complemented his skin tone perfectly. The eyes had caught her off guard.

William checked the French doors, then detoured through the kitchen on his way back. It was small, but had all the necessities. Appliances, table and chairs and an antique china cabinet, and another door which led outside to the dumpsters as well. Three means of escape if anyone had gotten in.

James took her statement while William called for a print crew, William's mind drifting. Even in blue jeans and a crop top she was perfect. He had never seen eyes as blue as hers, they hypnotized. He dropped his gaze, locking in on the smooth skin and firm muscles. The buzzer sounded and she trotted to the door to allow the print crew in, then she diverted up the hall. There was a light tap on his shoulder and James was grinning at him.

"We're on a call, buddy," James whispered. "But I agree, that is one hot chic!"

"Damn! Did you see those blue jea…eyes?" William said. He chuckled, realizing how lame that sounded.

"Here she comes," James said, his voice barely above a whisper. "Hold it together a few more minutes, buddy."

She handed James her ID and glanced at the floor. "I don't own a car so I don't have a driver's license. I don't usually call the cops for anything, either. I mean, it's usually pretty quiet around here. Um…I'm rambling, right?"

"You're fine," William said. He smiled, the sprinkling of freckles across her cheeks more pronounced when she dipped her head. "Cops can be intimidating if you're not used to talking to us. How long have you been in Salt Lake?"

"Three years," Amanda answered, twiddling her thumbs. She

looked away again not wanting to get caught up in the eyes.

James handed her a business card when he gave her back her ID and instructed her to call if she remembered anything further.

Once the print crew had finished, they drove to the station, James laughing in the passenger seat.

"I have never – been so nervous – on a call – in my years – on the force," James finally said, separating the words into groups.

William chuckled. "See something you like?"

"Yeah, buddy. Yowza! I could handle a night or two with her. I have never seen a woman that looked like that! Her name's Amanda Granger, and she wasn't wearing any rings."

"Are you going somewhere with this?"

"Yeah, I saw the way you looked at her. Did you finally find someone you could ask out? I've only seen you date a couple of women since your wife died."

"Maybe," William said, smiling broadly. "She was nice."

An hour and a half later they had finished their reports and were walking out the door. William checked the clock as they left. Seven-fifteen.

James pulled out of the parking lot and William's thoughts drifted back to the lady on the last call. He could handle a night or two with her himself.

William drove south from the station, taking a left off State Street onto Fifth South. At her complex, he did a slow drive through, checking the newly fallen skiff of snow for footprints, finding no indication anyone had been there. *'Just in case her intruder was hiding in the bushes.'* Then he laughed and hoped no one called the station about a stalker.

He caught movement out of the side window and Amanda trotted toward the street almost doing the splits on a sheet of ice.

"Yeah, I could handle a night or two with her," he said out loud.

2

Amanda stepped out to a fresh dusting of snow and frowned. The weather man said it had been an unusually warm spring. Then she shrugged. The snow would be melted by noon. As she walked briskly toward the street the crisp morning air took her breath away and she pulled her coat tighter about her. 'Cold as a witch's tit,' she thought then remembered her mother used to say that. Who started that? Who knew a witch had cold tits? Slipping on a thin sheet of ice hidden under the fresh layer of white she decided mornings like this it would be nice to own a car. Metal crunching and horns blaring while people cursed in the distance reminded her why she didn't own a car.

Seven forty-five and she hurried past the bus shelter and up the last half a block on Main Street, hearing the 'slub' of her Moon Boots echoing off the buildings. A bus pulled in behind her and she jerked to look over her shoulder, surprised at her sudden paranoia.

Amanda rushed through the doors at Berringer & Hardy and greeted the receptionist then stepped onto the elevator, relishing the warmth. The doors slid shut and she was enveloped by the smell of fresh paint, new carpet, and cinnamon rolls. Someone had brought homemade cinnamon rolls!

As the elevator crept up visions of stacks and stacks of files popped to mind, the cube in complete disarray. The doors whooshed open and the girls' friendly banter filtered down the hall. She moved into the work space, their ugly laminate counter tops were gone, replaced with faux wood cubes and mahogany desks. They were still cubes, but they were classier cubes. Gone were the previous iron clad rows of submarine gray. Rerouting to the break room, Amanda's co-workers already there.

"So what do you think?" Janice asked when Amanda joined them.

Just under six foot Janice had the broad shoulders and well-endowed fullness possessed by a lot of black women, and Amanda marveled at the aura of sexuality they projected while white women who wore larger than a size three cloaked themselves in tunics and whined about being fat. We really needed lessons in self-esteem from the black women of the world.

"A lot more than carpet has been changed," Amanda said.

A cup of coffee and a few minutes of chatter, and they filtered to the cubes. Amanda located hers next to one of the bay windows overlooking a fountain on Main Street. Not finding the expected stacks of files, she opened a drawer everything having been replaced in perfect order, and remembered her father's reference to 'an anal attention to detail'. She sank into the plush leather of the chair and brought her computer up to prepare for the day. While she waited for the computer to boot, she took the wieldy Moon Boots off and replaced them with her heels, discovering the notice offering anybody interested the opportunity to work overtime.

Keying in her password, Amanda took a few minutes to arrange her cube as one of the file clerks made her usual rounds.

Amanda gave the girl her reply and was handed an eight inch thick stack of brand new manila folders.

"First installment," the girl said with a laugh. "I'm glad it's you and not me."

Amanda smiled and did a sideways nod.

That night Amanda changed back into her boots and stepped outside to a wind, biting and strong, and people scurrying along the sidewalk. She pulled her coat tighter about her shoulders, her eyes drawn to the flicker of a street light as it flooded the stream of pedestrians below. No one appeared threatening. At the corner, one procession stopped when it reached the confluence of the concrete streams and the intersecting flow took over. It was the same every night, except tonight it was dark so they were red and white streams flowing in opposing directions.

The tributaries of humanity switched directions and began moving again as she rounded the corner onto Fifth South going east. A limo, driving east on Fifth South, caught her attention, the rear window rolling down while the passenger stared back at her. It drove down the block and took a left on State Street. When she reached the intersection, she pushed the button twice and waited for the signal to change. A furtive glance in both directions and she admitted it would be too dark to see the limo, then she jabbed the button again. This stupid light needed to change!

"Good evening," someone said beside her.

Startled, she looked over to see a man gazing down at her.

"The name's George," he said. He offered her his hand then pushed the button himself. "George Bonner. It looks like you're in a hurry. Do you mind if I walk with you? I never thought it was safe for women to walk home alone after dark."

"Thank you," she said. She sized him up in the light from the streetlights and shook the proffered hand. He was the man from the limo. Not bad looking, brown hair and eyes, and the t-shirt under the open jacket showed enough to hint at a well-muscled body hidden beneath. "I appreciate the concern, but I'll be fine."

"How about if I keep pace with you then? I would hate to see something happen to someone as beautiful as you. I'm going to the end of the block anyway."

"If you're already going that way, I guess it won't hurt."

"And your name?"

"Sorry. Amanda. I don't remember seeing you here before. Are you new to the area?"

"No. I'm usually at work by seven, but I made an exception tonight."

Amanda stared at the ground, confused. Offices in downtown were usually closed this time of night.

"I would offer you a ride, but you look nervous."

"It has to do with that walking alone after dark thing. I try to be careful."

They walked the block in silence then shook hands at the end of the block.

"Thank you for accompanying me."

"Forgive me if I sound forward," George said, "but would you like to stop for a cup of coffee? Warm up a bit."

"No, thank you," she answered.

"Are you sure? I would be more than happy to give you lift."

"I'm sure. Thank you." Would this guy just go away?

She crossed Second East and continued east, then glanced over her shoulder, George walking north on Second East, melting into the shadows of the trees surrounding the City County Building. Two minutes later a limo turned left off Second East onto Fifth South. The car hop scotched up the street, parking until she crossed an intersection then it drove part way down the next block and did a repeat. She picked up her pace, that unintended paranoia creeping in.

At her apartment complex she turned into the office to pay her rent. The secretary waved and signaled for her to wait while she completed her call. Amanda looked outside as the limo slowed and pulled in one building over. Her mind flashed to the piece on the news about the girl who had been found at Liberty Park then the newly introduced George Bonner stepped out. Was he casing the place, discovering its weaknesses? The piece about the victim in Liberty Park flashed across her mind again. She subsequently admonished herself for watching too much TV.

George walked toward the office and locked eyes with hers before he detoured and approached the entrance to the building next door, studying the security panel. As he glanced down the front of the building he pushed a button then stared down the hall, cupping his hands on either side of his face, his forehead pressed against the glass, turning his head, first to the left and then to the right. The secretary said something and Amanda smiled and took her receipt then glanced back outside. Another tenant passed the office and she used him for cover as she dodged out the side door.

"Looking for someone?" the tenant asked.

"Yes," George said. "I guess I missed her. She didn't answer."

Curious, and feeling a twinge of panic, Amanda jogged behind the building to hers then sprinted down the hall. Safely inside her apartment, she dropped her purse on the kitchen counter then peered around the curtains on the French doors.

George had moved away from the building and was standing with his back to her still studying the other building. Amanda followed him with her eyes as he walked back to the limo, looking inside the office once more before climbing into the car. A cop car did a slow drive through as the limo pulled out, then parked in front of the neighboring building. The officers stepped out, one surveying the parking area, his gaze following the limo while the second officer pushed the buzzer. They took a step back and surveyed the front of both buildings while they waited. Once the tenant admitted them, Amanda turned her lights on and removed her boots, tossing them on the floor of the closet and her coat over the chair.

She flinched when the buzzer sounded. The officers identified themselves and Amanda allowed them in.

"Good evening," James said. "Sorry to bother you, but could we ask you couple of questions?"

"Not at all," she replied. "Aren't you the ones who were here last night?"

William walked to the French doors and pulled the curtains to the side then scanned the parking lot and returned.

"Yes, ma'am," William answered. "We received a call about a strange vehicle in the parking lot. Your neighbors said there was a limo parked over here." He pointed outside.

"There was."

"Have you seen it before?" James asked.

"Just tonight," she answered. "I saw it first at Main Street and Fifth South. It turned left off Fifth South onto State Street then ended up here."

"And that's the only time you've seen it?"

She nodded, her mind a blank slate. The black dude's eyes did it every time.

William thanked her and they started toward the door, then she remembered George. The man made her nervous so she had dismissed him like so much useless baggage.

"I got a question." Both men stopped and she debated saying anything, but pressed on. "A guy named George Bonner offered me a ride home tonight, but I turned him down. Do you know him? I mean, is he a nice guy?"

"I would keep as far away from him as possible," William said. "We've heard a few things here and there."

"Do you work nights?" James asked. "Walking alone after

dark isn't the safest thing."

"Not usually. I'm just working some overtime now. I work at Berringer & Hardy on Main Street so it's a short seven block jaunt. Usually. It's an accounting firm downtown. Of course, I don't see limos and have strange men try to pick me up…." She stopped, taking a deep breath to calm herself. She was babbling again. "Sorry."

"You have one of our cards. If you need anything, call."

3

Amanda went to bed, her thoughts revolving around George and what the officers had told her. She hadn't been comfortable talking to George so they had verified those feelings.

Someone riding the wall in the hallway before falling into her door woke Amanda then the knob rattled. She climbed out of bed and frowned and looked at the clock. How hard could it be to get some sleep? She peeked through the peephole and thought about opening the door then changed her mind. It had probably been one of the neighbors sliding their way home. One of them had been caught climbing the stairs on all fours one night. She padded back to her room and stopped, debating locking her bedroom door. The outer door was locked. It should be fine.

Something woke her again and she looked at the clock. Three a.m. A faint click and her heart jumped, someone was in her room. She should have locked that door. A slow deep, breath to calm herself, and Amanda waited impatiently for her eyes to adjust to the dim lighting, the odors of greasepaint and alcohol assailing her nostrils. As she reached for the lamp there was the whoosh of air when something flew past her. She cringed and jerked her arm back, opening her eyes to a shadowy figure and moonlight glinting off the edge of a knife, buried in the mattress only inches from her face.

"Very slowly," he instructed her. "This way. Hands out."

A light pressure on the inside of her thigh and Amanda complied, holding her hands away from her body as she slid off the bed and onto her knees on the floor. The darkened outline of a pistol appeared to her right then there was the quick flash of light as he freed the knife from the mattress. Pinned between the man and the bed, she watched helplessly as the distance between the knife and her throat diminished rapidly. She flinched when the cold steel pricked the underside of her jaw; then she heard the deep, throaty laugh. She recognized that voice from somewhere.

"A woman," he said his breath hot and sticky on the back of her neck. "A nice one at that."

Amanda nodded not sure why.

He laid the gun on the floor then began a slow, methodical search for weapons. As he ran his hand down her side, his fingers slid across her breast, gently teasing as they moved, continuing down her back and over her buttocks. She gasped when he moved his hand forward, the fingers massaging the inside of her thigh, beginning an ascent up and over her abdomen. As he explored her body with one hand, he urged her tighter against him, the knife clutched under her jaw with the other. His hand moved back up her side his thumb caressing her breast once more.

"What's the matter?" he asked. "They've instructed you in the decadent behavior of us Americans, haven't they? You've been told how cruel and sadistic we are."

She nodded and averted her eyes attempting to find something to defend herself with.

"There's nothing out there, honey," he said as if reading her mind. "And judging from your reaction, we're the only ones here. You and me, we're going to have a lot of fun, aren't we?"

She nodded again and stifled a sob. She dropped her eyes to the floor and saw moonlight reflecting off metal.

"You won't get away that easily," he said, the warning clear. "It's just you and me."

He slid his hand under her nightshirt and lifted it allowing her breasts to fall free. As he probed their fullness, he moved his hand onto her abdomen rubbing his body against hers.

"I am going to enjoy this a whole lot more than I thought I would. This will be for all the G.I's your kind have mutilated."

This time she could hear the urgency in his voice and tried unsuccessfully to wriggle free as a sob escaped her throat.

"Not yet. I have a present for you." He slid his fingers under the top of her panties as he held her body against his. "Take them off. Just one hand."

Her mind raced back to the pistol while she slid them down. Leaning to the right, she planted her hand palm down on the floor to balance herself, and groped for the gun.

"The rest of the way," he ordered.

She nodded again and slipped the garments over her knees.

"You're going to be real nice, aren't you?" He dropped the point of the knife and grabbed her throat with his left hand then began to unfasten his clothes.

His grip loosened and Amanda pushed herself backwards and lunged to the right, knocking him off balance. Then she grabbed the pistol and scrambled around the end of the bed. There was movement behind her and the man had dove across the bed after her. With the gun grasped firmly in both hands she swung it in a wide arc, striking him on the side of the head and continued her crawl for the door and the freedom beyond.

He hesitated, momentarily stunned, but quickly regained his equilibrium.

There was the rush of air and she looked over her shoulder, the knife beginning a downward trajectory toward her. Chances of her making it to the door didn't look good. She raised her hands in front of her and rolled onto her back, using the gun to block the intended strike. There was the clang of metal on metal when the weapons met and her arms buckled from the force of the blow. The edge of the knife slid off the pistol, slicing into the flesh on her left shoulder. She bit her lip to avoid screaming and kicked him in the crotch. He emitted an explosion of air as Amanda leaped through the door.

She raced for the living room when her body went airborne and she slammed to the floor, the air ejected from her lungs then she slid across the worn wood. There was a stab of pain and the candy dish clattered when her body collided with the stereo cabinet. Dazed, Amanda lay in a heap on the floor, gulping for air, engulfed in a thick veil of pain. She continued to gasp for breath, straining to find her assailant in the darkness. She rolled to her right still clutching the pistol tightly to her chest then he kicked her. Amanda moaned from the blow, he kneeled beside her and rolled her over, lifting her nightshirt. One more painful inhalation and she flipped onto her back, planting her feet in his chest and pushing him away.

There was a slap when his hand struck the floor, stopping him from going over backwards. Amanda aimed the gun at his chest and took another deep, painful breath then flipped the safety off. She remembered the metallic click earlier. There was a round in the chamber. His shadow froze where he crouched, motionless; his hands raised, fingers splayed. She kept the gun leveled at his chest as she scooted backwards toward the kitchen and the phone.

"I suggest you don't move," she told him. "I learned how to use one of these before you learned how to use what's in your pants."

He kept his hands up and out then rocked up on his toes, his eyes glued to the muzzle of the gun.

Amanda continued scooting backwards, eyeing him cautiously until she pulled herself up to reach the phone. She dialed 9-1-1 then the door opened, crashing into the wall. The operator came on the line and Amanda gave her the requested information and was told officers and paramedics were on their way.

Wetting a paper towel Amanda folded it over the cut and started toward the bedroom. This was going to make a nice scar. At least tomorrow was Saturday. Stooping to pick up the gun, she stopped and surveyed the scene. Blood on the floor, a hole in the wall from the door handle striking it and another on the wall from the stereo cabinet. She hid the pistol behind one of the stereo speakers and continued to the bedroom, picking up her panties, the buzzer sounding and she darted for the button to allow them in, then the room began to spin.

A female paramedic was bandaging her shoulder when she opened her eyes. They had covered her and she raised the hand, holding her panties.

"How you doing?" the woman asked.

"Fine," she answered. "Can I get some clothes?"

"I grabbed the ones on the bedroom floor for you," she answered, patting the end of the gurney. "If you get up now all these nice gentlemen will get a peepshow."

Men laughed and Amanda noticed several officers standing off to the side. One of them was on his portable; two others said they would meet her at the hospital. The next thing she remembered was the inside of the ambulance and being jostled into emergency room and an exam area. Then a patrolman was shown in by a nurse.

"How are you?" James asked. "Officer Harrison will join us in a couple of minutes. If you feel up to it we'd like to ask you a few questions. If not, we can come back."

She shook her head. Every breath was agony and she hoped

this was another bad dream. She squeezed them shut for a second, opened them, still in the exam room, heavy curtains draped between her and the bed next to hers. Not a bad dream.

"Do you know the person who did this?"

She shook her head again.

"Did you leave your door unlocked?"

"No. The door was locked," she said. She pulled in another painful breath then exhaled slowly. "I'm sorry. I moved to Salt Lake City after a really screwed up marriage to get away from my ex-husband." Now she wondered why she had volunteered that.

"I understand," he said. "The nurse told us a gentleman called and asked if you were alright, but you just said you're divorced, correct?"

"Correct," Amanda answered.

She held her finger up to ask for a minute while she composed her thoughts. She wanted to remember every detail. Not because she wanted the memory, but because she wanted to tell the police as much as she could and be as accurate as possible.

"Did he say anything?" James asked. "Did he act like he knew you?"

"He talked like I was a Viet Cong whore out to mutilate an American GI. He asked if I'd heard about the decadent behavior of Americans. My ex told me stories about that."

"Is there anything else you can tell us? I hate to put you though this, but we need as many details as you can give us."

"Not really." She stopped and attempted to catch her breath again. "I'm sorry."

"You're fine."

The curtain moved then William joined them.

"Ma'am," William said. "From what the doctor's said you took quite the hit. I know my partner has probably gone over this, but can you tell us anything? Sometimes more is brought to light the second time through."

"We hadn't got that far," she said. She hesitated a minute, as she struggled to breath once more. "I woke up when I heard someone using the wall in the hallway to keep themselves upright and then they rattled my doorknob. I looked through the peephole, but didn't see anyone. After a few minutes of nothing, I went back to bed."

"You didn't let the man in?"

"No," Amanda said, laying her head back. "I thought he left. I woke up when I heard a click and the next thing I know a battle knife was in the mattress next to my head. I have no idea who the man was, I don't care who the man was, and I have no idea how he got in."

"You're sure you've never met him?" William asked noting her use of the term 'battle knife'.

"Well, I didn't actually get a good look at him. It was dark so I guess I could be mistaken, but what difference does that make?"

"It's alright," William said. "We understand. We just have to ask these questions."

"Did you strike him?" James asked. "There might be scratches we could use to help identify him."

"I hit him on the side of the head. He might have a bruise. It was on the left side. I think."

"Do you know where your ex-husband is?" James asked.

"As far as I know he's still in Chicago. I haven't seen him in three years. I remember he used to have nightmares. He said it was from *Delayed Stress Syndrome*."

"You said he had the same type of nightmares?" William asked.

"Yes. Well, no. Not exactly. Once he was screaming, telling someone not to do it. When I talked to him, he said he was trying to keep some guy from jumping out of a helicopter. The guy had lost both his legs to a landmine."

William and James asked a few more questions, using different words and in different ways, listening for any variance, but nothing changed. When they left, William gave her another card, telling her to call them at the non-emergency number if she remembered anything.

"Twice in three days," William said as they climbed into the black and white. "Not good odds."

4

Saturday morning Amanda's confusion threatened to settle in, to entangle her. She had moved to Salt Lake City to straighten her life out, but it was going nowhere fast. This apartment was the perfect example of that. It was only supposed to have been temporary. Yeah, three years worth of temporary, and she hadn't heard anything on the demo tapes she dropped off. She needed to pass more out, start working it, get her name out there, management changed frequently in these clubs. She started a pot of coffee then walked to the bathroom and a welcome shower.

There was the sizzle of her cigarette as it met its demise in the toilet then she turned on the water, climbing gratefully under its warm spray. She succumbed to the massage of the water against her skin and closed her eyes then she heard the click in the darkened room, felt his breath on her neck, saw the knife blade in the mattress, felt his hands – a stranger's hands – exploring her body. She choked back a tear and slammed the shower curtain open, stepping onto the cold tile, anger threatening to overcome her. It was time to go get out of here. She needed more cigarettes anyway.

On the way to her bedroom Amanda dropped the towel and eyed her reflection in the mirror. She was still in pretty good shape. Tall, slender and uniformly proportioned, she was pleased with her attributes. Her brunette hair hung to her waist and she only applied a minimal amount of make-up, preferring the sprinkling of freckles to the layers of pancake make-up she had seen other women so painstakingly apply. A quick twist to look at the tush, it was still firm and the boobs didn't sag. The eyes were sultrier than some. When she wasn't angry or scowling. Mother Nature had been kind to her.

A last inspection and she acknowledged it probably wouldn't hurt to start running again, but she hated running circles around the park. And running on the sidewalks had proven even more problematic. Invariably she tried to run over some unsuspecting pedestrian.

Throwing on an old pair of jeans and a sweater she headed for the kitchen and the coffee she was craving, her eyes falling on the tiny filing cabinet sitting forlornly in the corner. She took a hesitant step forward, allowing her fingers to caress the cold steel, sliding across its smooth surface, coming to rest on the handle. Those were her dreams, her desires. Everything from Billie Holiday and Ella Fitzgerald to the more modern tunes. Half her adult life had been spent lovingly tucking each sheet into its protective plastic sleeve. She jerked her hand away and reminded herself she was being selfish to dream about singing. Her anger bubbled again and she fought back the tears. Other people did what they enjoyed. Why should she be different?

"Dreams are fine," her mother had told her once, "but they don't pay the rent."

Right. He just couldn't handle having a kid so he buried his head in drugs instead. Where did people come up with this crap?

Amanda poured a cup of coffee then went back to the living room, looking down at the lonely file cabinet as she passed. She dropped wearily onto the sofa picking up the remote and unconsciously motioning around the room with it. All of this for the small price of her dreams.

"I feel like one of those characters in a 'Grade B' horror movie!" she spat, thankful no one was there to hear her.

She finished her coffee and snatched up her purse, as she shrugged on her coat and started out the door. Outside the trees stood barren and lifeless, the buds on the braver species just beginning to peek out. Another beautiful spring morning in Salt Lake City, Utah. She hunched her shoulders against the wind, her mind racing back to the dusty old file cabinet and its precious contents.

Afternoon found her comfortably ensconced in the armchair with a fresh cup of coffee, scanning the newspaper. Two ads caught her attention. One read:

Singer Wanted. Country and Western artists only. Prior experience appreciated, but not necessary.

The other said:

Singer Wanted. Must have professional attitude. No Country or rock-and-roll, please. Willing to work with new talent.

That last one sounded perfect. If she was serious about singing, she had to quit smoking. Clipping the ads, she slid them into her hip pocket and stubbed out the cigarette. She didn't smoke at work, anyway.

5

Sunday afternoon Amanda glanced outside, recognizing James when he climbed out of his car.

"What brings you here?" she asked, allowing him in.

"I was at the gym and remembered you said you worked at an accounting firm so I thought, since it's Sunday, maybe you'd be home."

"I thought only guys in the movies used the gym."

James shrugged. "I don't use the vanity equipment. I just need to keep up with the bad guys on the streets."

Amanda nodded.

"Anyway, I wanted to see if you had seen Mr. Bonner recently. Make sure he isn't harassing you." James was nervous. He didn't normally approach victims after the fact, but he knew George's interest wouldn't be coincidental. George had a reason for everything he did, and James didn't believe in coincidence.

"I haven't seen him, or the limo," she said. "I was going to have some lunch, would you care to join me? It isn't much. Soup and grilled cheese."

"Best offer I've had all week."

She felt self-conscious, hesitating, his coat hanging impotently in her hands. Maybe she should hang it up. She noticed him watching her then smiled and draped it over the back of the sofa next to hers. He followed her into the kitchen and the space felt claustrophobic with someone else in it, the walls collapsing in on her. There had only been a half a dozen times anyone had been in her apartment.

"Well, this is it," she finally mumbled. "There's not much here, but you've already seen it." Now what was she supposed to say?

"I take it you don't do a lot of entertaining," he said.

"Nope. No entertaining. I don't want you to think I'm easy or anything. I mean, we just met. I don't want you to think that or anything. It's been so long since I made love to anybody." Why did she tell him that? She had to quit prattling when she was nervous. "Of course, every man I meet wants to get me in bed the first time they talk to me. I guess that doesn't help. Now I feel dumb. I'm babbling away like an idiot."

"It's alright," he said, chuckling softly. "Just relax. It's only soup and grilled cheese."

She started to nod, caught herself and did a pseudo salute and laughed. She had to learn a better move than 'nod' when she was nervous.

"Touché," she said. That sounded awkward.

After James left Amanda scanned the parking lot through the French doors. This had become her new routine, checking for strange cars. There were none, but she noticed a new couple approach the building. They had just moved in on the second floor. It had only been two days since her assault and she was still uncomfortable, checking everything and everyone.

With nothing unusual she turned away from the window and grabbed a soft drink. Getting dressed for bed she was embarrassed by her earlier nerves still contemplating this sudden onset of paranoia. It had started just before her meeting with Mr. Bonner and the magical limo.

Amanda awoke when someone slipped between the sheets and covered her mouth. This only helped fuel the fears.

She tried to roll to the side, but he wrapped a leg over her then started to bind her hands. Something cold fell on her arm and she ran her fingers up one side, recognizing the metal closure as one her dad had used. She had used them many times since herself. He closed the clasps; she applied pressure on one side re-opening the clasp then slipped one hand loose. He forced his knee between hers to spread her legs and pull her into the position he wanted, she kicked backwards, then grabbed the edge of the mattress and swung the binding over her shoulder, knocking the phone off the hook as she moved.

A thud and a grunt echoed in the quiet when the hook struck then her body was flying in reverse. Another swing and the hook struck him once more, and she rolled to the floor, the lighted dial and dial tone drawing her attention. Amanda punched in 9-1-1 and raced for the door. She lunged through the door, tore the gag off then hooked one end of the nylon rope over the door handle. She darted for the bathroom door and was jerked to a standstill, painfully close to losing her balance. The rope was too short. She let it drop, sprinting across the living room.

In the kitchen she opened one of the drawers and reached for a knife. He slammed the drawer shut and her back smashed into the cabinet, her arms flying up to cover her face, knocking the phone off the hook. She fumbled for something to defend herself with as he wrestled her arms behind her, fighting to gain control. He spun her around; Amanda twisted and found herself bent over the counter, the receiver staring up at her close enough she could almost touch it. She pushed the '0' with her chin then she heard the operator, and she screamed.

As he grabbed for the phone, Amanda threw her head back, something crunched and blood spattered the countertop. He released his grip and she bolted for the living room, flung the door open and unlocked the knob as she raced for the main entrance. A door slammed behind her, echoing down the corridor and she kicked it up a notch. Then two officers appeared at the entry.

Amanda hit the main entrance at a dead run, ramming the door into James. William grabbed her while James grabbed the outer door to avoid being knocked to the ground.

"I'm sorry, I wasn't expecting you this quick," she said breathlessly. "I'm not even dressed." Yeah, she needed to start running. A blast of air caught her nightshirt and she flattened it down with her hands, her cheeks getting warm as she blushed. She sighed as caramel colored eyes stared down at her. "I'm sorry. Let's go back to my place so I can grab my robe."

She was already hurrying back to her apartment.

"You're fine. We received a call about an intruder," William said, noticing her behind as she tugged at the bottom of the pajamas. That was one nice tush!

James stepped inside, following them. He could handle seeing that view more often. They were on duty, he reminded himself, glancing up at his partner. William's smile told him he wasn't the only one.

"I wasn't sure how to report it," she called over her shoulder. "I guess I need to leave things as they are." She left the door open and headed up the hall, slipping her robe on and rushing back to the living room, running into James again. How embarrassing! "I'm sorry. I guess I wasn't paying attention to where I was going." That was an understatement. "I'm batting a thousand." She had to think of something better than, 'I'm sorry', when she was nervous, too.

"No problem," James replied. "What can you tell us? What

happened?"

"I don't know where to start," she said. "I woke up when a man climbed in my bed with me."

She offered an awkward smile and stepped aside, directing them to her bedroom. This felt like her first school girl crush. How stupid. They were only here because she called the police. She only called the police because of an intruder.

"I assume that's unusual, but I could see it happening."

There was a flare of anger as she glared at him then it was gone.

"Could you tell if it was the same man?" James asked.

"Maybe," Amanda answered. "I hit him with the metal hook on the rope."

"How'd he get in?" William asked. He noticed the exchange as he called for the print crew. James was going to get in trouble one of these days.

"I don't know. I keep an extra key in my purse, but he would have had to get in to get the key. I don't know how else he would get in."

"Can you check your purse for us?" James asked.

Amanda nodded and ran to the kitchen, dumping the purse.

James had followed and saw the blood, deflecting the purse and its contents into the sink.

"Is that from him?"

"Yeah. I smashed him with the back of my head. I think I hit his nose. He might have a nice shiner."

James watched her paw through the items in the sink, shaking her head as she searched.

"Is anything missing?"

She continued to shake her head. "Everything's here."

They started back up the hall, stopping when William stepped out of her bedroom, pointing to the section of rope dangling from the doorknob.

"Is that what you hit him with?" James asked.

"Yes."

"So he probably has a large bruise or cut on the side of his face," William said. "Right or left?"

"Left."

"Along with a broken nose and black eye."

"Other than what you just told us, did he touch you in any way? You didn't have intercourse with him?" James recognized the fear in the wide-eyed stare. "These are just questions we have to ask. We're not trying to pry and we aren't here to judge you. We just need as much information as you can give us."

"No," she answered. "I woke up when he climbed in bed with me and then he tried to pull my under things off...." She paused, looking away, embarrassed. "I tried to tie the bedroom door to the bathroom door. The rope's too short."

Frustrated and angry Amanda pulled her robe tighter about her, crossing her arms as if it would help her hide somehow.

William noticed her discomfort and thought about how he would feel in her place. "Maybe you should think about moving. Into a more secure building," William said. "Maybe even get a new phone number."

"I'm working on that."

"Good, because it sounds like he's either got a key or he's good with a set of picks. I called officers to check for prints again. We'll let you know what they find. You might want to have new locks installed. That could help until you get moved."

While William spoke James inspected the room. He pulled the covers back and scanned the bed, noticing the stain. A quick look up, Amanda had noticed the mark, shock and disgust morphing her features.

"I'll talk to the apartment managers tomorrow," she said. "If he can pick locks, that means he can get in anytime he wants to, doesn't it?"

"Yes, ma'am," William said.

She sighed loudly. "What else do you need to know?"

"Would you say this man was larger than the gentleman who was here before? About the same size? How tall? Muscular build or just big? Heavyset?"

"Kind of skinny. Not like you or Officer Thompson. About Officer Thompson's height. That leaves a lot of room, huh?"

"You're fine," James said. "About the same as the previous person?"

She nodded, almost a nervous twitch.

"Closer to six foot, then?" William asked. "That was your only spare key?"

"Yes and yes," she answered.

"Do you have anywhere you can stay for a couple of days. My suggestion is to stay away from here for a while. I would guess he's watching you."

"Watching me. You mean like following me around?"

"Possibly," William answered. "He's followed you enough to learn where you live. If he's been watching you this long he might even know where you work."

Amanda thought of the limo, scowled then looked up at him.

Once the print crew was gone, William and James surveyed the thick coating of black fingerprint powder before returning to Amanda.

"Okay," William said. "They found no prints ...."

"Not to mention all this black crap I have to clean up!"

"I know," William said.

She dropped her head in her hands and sighed.

"I'll see if we can get a plain clothes team to stake the place out for a few nights."

Amanda nodded, her palms pressed against her eyes, holding the tears in.

"I'm sorry. I wish we could do more."

She nodded again, following them to the door and locking it. Then she padded back to her room, pulled a blanket out of the closet and curled up on the sofa. She didn't want to even look at that bed tonight.

William and James drove to the station lost in their own thoughts. George Bonner was Salt Lake City's resident pimp and he was the only person they knew who owned a limo, but none of the information the department had, painted George as a psycho who entered homes to terrorize unsuspecting women. He had too many readily available ladies for him to work that angle. He was a pimp for heaven's sake.

They had just finished their reports when they were joined by a plains clothes officer.

"How's it goin'?" he asked.

"Goin'," William answered, puzzled.

"Just so you know, bro," he said, "you guys need to keep it low. Someone's gunnin' for you and none of us want your or your partner goin' down. Just an FYI." He slapped William on the back as he left.

"Appreciate that," William answered.

6

Amanda spent the next two weeks handing out demo tapes and introducing herself once more. As expected, a good part of the clubs managers had rotated out and she found herself talking to new people. Tuesday morning Amanda was rewarded for her diligence and received the long awaited message.

"Amanda," she said when she answered the phone.

"Hello, my name is Monica. I'm the bartender at Pearls on Main. The manager would like you to be here at seven o'clock tonight for an audition. Would that be convenient?"

"That will be perfect," she answered.

"We'll see you at seven," Monica replied.

Amanda hung up and stared at the phone. She wanted to scream. She wanted to hug everybody. She had nothing to wear!

"Yes!" she squealed instead. The rattle of wheels on desk chairs echoed through the space as everybody stood to check it out. "Sorry, guys. Just me," she called over her cube.

"What time is your audition?" Janice asked. "I know that's what that was."

"Seven o'clock tonight."

"I'll be there, girl. And I have a dress that would look great on you. Trust me."

The phone rang again and Amanda answered it still floating from the previous call.

"Good day, princess," a filtered voice said. "I just wanted to let you know I've been enjoying the scenery. I have to tell you, I like this dress better than the others. It's very sexy."

Amanda covered her chest with her hand, the officers' words echoing in her mind. *If he's been watching you this long he might even know where you work.* Then the voice laughed and she hung up. The phone rang again; Amanda reached for it then paused. She didn't want to talk to that man again, but she had few choices. If it was a client, she had to answer it.

"Don't be afraid of the phone, gorgeous," he said when she picked up.

Amanda dropped a hastily scribbled note over the top of her cube asking Janice to call the police.

"It won't bite, the voice continued. "I won't either. I only want to see you naked and watch your body move with mine. Does that make you uncomfortable?" There was a moment of silence. "No answer? Then I have another question for you. I know you're going to say it's none of my business, but I think it is. Do you prefer things hot and steamy, or maybe normal and routine? What do you say, princess?"

"You're right. It's none of your business. I wouldn't tell you a thing if my life depended on it!"

"It might princess, it might. Just to make it more interesting I'll tell you now, I enjoy watching your chest as you breath. The way it lifts with each breath is exhilarating. One day I will see you moving under me."

"Only in your wildest dreams," she replied. She turned her back to the phone, fear and anger vying for dominance. "You wouldn't be this brave if you knew the cops were tracing the call."

"They aren't. I know the sound of a trace starting. It won't do you any good to call the cops, either. They won't find anything."

"You could be right," she answered. "Of, course they might be smarter than you think. They might catch you. Is that what you're afraid of? Maybe I'm wrong. Maybe you just want attention. Is that it?"

"Only yours, princess. I want your undivided attention, every single night."

"It'll take more than some jackass on the phone to keep my attention. I want someone who is man enough to talk to me in person. It doesn't look like you fit that ideal."

"You'll find out soon," he replied. "Then we will see who has the last laugh."

The phone slammed and she questioned her decision to push that far. If he wasn't her intruder, she didn't want a second one. She had just placed the receiver in the cradle when William and James walked up. They stopped just outside the confines of her cube studying her.

"Is that why you called?" James asked nodding in the direction of her phone.

Amanda did a barely perceptible head bob. "Yes."

"What did he say?"

"He knew every move I made," she answered. "He said he wants to see me naked under him. He also said he will be seeing me soon."

"That sounded like a threat," William said. He scanned the windows across the street as he walked the length of the room. "Have there been any deliveries?"

Amanda shook her head and then shrugged.

"All deliveries go through the loading dock," she answered.

"Unless it's flowers, or something. Those are left at reception."

"No one brings things to your desks?" James asked.

"We have to pick them up. We handle people and businesses sensitive financial data."

James glanced at William, raised an eyebrow and chin pointed across the street. William shook his head 'no'.

"Next question, how would he see her? He would have to have a camera somewhere."

"And how would he have got it in here?" William asked. He turned to Amanda. "Where's the loading area? Who do we talk to?"

Amanda gave them the receiving supervisor's name and they took the freight elevator. Talking to the employee's they were told there had only been routine deliveries. Paper, office and cleaning supplies, things of that nature. When pushed, the men admitted coming to work a few days prior and finding a message that someone had bypassed security. No one had tried to access the computer system so they did a routine building check and found nothing missing so, no reports had been filed and authorities hadn't been called.

William and James stopped in the IT department on the way back and were told the computer system would automatically shut itself down if there was a breach. No sensitive financial data would have been compromised. But the bypass on that particular night hadn't involved the computer system. The security cameras had been brought down, which was odd because nothing had been taken. When asked about the possibility of a camera being installed, he told them the person would have had plenty of time, if he had known what he was doing. But without video, they had no way of knowing.

James and William stepped off the elevator and went back to Amanda's cube. William beckoned her to join him in the aisle.

"How often do they replace your equipment? When new things are introduced, or only if something quits working?'

"Usually when it quits."

"We need to talk to the lieutenant about setting up a trace. Is there a phone I can use in here?"

"No one's using that one." She pointed to the cube behind hers. "Just push one of the light up buttons for an outside line."

William called Lieutenant Ohlmet, waited twenty minutes, finally getting the message to call the lieutenant again.

"Everything should be set by eight a.m.," William told her when he hung up. "If he calls again we're going to try to catch him. See if you can have them bring you a new monitor."

"I don't think it's the monitor," James said, "but it might push him into calling again. Gloat over his ability to outsmart the cops. That could work to our advantage if she can keep him on the line long enough."

7

Amanda arrived at the club, Janice already waiting with her make-up kit and the dress. Amanda would be on stage so she needed to highlight her features better Janice told her. Then she handed over the dress and Amanda giggled when she held it up. A red fitted number with spaghetti straps. Amanda slipped it on and smoothed her hands over her hips, surveying her reflection in the full-length mirror then she did a quick turn to check the rear. She normally didn't wear anything this tight, but it felt good tonight.

Janice had just finished Amanda's make-up and stepped back to admire her handy work, when someone knocked on the door.

"The audition is supposed to be at seven p.m. tonight, not seven p.m. tomorrow night," came a familiar voice.

The voice sounded nice. Smooth, sexy, like the words were caressing the senses. Whoever it was, Amanda liked that voice.

She walked on stage surprised to see William at the piano.

"I had no idea the beautiful lady could sing," William said.

"And, I had no idea the officer could play the piano. I thought you guys were on graveyard?"

"With the audition tonight and now the trace in the morning, a couple a guys switched with us."

"That's why you responded this afternoon. I thought your shift had changed or something."

"No such luck," he said, laughing quietly. "We're still waiting to get rotated back to days."

The club manager watched them then turned his attention to the reason they were here. He'd had his doubts from the minute she dropped the tape off and those doubts were mounting. She looked good, but that didn't mean a thing. It was easy to doctor demo tapes. Making a couple of last minute notes, he moved to a table behind the stage and waved her over.

"For your audition," the manager said. "I want you to sing one of the selections from your demo tape, but without your music. I want to hear you, not your tape, so William's going to accompany you on the piano."

Amanda nodded and faced William.

"What do you want to hear?"

"Don't matter much to me," William replied. "I can fake most anything."

She dropped her hands, William laughing when he saw the look of exasperation then he started into one of the patron's favorites. A slow, smoky ballad that needed to be massaged and worked gently none of the previous entertainers had been able to pull it off. It wasn't on her demo tape, but if she could do this song, she could do any of them. And she nailed it. She started out soft and sultry then built until she dropped you over the edge. She picked you up and took you on the ride of your life.

With the audition over, Amanda joined Janice, while William conferred with the club manager. She tried to stay calm, but caught herself fidgeting in her seat. It was ten agonizing minutes before the manager waved her over. He agreed with William and knew as soon as the patrons heard her they'd be under her spell. Good music had a way of winning people over. Especially with form and tone like hers.

"I was ready to hire you the minute I heard you," he said. "And William's in agreement so I'm going to offer you a position as the headliner…"

"Yes!" Amanda exclaimed. She covered her mouth with both hands as she started off the chair, forcing herself back into the seat, laughter coming from behind her. Now she hoped she hadn't sounded like a child.

"Be here Friday prepared to perform a couple of songs," he continued. "We'll go over everything with you then. Your official start day will be Saturday. And the name is Eddie," he finished offering his hand.

"Thank you, thank you, thank you!" she exclaimed. "I'm so excited I could just kiss you!" Headliner! She was going to be the headliner!

She jumped up to shake his hand, the chair clattering behind her to the accompaniment of more laughter. She tried to upright the chair, tripping over one of the legs and reaching for the table to keep from toppling over.

"I guess I need to calm down," she said finally righting it.

Eddie laughed. She was going to be great.

Amanda rushed back to the table and kissed William on the cheek.

"I think I know the outcome without you saying a word," Janice said. "That squeal was a dead giveaway. I'm so proud of you, girl."

"Ah, man," Amanda said, "I don't know when I've been this excited. Man, I got the gig! I got the gig!" she repeated. Then she noticed the lipstick and wiped it off. "Sorry! Eddie said you agreed about making me the headliner. And that last performance was real graceful. I just made a fool out of myself."

"Don't let it bother you," Janice said. "You're just excited, girl."

"After that number, it would be stupid not to," William said. He waved the cocktail waitress over and ordered another round. "And, I'm going to have to side with your friend. I'm also going to have to bid you lovely ladies adieu after this. I have to be ready for tomorrow."

"Me, too," Amanda said. "I don't want to be nonfunctioning in the morning."

"This will be the last drink and I'll give you a ride," William said. "Deal?"

"Deal," she answered. Good looking and the sexiest voice.

At her place, she offered to fix something to eat, but admitted she hadn't been to the store. She didn't have much.

"I used to make a pretty mean omelet," he said. "What's in your fridge?"

"I think I have enough for that. Unless you want ham or bacon. It'll have to be veggie or cheese."

"How about veggie and cheese?" he asked.

Amanda started the coffee and helped chop vegetables while William grated the cheese, then banished her to the kitchen table. When everything was done, he set the plates down and sat across from her. Before they realized it, it was after one a.m. They had spent more than three hours talking and telling jokes. He apologized and pulled his coat on. He hadn't meant to stay this long, they both needed some sleep.

"We'll have to do this again sometime," he told her, grabbing the edge of the door. "I haven't had this much fun in years."

"I'd like that." Then she noticed the wedding band and glanced away.

"You okay?"

"Yeah, just tired."

She leaned against the door after he'd left angry with herself. She should have noticed the ring. Wouldn't his wife wonder why he hadn't come home? And why had she lied to him?

William had barely made it back to his apartment when the phone rang. He looked up at the clock, the possible reasons for someone calling this late racing through his mind. It was James – for the fourth time – his partner told him. How had the audition gone?

"It was great," William answered. "I gave the lady a ride home and made omelets...."

"Wait! You took someone home? I'm seriously impressed."

"Yes, I did," William answered. "We talked until about fifteen minutes ago. She looked embarrassed when I left, though. She said she was tired."

"What did you say? You had to say something."

"Nothing. I told her we'd have to do it again. She said she'd like that."

"Did you take the ring off? You probably forgot to tell her you're a widower, too."

"She probably thinks I'm a complete ass," William said with a sigh. James had told him he needed to quit wearing it, but he didn't want to let go. And he liked the safety it afforded. It helped keep some of the women at bay. "You're right. I forgot the ring."

"It looks like you got some serious treading water to do there, buddy," James said. "See you in the morning."

8

William and James met at the station at seven o'clock the next morning, William grinning from ear to ear. James was curious. First Amanda and now this lady who auditioned at the club. When pushed William only laughed.

"Come on, buddy," James said. "Who is she? She must be nice if you cooked her breakfast."

"Nice isn't the word for it," William replied. "Perfect, is the only description that will suffice."

"Have I met her?"

"Oh, yeah!" William laughed harder when James straightened up and stared at him.

"Well, come on! Let me in on the secret. Damn! You're killing me!"

"Our lady with the hypnotizing eyes," William answered, noting the surprise on James face.

"Amanda? I gotta learn to like this jazz stuff."

"The one and only," William replied. "I get to work with her every Friday and Saturday night! I'm not sure how this is going to work, though. The way she looked last night, it was all I could do not to sweep her off her feet and take her straight to that bedroom. She is…. I can't think of anything except *perfect*. But now she's probably pissed. Damn, James! I gotta fix this screw up."

"You got that right, buddy."

At ten minutes to eight they were at Berringer & Hardy, ready and waiting. Amanda called the tech to bring the new monitor and stepped out of the way, leaning on the low wall of the cube, sneaking glances at William. She was nervous, not sure what to say or do, and noticed he acted the same way, until the tech brought the monitor. Then it was all business.

"I need that boxed so we can deliver it to the department," William told the tech.

Three long hours went by and they had heard nothing. It appeared James was right. The camera wasn't on the monitor. While they waited a clerk brought a box of supplies, Amanda signed for them then stacked them in front of her phone while she opened a drawer to make room.

Within seconds the phone rang. Amanda answered it and put it on speaker. If it wasn't her caller, she would pick up. William recognized the sound of a filter and picked up the phone in the adjacent cube, instructing the operator to start the trace.

"Why are you blocking my view, princess?" the voice asked. "I can't see you. And I wanted to tell you, you only have a short time before we see each other. I also want you to wear something a little more risqué for my viewing pleasure from now on. I want to see the merchandise."

There was silence for second, Amanda uncertain if he was waiting for a reply.

"I know you called the cops yesterday," he continued. "When you call them today, make sure you spell the name correctly. It's J-e-r-r-y T-h-o-m-a-s," he said, spelling the name out. "Get ready to kiss the frogs my princess."

Amanda moved the files and looked up at William.

"Is that better, Mr. Thomas?"

The line went dead; James giving William a high five. The camera was on the phone. William called the operator and was told they hadn't had time to complete the trace.

"Amanda, request a new phone," William said. "We'll need the phone and we'll be here in the morning in case he calls. We want to try the trace again."

Eight fifteen the next morning and William and James met Amanda. The old phone had been boxed and was waiting with a note from the tech.

"You know there's a camera on the bottom, right?"

William called Lieutenant Ohlmet and told him they had the phone and the tech had found the camera. He wanted to know if they should keep the trace operator on standby in case the man called back. They decided to hold the operator for one more day. They would have to pay her for that day anyway. Then they pulled in plain clothes officers in case someone did show up. They didn't expect that, but they had seen criminals do stranger things. Common sense wasn't always a prerequisite for that profession.

By nine forty-five a.m. they had a plain clothes officer inside the bus shelter closest to Berringer & Hardy, one sitting on the edge of the fountain reading the sports page, as so many riders did when they were avoiding the crowded benches, and two roaming the street. Two more observed the rear of the building on Gallivan Avenue, a side street that ran north off Third South for a third of a block.

At one fifteen p.m. everyone met at the station. No one had entered the building, and no deliveries had been made. One of the officers who had been posted on Main Street said a man parked north of their location wearing blue jeans and a polo shirt. A Utah Jazz baseball cap pulled down over his face. He walked toward Berringer & Hardy, but didn't enter, changing course at the last minute, continuing south then going east on Fourth South. He thought the man had gone north on Gallivan behind the target building, but by the time he got there, the man had disappeared and the surveillance team had seen no one. The description the officer gave matched George Bonner, but they needed something more concrete than 'thinking George had walked by her office' to pull him in and make charges stick.

William returned at five minutes before five and offered Amanda a ride home. She thought about the wedding ring and decided this would be a good time to broach the subject. At her apartment, Amanda looked across the seat, suddenly nervous. How should she ask about the wife?

"Thanks for the ride," she said. Her voice held a slight tremble and she hoped he didn't hear it. "I hope your wife doesn't mind you giving strange ladies rides."

"Wife?" He looked at his left hand and the ring. He had forgotten again. "There's no wife. I'm a widower. I wear it to keep some of the women off me."

"I'm sorry," she said. "I didn't mean to bring up any bad memories … I mean…I assumed…"

"It's alright," he answered. "You didn't know." When they reached her apartment, he placed a hand behind her neck and kissed her.

"I have an idea," Amanda said. "How about I order pizza? My way of apologizing for the wife thing."

"I'd like that," he answered. "On one condition, I pay."

Amanda opened them each a beer and ordered the pizza. She was relearning the nuances of being an impromptu hostess.

While they talked William realized there was a reason he spent most of his free time playing at the club. The only thing at home was an empty apartment and lots of memories. He hadn't realized how much he missed having someone around. Someone who was easy to talk to, easy to look at and liked the same things he did. He wondered what his parents would think if he married a white girl. Then he thought about her folks and what they would think about her dating a black guy. Now he had gotten ahead of himself. Half the pizza later, he glanced at the clock, almost ten-thirty. It didn't feel like he had been here that long.

"I need to go," William said. "I enjoyed the evening and the company, very much."

"See you Friday?" she asked.

"Definitely," he said. It suddenly felt awkward. He didn't want to leave.

"Maybe I should be a good girl and let you go home," she said sporting a fake pout.

"If you must," he replied.

Searching her eyes for a hint of where she stood, he leaned in for a kiss. This wasn't in the law enforcement training manual, but he could handle a few of these lessons.

"After that kiss I might have to stay." He nuzzled her neck as she melted into him. "What do you think?"

"It's been a while," she answered. "And you are being pretty persuasive."

"I'll start the lessons slow and easy." He kissed her again, guiding her toward the bedroom. Once they'd made love, he lay beside her; Amanda snuggled up close, thinking about his job. It had got his first wife killed. Maybe he shouldn't involve Amanda. This might not be fair to her. He was pulled out of his thoughts by her fingers gliding up his side. "What are you doing?"

"Just feeling your skin. It reminds me of velvet."

His body did an involuntary shiver and he kissed her beginning the music once again. After they'd made love, he kissed her cheek one of her legs draped over his side. He checked the clock then gave her one more kiss.

"I hate to say this, but I gotta go," he said with a sigh. "I have that work thing tomorrow. Today." He corrected himself quickly and kissed her forehead. "You gonna be okay?"

"Yes. And you don't have to explain. I have to work, too. You'll be back on graveyard, right?"

"Right. Maybe I'll take you to dinner before I go in."

"I'd like that," she whispered. "Are you sure you have to go? I'll be up in four hours anyway."

"Yeah, I gotta go. James is supposed to call about an arrest we made. I'll pick you up for dinner."

"Okay." She mumbled, pulling the covers around her.

9

William was startled awake by pounding on the door and automatically checked the clock. Seven a.m. He had only been asleep a couple of hours. It was almost time for James' planned call. But with everybody in the building knowing he was a police officer he expected it to be a plea for help. It had happened before, and it would happen again. He stumbled to the door, flipped the deadbolt back, unhooked the chain lock and was slammed against the wall; his hands yanked behind him and put in cuffs.

"What the hell's going on?" William asked.

"You'll find out when we get you to the station!" one of the patrolmen barked. "It's officers like you who give the rest of us a bad name. As far as I'm concerned, we're doing the department a favor. Whine to Captain Jakes about any other shit."

Chief Vanders walked in then William was pulled off to the side and read his rights. A nod from the chief and he was allowed to dress under the officer's watchful eye. Once dressed, William was put back in cuffs and led to a waiting squad car. At the station, he was dragged out of the car and saw James being manhandled in much the same manner. This had to be somebody's idea of a sick joke. Once inside, they were placed in separate interrogation rooms where they were forced to wait until their superiors decided to join them.

When Captain Jakes finally took a seat across from him, William wondered who James was dealing with. Was it Lieutenant Ohlmet, Assistant Chief Robinson or maybe Chief Vanders? It might even be Captain Kirby. William reined his thoughts in, looked across the table at the captain and tried to grasp what was happening.

"I'm going to assume, since I was read my rights, this is a criminal complaint."

"Yes, you may," Captain Jakes answered.

"Then I won't say anything until I talk to an attorney."

"I wouldn't push that too hard if I were," Captain Jakes said. "Do you have any idea why you were brought in?"

"No, sir," William answered. He looked around the room, confused and angry. "Your threats aren't going to work, Captain. I call an attorney or I don't talk to you or anyone else."

"If you hadn't decided to sell drugs we wouldn't have brought you in. I want to know why you made that decision."

"I don't sell drugs," William said. "I never have, I never will. Captain, this is bogus!"

"We can make this very hard on you, William. We have witnesses who say they bought from you. Are you calling them liars'?"

"Yes, sir" William answered. He stared at the table, finding it hard to wrap his mind around the accusation. They arrested people for selling drugs, they didn't sell them. "Someone paid them off. I won't be going anywhere, and once this is cleared up I can request a transfer. I have the right to one phone call. I don't talk to anybody until I make that call."

"And I can deny that transfer. I can make your life a living hell if they're stupid enough to put your black ass back on the street. Now," Captain Jakes said, "why are you selling drugs?"

William heard the anger in Captain Jakes voice and his eyes flashed, but he wasn't backing down. Not after that last remark. The captain never spoke that way about anybody. Something had changed.

"You can't prove anything. Do you have pictures? Do you have video or recordings? If you don't, it's their word against mine. I have the right to an attorney. I want one."

"We have pictures," Captain Jakes said. "Are you refusing to cooperate with this investigation?"

"This isn't an investigation," William replied, staring at the table, stunned and trying to wrap his mind around this sudden turn of events, trying to think of how anybody could have gotten pictures. "This is a witch hunt. I want an attorney."

The remainder of the interview went much the same way with William refusing to talk. He knew his rights and was sticking to them. In the neighboring interrogation room, Captain Kirby was having the same problem with James.

It had been almost ten hours of being pushed, prodded, and otherwise interrogated by their superiors before he was left alone to think about his position. Everyone in the chain of command had attempted to coerce a confession out of him, now he was sitting here staring at the same stark walls and had been for what felt like hours.

Then Chief Vanders started it again finally ending the grueling session when Assistant Chief Robinson came in and requested both men be moved into the same room. Joining them, Assistant Chief Robinson leaned against the wall, watching them from where he stood, his look a disconcerting bore, cutting them to the core.

William pulled himself together and forced himself to return the assistant chief's stare, his head swimming, his mind going over the questions, feeling the pressure. All this to break them. Part of him wanted to give up and walk out, but the other half knew, if they gave up, they would never walk out. He let out a slow sigh, forcing himself to relax and looked over at James. His partner was angry and exhausted the same as him.

Assistant Chief Robinson finally pushed himself off the wall, taking a step toward them. "Officers," he said. "I'm going to show you one thing and ask each of you one or two more questions. Then we will make a decision as to where this is going. Right now it appears two of our best men have moved into the enemy camp."

Neither man said anything. If the department had pictures, something was wrong. They weren't guilty, but they weren't in a position to prove it.

"This," the assistant chief began, taking a photo out of his pocket, "was given to Captain Jakes along with a letter. The letter states this was taken the night you two responded to the call about the body in Liberty Park."

James sat up, smirking then the assistant chief dropped the photo on the table. It was a picture of James showing off his winnings. James smirk disappeared, he groaned and dropped his eyes. William hung his head.

"I take it you recognize the picture?"

"Yes, sir," James answered.

"Can you explain it?"

"The information is correct. That," he nodded at the photo, "was the night we received the call about the girl in Liberty Park. William and I were horsing around with Lloyd about going to Vegas to win some money. I pulled that out of my wallet because I had just won it in Wendover on my days off. That's all it was, gambling winnings. I got lucky."

"And you expect us to believe that?"

"Yes, sir. And I can prove it."

"I was told they found nothing in your car or your apartment that accounted for the money. It came to a little over fourteen hundred dollars."

"I had the casino give me a copy of the receipt when I cashed in. Just in case I needed it for tax purposes. If not I figured I could use it for a souvenir. You know, frame the receipt and hang it on the wall, the only time I ever won a jackpot at the tables. That sort of thing. But I don't keep my tax records at the apartment in case the place burns."

"Where is it?"

"I don't have to tell you anything. No disrespect, but after this morning I've probably said too much already. Either book me and let me call a lawyer, or release me."

"If that's what you want," Chief Vanders said from behind the assistant chief.

Assistant Chief Robinson spun, his jaw slack, a look of shock creasing his forehead.

"You are already aware of how this works," Chief Vanders continued, "but I have to inform you that you are being placed on leave until notified otherwise."

The chief walked out and left the door cracked. They could hear voices, one of the men was angry. It sounded like Captain Jakes. Assistant Chief Robinson swung the door to, and leaned on his hands on the table as he looked between the two.

"Are you sure this is how you gentlemen want to play this?"

William and James gave a weak nod, confused.

"How else are we supposed to play it?" William asked.

The assistant chief dipped his head for a half a second. "I wish I knew. But I'm afraid you may have just signed your separation papers with the department."

There were footsteps then Chief Vanders opened the door and asked that they be taken to his office. As they walked up the hall, they looked back at the assistant chief staring back at them. What the hell was going on?

Once they were outside his office, the chief faced the patrolmen.

"Undo the cuffs and have their personal effects brought up please. I want both of you outside my office. Lieutenant Ohlmet is the only one allowed in or out until I say otherwise."

"Yes, sir," the men answered.

One of the patrolmen left to retrieve William and James' belongings and the second officer unlocked the cuffs, stationing himself in the hall. After the door had closed, the chief took a second and stared at them.

"What did the assistant chief want?"

Both men shrugged, puzzled.

"I'm not sure," William answered. "He showed us a picture. I'm confused. Why the hell didn't you talk to us?"

Chief Vanders turned and stared into the darkness outside his window, his back to them.

"Gentlemen," he said. "I'm going to release you, but I want the receipt for those gambling winnings by end of today. Do you think you can do that?" He turned as he spoke and James nodded then he looked back out the window. "The search conducted of your apartments and your personal vehicles found nothing. Your squad car, however, contained drugs under the passenger seat. I want to know why."

"I haven't had a chance to call an attorney," James said. He stared at Chief Vanders back and thought about what he had just told them. How could anyone have found anything in their squad? "I'm not sure I want to say more. I know you could easily be recording this conversation. Sir!"

"This conversation is not being recorded gentlemen," Chief Vanders said. He turned to face them now. "And this is strictly off the record. We were told you had large quantities of cocaine and heroin hidden in specific areas of you apartments, but nothing has been found. I want to know why you would be so sloppy as to leave drugs in your squad car but your personal cars and your apartments were clean when we were given very precise locations."

"Off the record?" William asked. "I'm not sure I believe that."

"Off the record," Chief Vanders repeated. "After this morning, I understand."

An uncomfortable silence ensued while they debated how much they should say. James glanced at William, and shook his head in a 'what the hell' way.

"The men didn't find anything because we don't sell drugs," William finally replied. "I have no idea what's going on with the squad car, but anybody who can get into the station could have taken the keys to that ride and we'd be screwed."

"William's right," James said. He could feel his fatigue and rubbed the back of his neck, stretching his shoulders. "Who told you to search the squad? We were set up, Chief."

"Why would anyone set you up?" Chief Vanders asked.

"How the hell am I supposed know?" James answered. Then he exhaled loudly, frustrated. "All I know is men I have worked with for nine years think I'm a bad cop. I don't want to walk away from my job, but how am I supposed to face those men again?"

"Try to calm down," the chief said quietly.

"Calm down?" William exclaimed. "How are we supposed to calm down? When you came barging through my door, an officer I have worked with for ten years said, 'it's cops like me who give all cops a bad name'. I haven't done a damn thing wrong and I've already been judged guilty. And Captain Jakes makes the comment about the department being stupid 'if they put my black ass back on the street'. Think about it, Chief!"

The officer outside turned to looked inside.

"Where's the lieutenant?" James asked.

"He should be here any time," Chief Vanders answered. "Why?"

"We were told by one of the plains clothes guys to keep it low. Someone was trying to take us down. We told the lieutenant."

"And you think this might be what he was referring to?"

"Only thing I can think of," James replied.

Chief Vanders wasn't happy, but all they could do now was stand their ground. If they said any more it could undermine their positions. They were both concerned they had already said too much.

"I have someone you need to talk to," Chief Vanders said after a few minutes. "This will be between the lieutenant and the three of us and nobody else."

When Lieutenant Ohlmet walked in, Chief Vanders dialed a number and put the call on speaker.

"I'm having serious concerns about this. When your personal items are returned your weapons and your badges will not be in the box. Understand?"

"Yes, sir," they answered.

"Your home phones will be tapped…." Someone picked up on the other end cutting him off. "Jeremy," the chief said, his voice tight with tension. "I have a problem developing. I think I need your aid."

There was a knock on the door and the lieutenant answered, taking the boxes containing the men's personal effects. Once they had verified nothing was missing, they stuffed everything into their pockets then the chief returned to the call.

"I'm back, Jeremy."

"Thank you, Chief. I'm glad you think I can be of service. I am a tad concerned if you feel the need to contact me, though. What can I do for you?"

"I have two patrolmen who were arrested for distribution of

drugs," he said. "They were pulled in because of an anonymous tip and a search of the squad they used had drugs in it. The tip gave very specific locations in their apartments for the drugs, but nothing was found."

"Are they the only ones who drive that particular car?"

"They were the only ones who drove it in the previous twelve hours. The search was performed before day shift came in. We checked the tapes from the department's surveillance cameras," Chief Vanders said, "but we found nothing suspicious."

"That leaves it a bit wide open unless the vehicle was searched prior to their shift. Where do I fit into this?"

"I'm beginning to think the men were framed," Chief Vanders said. He looked up when William and James sighed. "Lieutenant Ohlmet and I have our suspicions that it might have to do with the problem we were discussing last week. Plus the men stated they were warned by a plain clothes officer about being targets."

"Can anyone get into their apartments now?"

"No. We have them sealed and taped. The patrolmen on duty have been given strict instructions no one goes in until I say otherwise. Once these men go home, if the tape has been compromised in any way I'm going to ask them to contact me."

"Are the men with you, sir?"

"Yes, sir. They are listening now."

"Good. Is there anything else I should be aware of?"

"One of the men had fourteen hundred dollars in his wallet. Someone took a picture of him flashing it to a friend and that is what was used as part of the proof for the charges against them. The officer said he won it in Wendover and has the receipt to prove it."

"He will need that, sir. It is after midnight now, so I will be in Salt Lake City this afternoon to talk to you. I want the men to meet us in the lounge at The Hotel America at eight p.m. tonight. Will that be satisfactory?"

"Yes, sir," the chief answered. He glanced between the two as if verifying the time and they nodded. "Thank you, Jeremy." The chief hung up and turned back to William and James. "What we discuss tonight cannot go any further than that table. If I hear anything I will make sure this morning feels like playtime in the park. Is that clear?"

"Yes, sir," they said.

"Good. I'll see you tonight. You heard what I told Jeremy. If the tape at your apartments looks like it has been altered in any way – call me. I'm going to have the lieutenant take you home and we'll see if we can get the plain clothes officer to confirm your story. Which officer gave you the warning?"

"Ortiz," William answered.

"Thank you. I hope this is corrected soon. Now, go home and try to get some rest."

10

William stared out the passenger window as the lieutenant drove, his mind rerunning the past fourteen hours, trying to work out what the assistant chief had told them. What had he meant, *'signed their separation papers with the department'*?

"Lieutenant, what's going on?" William asked.

"Captain Jakes brought us that photo and a letter and said he had witnesses willing to sign statements against you," Lieutenant Ohlmet answered.

William could tell the lieutenant was debating how much to give them.

"We were going to talk to you before we went any further, but Jakes already had everything set when we arrived yesterday. Chief Vanders decided to go along to monitor the captain."

"The chief mentioned things that you guys were talking about last week."

"I'm not at liberty to say anything, William. You'll have to be patient."

"Lieutenant…."

"William, I can only tell you, the chief is doing the best he can, but we have been backed into a corner. You have to wait."

The lieutenant stopped in front of William's apartment and looked at him and William knew the conversation had ended. William climbed out of the car and locked eyes with James, James doing a slight head dip.

Inside, William surveyed the mess. They had even gone through his late wife's belongings. Those boxes should not have been touched. As he repacked her things he could feel the anger intensify. When he placed the lid back on the last box, he sat on the edge of the bed running his hands over his kinky hair, the tears falling. Two years since her death and no one had a clue what had happened. He had left for work one morning and she was home, and when he returned, she was gone. Her car, with her body in it, had been found at the mouth of Big Cottonwood Canyon. A single tap with a .45 through the heart. Still, no suspects had been named and no one had been arrested. He was told the hit to the heart was symbolic. It was meant to hit him where it hurt. And it had.

Ten minutes later his phone rang. It was James. James had got the message.

"What's up?" James asked.

"I'm getting the feeling we could be in trouble," William said. "I don't know about you, but it sounds like the chief and the lieutenant think Captain Jakes is behind all this without saying it. Why would the chief just blindly follow the Cap if that's true?"

"Don't know, but you're right. Something's going down. I want to know what the hell the assistant chief was talking about, too."

"Same here. I wanted to see if you were picking up on the same things I am. Let's try to get some sleep. I have a feeling we're going to need to be on our toes. I don't want to miss a thing tonight."

"Did Jakes really say that about putting you back in a squad?"

James asked. "I've never heard him talk about any of the men like that. Even the screw ups."

"Yes, he did," William said. "And I agree. Jakes has always talked about everyone with respect."

James hung up and crawled into bed, his mind replaying their arrest and the conversation in Chief Vanders office. Things were painting Captain Jakes in a dim light and he didn't want to believe that.

A look at the clock on the bedside table and it read five a.m. If he got up, the only thing he could do was wait until the bank opened. He stared at the ceiling, subconsciously counting the holes in the ceiling tiles. How ridiculous was that? He took another look at the clock, five-fifteen. He rolled over and buried his head under a pillow willing sleep to come. This was not working. He finally threw the pillow off and looked at the clock again. Five thirty-five.

James gave up and made a pot of coffee then thought about calling William. William was probably having the same problem. He picked up the phone and stared at the receiver, then set it back down. He looked out the window and cursed to himself, picked the phone up again and dialed William's number.

"Yo, my man," William said when he answered.

"How'd you know it was me?"

"You're the only one who would call at five forty-nine in the morning when we aren't going in to work. What's up?"

"Just thinking about the phone call in the chief's office."

"Me, too. Want me to pick you up and we can go by the park, play some ball or something. By the time we get there the sun should be up."

"I'll meet you. I'll need to stop at the bank."

William hung up and stared out the window at the sun just peeking over the Wasatch Mountains. Shit! He was supposed to take Amanda to dinner last night. She was probably angry, but he owed her an explanation. And he wasn't going to call her this early.

William and James met at the park and alternated between discussing the events of the last twenty-four hours, running laps, and throwing a few hoops. They parted ways, exhausted and agreeing it was unnerving knowing their careers were riding on Chief Vanders faith in them, investigating on their own – without getting caught – and someone they had never met.

Closing his apartment door, William stared at the phone. What was he supposed to tell her? Sorry, I missed dinner; James and I were arrested for selling drugs. This just kept getting better. He finally gave up and called Berringer & Hardy.

She understood, she said, letting him off the hook, laughing softly as he fumbled through an excuse. They agreed to try another night.

11

William and James arrived at the hotel at seven thirty. They wanted to know more about this man their superiors had turned to for help. He had to have some deep connections, but to who? They walked through the lobby and Chief Vanders and Lieutenant Ohlmet had already arrived and been seated. There were two men stationed outside the lounge entrance and one of them raised his hand as they passed. The men were wired, but they didn't work for the department.

"So, who is this dude we're supposed to meet?" James asked when they had seated themselves. "And why not the station?"

"You're on leave," Lieutenant Ohlmet reminded them. "You'll meet Jeremy soon. His men have probably already told him you two are here."

"Yeah, we saw them. CIA or FBI?"

"No," Chief Vanders answered. His tone told them nothing further would be said. "Any questions so far?"

"A couple hundred," William answered. "Including why we were arrested and made to look like jackasses."

"Well, that's the reason we're here. You will know more

soon," Chief Vanders said.

"While we're waiting I brought this," James said. He handed a copy of the play receipt to the chief filled with conflicting emotions. He wanted to wad the paper up and throw at him. He wanted to stuff it down the chief's throat. But, if he wanted his job back, he had to keep his anger under control. "I kept the original. The department will have to deal with it," he said.

Chief Vanders took the paper and nodded. He understood James feelings. He would feel the same way.

It was about ten minutes when the chief and the lieutenant sat straighter up, more alert. A look to the side and a man could be seen walking their direction, sizing them up as he approached. He carried himself with an easy confidence. He knew his abilities and, they suspected, theirs just by looking at them. He had dark hair and blue eyes, and was an inch or two taller than William with a muscular, athletic build. He would not be taken easily if at all.

"Good evening, gentlemen," he said. "Chief, have you told the officers anything?"

"I thought I would leave that to you," Chief Vanders answered. "I'll fill in any details dealing with the department as needed."

"Very well. Introduce me to these fine gentlemen then."

"This is Officer William Harrison," Chief Vanders said, using his eyes to indicate William. "And his partner Officer James Thompson." He chin pointed at James. "William has been with the department twelve years. James has been with the us nine and they have been partners for eight. Gentlemen, this is Jeremy Hamilton."

"Glad to meet you," Jeremy said. He remained standing until after the introductions then sat, the chief and Lieutenant Ohlmet to his right, putting William and James to his left. "Why do you feel this is connected to our conversation from last week?"

"As I mentioned previously William and James were both arrested for sales and distribution," the chief said. "I was in on the interrogation and, even after close to twelve hours of being hammered by four of us, neither of them gave an inch."

"And who was in on the interrogation?" Jeremy asked.

"There was myself, Captain Kirby, Lieutenant Ohlmet and Captain Jakes. The men also said they had been warned by a plain clothes officer that someone was after them. We have spoken with that officer and he confirmed their story. The officer said he heard it through the usual channels, but thought William and James should be made aware of it this time. He said this one carried a deeper feel. No one thought of this being the method employed to take them down, though."

"You said Captain Jakes," Jeremy said. "Is he the one who had them brought in? Did they bring you the receipt you told me about?"

"Yes, on both counts," Chief Vanders answered and he held the paper up for Jeremy to see.

"I would like a copy of that, please, Chief. Any reason someone might want them out of the picture?"

"They were both involved in a large drug bust about three months ago, and they are the ones who gave us George Bonner as a possible suspect in the distribution of said drugs a few months earlier. Mr. Bonner has been observed by different officers at different times, handing off packages, but by the time officers pulled the men over the goods had vanished. Officer Thompson suggested we send plain clothes officers inside the bar Mr. Bonner owns on State Street."

"Has that happened yet?"

"I had vice send men in, but I get the feeling I may need someone with a little more pull in case this goes broader than George Bonner. Our information is showing a possible connection to the syndicate in Reno and I don't want to turn it over to the feds yet. I want to pull Bonner down, not let it drag on any longer than necessary."

'So much for the feds,' William thought as he and James listened, attempting to keep up with where this could be headed.

"Since we talked last week," the chief continued, "Captain Jakes has been seen in the company of one of George Bonner's known associates on two separate occasions. We tried to put a wire on him, but he found it so we don't have audio of those meetings, but in the pictures we have, they don't look like casual conversations. The captain was quite animated. If George Bonner is the man pushing the buttons, the captain might be helping him."

"So…You think Captain Jakes is in cahoots with George Bonner?" William asked, surprised. "He's been on the force twenty years."

"We received a phone call about a month ago," Lieutenant Ohlmet said. "Nothing accusatory. The person was looking for Edward Jakes. The captain wasn't in so, for whatever reason, the call was transferred to my desk. The person identified themselves as an employee of the bank Captain Jakes uses and said they had a question about a deposit they found in the night depository. This person said an envelope had been left in the night drop with Captain Jakes name on it but no account number. They didn't know which one of his accounts he wanted to deposit the money in. Someone having more than one bank account is not unusual and I assumed one was a savings account. He has two boys who will be going to college. What struck us as strange was the person continued and said it was an extremely large amount of cash. The person on the phone also said they have never had Captain Jakes leave deposits of more than ten thousand dollars in the night deposit before."

He paused, letting them digest what he'd just told them.

"Captain Jakes doesn't earn enough in his position to make

arbitrary deposits of that amount. Our concern then was the possibility he was embezzling from the department. As much as we hated to do it, we requested a warrant and went through his accounts and found one that has regular deposits of five thousand dollars or more going into it every week. And they are all in cash. We also went through our system and found nothing. We are not missing a penny. Since that time there have been five more deposits...."

"Five more?" William asked. He had interrupted the chief, but being polite was the last thing on his mind. Someone was trying to have them thrown out of the department and now they find out Captain Jakes might be dirty. "That means they're increasing the frequency of the deposits."

Jeremy observed the two, noticing William and James paid attention to details some might not.

"The last deposit was fifteen thousand," the chief continued. "There's close to a hundred and ninety thousand dollars in that account. Since we weren't successful planting a wire on Captain Jakes, we put a tail on him. That's when we caught him talking to the men who are suspected of working for George Bonner. Other than that incident, nothing has been discovered. He's a cop and recognizes our tactics."

"Holy shit!" James said. "Where do we fit in?"

"You're already on leave," Chief Vanders said. "Officers who are on the outs with the department are sometimes greeted warmly by undesirables."

"I'm in," James said. He needed no further explanation. "If we don't get our jobs back do I have any legal recourse with the department?"

"Once this investigation is over – barring more evidence being found against you – you will be reinstated," Lieutenant Ohlmet replied. "What about you, William?"

"I'm in," William said. "There's a reason I wanted to be a cop and it wasn't to wear the fancy uniform. I don't like investigating my own, but in this case I'll help."

"Let's get started then, gentlemen," Jeremy said. "Do either of you know much about George Bonner? I know you are the ones who fingered him for distribution. Other than that, what do you know?"

"We've heard some of the narcs talk about him," James said. "We know there are more drugs flowing on the streets. We also see more hookers floating in the clubs and bars. These ladies look like they are fairly well connected."

"Mr. Bonner is known for taking good care of his ladies. As long as they don't make him angry. If they fight too hard or withhold funds they have been known to disappear. That is part of what we need to find out."

"Does that have anything to do with the ladies we found before?" James asked.

"Possibly," Jeremy replied. "And your newest girl at Liberty Park. We also suspect him of being a large supplier of drugs in and around the Salt Lake City area. I am currently in the middle of an operation to get in good with the guys in Reno. George Bonner is one of the means to that end. No one knows exactly what happened but, up until two years ago, he was tight with the boys from Nevada. Around the same time frame an officer's wife was killed. Then George divorced himself from them."

William looked away attempting to focus on something other than his late wife.

"Are you alright, William?" Jeremy asked.

"That was my wife," William said. "It's good to know the department is finally getting some help."

"I think I understand," Jeremy answered. "We do not want George Bonner getting away so I will help you pull him in before I finish the other venture. I have several loose ends that still need to be worked on that front anyway."

"Why not send in plain clothes?" William continued. "Why us?"

"Because we don't want to take a chance that Captain Jakes will meet with Mr. Bonner and recognize one of the officers then tip George off," Jeremy answered. "We want this as unobtrusive as possible. You and James are under investigation by your own department and have been put on leave. You are no longer privy to what's happening inside, so he won't suspect anything if he see's you suddenly start hanging around the bars. You have a lot more free time. You will pass any and all information you gather off to me and, as your chief has said – barring new evidence against you coming up – you two will be reinstated. That brings us back to George Bonner and possibly Captain Jakes. Are you still in?"

Both men nodded and Jeremy stood to leave.

"In that case, if you will excuse me, I have some things I need to take care of. I will be in contact with you gentlemen in a day or two and we will start working out the details."

Jeremy excused himself, the men from the lounge entrance falling in behind. One continued with Jeremy while the other peeled off to cover the main entrance. William raised an eyebrow, asking the question he wasn't sure how to ask, Lieutenant Ohlmet and Chief Vanders shook their heads slowly and stood, leaving him and James alone. They watched at their superiors for a minute then stood to leave, Assistant Chief Robinson unexpectedly sliding up close to the table, leaning toward William.

"Watch your asses. I don't have all the answers, but if you make the wrong move you will be in trouble."

"What's going on?" William whispered.

"I don't know, but something is wrong. Now, I can't stand here like this. We're being watched."

"We saw the men. They left."

"Not them," the assistant chief said, sidling farther away. "It has nothing to do with the man you just talked to."

William tried to say something and the assistant chief's head jerked to the left, his eyes boring into William's.

"Just keep your nose to the ground. Watch everything. If this backfires, don't say I didn't try to warn you." He kept his eyes locked on William then turned and continued to the rear of the lounge, disappearing around a corner of the bar.

William wondered how much, if anything, the assistant chief had overheard.

"Let's get out of here," James said. He stood, automatically scanning the crowd for unwanted eyes. "This is getting scary all of a sudden."

12

As he passed the front desk Jeremy was told he had a fax. Scanning the pages as he rode the elevator up, he saw where George was advertising for primo examples of ladies on the west coast, confirming the rumors about the escort service. Areas he was advertising for were Reno and Wendover in Nevada, and Salt Lake City and Park City in Utah. Park City's ski resorts would be the larger draw for those services. Sources also said he was attempting to work the ladies – along with the drugs – onto the military bases.

Once in his room, Jeremy sat at the table, stacking the pages neatly in front of him, continuing his scrutiny. According to sources, George had a new man on his payroll. A man who had moved here from Chicago, but they had been unable to confirm that, or his name. It was also possible the man was using an alias. A person didn't need ID to pay cash for a plane or bus ticket.

Jeremy picked up the phone and called Chief Vanders. Since he was already in Salt Lake City he would talk to the officers he had just spoken with. They might be of help there as well. Jeremy was just getting ready to hang up when Chief Vanders answered.

"Good evening, sir," Jeremy said. "I was beginning to think I caught you at a bad time."

"Not at all," the chief answered. "How can I help you?"

"I need you to see if you can pull any information on a new man who is, supposedly, tied in with the Bonner organization. If it is him, his last known address was Chicago. Priors were California, North Carolina and other points east. There is also the possibility he is using an alias. Do you think the men we spoke with tonight could help?"

"Possibly, but I don't want any men getting killed tracking down an unknown."

"Right now we are only attempting to verify whether he is here or not. For all we know, he is still in Chicago, but there is a lot I am missing. I just need someone to help me locate him."

"I can call them. Tell them I have a few more questions."

"If you can, that will be perfect."

"How soon?"

"Obviously, the sooner the better. Let me know so I can plug into your system."

"I'll have them in my office at nine in the morning."

"Thank you, Chief. I'll have my people start the connection tonight."

Chief Vanders hung up and called William and James to set the meeting.

William and James had just walked into William's apartment when the phone rang. William trotted across the room, checking the clock on the stereo. 'Old habits die hard,' he thought, as he chuckled to himself. After he'd talked to the chief he told James.

They were at the station at eight forty-five the next morning, both hoping this dealt with the evidence that had been planted against them. Entering the squad room, Captain Jakes was glaring at them.

"Gentlemen," Captain Jakes barked. "My office! Now!"

They could feel all eyes on them as they crossed the room. In the captain's office, James noticed a stack of mail on the corner of the desk with a handwritten note partially hidden under it. He couldn't read the note, but he saw the name, 'Roger'. He didn't know anyone in the department named 'Roger'. Captain Jakes closed the door and lowered the blinds.

"What the hell are you guys doing in here?" he snapped.

The door opened before they could formulate an answer and Chief Vanders stood in the doorway.

"I'm glad to see you made it gentlemen," the chief said. He glared across the desk at Captain Jakes and directed the two back into the hall. "I'll meet you men in my office in a few minutes."

They moved past the desk, James brushing the stack of mail onto the floor with the tail of his windbreaker then he apologized and stooped to pick it up. As James collected the envelopes, he slipped the note into his sleeve, replacing the mail on the captain's desk, squaring the corners neatly.

"The last I heard, Captain," the chief said as they walked out, "this department was still under my command."

James glanced down the hall when they entered Chief Vanders office then pulled out the note.

"What's that?" William asked.

Angry footsteps came up the hall and James shrugged, slipping the paper into his pocket as Chief Vanders barreled through the door, closing and locking it. The chief sat behind his desk and watched them for an unusual length of time then nodded for them to take a seat.

"Jeremy will be calling in a minute," the chief said. "First, I have a couple of questions for you two. Do either of you have a weapon at home, one you used for back up?"

Both men nodded.

"Good. Have either of you worked undercover before?"

They shrugged then James pinched his thumb and index finger together.

"Well, I guess you get to learn. You'll find out why in a few minutes."

"Is there something going on here that we need to know about, sir?" William asked. "Things seem a little tense."

"Let's just say if this doesn't work half the heads in this department are going to roll and one of them is mine." The phone rang and he put it on speaker. "The men are here, Jeremy."

"Thank you, Chief. Gentlemen, as you can probably tell a few things have happened since our conversation last night. Chief Vanders and I discussed the issues just before your arrival and think we have come up with a solution. Originally I was only going to ask for your help to locate a person who may have recently moved to Salt Lake City, but it appears things have escalated. Has the chief told you anything?"

"No, sir," James answered.

"Would you like me to take it, Chief?"

"Please."

"Very well," Jeremy said. "Someone sent an interoffice memo to the mayor yesterday afternoon. In this memo the person said that Chief Vanders and Lieutenant Ohlmet are attempting to have Captain Jakes removed from his position. It also states that they employ drug dealers on the force. You two were named…."

"Bullshit!" William exclaimed, jumping to his feet. "Chief…"

"It's okay," the chief said. He raised a hand signaling for William to sit down. "Jeremy's getting there. Be patient."

"You two were named because of the tip that resulted in your arrest," Jeremy continued, "and because they went into your lockers yesterday and found the drugs that were supposed to have been hidden in your apartments. And that makes me nervous."

"You're shittin' me, right?" James said. "In our lockers? Can this get any worse?"

"That is what has me nervous. Things are beginning to look like you truly are the bad guys. My question is. Why would you be stupid enough to leave the contraband in your lockers? They are subject to search, are they not?"

"That's correct," William said. "I'll still bet this is what that plain clothes officer meant."

James unfolded the paper and read it then gave it to William.

"The plains clothes dude was right," James said. "We're in someone's crosshairs."

William read the note and tossed it across the chief's desk.

"What does he mean, Chief?" Jeremy asked.

Chief Vanders took a moment to look at the note and then leaned back in the chair.

"Where'd you find this James?" the chief asked.

"It was on Captain Jakes desk. I, kind of stole it." James gave a sideways shrug.

"What do you have?" Jeremy asked.

"We have a handwritten note that Officer Thompson stole off Captain Jakes desk," the chief replied. "It says 'Plant successful. Reno informed.' It's signed, 'Roger'."

"That makes my decision a tad easier. I have already tapped into the department's system to pass along information and two men from my organization will go in through that portal to see if there are more people in your department who could be involved. We have a team working on the memo, but they have just started. Electronic trails can be the most difficult to follow and this person covered their tracks quite well. That note makes reference to Reno so that is where we begin. Whoever is threatening Chief Vanders and Lieutenant Ohlmet are the same people who framed you gentlemen. Your unintentional involvement in that drug bust and your fingering of Mr. Bonner may have been your undoing. Since you gentlemen are already off the duty roster, our plan is to use you undercover. It may get dangerous."

"That's okay," James said. "They made this personal when they attacked me."

"Same," William echoed.

"Okay. Now for the other half of this game. We know Mr. Bonner runs the ladies and we have been given information he may also be involved with trafficking. He is currently advertising for ladies for a new escort stable. We also know him to be a man who is willing to go to whatever lengths he feels is necessary to procure a lady's cooperation."

"Is that where the trafficking comes in?" William asked, mentally reviewing what Jeremy had just said. A *new* escort stable hinted at the possibility George already had at least one. That could be where George had amassed the money to break from the syndicate.

"Yes," Jeremy answered. "We need to know if Mr. Bonner is involved in trafficking, or only drugs and prostitution. You need to hang around the clubs and any other locations Mr. Bonner is known to frequent. We need information. You gentlemen will pass anything you gather off to me and I will put it with what I feed your department and they will combine it with whatever your plain clothes officers can find."

"We might know his first target," James interjected.

"Excuse me?" Jeremy said, surprised. "What do you mean his first target?"

"There's a lady who is being harassed. She's had someone go into her apartment and attempt to assault her," James said. "And George Bonner has attempted to pick her up."

"In that case, she will also be one of your surveillance targets until we know more about what is going on. We want to catch him before he can approach her. To pull this off, any young lady George has his sights set on will be as perfect as a woman can be."

"That's her," William said.

"Then this is what we will do. You gentlemen have to find a way to show up to any calls regarding her. You will need to be available twenty-four seven along with your undercover work. If that is her, we need to know if Mr. Bonner approaches her about working as an escort or if he has already approached her. We know Mr. Bonner is dumping a lot of money into a new condo in Park City and a large estate or compound of some kind in Reno, Nevada. Mr. Bonner also has a new employee and we have been unable to pull up anything that would help verify the identity of the gentleman. He doesn't appear to own a car or have a Driver's License, and we don't find any utilities under his name. There are plenty of apartment complexes who pay the utilities so we suspect he has rented one of those."

"If she is on George's radar," William said, "I don't think she's working for him. Not yet."

"What makes you say that?" Jeremy asked.

"We responded to a call about a strange car at her apartment complex. The person who called it in said it was a limo and after we talked to the caller we talked to a few of the other tenants and the lady we're talking about was one of them. She said she saw the limo that night and it followed her home. She is the one George Bonner stopped her on her way home."

"I have a question now," James said.

"Okay." Chief Vanders answered. He looked across his desk and saw James' grin. "Why do I get the feeling I could be getting into even more trouble than I already am?"

"I just need to know if it's legal to wear wires," James replied.

"And how would you explain that? It's official equipment," the chief said. "You aren't working. Technically."

"It isn't official equipment," James said. "I bought them from a police wholesaler a few months ago. I thought they might be fun party toys. I carry them with me everywhere I go. Just in case."

"Unofficially," Chief Vanders said. "You can play with toys all you want as long as you're not crossing any legal lines. Officially, I have no clue what you're doing. You're not on duty."

"Too bad you can't record the conversation," Jeremy said.

"We can," James answered. "I just recorded this entire thing. I know it probably won't be admissible in court, but it might give us a little leverage with some of these guys."

"Since my rules bend a tad more than yours any recordings will be legal in a court of law."

"What if they find the wires?" Chief Vanders asked.

"They won't," James replied. He pulled a piece of paper out of his pocket with an eighth inch dot on it. "This is one of my toys. They're wireless, come with several of these little babies, plus the listening and recording station."

"Okay, gentlemen," Jeremy said, "You will be working outside the guidelines of standard law enforcement, but you still cannot break the law. Understood?"

"Yes, sir," they answered.

Chief Vanders opened the top drawer on his desk and took out a box, sliding it across the desk.

"These are your badges, your department pagers and two brand new portables. Do not let anyone see these. Do not use the radios to call anything in. Use them for monitoring calls only."

They removed the items from the box, slipping the portables and badges in an inside jacket pocket.

Once they were outside the men stopped between their cars and examined the station. James dropped his eyes then looked at William. "I hate to say this," he said. "But it looks like Captain Jakes is doing everything he can to get us drummed out."

"Have faith, my man. I have a feeling Jeremy wields a lot more power than he lets on."

13

Amanda stood behind the stage Saturday night looking over the audience, trying to get a read on the crowd. They weren't here to prove a point or make themselves look good; they were here to enjoy an evening of music and fun. There was also a feeling of expectancy. A curiosity. Except for last night, it had been five years since she'd sung professionally and she found herself equal parts terrified and excited. She caught movement out of the corner of her eye and recognized William walking her way.

"Just relax and sing," William said. "You did great last night, you'll do fine tonight."

"It was only two songs."

"The best two songs we've heard."

She held her breath for a second and placed her hand on her diaphragm.

"Anything wrong?" William asked.

"Butterflies," she whispered. Then she exhaled slowly and walked onstage, hoping she'd get through this.

'Butterflies,' he thought, but didn't to ask.

She glanced back at the piano and William gave a slight nod of his head. One last look over the crowd as the music started and all jitters disappeared. She was in her element.

Amanda finished the set then joined the girls from work and waved James over. James wasn't normally shy, but she noticed he paused before he sat down and Karen dipped her head then looked back up. James smiled, gazing at Karen. Amanda understood James being interested. Karen was a petite, pretty girl, her soft brown hair cut in a bob to frame her face, highlighting her eyes. One more glance at Karen, and Amanda saw the flirty smile and the slight blush. Something was definitely going on there.

When William and the back-up singer finished the last set, William joined the table, buying a round and offering Amanda a ride.

It was one a.m. by the time they pulled in at her apartment.

"How about lunch tomorrow?" he asked. "I promise not to be late."

"I would like that. How about a beer before you go?" she asked.

"Amanda, after the last time I was here, I know what I'm going to want to do," he answered. "And I don't want you to think that's the only reason I'm seeing you."

"I understand." She shrugged and smiled, looking at him from under her lashes. "I wouldn't mind tonight. That makes me sound so easy, doesn't it? I don't usually go to bed with someone just because they're here and now I'm babbling like a fourteen year old virgin. Please forgive me."

"Just relax. This is the eighties and I wouldn't tell anyone, anyway."

William noticed the slant of her nose highlighted by the outside lights and the electric blue of her eyes, the play of shadow below her cheekbones and on the curve of her jaw, remembered her body moving with his, and thought about his sanity. The perfect woman hustling him and he turned her down.

"Let's plan on lunch and go from there," she said, untangling his thoughts.

"I'll be here at noon," William said.

Amanda gave him a kiss and climbed out of the car, entering the building as he backed out. He stopped and looked down the hall one last time. Maybe he was losing his sanity, that was one good looking lady!

Amanda waited anxiously the next morning. She was early she told herself, give him a break. She walked to the window, moving the edge of the curtain aside for what felt like the hundredth time then checked her watch. Eleven fifty-eight. Why was she so excited? So nervous? She looked outside again as a limo parked on the east side of the parking lot. It was that George guy.

William drove in behind him, parking one car away. She would deal with George outside. The heat when she opened the door hit her like a blast furnace and she lifted her hair off the back of her neck. Ten seconds and she was perspiring. Hooking her hair back in a ponytail, she looked up to see George approach, William a few paces behind him.

"I thought we might do that coffee you refused," George said. "Maybe lunch."

"I don't think so," she answered. "I already have plans."

"I have something I would like to discuss with you. Something that could be quite lucrative for both of us. Give me ten minutes and I'll bring you home."

A glance behind George then George reached out to grab her arm and Amanda took a step back.

"Hello, George," William said. "I hope I'm not interrupting anything."

George jumped, jerking his hand back. "My apologies. I only wanted a few minutes of her time."

George glared at William then stepped to the side and looked in the direction of the limo, giving his head a tiny shake. Amanda followed his gaze, the driver had climbed out, his hand inside his jacket. With George's move the driver dropped his hand to his side.

"Forgive us if we don't believe you George," William said. He stopped and held an arm out for her.

"I'm afraid this isn't at all what it appears," George continued.

Amanda moved over by William while George lowered his eyes, his mind working behind them. Planning his next move.

"Perhaps I'll talk to the lady another time," George continued, his eyes smoldering. "Perhaps after work one of these nights?"

"Perhaps not," she replied.

Amanda wondered if George had taken that as a challenge. Could she back it up if he had? He walked back to the limo and she nodded to herself, the huge car pulling out, her and William's gaze following it.

"Now what?" Amanda asked.

"I don't know," William answered. "You need to watch your back, though. James and I are still here but, please be extra careful."

"Well, it isn't much, but thank you. I'll never be able to repay you."

"No problem. I wear a badge for a living. It's one of those twenty-four seven things at times." 'Technically,' he thought. "Now, how about we grab that lunch?"

"I'd like that. Do you know how to spit?"

"Yes," William answered, puzzled.

"Will you teach me, please?"

"Of course." That would be a real romantic date, wouldn't it? Teaching your girlfriend how to spit. She wasn't even his girlfriend!

14

William dropped Amanda home berating himself silently for taking so long at lunch. He had to meet James and they had added a stroll around Liberty Park and a trip through the Aviary to their agenda. Now, he was pushing the boundaries of time.

Driving out, he thought about what Jeremy told them. Would George really go to the lengths Jeremy had hinted at just to hire a woman? There were probably thousands of women willing to make the kind of money an evening with a high end escort commanded. But none of them, he admitted, would be as perfect as this one. And if George was dropping that much cash into two different locations he was either still connected to Reno, or had a much larger client base than the department was aware of. That brought up another possibility. If George hadn't broken ties with the syndicate, was he skimming off them? But how? How would he pull one over on the big boys without getting caught? But, if he wasn't connected to Reno, where was he getting his money? He kept coming back to the words *new escort stable* in Jeremy's information.

William walked into the bar and was assaulted by the smell of skunky beer, sweat, cheap perfume and urine, and the cigarette smoke burned his eyes. There was a reason he didn't frequent these places.

James was seated at the farthest of three small round tables spaced evenly along the run of plate glass windows at the front, two plain clothes officers seated on the left wall at the end of the pool tables. Their smile told him he had not kept his expression as clear as he had hoped. That and word had gotten out through the pipeline that he and James had been suspended. There was no such thing as sealed when it involved the department. It did no good to dwell on it so William ordered a beer and joined James.

"What's up buddy?" James asked.

"I took a slight detour" William answered. "I took a beautiful lady to lunch and the Aviary."

"I'm lucky you made it then."

"You got that right. Plus George showed up. I'm not sure, but it looked suspiciously like he was going to grab her."

"That's not good. Makes you wonder about that info Jeremy gave us."

A short time later a man they had previously seen with George walked in followed by several of his buddies. The guy was a regular and information the department had said his name was Royce Warden, and hinted that he worked for George. Word on the street said he had been in the military and still had some fairly decent connections. If so, Royce could get on any of the areas military bases and make George even more money. That could be how George's little empire had grown so rapidly.

While Royce and his buddies played pool and made way too many trips to the restroom they thought about the stories floating around about George supplying Royce and his cronies with a few extra benefits. There was a reason everybody loved Royce. They just didn't have enough to arrest him. They needed pictures of Royce taking the drugs on base and distributing those drugs. They also needed pictures of George handing them off inside the bar, and they had to discover where George was hiding the drugs. Jeremy's instructions had been very precise. They also wanted to attach a few more strings to both men. Strings that would nail George for his suspected participation in the sex trade industry and Royce would be along for the ride. When Salt Lake City took George Bonner and Royce Warden down, they wanted them down for good.

Royce didn't mingle for long, leaving with a plain paper bag that held a six-pack of beer and, possibly, other product. William gave James a mock salute and headed out. Information they had been given said Royce left here and went to Lilly's, a bar on Main Street two blocks south of where William played. He would catch up to Royce there while James monitored George. This might be a long night.

William pulled up in front of Lilly's and recognized the car Royce had left in. Taking a peek at the interior as he walked by, he saw the paper bag still sat on the passenger side front floor boards. He walked inside and was greeted by the usual odors of cigarettes and beer. The lights were dim, except for those hanging over a pair of pool tables. That was where any resemblance to George's bar ended. This one was clean, neat and the mirrored walls by the dance floor held no speck of dust. The walls near the entrance were covered with etched mirrors depicting leprechauns, four leaf clovers and mugs of beer. They were immaculate as well.

Royce's friend sat at the far end of the bar next to where the bartender stood.

William took a stool at the end of the bar closest to the door, but he didn't see Royce. Maybe he had gone to the Men's room. Twenty minutes went by and still no sign of Royce. William pulled the pager and keyed '000' and pushed the send button. Their signal Royce hadn't made it. He ordered another beer as James walked in, strolling over and taking the stool next to him.

"No sign of Royce," James said stating the obvious.

"Nope. He wasn't here when I got here, and the paper bag is still in the car."

"I noticed that. Any sign he's been here?"

"Not even an empty glass. I don't think he's been here."

"It's kind of late to be visiting," James said. He checked clock behind the bar, it read eleven.

They had just finished their beer when Royce bounced in carrying his paper bag and took a stool at the far corner, the bag on an empty stool between him and his friend. James and William ordered another beer. People started crowding Royce, ordering more drinks and giving him and his friend pats on the back. Once the crowd had died down, Royce and his friend left empty handed. Not even the bag. William and James finished their beer and left.

"Now we know how it works, we'll get the pictures," James said when they topped the stairs.

15

William was up before ten, showered and wandering the malls. He wasn't much for shopping, but he had to do something, anything to kill time. It had only been three days and not going to work was already taking its toll. He stopped for lunch at Dee's on North Temple and thought about the evidence that had been planted against them. He could think of no one who had a grudge against them. He had worked with some of these men for twelve years. And, except for the jokes about him and James being the modeling duo, no one had said anything against them.

Bored with his own thoughts, William stopped at a 7-Eleven and bought a six pack of beer and some chips, then headed home. Munchies for when James came over to watch the game. The phone was ringing when he walked in. It was James.

"Is there some good news?" William asked.

"Maybe, maybe not," James replied. "The lieutenant called earlier. He said he called you, but you weren't home. He wants to meet at your place in the morning. Jeremy dug up some info. He's going to call at eight-thirty. Chief Vanders will be there, too."

"I'll be here. I might even make coffee. I thought the chief said our phones were tapped?"

"Jeremy has it covered. We're good."

Eight-fifteen a.m. and everyone had arrived. Jeremy called at precisely eight-thirty, moving quickly to the reason for the call.

"I ran another search using a different set of criteria," Jeremy said. "The name we have is correct. It is Royce Warden. I show him being shipped to Vietnam in nineteen sixty-seven. He was only in country six months then he was returned to the states pending a psychological evaluation. The Army ran some tests, and he was released."

"Why did they put him in a psyche unit?" William asked.

"Supposedly a few of the nurses reported him for obscene advances, but nothing was done. There were men and women working side by side in a highly stressful environment and the military deemed it nothing to be concerned about. Kind of like one of you gentlemen walking into a bar and picking up a lady. A few of the men in his unit said he used to head into the jungle on his own and they thought Royce was just settling a score because he would carry an M60 and a pack. Medics saw the worst of the worst and they routinely came back with some pretty mangled bodies and he was a medic. They did have questions about him being brought stateside. That was the unusual part. Once in the field – especially a medic – you usually stayed in the field for the duration of your deployment."

"Why would he wander off on his own?" James asked.

"How long was he in psyche?" William asked.

"That depends upon the document you read," Jeremy replied. "That is where I am having issues. There should not be the discrepancies I am seeing in his records."

"But why was Royce brought stateside?" James asked. "I'm stuck on that. It's not how things were done. I know a few guys who were certifiably crazy over there and no one brought them back. And the nurse issue is total B-S. The nurses pushed that as hard as the men."

"That is being kept under wraps. The military brass has not released any details whatsoever. Even my commander has been unable to unlock anything. We're still working on it, though. We do know the government worked a lot of operations over there that the general public was not aware of."

"What about after he was released?" James asked.

"Within a month of his release a woman reported waking up to a man in her apartment and he attempted to accost her. They think whoever it was picked the lock."

"So far that sounds pretty close to what we have," William admitted. "Did that occur again?"

"Not there. Royce moved to California and shortly after his arrival, a lady reported someone watching her," Jeremy said. "The lady went home a few nights later and thought she smelled cigarette smoke. She woke to a man on her bed touching himself inappropriately. She told responding officers when she reached for the phone, he attempted to grab her. She managed to keep one hand free and called 9-1-1, and he fled. An inspection of her apartment revealed stains on her bedding where he had ejaculated. They think that was what woke her. Her locks had been picked. She promptly moved. There were a few others after her, but nothing was ever found."

"Let me guess," James said. "Extremely beautiful ladies."

"You are correct," Jeremy answered. "And nothing further happened with any of the women so they assumed it had been a drifter. Just someone passing through."

"So, what about this DNA shit they've been working on?" William asked. "How close is that to us being able to use it?"

"DNA is too new to use in court yet. However, some localities are voluntarily taking samples from inmates or detainees and keeping them in a database for future possibilities. Some states are using it to help connect cases and using that to squeeze their suspects. But nothing says Royce was responsible. I ran a search on sexual assaults and calls for breaking and entering because of your incidents and noticed those occurred during the same time period Mr. Warden had been living in those areas. Then he moved to Chicago and married a lady named Amanda Granger...."

"Amanda," William said. "I wonder if she's the reason he's here."

"Is she the lady who has been having issues?" Jeremy asked. "Is her name Amanda?"

"Yes, and she said she moved here to get away from her ex-husband," James answered. "She said it was a really screwed up marriage."

"Did anything happen in Chicago?" William asked.

"They had a few break ins," Jeremy continued. "Which they assumed were attempted burglaries at first, except the burglar didn't come in until after the ladies had gone to bed. In the first couple of instances the ladies had phones by their beds and called 9-1-1. As soon as they picked up the phone, the intruder left. In the next ones he did the same as your lady in Salt Lake City. He attempted to accost them, the ladies being successful in fighting him off. In a couple of the instances he ejaculated on their beds as well."

"And none of these women saw their intruder," William said.

"Correct. Now you have an Amanda living in Salt Lake City and you have a man breaking into her apartment. And she happened to have moved there from Chicago."

"And from what you just told us, the other women were unable to press charges because there was no one to press charges against."

"You are correct again," Jeremy said. "I know that isn't what you wanted to hear, but it might give us a little more to work with.

The lady needs to watch her back a lot more carefully. Especially since we feel she may be in Mr. Bonner's sights as well. So, I want you gentlemen to concentrate on keeping her safe, but we don't want it to look like she's being guarded. And find out anything you can about this ex-husband. We have also learned George may have a new man on his payroll. A new face in the crowd. This gentleman's name is Royce Warden."

"And I think her ex-husband is Royce Warden," James said. "The strings aren't attached too tightly yet, but that's where it's leading."

"Her ex is Royce Warden?" Jeremy asked. "The same person we were just discussing?"

"I'll check on that further. She told William and I she was from Chicago and she left there to get away from her ex. She thought he was still in Chicago. I had lunch with her once and that was the name she used. How many Royce Warden's would be in Salt Lake City?"

"We still need to catch him in the act, though," William said. "We need witnesses – proof. Correct?"

"Yes," Jeremy answered.

"Did you get the update we sent you? We're waiting for Royce to make another run to get the photos."

"Yes, I did. As soon as you can get those it will be appreciated. Have you seen him recently?"

"He was at George's Sunday night," James answered. "Nothing happened then. We have photos of him picking up bags at the bar on other occasions, and we're trying to get pictures of him handing things off, but he's good at hiding his actions. We want some that are more definite on what he is doing. Do you want us to follow him? We hang more inside right now."

"No," Chief Vanders interjected. "Jeremy has requested men to put on that, but it might be an idea to keep a closer eye on him when you do see him. They think he might even be helping

George push the ladies. William, we know George frequents the club you play in from time to time. Have you seen anything suspicious while you were on stage?"

William glanced at James. Nothing like pushing Jeremy out of the way.

"I've seen him a couple of times, but it's usually after I'm through," William answered. "From the piano it's hard to see the tables in the back with the lights glaring in your eyes. George and his entourage usually leave early. They were both there about a week ago. Royce was there Saturday night. James and I followed Royce to Lilly's Sunday night. He had lots of buddies then. That's the night we think Royce was making the exchanges under the lip of the bar. That's why we're waiting for him to make another run."

"Fill us in on this lady you are so positive George is after," Jeremy said.

"The first time we talked to her someone had tried to break in," William said. "The first of the other incidents, a man entered her apartment, but she has no idea how he got in the building...."

"Damn!" James suddenly exclaimed wide-eyed. "Royce!"

"What?" William asked. "You think Royce is our resident psycho?"

"Fill me in guys," Jeremy said.

"I'm sorry. We've been setting here talking about Royce and about George and now it clicks," James said. "With all of the surveillance on him, George has shown no interest in Amanda at all. He has never been seen near her, never tried to talk to her, nothing. All of a sudden, she not only has some pervert trying to assault her in her own apartment, but George Bonner is all over her. What are the odds?"

"I think the info helped us put some things together Jeremy," William said.

"Do you think her attacker might be this Royce Warden Jeremy was just telling us about?" the lieutenant asked.

"Thinking about it now – possibly. The guy who attempted to rape her sent her to the hospital with a pretty good gash on her shoulder. It looked like he had a key, but she swears she hadn't given anybody a key. The complex was one with a secure entry, too. You had to buzz her apartment for her to allow you in, but it was a retrofit. Some of those are easy to bypass. She has since moved and had her phone number changed."

"Someone placed a camera on her desk at work, too," James added.

"Keep working on that," Lieutenant Ohlmet said. "We would like to get one or two counts of trafficking and we'll pull George in."

"If we have enough proof," Chief Vanders cautioned.

"Are you guys going in tonight?" Lieutenant Ohlmet asked, giving the chief a sideways glare.

"No, sir," James answered. "We only pop in now and then Monday through Wednesday. Weekends are the best."

"Understood. You want to take it again, Jeremy?"

"Thank you," Jeremy answered.

They heard the frustration in Jeremy's voice and thought about Chief Vanders not so gentle push a few minutes earlier.

"We caught the person dropping the cash at Captain Jakes' bank," Jeremy continued. "He was carrying ID that says he is an officer with the Salt Lake City Police. His name is Roger Portman. Do you gentlemen recognize the name?"

"No, but before we were hauled in I saw a new man hanging around the station," William replied.

"Roger was the name on that note I found," James said.

"He's not one of ours," Lieutenant Ohlmet said.

"He is not a known associate of Mr. Bonner's, either," Jeremy said. "But that doesn't mean anything. We are aware of several people who only work for George occasionally. However, we are leaning more toward the syndicate due to the note James heisted. My organization was able to get pictures of this Mr. Portman dropping the envelope. My commander pulled some strings and the only envelope dropped that night was the one he left and it contained almost thirty thousand in cash. Also, Captain Jakes isn't using any of the funds in that particular account. Whoever is behind this may be using it to bank extra money for an upcoming project. Who is doing it, we don't know. What Captain Jakes is doing, or why Captain Jakes is in on this, we don't know. If it deals with the drugs coming into the valley, we need to find out. Any chances you could start mining that arm of this venture, gentlemen?"

"We can try," William answered.

"Good. Do you gentlemen have any further questions?"

"No, sir," James answered.

"In that case, I will call again when I have more details."

The line went dead and they were even more curious about this man Lieutenant Ohlmet and Chief Vanders dropped everything for. He wielded some serious power. They still thought he was connected to the feds.

"So, what's the deal with Jeremy?" James asked. "We asked you before and you didn't answer."

"Jeremy will let you know when he needs to," Chief Vanders replied.

"Are you any closer to finding out who set the trap for you?" William asked. He hated to think he had been working under Captain Jakes all these years and the man was undermining the department.

"We know it was from inside the department," Lieutenant Ohlmet said. "The crumbs are getting bigger and there are more of them. With Mr. Portman in custody we learned a few tidbits, but he's clammed up. We're pretty confident he knows who's behind it, which means he also knows the man behind your arrest. Just keep your heads on a swivel. Now, enjoy the rest of your day, gentlemen."

When the lieutenant and the chief left both men agreed this wasn't what they had wanted to hear. It was like being given a bite of the appetizer when you wanted the main course. And they wanted to know why Chief Vanders appeared to be steering them away from George Bonner. They had even more questions now.

"When you goin' to George's dive again?" William asked.

"When you want to go, bro?" James answered.

"I just can't do Friday or Saturday," William reminded him.

"I'll pick you up Thursday."

"Thursday it is. You're not trying to set me up, aren't you?"

"William! Would I do that to you?"

"Yes," William said with a laugh. "I remember this one blind date…."

"Never mind. You don't have to remind me. That was not a good set up."

16

William picked James up at six-forty-five sharp Thursday night. It was a boys' night out.

"What's the game plan?" William asked. "Just two dudes out hustling the girls? You trying to hook me up with a hot mama, ain't ya dude?"

"Hey, if it happens it happens. But I hope with both of us inside and both of us acting like we're on the lookout maybe we'll find out something. Information, I mean," James added when the smirk appeared on William's face. "I want to mingle with the clientele not just sit by the door like I'm waiting for someone who never shows up. Some of those girls work for Bonner and they are fonts of information when they want to be."

"And how would you know that?"

"Not the way you're thinking," James replied. "Hang back on the fringes and listen. Not all of them like their job."

They pulled up at the bar and William took in the pools of scantily clad women. The days were getting warmer and the clothes were disappearing. Too much make-up, not enough self-respect. He also understood – like a lot of people – these women had bills to pay. For some this was just the end result of a screwed up life. Maybe they'd had too few choices. Maybe they'd made too many decisions that had gone south in a hurry. Maybe a few too many nights in some mans bed only to find out he had been married all along and had no plans on ever leaving his wife and kids. Maybe it was too many nights alone. Desperation wasn't always a good thing.

"Okay. What's up?" William asked. "You got something more than that on your mind."

He forced his mind away from the clusters of bodies and they headed for the door.

"Yeah," James answered. "We're missing something. We both think we might have two different people with two different agendas. We both know Royce and George are working together. When we walk up to get a beer, we need to eyeball the place. Especially if George is behind the bar. No one has seen him work it. We'll compare notes once we're done. I also want your opinion on some of the people who frequent this joint."

"I can already tell some of these people are only here for the alcohol," William answered. "They have no other life."

"That I know, too," James said. "I'm talking about the other people."

When James opened the door William was hit again by the odor. This place was foul.

"Grab us a beer and I'll find a table," James said. "George is behind the bar. I think he's replenishing his dealers' goody bags. By the way, you're already being tracked."

"By what?"

"Funny, William! Now go."

At ten p.m. Royce walked in and joined George at his usual table near the back. The bartender handed Royce a beer, Royce pulled an envelope out of his pocket and slid it across the table to

George. James walked up to the corner of the bar closest to the two and ordered two more beers and two bags of chips.

"Here's the money from that last bunch of fun," Royce said. "More men transferred out at Fort Douglas and Hill Air Force Base this week and they won't rotate back in for another two or three months. Maybe longer. Not sure about Tooele. I'll get back with you when I need more."

"Thank you. How's the information gathering?" George thumbed through the cash and slid part of it back to Royce.

"Going," Royce said. "I tried to get farther than the Men's room last night, but they caught me. They don't like people snooping around, I guess. You're sure nothing is going to happen?"

"I promise," George answered.

Royce got comfortable in a booth with one of the ladies and William and James debated the wisdom of staying. When William left to get another beer, George approached James.

"May I?" George asked. He didn't wait for answer, just grabbed an empty chair from the adjacent table and slid it over.

"Not at all," James answered. "What brings you here?"

"I need to talk to you. Without your buddy."

"What's wrong with my buddy?"

"Nothing," George said with a slight hike of his shoulders. "I was wondering. I might be in need of some assistance and I was curious if you might be interested in earning some extra money. You and your friend are here quite regularly lately. And the women seem to like you."

"Possibly," James answered. He scanned behind George at William still waiting at the bar. "You haven't answered my question about my friend."

"Sometimes they're singled out by law enforcement," George said. "I don't want to attract more attention. If you catch my meaning."

"I think so. What do you have in mind?"

"I want the ladies to spend less time on the streets," George said. "I need someone who will collect and not trade favors. You know, let them keep more of their cash while getting something in return. Follow me so far?"

James nodded and William started their direction.

George noticed James gaze and stood. "We can finish this conversation later."

James pulled out a business card, and set it on the table.

George's eyes grew wide at the sight of the police department insignia and James laughed.

"Don't worry. My *friend* and I are on suspension for selling drugs. My friend knows how to keep it low, George. Give me a call. My home number's on the back."

George saluted James with the card as he stood, returning the chair to the table he had taken it from. He nodded at William in passing.

"What was that?" William asked, sitting a bottle in front of James before sitting down himself.

"We have officially been approached. We just might be on our way."

They finished their beer and drove to James'. Royce hadn't left and George hadn't given him a paper bag. Royce wasn't making a delivery tonight.

James unlocked his door and waved William in then headed for the refrigerator.

"So what do you think?" James asked. "I'll grab us another brew."

"About the place, the women, or what our Mr. George Bonner is doing?"

James popped the top on a beer and set it on the table in front of William then flipped a chair around so he was straddling it and leaned into the back.

"George," James said. "I thought that one girl was going to rape you right there at the table, dude. I knew you'd attract attention."

William reflected on the woman his partner had referred to. It was going to take more than one laundering for the clothes and two or three showers to get the feel of that woman off him. He didn't want someone hanging on him like a piece of jewelry.

"I want to know what Mr. Bonner was talking to you about," William said. "And that one 'girl', as you call her, was way scary. I think I'll stick to the club where I play, thank you."

"It seems he's looking for some help collecting from the ladies. Someone who won't partake of the goods in lieu of the cash."

"And?"

"I gave him one of my business cards. You should have seen his face when he read Salt Lake City Police Department. I thought he was going to choke."

James laughed and William leaned back, thinking about the possible ramifications of getting caught working for George. They were trying to go back to work, not get arrested again.

"What if we get caught?" William asked.

"I want to talk to Jeremy about that, too," James admitted. "I don't want to go down that path again. With my toys, though, we can use the recordings as evidence and cover our butts. Now, did you get any new insights on George?"

"George isn't running things like a syndicate affiliate. It's too much of a dive. The syndicate usually likes things more upscale. I did notice when I walked up to the bar he's got some hidden storage under the rear corner of the bar. A couple of times it hung open like there's a cabinet or a door. I didn't see a handle, though. The last time I was up there it was M-I-A."

"I've seen the same thing. I also want to know how he gets his goods. Where's the stuff dropped, or does he have someone pick it up?" James hesitated for a minute. "I don't know. There's still a piece or two missing."

"Understood." William watched James and recognized the gaze. His partner was thinking. "I've never known your instincts to be wrong yet."

"We got some free time now. I want to follow Georgie boy around. I also think we need to take the offered position."

"We can follow him. The other...I'm not sure. Let's wait until we talk to Jeremy before we make that decision. What about that conversation you were listening to?"

"Oh, that was interesting," James said. "Royce gave George information on troops being rotated out at the military bases. He also handed George an envelope full of cash and George gave him three hundred bucks back."

"That makes the evening worth it."

"They were also discussing some building. He said the people wouldn't let him past the restroom. Then Royce asked if anything was going to happen. I wonder what he meant."

"Makes you wonder," William commented. "Any ideas?"

"Nope. You?"

"Nope."

17

The next week William and James met at George's again. Instead of sitting at the table near the front, they sat at the end of the bar closer to George. They straddled the bar stool, telling jokes and listening to the myriad conversations around them until the hinges on the back door complained and Royce walked in. Royce met George and ordered a beer. They decided to hang around, ordering another beer and a pack of jerky.

They could see the table through the mirror behind the bar and watched Royce take a napkin and draw a map while describing the interior of a business. The discussion turned to the positions of roads and alleys, sounding like the area near Regent Street. After the two were finished George slid a manila envelope across the table to Royce. Royce picked it up and counted the money then saluted George with the envelope and George laughed.

After Royce walked out George approached them and waved for the bartender to bring them each a beer, on the house.

"Have you given any thought to my suggestion?" George asked.

"William and I have discussed it," James answered and noticed

George glance at William. "We don't meet you here. We don't want the plain clothes guys seeing us. Deal?"

"Deal," George answered. "I'll tell the ladies to meet you elsewhere. Where should I have them go?"

"We'll find them. It'll draw less attention to us, and to you. William plays at Pearls on Main on Friday and Saturday nights so if they want to, there's an outside mail drop for the club. They can drop the envelopes there with one of our names on it and a note telling us who is or isn't paying so we can tell you. But they need to keep it discreet. We want no complaints from the club manager. Don't screw it up."

"I'll make sure they know."

"One other thing, George. If they come by the club, we don't want them inside."

George agreed, whispered something to the bartender then returned to his table.

"I thought we were going to talk to Jeremy?" William asked.

"We are," James answered. "Just setting the hook, reeling in the bait."

Eleven-thirty Friday night, William and James arrived at the club. With the normal rotating shifts of a police officer, Eddie had a replacement in the wings for William, her name was Julie Barron. Since they were attempting to maintain the illusion of working, William had told Eddie he would be on swing for a while so Eddie had called her in. But with Julie filling in, George had turned the club into his new hangout, making the undercover part difficult.

William told Eddie they were going back to days next week. He and James would go back to hanging in George's bar and maybe George would go back to hanging out in his part of town.

Amanda and Julie completed the last set, and Amanda joined the group, saying she didn't want to hang around. It was late and she was tired. Working full time and singing two nights a week were catching up to her, and James offered Amanda a ride. Surprised, Amanda glanced at Karen, who looked disappointed. James was then told he had a call, and he automatically tried to think of any new accusations that may have been leveled against them, but they hadn't been in the station, and William was the one who normally get the calls here, not him.

"What's up?" James asked when he answered.

"I need you and William to meet me at the Sambo's on State Street," Lieutenant Ohlmet said. "I'll be in the rear dining area."

"On our way." James hung up and tossed his keys to Amanda. "Here take my car. William can drop me by to pick it up. It might be late."

"No, Karen can give me a ride," Amanda said and tossed the keys back.

"My cars in the shop," Karen said. "I rode with Janice."

"Take James car," Amanda replied.

James raised an eyebrow as Amanda snatched the keys from his hand and tossed them to Karen. She wrote something on a napkin, and then turned back to the group.

"Janice, can you give me a ride home?"

"Anytime," Janice answered.

James only looked confused.

"This is Karen's phone number," Amanda continued. She stuffed the napkin into James pocket and pushed him toward William and the stairs. "Go! You'll be late!"

James glanced between the women, his mind revolving around the *'Who's on First'* skit by Abbott and Costello, then he followed William up the stairs.

They walked into the restaurant and found the lieutenant in a far corner and took seats across from him.

"Lieutenant," William said. "Problems?"

He shook his head and pulled a picture out of a folder. "No, no problems. I just have a couple of quick questions about the girl who was found at Liberty Park. You two responded to the call."

"Yes, sir."

William and James glanced at each other trying to think of something they might have done wrong, but could think of nothing. They had followed procedure right down the line.

"Another body has been found," Lieutenant Ohlmet said. "This one at Silver Lake and the sheriff thinks the two might have been committed by the same perp. I want to hear your observations. Reports can be a little dry when it comes to details."

"Shoot," William said. "We'll do what we can."

"When you found the girl at Liberty Park, she was naked and laying in the same position the detectives found her in," Lieutenant Ohlmet said. He slid the picture across the table to them as he spoke. "Nothing had been moved that you know of, correct?"

"Correct," James answered. "As soon as we saw her William made the requisite calls and we set up the tape and secured the perimeter per procedure. At that time there were a few citizens beginning to take an interest. Something about flashing lights on a squad car draws them out of the woodwork. There were a few foot prints but Lloyd determined part of them had been made by the couple who found her. There were some that were different, but they were too badly smudged to be useful. I think Lloyd had the techs try to pour a couple of casts anyway."

William looked up from the picture. "This one's in the same position," William said. "Except for the decomp she's almost identical. Who found it?"

"A fisherman was backing his boat in, getting ready for a day of fishing with his buddies. They were supposed to meet at five in the morning so he thought it would be easier to put the boat in the water tonight. He almost ran over her. His dog started barking and he stopped. That's when he saw her."

"Is she a runaway?"

"Doesn't look like it," the lieutenant answered. "She lived in Brighton and worked at the resort and the campgrounds. Has for several years. Her parents said she met some guy who had lots of money and has been hanging around Salt Lake City more than usual. The last time they heard from her was last week."

"Last week?" James echoed.

The lieutenant nodded. "They found her car at a restaurant here in Salt Lake City, but there was no sign of her. Then her body was found tonight. This is the second one and they are eerily similar to the ones that ended two years ago. As you can see, it looks like some animals got to it."

James looked away and slid the photo back across the table. He couldn't get used to seeing that. Why would someone hurt a woman and then just dump her like that? Why would someone hurt a woman?

"That's it. I just wanted to know if there was anything new you might remember. You were the first ones on scene." He looked across the table at them. "Well, unless you can think of anything else, that's it. If you do think of anything. Let me know."

His eyes looked tired.

Both men nodded and watched the lieutenant leave. There hadn't been a single girl murdered in two years and now there were two plus one being assaulted.

"Do you think it's starting again?" William asked James. "Do you think the dude's back? Or maybe he never left. He just went into hiding."

"I was thinking the same thing," James answered. "It's been two years. He could have left and moved back. I wonder if Lloyd will help us. Give us a few answers."

"Maybe. We're not detectives, my man."

"Just curious, buddy."

"I'll give him a call. If these were done by the same person as the previous women, the department might be in for a bumpy ride."

James called Karen and got her address then had William drop him off. He closed the car door and looked up at the lights still on in one of the apartments. Some nights he hated this job. This was one of them.

He walked up the hall, fighting his own emotions, pictures of his mother and sister flashing through his mind. He tapped lightly with a knuckle; Karen opened the door and waved him in. She took a hesitant step forward, James put his arms around her and she returned the embrace.

"I think you would make coming home a definite pleasure."

"You think so?"

"Yeah, I think so," he said. Nights like tonight reminded him of how lucky he was to still be alive. "I wasn't sure what you thought."

"I think I'd like to find out," Karen whispered.

Karen backed slowly toward the bedroom, sliding his shirt off. They sank onto the bed and James pulled her close, felt her breath on his chest, her heart beating against him. He ran his hand down her back and kissed her, thinking about the girls who would never have the chance to get married or raise a family. And two families who had been robbed of their daughters. Friends who would never see them, or talk to them, again. They had to catch these men and they had to catch them soon. Karen or Amanda could be next.

Karen woke the next morning to James kissing her softly while tracing her hip and the curve of her side with a finger.

"Don't you have to work today?"

"Huh-uh," he said his voice soft. "Time off."

"For good behavior?" She laughed a wisp of hair caught on her cheek.

"Something like that. Now, quit talking and kiss me."

James lay beside Karen after they'd made love, watching her heartbeat in the hollow of her neck, a leg draped over her belly. Light olive skin, tan lines barely visible, petite and perfectly proportioned, and dark eyes he could get lost in. She would make beautiful babies and be a perfect mom.

After they'd dressed, he took Karen to breakfast. They were joking and talking about stupid things they'd done as kids when James' pager chirped. He checked the number, excusing himself to use the payphone.

"What's up, buddy?" he asked when William answered.

"I called Lloyd," William said. "He pulled a copy of the report on the girl at Silver Lake. He says her and the girl we found in Liberty Park were killed in the same way and probably by the same person. He also said it's the same as the previous women. Our man only took a long hiatus. Both girls had had sex before they died. There was semen in both. No sign of rape. It looks like it was consensual."

"Could they tell if it was from the same man?"

"I asked if we could have a DNA test done to check that. He said they are expensive, but he'll see what they can do. He reminded me it's new and not admissible in court."

"Did you tell him we just want to connect a few dots?"

"I did. He understands but – like us – his hands are tied. Plus we're on leave. He's got to dance around that."

"Damn, I wish we were back on duty," James said.

"Hear ya," William answered. "Hey, where you at?"

"I took Karen to breakfast. Did Lloyd tell you anything about cause of death? They weren't strangled so how did they die? Were they suffocated?"

"He said they weren't strangled with ligature, but they may

have been choked. This girl has a bruise on the underside of her jaw. Not all of the previous victims had that mark."

"But some of them did?"

"It sounded that way. I want to see if Jeremy can pull those old reports for us. I want to see if there are any other common traits. So far we have the panties and the pose. There has to be more. One person they all knew or had recently met. Like that girls new boyfriend. Lloyd said to put in for a detectives slot again. We're too nosy for our own good."

There was several seconds of silence as they thought about the possibilities. Neither of them liked the path this was leading down. James finally broke the silence.

"Let me know if you find out anything else. I should be home in about an hour. I have to drop Karen off."

"Meet me at the park," William said. "We can go over this and shoot some hoops or something."

18

William pulled in at Amanda's, looked up at her window. This undercover crap was harder than he'd thought. His mind shifted back to their psycho and everything that had happened recently. He couldn't get past the feeling they were connected.

He pushed the buzzer and identified himself the lock releasing. Two steps up the main stairwell he diverted to the hall, inspecting the area. When he passed the side door, he backed up, opened it and leaned out, checking along the wall and the outside of the door. No security panel. If Amanda's attacker had a pick, and was any good, this had been his point of entry. But how had he got away without being seen? A scan of the street and William remembered a convenience store a block away and two apartment buildings - one north of here and one west. Plenty of places to disappear.

William trotted up the stairs, his mind racing.

"What's up?" she asked. "You look like something's bothering you."

"Just thinking about things," he answered as he put his arms around her and gave her a kiss.

Amanda threw together some lunch then they turned the stereo on and a couple of hours later, William decided he needed to get cleaned up. They had to be at the club tonight.

"So," she said, hesitantly. "I got a question for you."

"Okay," he answered. "I'll do my best to answer."

"Promise?"

"Promise," he replied. "What's going on?"

"That's what I want to ask you," she said, noting the surprise.

"I don't know what you mean," he answered, hoping he sounded convincing.

"William, I'm not ten years old. You never wear your uniform anymore and your schedule seems to have flown out the window. It's rotating faster than a merry-go-round."

"Well, we aren't doing anything illegal," he stammered, unsure of where to go from here.

"And if I call the station are they going to tell me you guys have been suspended again?"

"Aw, shit! You called the station?" Her eyes skewered his, searching for an answer then he glanced at the television, its screen black. No help there. "Yeah, they will. There are only three people – besides James and me – who know what's going on and they won't tell you anything. This is one of those times you have to trust me."

She frowned and searched his eyes a tic longer than usual, then shrugged her left shoulder. "I guess, I have to," she said. "I know with cops there's a lot about your jobs that can't be said."

"I promise I'll tell you everything as soon as I can."

"You're sure?"

He nodded and smiled. "Trust me," he whispered, pulling her in for a kiss.

"You definitely don't play fair."

"Good. I'm glad."

After they'd made love, Amanda rested her head on Williams'

chest, listening to his heartbeat.

An unfamiliar chirp startled her and William sighed and picked up his pager. He excused himself and went to the kitchen to use the phone. She wanted desperately to pick up the extension and eavesdrop, but it was his work. He hung up the phone and climbed in the shower then he was standing in the door wrapped in a bath towel. He even looked good out of uniform.

"Hello, sunshine," he said.

"Mm-hmmm," she said. "Like that girly soap?"

"It brings out the softer side," he answered, walking over and curling up beside her again.

Amanda stroked his chest gently. Caramel colored eyes that looked into her soul, a sexy voice that caressed her senses, and skin like velvet. The perfect package!

"Keep that up and we won't make it out of this bedroom."

"Promise?"

"Promise," he answered. "You know, you're the sexiest woman I've ever met. We're going to have to do this again."

He ran his fingers along the scar on her shoulder his mind already thinking about her assailant.

"Sounds like an idea. Don't you have to work tonight?"

"Nope," William replied. "It has something to do with that schedule flying out the window. You know it's rotating faster than a merry-go-round. I have to meet James, though. I'll see you at the club and maybe we can do more exploring tonight."

"Where are we going?"

She reached over and unhooked the towel, running a finger across his hip and up his back, his body doing an involuntary shudder.

"To the moon." Then he popped her playfully on the rear and gave her a kiss. "Damn, I hate to say this, but I gotta go. I'll meet you at the club."

Amanda checked the clock as William dressed. Five p.m. She had to get dressed, too.

"*You* do not play fair," he said. He gave her one more kiss then trotted out.

William was at the club when Amanda walked in, and the place was packed. Word had spread rapidly about the 'white lady who could belt out the tunes' and everybody wanted a good table.

Amanda had worn a summer dress with spaghetti straps, William smiled when he saw her and winked. She walked onstage and sat on the bench beside him, giving him a kiss. His skin tone changed and she was curious if black men blushed. It did look a little rosy.

"I already don't like this not working thing you're doing. Except for this afternoon, I haven't seen you much lately," she whispered. "So I decided to take you up on your offer to do some exploring tonight. What do you think? Are you up for a journey to the moon?"

William threw his head back and laughed silently. "Boosters on standby!"

Half way through the second set, Eddie approached William, whispering in his ear then the two hurried off leaving Amanda mid-song. The sound man quickly spooled up the music and Amanda finished the piece then excused herself. William stopped her in the hall and nudged her gently back to the front, Eddie giving the bartenders instructions before walking onstage and picking up the mike.

"I'm sorry, but I'm going to have to bring the evening's festivities to an abrupt end," Eddie said, his voice betraying his apprehension. "There's a fire in the rear of the building and we need everybody out as quickly and safely as possible. Don't panic. Please, follow the directions from the members of law enforcement who are here tonight. The fire department is already on their way. Again, please follow the instructions given by the officers here tonight."

While Eddie talked, William enlisted Timothy and James' aid.

After the bartenders had cleared the restrooms, the men slid two tables across the hall blocking it, pushing the remaining furnishings against the walls while James and Timothy began evacuation procedures.

William took the microphone, repeating the precaution then moved off stage to help James and Timothy with the clientele. With the customers out safely, William took Amanda's hand and started up the stairs. One of the firefighters stopped him and Amanda's hand slipped out of his.

William took the steps two at a time, expecting to find her outside. No one had seen her. He returned to the club and began a search, starting in the dressing room, thinking she had gone back to get her clothes. The fire department kicked him out telling him that, if they found any sign of her, they would let him know. At this point that didn't look promising.

The next two hours passed slowly, the fire was out and still no sign of Amanda. William remembered Royce and George's conversation and walked the length of the hall, realizing Royce had given George the layout for the rear of the club. William topped the stairs on his way to tell James, halting on the last step than looked back down the stairwell. He hadn't moved anything to get down the hall.

James noticed William's move and rushed over, his curiosity piqued. William explained and they raced back down the stairs, William being jerked backwards.

"You can't go in there," someone said, sounding eerily like one of the divers on one of those *National Geographic* shows.

William wheeled around to face a firefighter still wearing his breathing apparatus as James barreled into them.

"We have to check one thing," William replied. He held up his index finger to accent his statement. "Just one thing. You can come with us if you'd like. Please," he added when the man hesitated.

"Go," the man said, waving them forward. "I'm with you."

William and James stopped at the entrance to the hall, the tables had been moved. At the end of the hall, the emergency exit was cracked, but the alarm was quiet. It should have gone off the minute that bar had been pushed. A search of the street and William found a diamond bracelet next to a fresh set of tire tracks. It was Amanda's. He waved a patrolman over and explained what they'd found.

There were several sets of prints and one belonged to a big man, but further investigation showed no trace of blood and no sign of a struggle, the officer's explaining that the bracelet had probably fallen off when she entered the car. '*When she entered the car*' made it sound like she had gotten into the vehicle voluntarily. William understood the officer's stance, he had been there, but he knew differently. He had started back inside when James tapped him on the shoulder.

"We both know that's bullshit. There are no women's prints. Amanda was wearing heals."

William spun and looked behind them at the tire tracks. James was right. Rushing inside William grabbed Amanda's purse and clothes from the dressing room then they charged up the stairs. Now they had to tell Jeremy.

James volunteered to make the call and while he called Jeremy from a payphone across the street, William leaned against the front of the building holding Amanda's clothing. Three of them inside and she was gone. Could this thing go any farther south?

William shifted her clothes in his hands and dropped her purse. Picking it up, he cursed silently to himself and then stared at it. Women didn't go anywhere without their purse. He waved the purse, locking eyes with James. James immediately stood up straighter. His partner had got it. Then James turned, facing the phone.

"Is there a problem?" Jeremy.

"You might say that," James said. "We lost her."

"You lost her," Jeremy repeated. "How so?"

"There was a fire in the club and someone grabbed her. I'm sorry, Jeremy. We're not sure what happened."

"You're fine," Jeremy said. "I'm on my way. I'll meet you gentlemen along with the chief and Lieutenant Ohlmet at the restaurant in The Hotel America. Be there by nine a.m., please."

Jeremy checked the clock before he dialed the chief's number. One a.m. A short message letting the chief know he was coming to Salt Lake City and asking him to call the lieutenant, and Jeremy packed his overnight case. One more call to make sure they had a room available at the hotel and he threw his bag and his briefcase into the Land Cruiser and headed north. He would pull into Salt Lake City at approximately four a.m.

Once he was on the road, Jeremy pushed the button on the pager.

"Is there a problem?" came the commander's voice.

"Yes, sir." Jeremy replied. These occurrences were rare, but he always felt as though he had failed. He didn't allow himself the luxury of being unsuccessful. "The girl is gone. Pulled out from under their noses. Just giving you the normal heads up, sir."

"Keep my informed."

"Most definitely," Jeremy answered, the connection already severed.

19

Jeremy made good time and was in Salt Lake City before he expected, grateful for that extra hours sleep. He had to be focused when he met the men.

He walked in the restaurant that morning and all four men were waiting.

"Good morning, gentlemen," he said. "Are we ready to get this over with?"

James and William shrugged.

Jeremy waited until after everyone had ordered to get things started.

"Okay," Jeremy said. "Before we go over last night I want to know what the press has been told. How much information has the department given out?"

"Officially, nothing," Chief Vanders answered. "They know about the fire, but we haven't said anything about the abduction. I asked the manager not to say anything until we can find out more details on her disappearance, but I would like to release something to help pull in leads."

"Understood," Jeremy replied. "I'm going to ask to use a

different tact on this one. Let's keep this as quiet as we can until tomorrow. If asked do not deny you're looking for her, but don't offer anything. If George is responsible I want him to think he has had enough lead time he doesn't need to worry. I want him to get sloppy."

The chief and the lieutenant nodded and Jeremy turned his attention to William and James.

"Now, exactly what happened last night?"

They spent the next couple of hours going over everything that had happened up to, and including, the fire and the conversation between George and Royce two nights prior.

Jeremy was amazed at how quickly and easily the abductors had moved her. If they had taken her out the front someone would have seen them. Especially if she had been fighting. And they would have had to drag her around the block to get her to where the bracelet had been found. Unless they had the car waiting on First South and someone dumped the bracelet as a decoy. Still, someone on the street should have witnessed them moving her. Plus that didn't explain the tire tracks. There was also the possibility they had taken her through the back door. That would have forced them to pass the firemen and the fire. Then there was the alarm. This had been well planned and executed.

"Unless…" William said gazing out the window. "Unless they waited until everyone was out of the building. The room that fire was in is at the end of the hall past the restrooms, and the kitchen is just before the restrooms. There's a walk in beer cooler in the kitchen. That's where they store the kegs. I pull them out for the female bartender's once in a while. We blocked the hall with two of the smaller tables just past the restroom doors, and when I walked down that hall someone had moved one of those tables. If they kept her in the beer cooler until everyone was gone, then they could have just moved a table and slipped out the back door."

"Anyway to check that? Find some hair or an earring? And w still need to discover what happened to the alarm."

"Possibly," James said. "Eddie will let us in, but we'll have to do it without any other officers being present."

"I will let you gentlemen work that out."

Jeremy dismissed Chief Vanders and Lieutenant Ohlmet, telling them he would be in Salt Lake City until the next morning if they had any concerns. Once they'd left, he turned back to William and James.

"Any news on George?"

"George approached James about working for him," William told him. "We gave him our conditions, but we still aren't sure about it. We don't want to get nailed for working for George."

"What are your concerns?"

"If we do this and one of the plains clothes guys sees us, where do we stand? What can they do?"

Jeremy hesitated, taking the time to choose his words. "You are currently running under my organization's umbrella," he said. "But, if your plain clothes officers catch you, they can arrest you. It will then be up to your chief. If you use your 'toys' as you call them and have recordings to back up your claims of working undercover, the chances of your department making the decision to file charges are slim. With my organization backing you, it will make it difficult to make any charges stick. That also depends on how bad the people pushing this want you out."

"So....fifty fifty," William said.

"No. Probably more like eighty twenty in your favor, but I can't give you an exact answer without knowing what Mr. Bonner has you doing."

"Collecting from the girls," James said.

"In that case, you needn't worry about it. Just take plenty of pictures and record everything. Anything else?"

William and James shook their heads and Jeremy excused

himself.

The two had barely made it back to William's when they were called into the station. The building the club was in had installed exterior security cameras and one of the cameras had video of a woman being carried up the rear stairs to the alley and loaded into a waiting car. The department had been given a copy of the video.

In the lieutenant's office Jeremy had seated himself across from Lieutenant Ohlmet. William entered and Jeremy glanced at the chair next to his. William sat down and was handed a still of the woman in the video. She was wrapped in a blanket, which validated his idea about the cooler. He studied the picture closely, confirming it was Amanda.

When James arrived the lieutenant played the tape. At twelve forty-five a.m. a car drove up and a large man carried a woman up the rear stairs, draped over his shoulder, putting her in the backseat. A teen with short cropped blonde hair accompanied him. When the man laid the woman in the car, something fell. The teen climbed into the passenger seat and the big man slid into the backseat with the woman. The car drove away and another boy, standing off to the side, left. He had dark hair and a small scar on his jaw. Their look out.

"Back up," William said. "I want you to back it up and zoom in. Play it in slow motion."

Lieutenant Ohlmet rewound the tape and everyone leaned in closer, examining the picture as it crawled across the screen. The lieutenant froze the tape when he was instructed and William stood to examine the picture then showed them a small scar on the blonde kid's cheek.

"I want to see a closer shot of this kid here," William said and he tapped the screen where the dark haired youth stood.

"I got something better than that," the lieutenant answered.

The lieutenant inserted a new video and fast forwarded to the nine p.m. time stamp, going to normal play. The camera showed a dark haired male teen, with a small scar on his jaw, exit through the back door. Lieutenant Ohlmet froze the tape on that frame.

"This is shortly before the fire was discovered. We have files on him and the blonde in juvenile. Now, we need to find those kids and find out how this kid got in and disabled that alarm."

William stared at the grainy image. George was behind this. He knew it as well as he knew his own name. They had no proof, but this was perfect George Bonner. He hadn't abducted her, but it had been masterminded by him. Just like Amanda's intruder, George had learned Amanda's habits. He knew when she went to work and when she got off. He knew which way she walked to work and when she took her lunch. And who with. George had learned more about Amanda than Amanda knew. They were also convinced George hid the camera at her desk. Jerry Thomas was leading them nowhere. He had only been thrown out to confuse them. Now they had to find her before her kidnappers got her across state lines, if they hadn't already. It was less than two hours to Wendover and the Nevada state line, and less than an hour and a half to Wyoming or Idaho.

"This explains the lack of Amanda's footprints," James added. "And why she didn't take her purse. Someone needs to work with the new recruits a little more."

20

William and James drove in at Amanda's apartment complex at four thirty-five the next afternoon in a rental car. They wanted answers to a couple of questions before they put a noose around their necks, and they thought it best if any officer's who might show up didn't see either of their vehicles. They parked in a space in front of the building next to hers and climbed out then began an inspection of the exterior of her building; hoping officers didn't arrive while they were here. This was a huge risk, but according to Jeremy, the police hadn't been given access by complex management yet.

At ten minutes after five a car drove in and they checked the parking lot for a detective's car or a black and white. It was neither and they continued their examination. William checked his watch when they'd finished their survey. Five twenty-five. Right on schedule. Time to check in at the office. Only one person remained, and she would be in a hurry. They walked in and showed her their badges, explaining they were investigating Ms Granger's disappearance and asked about the possibility of checking her apartment. They had found no clues at her place of employment or the club where she performed. The clerk hesitated; James glanced at the clock, gave her the once over with his eyes and a sexy sideways smile and assured her they would make sure they dropped the key in the rent depository. She gave in, beaming deliciously.

"Well, I am running late and they don't pay overtime," she said, giggling nervously.

James kissed her hand, held it a tic longer than was necessary when he took the key, then thanked her and escorted her outside. As soon as her car was out of sight, they raced for Amanda's building.

"You gotta teach me that trick," William said.

"It's all in the eyes," James answered. "I just think of Karen without her clothes. It gives just the right vibe."

They rushed through the door, walking the hall checking for anything that may have been out of line inside, but only found the usual path where people came and went. Half way up the stairs they heard men arguing, then a shot reverberated in the void and a door slammed, followed a few seconds later by a second door. The multiple echoes in the narrow space made it impossible to tell if it was coming from one of the upper floors or if it was behind them. Then the call came across their portables, shots fired and it was at this address.

They raced up the stairs, taking a minute to check the hall on the second floor. It had citizens milling around or peering out of their doors, curious as to what had occurred, but no one admitted to making the call. On the third floor, tenants from the top floor mingled with the inhabitants below, checking things out for themselves. William and James found the person who called and he told them he lived on the fourth floor, but the shot sounded like it had come from this floor. They quickly sent the people back to their apartments and continued toward Amanda's. It was the only apartment without occupants.

Outside the door, James and William positioned themselves on either side of the door, hugging the wall, weapons drawn. James knocked on the door and identified them as police. William chuckled as James shrugged. Minor technicality. James unlocked the door, William thrust it open with his foot then they ducked back against the wall, James calling again. Hearing only silence, James nodded and stepped around the door frame and inside. They were greeted by the telltale odor a smoker had been there, but Amanda didn't smoke.

They did a quick scan of the living room before moving up the hall, William staying to James left as they moved toward her bedroom, each man on opposite sides of the hall. James stopped outside the bedroom door and peeked inside before he crept into the room, pressing himself against the wall. William remained where he was, covering the hall, until James gave the signal to move in or drop. James turned the light on then waved William in. William took a position against the facing wall, his gun held in front of him, scanning the room. Finishing the sweep, William nodded at the open door, its reverse side to the wall, and James positioned himself so his weapon was aimed at it as well.

William swung the door closed with his toe, no one was there. James crept past him and opened the closet, dodging back against the wall. No sounds emanated from inside so James peered into the confined space, empty. The only sign anyone had been here was the smell of cigarettes.

They moved back down the hall and continued their hurried inspection of the apartment, finding a pistol on the dining room table. Who shot at whom, or what, and why?

"We have a hole in the sofa," William said.

James pulled a glove out of his pocket and picked up the gun. It had been fired. He flipped the safety on, turned the glove inside out over the weapon and tied the top closed, sliding it into his waistband. He turned to say something to William and a blur shot toward him.

James sidestepped as the man lunged at him with a broom, ducked then drove his shoulder into the man's midsection, the man exhaling loudly, the air knocked out of him. Then the attacker swung the broom again. The broom was high, missing James, and struck William on the side of the head when he jumped in to help. The assailant drove an elbow into the back of James head and raised the broom again. James struck back, knocking him off balance then the man jerked his leg up, catching James in the abdomen with his knee. James went to the floor, William lunging at their assailant. The attacker swung the broom once more and took a step back, William brushed the intended strike away and the assailant threw the coffeepot at them, fleeing through the back door as they dodged splinters of glass and plastic.

"You alright, partner?" William asked.

"I'm fine," James answered, dabbing at his face and checking for blood.

Sirens drew closer, the buildings occupants making their appearance once again.

"Let's get out of here," William said.

They took the rear stairs three at a time, exiting near the dumpsters. James bolted for the car while William raced for the office. Dropping the key in the box William jumped into the car when James screeched to a stop beside him, the blues and reds of a squad visible through the trees as it barreled their way. They pulled off the complex grounds thirty seconds before a black and white raced in. That had been close. Now they had evidence and they weren't even supposed to be here.

"Who the hell was that dude?" James asked, automatically checking the mirror for signs of a black and white. "He wasn't big, but he could move."

William shrugged while James fell quiet, William recognized the look as James processed what had just happened.

"What's on your mind?" William asked.

"More questions," James answered. He stared out the driver's window for a minute before he finished his reply. "Why all the crap now? We didn't even know Amanda existed three months ago."

"I was thinking the same thing," William replied.

"But where does her ex fit into all this? Or does he? I know there's nothing definitive, but I can't get past the idea he's in there somewhere. But where? Is he really her psycho?"

"Royce might be the key that opened that door," William said. "Maybe he told someone that we both know and love to hate that they were married. Maybe he said something in front of George and George got curious. There are hundreds of possibilities. We both think George is behind her abduction. It would fit. Someone called the hospital the first night she was attacked. It might have been him."

"You are probably right," James said. "We need to talk to Jeremy."

William paged Jeremy as soon as he got home. Jeremy returned the page within minutes and William explained what had happened, then set up a time to meet. They would give Jeremy the pistol and Jeremy could explain it to the lieutenant.

At eight fifty-five the next morning they were at Harmon's Cafe on State Street. Jeremy walked in and he didn't look happy. William slid the plastic glove across the table to Jeremy.

"That's the pistol," William said.

Jeremy stared at it a second then looked at James. "You look like you were in a bar room brawl."

James shrugged and chuckled. "Minus the bar room."

Jeremy slid the pistol in his briefcase. "I'll handle that through our channels. The fewer questions the better. We'll also check the serial number in case it's stolen."

"Now, what have you got?" William asked. "Please don't tell us you have more bad news."

"It's a little of both I'm afraid. I talked to Chief Vanders this morning and he said they went through the apartment and found prints, but most of them were hers and you gentlemen's. They found several sets of prints that belong to her friends from work so those – along with yours – have been eliminated."

Both men expected the department to find their prints. They had helped her move.

"They also found one set of prints," Jeremy said, "that don't belong to anyone else and they aren't showing on any database anywhere. He will probably be your suspect when you find him. He is also curious about the secretary asking why they were there. She said two officers were there last night and she gave them a key." He paused and watched the two. "It also seems one of those men had the sexiest green eyes she has ever seen. I won't say anything gentlemen, we all know who those officers are and you were only doing your job."

They sighed then James gave William a high five.

"It looks like your theory is right, buddy," he said.

"An examination of the grounds near the side entrance showed broken branches on one of the bushes. They also found boot prints under said bush. The boots came back as standard military issue," Jeremy continued. "There are an estimated eight to ten thousand men, maybe more, who wear that particular boot in the Salt Lake City area alone because of the military bases. About two-thirds of those men wear that size. What's this theory?"

"We were talking," William said, "and we think she's being targeted. She told us the man who attempted to rape her got careless when he had her pinned against the bed and dropped a pistol on the floor. We now assume she has kept it hidden and the pistol we just gave you is that gun. The man who attacked us may have gone back to find it. We don't know if it was him or not, but something happened before we got there. We heard arguing and then the shot, and so did every other person in that building."

"But you only saw one man," Jeremy said.

"Someone else left before we reached her apartment," William answered. "Check the reports and see if there's mention of a hole in the sofa, too."

Jeremy nodded. "Continue."

"Now, we add in Royce. Royce is almost James height and he is on the skinny side, which matches the description Amanda gave of her assailant. And it matches the man we fought off. If he hadn't surprised us and been swinging that broom like a battle ax, he wouldn't have gotten the better of either of us. Plus George has tried to grab Amanda himself. Add in that George didn't seem to care about her until recently, we think George heard about her through Royce."

"It sounds like you're on the right track," Jeremy said.

"What about those other prints?" James asked. "You said they aren't showing on any database. Any way to check through the military?"

"My commander is working on that angle. He is attempting to convince the military to release the information. It all comes back to those ops our men didn't do because they weren't in some of those areas they were in during those times."

"And Royce followed Amanda from Chicago," James said.

"You know that for sure?"

"Well, no. It's another one of those hunches, but she moved here from Chicago to escape her ex plus we think he's in Salt Lake City."

"And Royce was in the Army."

"Yes," James answered. "I think she mentioned he got kicked

out of the reserves because of his drinking."

"Anything more from Mr. Bonner about that side work?"

"He has us collecting from the ladies," James answered. "They deliver the funds to us at the club part of the time. Eddie's letting us use the mail drop out front Friday and Saturday's. William and I count out the money in each envelope and take photos of the cash and any notes that are left telling George who still needs to pony up." James handed Jeremy an envelope. "These are from the first few pick-ups. We have another set off site just in case. We think the girls are being given too much leeway, too. They aren't being pushed into paying. We've watched them, and there are more girls disappearing with men than we have money being accounted for."

"You think they're bilking George?" Jeremy asked.

"Absolutely," James answered. "One night we counted fifteen out of twenty of the girls we visited entertaining johns. When we got to William's and counted the cash there was only five hundred bucks and a note that showed sales of four nickel bags of weed. George told us they were getting a hundred a pop and they keep forty which should have given him nine hundred bucks that particular evening, if they only turned one trick. That's not counting the weed. Some of the girls turned two and three tricks. We should have had twenty-one hundred bucks. Add in the nickels that would have been just over the twenty-one. And we're supposed to get fifty bucks a pop – each – for making the deliveries to him."

"So George makes over two grand a night for allowing them to ply their trade," Jeremy said.

"And providing them a place to live," James said. "We went through city records and discovered a few of the old buildings he owns are slated for demolition so the city doesn't know they are being used. He maintains the interiors, and the girls live there rent free. Obviously, that will change here soon."

"This is also giving them the opportunity to tell George they put the cash in the envelope and we're keeping more than our fair share," William added. "They're taking advantage of the change in manpower. We told George and he didn't seem surprised."

"He's probably seen that before," Jeremy said.

"We're going to start making rounds to locations where the ladies won't expect to see us," William added. "Knock on their doors and keep them random and irregular. James and I won't split up so they can't say we're working off the money, either."

"Will that make your a bigger target?" Jeremy asked.

"That's why we're keeping it away from George's," William said. "We want to keep the attention off of us. I don't mind helping you get the dirt on George, but James and I aren't their pimps. We've done some scouting and know how to get in and out with vice catching us."

Jeremy opened the envelope and looked at the photos.

"Any word as to how George will recoup what the girls are stealing?"

He slid the pictures back into the envelope and placed it in his briefcase with the pistol.

"He has a man who does all his accounting for him." William laughed and noticed Jeremy grimaced. "He guaranteed the girls won't be hurt."

"Do you believe him?" Jeremy asked.

"Not completely," James replied. "We know to push now and we'll keep an eye out for that, too. We're doing everything else."

Jeremy noted the phrase choosing to ignore it. "Keep working it as close as you can gentlemen, but you're flying solo so watch your backs. Unless you gentlemen need to speak to me, the next batch of information will come in the mail."

21

The blare of the telephone woke William from a sound sleep. He checked the clock as he answered it and wondered what had happened to warrant a call at three a.m.

"Officer Harrison," he mumbled. Then James chuckled. "What's up, my man?"

"Chief Vanders and Lieutenant Ohlmet want to meet us at the hospital."

"What the hell?"

"Don't know, buddy. Lieutenant Ohlmet said something about Captain Jakes has been shot. He made a run for it. See ya in a few."

William climbed out of bed, dressing hurriedly then bolted out the door and down the hall. Why had Jakes run? Unless he was guilty. He didn't want to believe Captain Jakes had really got caught up in something. Who was Jakes running from?

William arrived at the hospital and he and James were told to meet the lieutenant in the cafeteria. Once they were seated, the lieutenant told them a vice officer had been tailing Captain Jakes, walking east on Fourth South when Jakes stopped on the corner with Fifth East. He thought Jakes had picked him up, then Jakes started south on Fifth East. Captain Jakes made it as far as the end of the Safeway parking lot when he went down. He suspected Jakes saw something, or someone, and had tried to make a run for it. The vice officer hadn't heard a sound.

"Shit," William said, his thoughts drifting to Captain Jakes wife and boys. This was something he would never want anyone to go through. "How bad is he?"

"Not as bad as it could have been. The officer knew enough to keep pressure on the wound until paramedics arrived. We have men scouring the area, but no one has found anything. No brass, no witnesses, nothing."

"When did this happen?" James asked.

"About seven p.m. He was on a busy street, in broad daylight," the lieutenant said. "Nobody saw a thing."

"Is Jakes going to be okay?" James asked.

"The doctor said if he makes it out of surgery, he should be good to go in about a month. We're going to make him take some extra time off as a precaution."

"But why did Jakes run?" William asked. "That makes it look like he's guilty of something."

"Hopefully this will tell us," the chief answered. He handed William a floppy disc. "This was in his inside coat pocket. Our computer department looked at it, but it's heavily encrypted…" The lieutenant let the sentence drop his gaze falling on a sign on the wall behind them before returning it to them. "Jeremy will be here sometime this morning to pick that up. He'll page you to set up the meeting. Give him this, too." He slid a piece of notepaper across the table to them. The words 'Silver Lake' and 'Liberty Park' had been written on it. "Before they took him to surgery, Jakes wrote this. We think he was letting us know the same perp who killed the girl at Silver Lake is the man who killed the girl at

Liberty Park. That or his hit was ordered by the same person who did those."

"Or both," James said.

"I don't think so," the lieutenant answered. "I went through his desk after we heard about the shooting. Captain Jakes had started taping some of his calls at the station. It looks like he was approached by someone with a few more teeth than George and, instead of coming to us, Jakes decided to do this on his own. I found this." The chief laid a manila envelope on the table and slid it over to William. "It's all in there."

William picked it up and looked inside. There was a cassette, several 8 X 10 glossies, a Polaroid and a letter. William looked at each photo carefully then handed them to James. The Polaroid of them at Liberty Park and pictures of Captain Jakes' wife and kids. That wasn't Bonner's style. This went higher.

"Apparently Jakes was told his family would be taken out one by one starting with the youngest if he didn't cooperate." The chief gestured to the pictures. "We're leaning on Mr. Portman. He knows more than he is telling us. The cassette will explain it all."

William stared across the table at the lieutenant. They knew his wife's murder had been a hit, but they'd had no leads. If they could connect her death to the threat against Captain Jakes family, they might have a case again.

"We know, William," Lieutenant Ohlmet said. "We're looking closer at that, too. It has never been closed, but with no leads it's been collecting dust. I hope we can bring all of this to a close, and soon. Especially for you."

"Thank you, sir," William said. His throat had constricted with emotion, words refusing to come.

"This Portman guy, has he said anything about who he worked for, or who might have talked to Jakes?" James asked.

"Nothing, yet. We went to a judge and got a court order to impound the cash in Jakes questionable account. The last we'd heard there was close to three hundred thousand dollars in it. When we got to the bank, it was gone. Account closed."

"When was it closed?" William asked.

"Four-thirty yesterday afternoon," Lieutenant Ohlmet replied. "There had to have been a second person on it, but all signature cards associated with the account have disappeared. We're going back to the judge this morning and see if we can force the bank to allow us to trace the trail. If we can't, we'll go to Jeremy. We'll talk again later, but continue to stay in contact with Jeremy. Now, if you don't mind. I'm going to desert you. I have someone very important I need to talk to."

William's thoughts drifted to Captain Jakes decision. The Polaroid of them, combined with the letter and the pictures of Captain Jakes family left no doubts regarding the consequences of the captain's choices. It also told them the people involved would have carried out the threat. He understood, but the captain should have gone to the chief. Then he thought about Captain Jakes wife and kids. If Jakes hadn't cooperated there might have been three funerals. That was a possibility none of them wanted to entertain.

Chief Vanders met them few feet from the elevator.

"Chief," the lieutenant said.

The chief paused, avoiding their eyes.

"Gentlemen," Chief Vanders said. "I wanted you to know…." He paused again. "Jakes didn't make it through surgery."

"Damn it!" William exclaimed.

James and the lieutenant sighed, James dropping his head as he turned to face the wall.

"I wanted to tell you in person. I know you respected Jakes. He was a fine officer and man…."

He didn't complete the sentence, a choking sound emanating from his throat. He gained control and silence filled the gap as they climbed onto the elevator and it started its climb. This was something no officer wanted to hear. The elevator stopped and they stepped off, the lieutenant tapped the disc.

"We need that info," Lieutenant Ohlmet said.

"Are you asking us to help with this, too?" James asked.

"If you hear anything, I want to know. You're on your own schedule gentlemen. Do what you have to do. Just keep it legal. Remember, Jeremy is going to page you this morning."

22

They sat in William's car and slipped the cassette in a portable cassette player they had had the forethought to take it out of their squad car their last night on duty. A quick glance at James and seeing James' nod, William pushed the play button.

The phone rang and there was a click when it was answered.

"Jakes," the captain said.

"Good afternoon, sir," someone said. "We have never met but I wanted to talk to you about a FedEx package you have just received."

There was several seconds of silence then the captain spoke again.

"What makes you think I received anything from FedEx?"

"It was dropped at the front desk approximately five minutes ago," the person replied. "I suggest you make sure no one is with you when you open the envelope, sir."

"Is that a threat?"

The man ignored Captain Jakes. "Once you open it let me know. There are two manila envelopes inside."

Paper ripped then more silence.

"I suggest you leave the larger envelope for last," the voice instructed him. "Open the smaller of the two, please." There was a pause and the person spoke again. "I trust you have opened it."

"Yes," Captain Jakes answered.

"As you can see that is two of your officers."

William pulled out the photo of them at Liberty Park. It was the only one of police officers.

"Yes. So what is this?"

"Your questions will be answered shortly. Please be patient. There should be a note in the envelope with the photo. Have you seen it?"

"Yes."

William unfolded the letter and laid it on the seat. Instructions along with floor plans of his and James' apartments, containing several bright red 'X's'.

"Good," the person said. "Now what I need you to do is make sure those men are arrested for possession and sales of a controlled substance. The note gives you the precise locations where the drugs will be planted."

Chief Vander's words after their arrest came to mind. *We were told you had large quantities of cocaine and heroin hidden in specific areas of your apartments, but nothing has been found.* The set up.

"A package is on its way," the voice continued. "Any changes to these instructions will be included in that package. Once it arrives a portion of it will be placed under the seat of their squad car...."

"And why do you think I would do that to my own men?" the captain snapped. "What kind of man do you think I am?"

"I already know what kind of man you are. You are a man who will do everything in his power to protect his family and his men. You are a man who does what he says he is going to do. You are a man of integrity, sir. With that said, I didn't expect you to handle this well, but since you have started with the unpleasantrie's so soon I will ask you to open the larger envelope."

"And if I don't?"

"Open the larger envelope," the voice warned harshly. "And I suggest you do it soon. We have five minutes to finish this conversation or you will regret not listening. Is that clear?"

More silence ensued and papers rustled.

"That's your wife and your two boys. Am I correct, Captain?"

"What does my family have to do with this?"

"I believe there are several pictures of your family at the mall, and the park. I believe your wife is a very good driver, too. Isn't she, sir?"

"Yes, but what do they have to do with it?"

"All I ask you to do is cooperate and you will save yourself and your family a lot of grief. Is it becoming clear now? You cooperate or they die. One person at a time. That way the others will know how bad you screwed up. First the youngest boy, then the oldest. We might wait a few months between, give you time to make a decision and let the family begin to get their life back together. I imagine your wife would be pretty upset. I really hate that part. I hate seeing women hurt. I would rather have them done away with quickly. You know, no pain, no suffering. Of course, if you still refuse to cooperate, we can always pull your brother's family into it."

"YOU ASSHOLE!" the captain yelled. A door slammed in the background. "HOW DARE YOU?"

"Do I take that as a 'no'? I'll hang up now and your youngest will be gone before morning." The voice hesitated a minute and then came back, but it was cold and hard. "What's your decision? I believe there is an officer waiting for your reply. You either nod 'yes'. Or you shake your head 'no'."

"Why are you doing this?"

"Have you given the officer your answer?"

There was several more seconds of silence, no words and no background noises, then a squawk like Jakes had lowered himself into his chair.

"I told him 'yes'," the captain answered. "What do you want?"

"Good for you, Captain. I'm glad you decided to see things our way. I know that was a difficult decision for you. Now, as I was saying. There is another package coming in. The officer you just saw will distribute the product in the target officer's apartments or lockers. A small portion will also be placed under the passenger seat in their squad car. Then he will let you know everything is set. Once that is done I want you to take the picture and the letter and go to your chief and tell him you have received an anonymous tip and you need to arrest said officers. That's all there is to it."

"Why am I doing this to those men? They're the best men I've got."

"That's exactly why," the voice answered. "We are trying to build a business in your fair city, but they are sticking their noses into it and we can't have that. Also, if any of this comes out, our agreement is off and your family is gone. Is that plain enough?"

There was a single syllable whisper in the silence then the man spoke again.

"You might want to change their shift when the time comes. Make sure they're working late so it's easier to plant the evidence. You will also start receiving cash drops in the night depository at your local bank. You will need to open a separate account for those funds. One your wife does not know about. When the funds reach three hundred thousand you will begin helping us with the distribution of a certain…"

There was a long pause.

"…product, shall we call it. You will also be compensated

quite nicely for your aid, Captain. When putting children through college extra cash is always welcome. I will let you go now. Oh, you should begin to receive the cash drops within the week."

There was the sound of the call being disconnected and William stopped the cassette.

"What the hell?" James said. "Why are we still on suspension if they have this?"

"We really do need to talk to Jeremy," William replied. "I'm ready to confront the lieutenant and the chief. Captain Jakes wife is the only reason I won't. She's going through enough hell."

James dropped his chin and looked back at the ER entrance, eyes blazing as he stared out the window. "I don't understand. Why haven't the charges been dropped, William? Why are we still on leave?"

"I have the same question," William answered. "I also want to know why Jakes didn't follow the instructions."

James looked over, angry and confused.

"We had the night off. I was at Amanda's."

"And I was at Karen's," James replied. "How'd they know we weren't home?"

"Exactly, my man."

23

Jeremy picked up the disc, William locked eyes with his, sliding the envelope across to him. William recognized the question and shook his head.

"Just listen. With the pictures it's fairly self-explanatory. We have some serious questions we need answers to. I'm not sure I trust the lieutenant or the chief."

Jeremy did a slight nod, alarmed, and put the package in his briefcase along with the disc.

Tuesday William and James received separate calls. Meet Lieutenant Ohlmet at the diner across from the station at seven a.m. Wednesday morning. They walked in and recognized the lieutenant, but there was a new man with them. He wasn't IAD. He was in uniform. They automatically sized him up as they drew closer. He was about five eleven, dark coffee complexion. Kinky hair cut close like William's. Not as muscular as them, but had some descent muscles. He would hold his own on the street.

"Officers," Lieutenant Ohlmet said. "Sorry this is last minute, but I thought you might like to know what Jeremy found on that disc. I also wanted to introduce you to the newest member of the department. This is Officer Timothy Johnson. He will be helping you two once in a while since you're not officially back on duty. He's doing good work. Officer Johnson, this is Officer William Harrison, he nodded in William's direction, and his partner, Officer James Thompson, another nod this time at James. I know you've heard the rumors. Don't listen to them. These are the best men on the department."

They shook his hand, nodding in greeting.

"He worked military security for almost ten years before coming to us," Lieutenant Ohlmet added.

The lieutenant was nervous.

"Glad to meet you," Timothy said. "Any place for good music around here?"

"William plays at a jazz club – Pearls on Main – Friday and Saturday nights," James answered. "If you don't like jazz, there's Bourbon Street on Fourth South or The Dead Goat Saloon on West Temple. Most of the bars have some kind of music on the weekends. It just depends on what you like. The private clubs have the best."

"Officer Johnson, if you'll excuse us now," Chief Vanders said.

"Yes, sir," Timothy said. "Maybe I'll see you guys Friday."

"First drinks on us," William said. He watched Timothy a minute then turned back to the lieutenant. "So what was all that?"

Lieutenant Ohlmet glanced over his shoulder and shrugged, then looked back at them. "Have you found out anything new on Mr. Bonner or what's happening with the lady?"

"Not much," William replied. "We're still leaning toward two perps. We've learned nothing that would make us think George was doing the psycho stuff. He has a whole harem of hookers, plus a steady girl so that doesn't make sense. You said you have something on the disc?"

"We received a call from Jeremy yesterday afternoon."

"And?" William said. He hated prompting the lieutenant, but he wasn't as patient as he used to be.

"It's an organizational chart. Names, addresses, duties, almost everything we need to pull an organization down. We just have to figure out which organization. We don't know if it's Mr. Bonner or higher up the ladder. It's incomplete. We think that's why Jakes was killed. They may have been onto him. We also wanted to give you a heads up. Keep your eyes and your ears open and start watching your backs a lot closer. The station pipeline is beginning to hum again. We don't want anything happening to either of you. And keep it professional. There are already rumors going around. Someone is of the opinion one of you has been spending too much time in her company." He stared at William as he made the last statement.

Both men looked outside. Rumors and the station pipeline were one in the same thing. The lieutenant wasn't out of the loop. Would Officer Johnson be helping them or helping the department keep tabs on them?

"We don't want anything coming back on either of you or the department," the lieutenant continued. "Jeremy said to tell you he'll call you in a day or two at Williams."

"Yes, sir," Williams said.

24

Amanda opened her eyes, the odors of stale beer, cigarettes, urine and cheap perfume insulted her senses and made her eyes water. She lifted a hand to cover her mouth and nose, and curb the stench and hold the nausea at bay, and found her hands bound in front of her.

She stifled the urge to gag, thoughts of her dad intruding. Had he run to places like this when he and her mom had fought? She remembered the fights, her mom and dad's yelling, the door slam and the angry footsteps as he stormed down the hall. And she remembered her mother's tears. They didn't have enough money to buy clothes, but her dad had enough for his drugs. She wasn't old enough to understand all of that, but she was old enough to know they were tearing the people she loved apart.

Then she remembered the last time she had seen her father. She had trudged home from school, snow on the ground – normal for a Chicago winter – an ambulance parked out front. Paramedics were working frantically on her father, the tension palpable, a great weight in the air, their faces grim. Her mother ran to her, but she fought, struggling to reach him. Her mother had finally pulled her away, the gurney rolling out with her dad, his body draped in a sheet.

Memories of their camping and fishing expeditions filtered through. All before he had got mixed up with the people who killed him. In her mind, it was as much the fault of the people who sold the drugs as it was his for using them. She wished she could go back and tell him how much she loved him and warn him about what he was doing. Keep him from ruining their lives and ending his.

Blinking back the tears, she focused on the harsh halo of light over a desk. When she'd composed herself, she peered out through a doorway to where George sat at a table a few feet away, a door in the far wall behind him, and noticed the outdated red shag carpet on the floor and half way up the walls. Laughter and a loud clack, followed by softer clacks and dull thumps, echoed in the building and she closed her eyes to hear better, listening intently. *Thwack, clack, thump, clunk, clunk, thump.* Pool balls. People were playing pool. She was in a bar somewhere, but where.

The hinges on a door complained and a huge man joined George and smiled, locking eyes with hers through the opening. George followed his gaze and Amanda pulled her eyes away as he stood and worked his way toward her. George sat on the cot in front of her then brushed the hair off her face and she wondered what her chances were of getting out of here alive.

"Would you something like to drink?" George asked.

"No, thank you," she said, her tongue sticking to the roof of her mouth like cotton candy. Sticky and sickly sweet. It would probably be advisable to drink something.

"Are you sure?" he asked. "I thought you'd be thirsty by now."

"Water would be fine," she answered. Her voice was hoarse, and when she licked her lips her tongue felt like sandpaper.

"Relax," he said. "All I want to do is to talk to you. I have an idea that could benefit us both."

"I have nothing to say to you." She saw the flash of anger, deciding it would be best to stay quiet.

George looked away, waved his hand then turned his attention back to her.

"I could use someone like you. You're different than the other girls who frequent this place."

"There's a reason for that. It probably has to do with the smell, and I can imagine the clientele."

George stood and pulled her into a sitting position, seating himself on the cot once again. As he moved, the muscles in his arms rippled beneath the sleeves of the t-shirt. George wasn't her intruder; he was too muscular. Then she wondered if men bought shirts that were too small on purpose, shirts tight enough to make them appear more intimidating than they actually were. Amanda shook her head to clear the fog, George continuing to talk in the background.

"I think we could make some serious money together," he said. "We just need to sit down and work out the details."

Amanda could imagine the proposition George had and clutched her hands to her chest, then the door on the far wall creaked and Royce walked in. What the hell was he doing here?

George jerked his head toward the door and one of the men pushed Royce back outside, sliding a bolt into place. George Bonner definitely wielded some power and he did it with impunity.

One of the men finally returned with that glass of water and George held it out to her. Her hands shook as she tried to grasp it and he steadied it for her. She took a long drink and then leaned against the wall, closing her eyes. George laughed softly when her stomach complained and left, returning with a bag of chips and a sandwich.

"I'm not heartless," he said. "I knew you would be hungry and I didn't think you were the pickled eggs and pastrami type."

"Thank you," she replied.

"Will you be alright if I leave you here for a minute?"

She looked at her wrists, zip ties encircling them, and nodded, continuing to eat. It was only a sandwich, but it tasted so damn good. How long had she been out? She looked down at the zip ties and sighed. How was she going to get out of here?

As soon as she finished the sandwich, the huge man walked in and put his arm around her. Amanda tried to pull away, but there was a poke and then everything went dark. William and James had been right. George was heartless.

"Close the damn door so customers don't see her," were the last words she heard.

25

A sharp pain cut through Amanda's temples to the base of her skull when she rolled over. She rubbed the back of her neck, and found a lump where something had penetrated the skin, then remembered the poke. She continued to knead the spot as she opened her eyes and scanned the room. A stand sat on either side of the huge king size bed, heavy velvet drapes hung on the lone window – conveniently placed near the ceiling – and a wardrobe was centered against the opposite wall. When she got her mind out of this haze she would push the wardrobe under the window. She attempted to sit up and the room began to swim, her body floating into emptiness.

Amanda awoke again to moonlight filtering in from outside and wondered why anyone would put a window that high?

She sat up and hung her feet over the edge of the bed; her head going in circles, her hands braced on either side of her, and remembered the bar. Once the vertigo had subsided, she looked at her clothes. At least she was still dressed. Lifting her head, she inspected the room closer. No phone, no television, and no magazines, not even a window low enough to see out of.

A closed door sat directly in front of her and she weaved to a standing position, balancing precariously as she grabbed its frame. She opened the door slowly, a closet filled with clothes that belonged on a hooker. She would be fine in the dress she was wearing. Keeping her shoulder on the wall, Amanda eased the door closed and rolled to her right. Another door. This one led to a bathroom with plenty of towels and toiletries, then she rotated slowly back to her left where a third door – with no handle – teased her from the wall. She assumed that particular door locked on the outside. A sweep of the room revealed several cameras hidden in different locations. Now she understood why the clothes looked like a hookers and why there was no outside access. Even the velvet drapes added to the feel.

She continued to lean against the wall, what energy she'd had gone. Already exhausted. She yanked the pillows off the bed, tossing them onto the closet floor then dragged a blanket from the bed, folding it over her and closing the door. She curled up and tried not to think about what would be expected of her. She fell asleep willing the drugs to wear off the helplessness settle in.

Amanda climbed out of the closet the next morning and sat on the edge of the bed, finding it difficult to keep her mind focused. She wanted her life back. And she was starving. A glance at the door with no handle and a small table sat next to the wardrobe. It held a bowl with a spoon, a single serving box of cereal, a cup of coffee – which was probably cold by now – and a small carton of milk sitting in ice. When she picked up the cup, it was still warm. The ice in the bowl hadn't melted yet, either. She sat on the side of the bed as she ate, working on a plan to get out of here then rinsed out the bowl and cup and sat them on the table once again, her mind still working on her circumstances. A hesitant knock interrupted her thoughts. Terrified, she looked up as Royce poked his head around the door and stepped into the room.

"DAMN YOU!" She exploded at him, swinging wildly. "I

should have known you were behind this! How dare you come in here! HOW DARE YOU! WHAT in the HELL are you doing in Salt Lake City? I left Chicago to get away from you!"

"It's going to be alright," he said. "You're only going to be here for a day or two. George has an idea, but it'll require some training. Just calm down. You have to trust me."

"TRUST YOU!" She was kicking along with the swinging now, forcing him into a defensive posture, covering his face with his arms. "Excuse me. Look at this room. How do you expect me to trust you after this?"

"It's only temporary," he said, finally restraining her. "George promised. You should be out of here in a couple of days."

"George?" She stared at the ceiling in disbelief, memories crowded her mind of waking up in that bar, and George telling her he had a job he wanted to discuss with her. "You trusted that man? What did you do, trade me for drugs?"

"Well, no. He paid quite handsomely for you actually. I'm now twenty grand richer and I have my choice of evenings with you. You have no idea how much I've missed you. We have a lot of catching up to do."

"Oh, hell no! We have nothing to catch up on!"

Royce pulled her tighter against him, rubbing her body with his. "George said he has something special in mind for you," he continued, his voice barely above a whisper. "He said you will both make lots of money. He said all you have to do is go to dinner or dancing with guys. Can I let go of you now?"

"Yes," Amanda answered. She fought to keep her voice calm, attempting to control the anger and surging emotions. But she didn't want to. She wanted to beat the man to a bloody pulp. "Please."

"I don't want to let go," he said. "I want this to be our first night together."

"Royce," she said, "please let me go."

There was a second's hesitation then he allowed her to step free. She turned to face him and sighed heavily.

"What do you think he had planned for me?" Amanda asked. "If this is so legal and above board, why isn't there a handle on that door, Royce? Why did he have to drug me to get me in here? Why can't I go home?" Then she flung the closet door open and gestured toward the clothing. "Why do the clothes look like they belong on a hooker?"

"Royce," George spoke from the doorway. "She's right. What did you think I wanted with her?" He walked in, pushing the closet door closed then he reached out to caress her cheek only to have her recoil from his touch. "Look at this face. And this body. I already have men lined up to meet her. They're going to pay me three hundred bucks an hour for the privilege of being with this beautiful lady. Of course, I'll keep a close eye on them." He pointed to the cameras. "And I'll have to sample the merchandise first. I have to make sure she's as high a quality as I advertise. I can even sell the tapes and make more money."

"You said you only wanted to train her as an escort," Royce said, confused. "You didn't say you were going to pimp her out! You said she would only accompany men with money to plays and to dinner."

"What kind of an escort do you think George had in mind?" Amanda asked. "Think for once, Royce!"

The soft clatter of the dishes being moved drew Amanda's attention. The table with her breakfast utensils had been removed, but the door hadn't closed completely. They had left a gap. She shoved George backwards then lunged for the door. George grabbed one of her wrists, launching her against the opposite wall, the air forced from her lungs.

Royce dove across the bed for her, George yanked him back as the door creaked open, waving for the guard to remove Royce.

George strutted toward her, Amanda sidling to her left, her back scraping the wall, trying to get out of the corner. Two more feet and she could make the jump to the bed then the safety of the bathroom. One more glance away from George and he grabbed her, forcing a knee between hers, pinning her between him and the wall, her arms stretched above her head.

"I suggest you don't try that again," George said. "I'm the one who controls you."

"Nobody controls me," Amanda spat, "especially someone like you."

The door opened again and George thrust his head back, indicating that the person should leave. "We have everything under control don't we, Amanda? You're going to be a sweet little princess and kiss the frogs, aren't you?" The door closed quietly again.

Princess! George had planted the camera! She glared defiantly as he moved both her wrists into one hand then grasped her jaw tightly, squeezing her cheeks and kissing her. He released his grip on her chin and reached into his pocket. There was a click and his switchblade moved closer.

The blade was only inches from her neck when she closed her eyes and turned away. A tug on each strap of her dress and the bodice fell, wilting to her waist. George folded the knife then his hand dropped as he put it in his pocket.

Amanda kneed him between the legs, his grip loosening as he fell into the wall, the air driven from his lungs. She struck him in the throat then twisted out of his grasp, as George collapsing to the floor, gasping for breath. She scrambled across the bed, slamming the bathroom door behind her. Crouched on the floor, her back braced against the door she waited, thinking about George's next move. The next few seconds lasted forever then he staggered closer.

"Don't get comfortable, you're moving tomorrow," George said his voice raspy, tone cold. "Your new home won't be quite as spacious." The outer door opened and closed and the room grew quiet.

Confident she was alone Amanda moved to the edge of the bed, her mind repeating George's last words. She let her breath out slowly and examined the bathroom. The usual, toilet, sink and shower with a small window five feet above the floor. The wall below the window was blank. A furtive look around the room and she tossed the lamp onto the bed then grabbed the stand. She was tall enough she could reach the window from it. She tried to lift the stand, but it slipped out of her grasp sending her tumbling into the wall. She grabbed the stand again, it wouldn't budge. It was fastened to the wall. She whirled checking the rest of the furniture and found the same thing. They were all screwed to the floor or the wall.

Collapsing onto the edge of the bed she stared into the other room. George said she was leaving tomorrow. She had tonight to get out of here. The tickle of an idea started to form and she sat up straighter. The window would be in reach if she stood on the toilet. She lowered the lid and stretched until she leaned on the sill then she unlocked it, sliding the pane up. She hooked her elbows on the window frame then the lid slid to the side leaving her hanging by her forearms. That was graceful.

Amanda braced her elbows against the window frame, using her toes to crawl up the wall until she'd worked her head and shoulders through the narrow opening. Fourth floor and only a three inch deep ledge six feet below. Straight down from there. Three more windows below this one. However she achieved this, she needed something to hang on to and she had to work around the upper accessories. Boobs were a pain in the butt.

She pulled herself out farther, straining to locate a hand hold when she was grabbed and yanked back inside, both of them tumbling to the floor. The man wheezed painfully when she landed on him, squashing the air out of his lungs then he rolled from under her.

"Nice try, girly, but you forgot the cameras." He slammed the window shut and locked it, then dropped a pin down one side.

Frustrated and angry Amanda curled up against the wall and let the tears fall, cursing herself silently. This wasn't going to work. The police would be looking for her and she had to help them find her.

26

Amanda woke the next morning, the previous fiasco a giant loop feeding through her mind. She couldn't allow that again.

The door opened, breaking into her thoughts and the guard laid new clothes on the wardrobe, nodded and smiled. Jeans and sandals, and a t-shirt. She looked at her dress straps where she had tied them together then looked back at the new clothes. If she did this right, she could be home tonight!

"Come on, lady," he said. "You're moving. I'll be back in ten minutes."

He closed the door and Amanda wondered if he had been the man at the bar. He had to duck to walk under it. She grabbed the clothes, dressing quickly then sat on the end of the bed and waited. When he returned, she fought her impulse to run. She had to get out of the building first.

Downstairs, he planted her at one end of a high counter with a desk behind it. Guards stood inside the double entry doors, one stood next to her at the desk plus one seated at the desk, and one outside the side door. She took a step back and the man beside her grabbed her arm and pulled her forward again. A nondescript older Ford drove up with two men inside. The passenger climbed out and walked around the rear of the car. The guard who had just brought her down. As the guard dragged Amanda toward the entrance, she forced herself to be patient, waiting for the hand off. When the bigger man reached them the guard holding her released his grip, she jerked her arm away, racing for the street. Then she felt her body flying and the larger man yanked her backwards. Then the car hurtled backwards toward them, squealing to a stop. The door flew open and the huge man fought her into the front seat.

'Must make mental note. Do not fight someone twice your size without help.'

He slid in beside her, wedging her between him and the driver. The driver blindfolded her and the larger man bound her wrists with zip ties. The car dropped into gear and turned right out of the parking lot, taking a left a short time later, then a right. She guessed they were heading north now, the guard still gripping her tight. The traffic sounded heavier so they were probably on a main thoroughfare. A few blocks farther they made a right turn and another right then they slowed to a crawl and drove over a hump. When the car stopped she was hauled out, the guard continuing to grasp her firmly.

"Step up," he instructed.

Three steps in and they jerked her to a stop. She heard a buzzer and hinges screeched then they were moving again. The place smelled old. Not old as in dirty and musty, but like a well maintained older building. Inside, the guard removed her blindfold then she noticed a large ornate staircase that climbed three floors. The carpet was clean and showed a minimal amount of wear, but appeared to be from the thirties or forties. The stairs had been solidly constructed around a square central foyer with a common curled balustrade at the base.

On the top floor they cut the ties and shoved her into a room, quickly closing and locking the door. Old fashioned lace curtains hung on the lone window and a mattress and box springs sat in the center of the room. She sighed, fighting the renewed swell of emotions. She buried her face in her hands attempting to collect herself. She would be no good to herself, or anyone, if she didn't control this. The guard brought her a sandwich and something to drink then tossed her a set of sheets and two blankets.

She ate, inspecting the window, and noticed a metal grate on the outside. Narrow metal bands spanned the top and the bottom of the window on the inside, each one screwed into the side of the frame and painted the same color as the wood. She wouldn't get out of here that way.

The guard returned, took her by the arm and led her down the hall to the 'john'. It had been years since she'd heard it called that. A quick glance and she noticed there weren't many guards up here, but guessed they didn't worry about people jumping. The sudden stop could be terminal. When she walked out he was waiting and escorted her back to the room.

He closed the door and Amanda snooped through a closet and found a lone book lying on the shelf. If nothing else it would beat the boredom. Finishing the book, she looked out the window, it had grown dark. A different guard opened the door and took her to use the 'head'. She laughed softly and wondered where that name had come from. Back in the room, she turned the overhead light off and removed her sandals, tossing the blankets over her on the mattress. She drifted off to sleep thinking about how long she might be here and where they would take her next.

The door opened the next morning and she looked up to see George enter. That wasn't who she wanted to see.

"I need to use the restroom," she said quietly.

George smiled and stepped back, nodding in the direction of the door. The same guard who had brought her the day before stood outside, another man posted facing the door. She walked back to the room, George sitting on the edge of the bed.

"How are you feeling this morning? I trust you slept well."

"Must have," she said, remaining standing.

"It's alright," he said as he patted the edge of the mattress. "There's nowhere else to sit and I promise not to make a jackass out of myself. I have your breakfast coming."

"How long will I be here?"

"We're leaving this morning. I didn't want to put you where I'm being forced to, but your new home hasn't been completed."

"George, why don't you just release me?" A pause and nothing so she pushed. "I promise I won't tell anyone."

He ignored her, looking up when the guard brought her food. "I trust you like coffee?"

"You know, I will never co-operate with you."

"You need to remember one thing. All you have to do is look beautiful and be nice. I do the rest."

"That's not how I see it. What you're asking me to do is more than just being nice. Do you think I can finish my meal, now? I would hate to ruin a perfectly lovely breakfast talking about your ideas for my employment."

"You will eventually come around."

When she'd finished her breakfast, Amanda stood to use the restroom again. In the hall she took a detour to glance over the rail and the guard guided her back to the center of the hall.

She walked out of the restroom; George draped his arm across her shoulders then felt a poke and the guard retracted his arm. Damn the man!

"You know I hate you, don't you, George," she said then everything went black.

27

Amanda awoke with a splitting headache in a cramped little room that smelled of mold, dirty carpet and urine. Why did all of these places have to smell like urine? She rolled over and opened her eyes to see mildewed walls and tattered sheers hanging on a filthy window. What little light filtered through the window hurt her eyes. There was a cold draft and she reached down to discover there were no sheets on the bed. She swung her legs over the edge of the mattress and massaged her scalp gently, hoping to ease the pain. Finally pulling herself up, she faced the new Amanda in a huge gaudy mirror that didn't look like it had been cleaned in years.

Eyeing her clothes – if one wanted to call them that – the top barely concealed her breasts and the bottom almost didn't cover what it needed to. Whoever dressed her had pulled a pair of black fishnet stockings over her legs and fastened them with a garter belt. A pair of stiletto heels completed her new ensemble. She was about to take the heels off when she saw the filthy shag carpet. It was probably healthier wearing the heels.

An inspection of the room revealed the bed with a night table and lamp, and one broken down chair in the corner facing the bed. That first room had had a chair facing the bed, too. She didn't want to think about the reasoning behind that. Staring at the chair, she noticed the feathered 'V' stain on the cloth seat and tried not to dwell on what could have caused that particular mark. Maybe some poor unsuspecting woman had gone into labor. That wasn't comforting, either.

The hinges groaned and she looked around, trying to find something to cover herself with, but only found two badly stained pillows. Staring at the door, one pillow covering her torso and the other gripped for use as a torpedo, she watched a tiny hand reach inside and grope for the light switch. She cringed when the light came on, releasing the pillow and shielding her eyes. The door swung open and a tiny girl stood framed in the doorway holding clean bedding and towels, a guard in the hall behind her. The girl eyed Amanda in silence for a moment, emerald eyes reminding her of James, then the girl closed and locked the door before walking to the bed. Amanda stood and the girl put clean – well almost clean – linens on the bed. When she had finished, she left and made sure the door was closed and locked once again. The same girl reappeared in a few minutes carrying cleaning supplies.

"I didn't know you were coming or the room would already be cleaned," the girl said.

Amanda bobbed her chin and the tiny thing scrubbed the commode and the walls. Once she was done, the girl left and returned again with a plate of food. She handed Amanda the plate and a drink, then cleaned the mirror and the lone window.

Amanda looked at the food and realized she was starving. "Is this how all you girls live?" Amanda asked between mouthfuls.

"Oh, no, not the expensive ones like you," the girl answered. "Only the ones who turn tricks for drugs use these rooms. When they high, they don't care. You here because Mr. George doesn't have your new home finished."

"That's a relief," Amanda said unsure of where this was going. "So you work with the men, too?"

"No. Mr. George says I'm too little. He says I look like a kid and he don't want no trouble with that, so I get to clean the rooms."

Amanda thought about that for a minute. The girl sounded like she was proud of her work. And it sounded like George had a few more morals than she had been aware of.

The girl left only to return a few minutes later and retrieve Amanda's now empty plate. When she left she made sure the door was closed and locked securely once more.

Amanda walked to the window, and gazed out into the early evening light. The window was set back in an alcove, brick walls on either side and another, taller, brick wall directly in front of her. Horns honked and a filthy plume of black smoke rose from below, telling her an alley ran between the buildings. Amanda lifted gently, the window had been nailed shut. Hopefully there wouldn't be a fire.

As the light outside faded, Amanda reflected on her situation. She was in a room with no way out, dressed like a porn star. This might prove more difficult than she had thought. She was curious, though. How long could George keep up the charade? How long before all this came tumbling down? Because it would. Money and drugs had bought George everything he had and empires like this didn't last forever.

Keys rattled in the lock the next evening, surprising Amanda. She lunged for the tiny bathroom only to be jerked backwards and spun around to face her visitor. Her back slammed against the wall and she caught herself staring into azure blue eyes. He held her hands above her head, one of his legs forcing hers a few inches apart his hip pinning her against the wall.

"I see you have some spirit," he said. "I was told you were a bit of a fighter, but I won't hurt you. I have strict instructions not to damage the merchandise. George will make a lot more money on you that way. I didn't say I wasn't going to enjoy my time with you, though"

"I'll do everything in my power to make sure you don't," she said, as she kicked feebly.

"It's going to take more than that," he said with a laugh. "I'm going to start the introductions. George said your name is Amanda. Is that correct?" He waited a minute and shrugged one shoulder when she didn't answer. "Very well. My name is David. Remember that name. I might be the only thing that keeps your ass out of the ground. Now, shall we see what you've got?"

"Damn you!" she snapped.

"That's not the answer I want to hear," he said. "You're supposed to say 'Yes, David'."

"Ain't happening," she answered.

"We'll see," he said. Holding her hands above her head with one of his, he slid the other hand down and unhooked her top. "See how easy that was. One simple hook and it's open."

He slid the top to the side and caressed her breast then moved his hand down, pushing her bottoms lower, taking his time, moving slow and easy. He took a step back to giving Amanda space to move. She kicked and he danced to the side, avoiding the strike. The move loosened his grip and she jerked one arm out if his grasp and swung wildly, striking him a glancing blow on the shoulder. He tried to force her back against the wall, but she twisted to her left and swung again while attempting to pull her other arm free. He ducked and jerked her toward him, she kicked once more, her foot connecting with his leg. She kicked again but he grabbed her ankle, pulling her off balance. She landed on the end of the bed then bounced to the floor, jerking out of his grip.

Amanda clamored for the opposite side of the room then he lunged forward to slap her. Amanda ducked, dodging the attempt, racing across the bed for the bathroom. She slammed the door, heard a scream and looked down to see a hand squeezed between the frame and the door, one finger pointing awkwardly to the side. David rammed the door with his shoulder, shoving Amanda into the sink. She tumbled backwards, fighting to catch her balance. David grabbed her hair with his left hand, pulling her into him.

"We will meet again," he hissed between clenched teeth. "And I will remember this." Holding his hand up where she could see it, he thrust her away from him and stormed out, cradling his broken hand.

A single tap and the outer door opened. She thought about making a run for it, but both David and George were standing in the open door. Instead, she leaned against the wall and listened.

She stared at the floor as they casually discussed their options, make money off her or having her disposed of. It was hard digesting the meaning behind 'having her disposed of'. She didn't want to accept that that could be her fate. She had to get out of here. No man was going to use her like this.

The man who called himself, David, spoke again pulling her back to the present.

"If you can break her spirit," David continued, "she will make you a fortune. If not, she will only cost you money."

After what felt like forever, someone started to walk away. She dropped her eyes, thinking about the conversation again. Give in or die. She didn't like the sound of that.

Amanda closed the bathroom door silently and leaned against it then someone walked over and tapped on it.

"I know you were listening, princess," George said. "You may have even been contemplating your escape. Don't try it. The consequences will not be pretty. I also suggest you make a decision and you do it soon. The harder you fight, the harder this will be. And just so you know, you could have a great future ahead of you. It's no different than being married. In a marriage the man supports the woman in exchange for sex, meals, and a clean house and clothes. Only this is as safe and you'll have multiple husbands."

She hesitated debating if she should answer. "There's a big difference," she finally said. "It's not at all the same as selling your body to some unknown. If it's so safe, why do so many hookers end up dead?"

"You are stubborn, aren't you?" he said.

28

David walked in a couple of days later grinning from ear to ear. Amanda's expression must have betrayed her surprise and he started laughing. She looked away, angry because he had been able to read her so easily.

"Good day lovely lady," he said, saluting her with his casted right hand. "I am not hearing nice things. George says he hasn't made a dime off you yet."

Amanda lunged off the bed, then David reached out with his foot and tripped her. She landed face first on the floor then he grabbed her arm with his left hand and jerked her up, thrusting her back onto the bed. He swung the bathroom door closed, positioning himself between her and it.

"I'm at a bit of a disadvantage," he said, holding the cast up, "but I'm not helpless. I also admit when I saw you before I assumed you would see things my way. I have never met anyone who would rather die than make love. Now that I have said that, I propose we make a deal."

Amanda glared at him and scooted across the bed keeping her eyes locked on him.

"I'll take this as a good sign," he said. "You haven't out right attacked me, yet. So what do you say?"

"Depends," she answered curtly. "What's the deal?"

"George let me bring you your new outfit," he said. He tossed a small paper bag onto the bed in front of her. "I imagine the one you're wearing is getting a little ripe. It's been three days, hasn't it?"

"Four," Amanda corrected him.

She took the bag and peeked inside, but only saw feathers and chiffon. It didn't look much different than what she had on. A quick glance up at David and he hadn't moved, so she pulled it out. This one was longer and looked like it would cover her behind.

"Four," he repeated. "I imagine you'd like to change."

"What's the occasion?" Amanda asked, trying to reel the emotions in.

"George has set you up with a date," David replied. "Someone we hope will help you with your attitude."

"A date," Amanda repeated.

"A special date," David said with a smirk. "Your learning curve is going to go up rather rapidly. If not….I might have more fun than you could ever dream of. Have a good evening, my lovely Amanda."

"But what's the deal?"

David only gave her another salute with his cast.

As the lock engaged, David's words echoed in her mind like a demonic taunt. Her worst nightmare was coming to pass once again. But why was this one so special? Amanda paced the floor, the room growing smaller with each pass. She stopped by the window and grabbed the sash, shaking it violently. It remained solidly where it was, mocking her, and she fought the urge to smash it. Then what would she do? Jump? She didn't even know what floor she was on. The door opened behind her and she whirled around, the guard standing in the opening.

"Cameras," he reminded her. "Be a good girl tonight."

She recognized the leer, then he backed out, closing the door and she was alone again. Amanda showered and dressed, it wasn't much, but David was right, it felt good to wear clean clothes. Combing her hair, she stared at her reflection in the mirror. Why had David brought her the message and the clothes? Maybe they were going to move her again. Maybe not. Not dressed like this.

Amanda sat on the bed, remembering prior meetings. Were all nights going to be like that? The door opened and a distinguished looking gentleman walked in, jolting her out of her thoughts. He sat opposite her on the bed, inspecting her. Amanda clasped the blankets tightly over her chest, her body immobile, frozen in place.

"Sshh," the man said, putting a finger to her lips. "There is no need to panic. I have no plans on taking advantage of you."

"I've heard that line before," she said sarcastically. "Every man I meet says the same thing. It usually lasts about fifteen minutes."

"The way Mr. Bonner has you dressed, I think I understand." His eyes wandered across her shoulders and back once again. He laughed softly then and pulled his hand back. Something about her looked familiar. "What little I see would make it difficult for any man to keep his hands off you, unless he is not into the ladies. Since there are no decent chairs, I'm going to sit here, if that is alright with you."

"And if it isn't?" she asked.

The man ignored her, taking his suit coat off, and tossing it on the pillows, revealing a Jade grey brocade vest.

"Mr. Bonner said you were an exquisite creature. He didn't lie. Any man would be proud to have you accompany him. Mr. Bonner also said you have only been working this business a short time. Is that true?"

"One might say that. I think I need to go." She jumped for the bathroom door, confused about why she had bothered to say anything, and she definitely didn't want him getting a good look at the rest of the outfit she had been given.

"I don't think so," he responded, pulling her back. "You were placed at my disposal by Mr. Bonner for a mutually agreed upon amount. You are mine to do with as I please for the next hour."

"I don't think so," she said mimicking him.

Amanda rolled onto her back, planting her feet firmly in his chest and pushed, her body following his. They hit the floor and she squirmed to her right, but he had his legs hooked around her waist, his arms enveloping her torso, holding them at her side.

They stayed in that position for an indeterminate amount of time, Amanda refusing to speak and continuing to struggle, him refusing to release her while trying to remember where he had seen her. One thing he knew, she couldn't display this type of behavior with her clients.

"I told you I wouldn't take advantage of you," he whispered, finally breaking the silence. "I meant that. Please, relax. Do you think you can do that?"

"How am I supposed to relax?"

"I meant what I said, but I will sit here all night if I need to."

"Then it might be a long night for both of us. I thought you said you only had an hour?"

It felt like hours passed, her shoulders aching then her head and shoulders finally drooped, and he loosened his hold.

"I am going to let go," he said, his words slow and deliberate. "You will be free to do as you wish. I just ask that you do not attack me again. Do you think you can do that?"

Amanda nodded and he let her go then she scurried off, slamming the bathroom door behind her.

He had to talk to George. He had to remember where he saw her.

When the outer door closed Amanda moved out of the bathroom and back to the bed, listening to the men talk. Creeping to the door she leaned her ear against it, the voices were muffled, but she clearly heard George ask if he'd made a bad choice with her. The response took her by surprise.

"Perhaps," the man replied. "She is indeed exquisite. She will be perfect, if we can convince her to be more compliant. You will need to start soon if you want her ready for the winter events," the gentleman continued.

"I would like to start her training as soon as possible."

"As you wish," the man replied. "Let me know when you want me to perform my normal interview."

"I was hoping you could do it in the next day or two."

"I will see you day after tomorrow then," the man said.

Footsteps receded down the hall then keys rattled and Amanda sprinted for the bed. The door opened and she looked up to see George walk in. He sat next to her, studying her for a minute before attempting to caress her cheek. Amanda turned her head away and slid further up the bed.

"It would be much easier if you would just cooperate," George said.

George waited a minute and Amanda thought he might expect a reply. She said nothing.

"You really don't have any idea the effect you have on men, do you? You are the kind of woman men would die for. That's what makes you so valuable in this market. But now I'm curious. How much longer can you continue to fight?"

"Until the day I die," Amanda answered. "It's my body, I make the decision, you don't."

"Is it really worth that, princess?"

29

William walked into the restaurant the next morning hoping for good news. The four walls at his apartment had begun closing in. He smiled as he stood in front of the wall of windows and stared outside, thinking about the lieutenant's promotion. He was glad they had decided to put Lieutenant Ohlmet in the late Captain Jakes position. He would be a good captain.

Neither Jeremy nor James had made their appearance yet and William took a seat at one of the tables, reflecting on the last week. This was day seven without Amanda, and so far they had learned nothing new. He was getting good at waiting. He'd been waiting for six nights. Six nights sitting and staring at the phone, hoping to hear something. Six nights of wondering if they were going to find another body in one of the canyons and it would be Amanda. Six nights of wondering how he would make it through that night and the next day.

It had also been the end of their first week making their obligatory pick-ups for George. As they made the rounds and talked to the girls, they got a more personal insight into why some of these women did what they did. And it brought the heartbreak some of them felt more into focus. They had also learned how to push each woman, convincing her to fork over so she wouldn't have to talk to George's '*Accountant*'. None of the women wanted to tangle with him.

"How you doin', buddy?" James asked when he sat down.

"Doin'," William answered. "I never thought I'd go through this again."

"I hear ya," James said, not sure what else to say.

"How are you gentlemen holding up?" Jeremy asked, taking a chair on the side between the men. "Still hanging in there? Don't blame yourselves for this. I know that sounds easy and it isn't."

"Still hanging in there," William answered. "It's hard since we were supposed to keep her safe. We didn't do a very good job of that, did we?"

"You did everything you could. Now, to the reason for this meeting. Royce Warden was observed by one of my men entering a rather pricey apartment hotel in South Salt Lake…"

"So she's still in Salt Lake City," William said.

It was almost a question, but more of a statement and Jeremy heard the hope. He nodded and continued his explanation.

"A few minutes after that, Mr. Bonner arrived. Mr. Warden left approximately ten minutes later and Mr. Bonner was seen leaving thirty minutes after that. According to them, Mr. Bonner was not moving too fast."

"Amanda can fight," William said attempting not to laugh, but the picture of Amanda kicking George between the legs proved distracting. "Sorry. Did they go in and check the place out?"

"One of the men followed Mr. Warden but they lost him a few blocks north on State Street. His time in jungle was well spent; he knows how to evade a tail. My remaining man acted like he was looking for someone, but there were guards at every entrance. They continued to monitor the building and saw no further activity."

"Has the department requested warrants?" James asked. "Are they going in?"

"Warrants were requested," Jeremy answered, "but the judge isn't in agreement. He said they don't have enough evidence. Have you two seen anything recently?"

"George hasn't been at the bar for a couple of nights. We dropped our proceeds with one of the bouncers. He's George's right hand man. His name is on the list," James said, he slid an envelope across the table to Jeremy. "We're going to stake it out tonight."

"Please, do," Jeremy said as he took the envelope. "Were you able to get inside the club?"

"Eddie let us in," William answered. "The fire department was still doing their investigation but, according to Eddie, detectives had already been through and collected several bags with hair and other evidence. I found a button under one of the wire shelves, but it could go to clothing from anybody who worked there." He handed the bag across the table. "I found it when I moved one of the full kegs. Almost missed it then. It's grey like the concrete floor."

"Thank you." Jeremy opened his briefcase and placed the bag, along with the envelope inside. "Mr. Bonner called me in to do a meeting with a new lady. He told me the lady is beginning to have a few issues doing the work. He said she was scared."

Both men lean forward, instantly alert.

"I was under the impression she has already been working. She has not. Not the way she was acting. Do you have a good photo of Amanda? Not the still from that video."

"No," William said. "I can see if Eddie has a promotional photo. Do you think this is Amanda?"

"I believe so. Either way, she is coming out. I do not leave anyone in who does not want to work in that profession. We just have to make sure when this lady is pulled out, it is done safely. If Eddie has a picture, get it to me as soon as you are able."

"We received some information through this taskforce we're working with," James said. "It confirms what you said about George amping up for the escort side. We have hints that George is already involved, but not here. We don't know where the other stable is located. He has it hidden pretty well. But Amanda would be his first 'Class A' in the Salt Lake City, Reno area."

"And, this lady would be worth a small fortune to him, if she cooperates," Jeremy said. "She is exquisite. For now, I want you to continue watching George. Mr. Warden has been showing up at the bar about five or five-thirty, depending on which bus he rides. Do whatever you need to. Remember, I have men inside. They know who you gentlemen are so if you need back up, use them. And I agree with you about that information from Captain Jakes. Captain Ohlmet and Chief Vanders should have dropped the investigation against you. I will make more inquiries on my end."

They had just finished their breakfast when Captain Ohlmet walked in. Jeremy shook the captain's hand, directing the captain to seat himself. Their eyes locked for a half a second, and Jeremy's head dipped, but his expression was that of one humoring a child. Captain Ohlmet mirrored the move.

"I will leave you, gentlemen," Jeremy said. "I need to prepare for a formal interview with this lady."

William observed the exchange, remembered the cassette of Captain Jakes, and thought about the relationship between Jeremy and the department now. It appeared to have changed.

"Men," Captain Ohlmet said. "I have something I need to discuss with you before you go."

William waited.

"Remember when I asked you to keep it professional?"

William nodded and Captain Ohlmet leaned back in the chair then waved the waitress off.

"That was a request to keep your ass out of trouble. We have been told – again – that there has been inappropriate behavior between one of you and this lady. There's no clear cut line about getting involved with a victim, but if she files a complaint once this is over it can mean trouble."

"If you reprimand William, you may have to include me," James said. "I dated her. We didn't sleep together, but if you had someone following us they wouldn't have known that."

William looked across the table and watched Captain Ohlmet.

"I'm guilty, sir," William said. "If you decide to reprimand me – so be it. I don't want to screw up my chance to get back on the force, but I won't let James go down for something he didn't do. Are we free to go?"

"Do you believe James?" Captain Ohlmet asked.

"At this moment, I'll believe him before I do you or the chief. Anything else, sir?"

"Look, the chief and I are the ones who hooked you up with Jeremy…." Captain Ohlmet started.

"And you're the ones who have left us hanging when you have proof we were set up," William retorted. "Thank you very much, sir!"

Captain Ohlmet held his hands up, exhaling sharply. "We'll see how this works out. Just bring us some good news. I'll let you know if anything more is said."

Leaving the restaurant, James popped William's shoulder.

"She is exquisite," James said, mimicking Jeremy. "We knew that, huh, buddy."

"Got that right," William answered. "And the Cap just told us how they knew we weren't home."

30

The two met across the street from George's bar at five p.m. No one had been there James told William when he climbed into the car. Only one bus had gone by. Handing William a soft drink James hoped tonight wouldn't be a bust. They hadn't helped on any stake outs in a couple of years. He hadn't missed them, either.

"How you doin'?" James asked. "You think they'll do much over this?"

"Don't know," William answered "I knew better, but I couldn't stay away from her. And she never tried to lead me on."

"I understand," James said. "What are you going to do if she does say something and they kick you off?"

"I haven't thought about it. What are you going to do if they push this shit with you? You didn't even sleep with her."

"Get drunk as shit. I haven't thought about it, either."

They spent the next few minutes in silence, each man contemplating the outcome of his actions. Neither of them willing to back down. They weren't going to let their partner take the fall by themselves.

"Guess who?" James said, a car pulling in across the street. "It looks like Royce has wheels."

Silence descended on the car again as they settled in for the possibility of a long wait, but Royce returned in less than five minutes, slamming the door angrily.

"It looks like our boy's on the move already," William said. "He's empty handed and he doesn't look happy. The limo's in the back so I wonder what old Georgie boy said to him."

"Makes you wonder," James replied. He started the car and waited for Royce to pull out. Royce made a U-turn and headed south, James and William two cars behind him. "Looks like he's in a hurry."

They followed Royce to an apartment hotel and parked across the street, as he ran in. This was the building Royce and George had been at. Tonight there were no guards. It might be too late for that warrant.

Royce rushed back out and jumped into the car then peeled out. James checked traffic, made a U-turn and followed. Royce only drove a couple of blocks before he took a left and then a right onto State Street weaving dangerously between cars as he sped north. A few blocks farther and Royce turned right again. He made another right and pulled into a parking lot beside an older three story brick building and bolted for the door. They pulled into an adjacent parking space and approached Royce where he stood rattling the door.

"You were in a bit of a hurry," James said. "We followed you doing sixty up State Street. Would you care to enlighten us as to your reason for driving so recklessly? You know, you're lucky you didn't pass a black and white."

William studied the entrance and listened.

"I'm just trying to find someone," Royce answered. "You can't arrest me for that."

"Who said anything about arresting you?" William asked. He

pushed a button beside the door and a buzzer sounded in the rear of the building then an older man appeared.

"Actually, you're right. We can't arrest you," James said. "You see, Royce, we're no longer cops. So we can, kind of, do whatever we want. As long as we don't get caught that is."

William smiled as the man opened the door. "Police officers, sir."He showed the man his badge and nodded in James direction. "We're looking for a missing person and this gentleman seems to think she has been here, so we hoped we could take a look around. If you would rather not I understand. We can come back with a search warrant and more officers."

That usually worked. Nobody wanted their neighbors to see cops swarming around their home or place of business.

"No problem, sir." The gentleman stepped back and allowed them entrance. "We had a lady here a few nights ago. She stayed in one of the rooms on the top floor. We thought it rather strange since she was quite heavily guarded and they put her in one of the rooms we haven't finished yet."

"Would you be kind enough to show us this room?" James asked.

"They bring ladies here from time to time," the man prattled, "but this is the first time I have seen one being guarded this closely. Do they help government informants escape?" he asked, an excited, boyish light in the old eyes.

"Something like that," James replied, turning to see William grab Royce by the arm and pull him along after them.

"If you don't mind," William said speaking quietly. "We would appreciate it if you accompany us."

James chuckled softly. Oblivious.

"I thought you said you weren't cops," Royce said.

"Maybe I lied."

William dropped his gaze to the stairs, recognizing standard issue Army boots. James was two steps ahead and William tapped him on the back, nodding at the floor. James followed William's eyes to the boots then looked back at William. There just might be something to William's theory. On the top floor, the gentleman opened a door and stepped back, directing them in with a wave of his hand. It was more of an automatic move than guidance, they noted.

William dragged Royce inside with him and saw the mattress and box springs on the floor and lace curtains on the window. If Amanda had been here, what had it been like?

William sighed and James did a sideways nod at the door then he walked Royce into the hall. William remained behind and walked the perimeter of the room, opening the closet door when he reached it, and found the book. If Amanda had been here, there could be some prints here. He closed the door and walked out.

"Do you have any idea what I would like to do to you today, Royce?" James asked. He leaned over the balustrade and looked straight down three floors. "Long drop, don't you think?"

Royce nodded his head impotently and stared down at the foyer below.

"What's the matter?" James asked. "Getting a bit of vertigo there, buddy?"

William leaned against the wall behind them and observed. He could tell Royce knew more than he was letting on. It was written all over his face. Royce wasn't a good player.

"Royce," James said, "you're a smart man, but you're hiding something. We know you're completely aware of what happened, and probably even know where Amanda's at, so we think it would be nice if you would help us find her. Can you do that? We heard you were married to her once, so you must have cared about her at one time."

"I don't know a whole lot," Royce answered. He glanced over the banister again then behind them at William. "I know what I heard on the news. I'm really sorry this happened. All I can do is let you know if I hear anything. You just said you can't arrest me."

"You're lying," William said. He pushed himself off the wall and walked over, placing Royce between him and James. "We don't have to arrest you. We don't have to request a search warrant, either. We've been doing this long enough we know how to work this so we'll go free. It'll be your word against ours…."

"You have lost your mind!" Royce exclaimed.

"…so, what can you tell us that will keep your ass out of jail?" William finished. "I'll give you a hint. It has to be a lot more than you just told us."

William watched Royce, his frustration mounting. Time to play hard ball. He jerked one of Royce's hands behind his back and slapped a handcuffed on his wrist, sliding the other end of the cuff behind Royce's belt then pulled it up; fastening it around Royce's other wrist. Royce jerked powerlessly at the restraints, panic setting in.

"What are you doing?" Royce said, looking around frantically. "You said you weren't cops!"

William ignored Royce and grabbed a handful of Royce's shirt at the neck and the waistband on his jeans then lifted Royce over the rail, his airway obstructed as the fabric dug in.

"I didn't. James did. Are you sure there's nothing you can remember?"

"Wait!" Royce choked out his eyes wide in terror. "Fuck man! You trying to kill me or what? This isn't funny."

"You need to hurry. My arms are getting tired." William heard fear, combined with surprise and confusion, Royce was trying to decide how much to tell them. "And just so you know, I'm not trying to be funny."

"Alright! Alright! I'll tell you what I know!"

James grabbed Royce's arm then they pulled Royce back in.

Footsteps echoed below and the man who had let them in walked away.

"What led you to that place in South Salt Lake?" James asked. "Why there?"

"George took ladies there before."

"Amanda's not the first lady George hired this way? How'd you know about this place?"

"That's not what I meant. George entertains women there from time to time, ya know?"

"No, we don't know. That's why we asked. Please explain. Does George get deliveries there, too?"

Royce jerked his head up quickly looking the other way.

"He does, doesn't he?" William said, chuckling.

"Look, you guys can't prove shit. Let me go or I want a lawyer."

"If you don't know anything why do you need a lawyer? Besides, you aren't under arrest. We can't arrest you, remember?"

"Because it's my right! And if I'm not under arrest, why am I cuffed?"

"Because we're tired of trash like you playing games with people," William said. "See, the thing I don't like is, a young girl was killed and her body was dumped at Liberty Park. She was left naked for everyone to see. That's disrespectful. Then a girl comes to Salt Lake City, presumably for a date with her boyfriend, and her body is dumped at Silver Lake. And guess what? She was naked, too. No man should treat a woman like that. And now, a woman has been kidnapped and we think you know what happened in all three cases. You might even have been in on them."

"Officers have pictures of you leaving that hotel two days ago," James said, taking over. "We have enough to put you in the middle of soliciting and prostitution. We have pictures of you distributing drugs at Fort Douglas and Tooele. Both of those are federal property so that makes it a federal offense. We heard the folks at Hill are looking for you, too. If we don't hear something that will help us, we'll add unlawful entry and attempted rape along with kidnapping. You will be gone for a very long time. You shouldn't have gone into Amanda's apartment. What's your decision? Oh, and did I forget? We're recording everything."

"You're lying. You have nothing. The only time I was in her apartment was the night I was drunk and she let me in. I don't even know where she moved."

"There were a lot of nights you were in her apartment, Royce," William said. "According to her she didn't let you in on any of those occasions."

"How do you know she moved?" James asked.

"Look. I'm not telling you anymore. I'm drawing the line here."

"If that's what you want," William said. He shrugged and picked Royce up again. "What about the times you let yourself in her apartment?"

"Alright! Alright! Alright! I was drunk and tried to make love to her the first time. But that was the only time I was in there. And she let me in. I still want my lawyer."

"The first time?" James said. "According to her she didn't let you in at any time. And trying to make love to a woman without her consent is rape."

William's pager vibrated and he pulled it out, checking the screen. Royce was continuing to plead his innocence as William walked away.

"What's up, Cap?"

"We had a citizen call about two men harassing someone in their building. He said the men identified themselves as police officers before he let them in. What you are doing?"

"Just pushing a little. Royce might be Amanda's attempted

rapist. He admitted he's been in her apartment. He led us to her first suspected location and then he led us to this place. You might want to send a print crew over. According to the man who let us in, a woman was kept in one of the rooms upstairs. The man here said she was heavily guarded. It isn't the only time, either. I'll bet this is a transfer point. If it is the people who own the building are probably unaware of it. I know it's not bullet proof, but it's more than we had. And you said to use whatever means we needed to, as long as we don't break the law. What are you going to do, fire us? Besides, we're still on leave."

"I can do without the attitude. My ass is already in the grinder. Someone told the chief they have recordings of you at George's dive. I was told the recordings detail a business transaction of some kind. So far they haven't turned over the tapes."

"How the hell could anybody do that? We've never made any business transactions. Especially at George's…"

He stopped, his mind reverting to the night George approached them. But who could have overheard them? None of the plains clothes guys had been there.

"Did you remember something?" the captain asked.

"Just trying to think," William said. "If someone has a recording they could have picked up anybody talking to anybody about anything."

"Somebody also told him about you guys and this chic. I know Chief Vanders is pretty pissed. He's afraid somebody will think you're playing favorites for a little tail on the side."

William gave the captain the address where they were and the number of the room Amanda may have been kept in then the line went dead and he thought about what he had just been told. He needed to talk to James. They would have to pick Royce up again later.

"I helped George find out where Amanda moved," William

heard Royce admit when he returned. "That was all."

"We don't believe you," William said, "but we're going to let you go. If we hear anything that makes us think you're more involved than you say, you're ours. And I won't pull you back next time. Any last words?"

"I promise," Royce replied. "I'll call if I hear anything."

"I don't believe that, either, but we have to accept it. We'll even be nice and take the handcuffs off. One last question, Royce. Is Julie good enough in bed to risk getting shot over? Because you know that's what George will do."

William undid the cuffs and they followed Royce outside. On their way out, William made sure to thank the gentleman for his co-operation, and let him know other officers would be by to take prints in that room.

James stared at William as Royce drove off.

"What was that about George's girlfriend?" James asked. "We don't know that."

"So I lied," William said. "And what was all that shit about pictures of him on post?"

"Maybe I lied, too," James answered. "Why'd we let him go?"

"We need to talk. That was Captain Ohlmet. The old sucker who let us in called the station and complained about us harassing a citizen. Captain Ohlmet also said someone went to the chief about us and Amanda."

"The Chief? How the hell'd they find out? And what does the Cap mean 'us'? I didn't even sleep with her!"

"Don't know, but we're in deep shit if this doesn't turn around soon. The chief is worried we'll screw up because we're only chasing a piece a ass. He also said someone has recordings of us talking business at George's."

"Bullshit! He knows better than that!"

"Tell the captain that," William said. He glanced around their surroundings then put his finger to his lip. "You got your badge?"

he mouthed.

James nodded vigorously.

William held his hand out, wiggled his fingers in a 'give me' move.

James set his badge next to William's in his partner's hand and William turned them over, recognizing the button on the back. That explained the business transaction with George.

James covered his badge with his hand his eyes conveying the question he didn't want to ask. William shrugged surveying the area, his eyes landing on the door buzzer. They took the devices off their badges and William did a checked for the old man then wedged the bugs between the building and the faceplate. A quick thumbs up and they walked to the car.

"How long do you think these have been there?" James asked once they were out of earshot.

"Since our arrest," William answered. "We were warned, but I never thought of anyone bugging my badge."

"Or of us being arrested for sales," James added sarcastically.

They were angry now. They hadn't discovered anything new because they had been one step behind the people the entire time. They wanted to know if it had been Captain Jakes, or could it have been Chief Vanders or Captain Ohlmet. Neither of them wanted to believe it had been either of their superiors, but the way things were going, they didn't know who to trust.

"That buzzer should set them on their toes," William said dryly.

"Something else is on your mind," James said.

"Yeah, one of these Domino's is way out of place. We gotta talk to Jeremy. And Amanda isn't the only lady George has brought here."

31

William and James stood in the alley behind a warehouse off Forty-Five Hundred South and Third West waiting for a man they had never met, might never meet, and would probably never meet again, if they met him today. He had called William at home and told him he had information regarding Royce Warden. Royce had been his roommate at one time and had worked with him. All of that changed two weeks ago. So here they were hoping this wasn't a wild goose chase or a set up by George to take them out. At this stage of the game, either of those was a viable possibility.

At two-fifteen p.m. a man started up the alley toward them. It was Royce's friend from the bar. Approximately six foot tall one hundred and thirty pounds, maybe. Skinny as a toothpick. He looked to be in his mid-twenties, but was already sporting an extreme widow's peak. And acted nervous, glancing over his shoulders every few seconds. When he spotted them, he slowed momentarily then jerked his head to the right, indicating a small alcove between two sets of double doors on this particular warehouse.

William and James sauntered over and sat down on one of the

benches by a picnic table. He sat down opposite the two, seeming to relax now that he was out of view. He played with a pack of cigarettes for a second before taking one out and lighting it, then offering them one. The guy was scared to death.

"I'm William and this is my partner James."

"Glad to meet you, the name's Dan," he answered.

"Would you prefer to do this at the station?" If they called Captain Ohlmet would work something out for them.

"No, thanks. I just don't like squealing on my friends or co-workers, but I think Royce is going to get his ass in trouble, if he hasn't already."

"Explain what's going on," William said, keeping his voice calm. "Has Royce said anything that would make you think that?"

"Not really," he answered, taking a long drag off his cigarette then blowing the smoke skyward. "It's more what he's done, not said." He took another pull on the cigarette and sighed. "Royce and I were roommates. Almost two years. 'Were' being the key word here."

"And?" James prompted when Dan took another drag on the cigarette.

"Well, he came into a lot of money and then just moved out," Dan said. "He bought himself a car, rented an apartment and disappeared. He left me high and dry with only half a month's rent. Now, I'm screwed. Anyway, I got that worked out with the landlord, but I got to thinking about it and it isn't right. Not just the moving out part, but the part about that lady." He hesitated, taking another drag on his cigarette. "Royce has been working with George Bonner, making extra money on the side. Then that lady disappeared and I remember he said once his ex-wife was named Amanda."

"Is that what made you suspicious?" William asked.

"Kind of. Royce talks about anything that comes to mind when he's had a few, and he doesn't think about what he's saying, or who he's saying it to and he's let a few things slip. And I drove him around to all those appointments which puts me in the middle of it, too. I don't use drugs and never considered myself a dealer, but – I guess – technically the cops could say I am. I don't like that. I don't want to go to jail or anything."

"Would you be willing to sign a statement detailing what he was doing for George?" William asked. "We could go to the DA on your behalf, tell him if you're forced to testify in court George will have you killed. That would keep you out of trouble and help us nail George at the same time."

"Nailing George is the scary part," Dan replied. "I don't mind helping you, but I don't want to die, either."

"We understand that," James said. "What about Royce?"

"Yeah, well, he was on the telephone at work a couple of weeks ago and someone said something that pissed him off. He threw a temper tantrum, yelling and hollering about George not keeping his end of the deal. Royce told the person he didn't like being used and he was going to go the cops, and then he stomped out."

"Do you think George is after Royce?"

Dan shrugged. "Royce is always mouthing off, but no one's seen him since. I called his apartment complex and they haven't seen him, either. And now he hasn't been at work. No call, no show, nothing, and I'm the one who got him the job so they're pissed at me. It ain't my fault, but I'm hearing about it because I vouched for him."

"Did you know Royce very long?" William asked. "Before he moved out here?"

"Nah, I met him when he moved here," Dan answered as he shook his head. "He moved from California and needed some help so I helped him."

"Are you sure it wasn't Chicago?"

"Yeah. He told me he lived around Stockton somewhere. He said he visited Chicago once."

"But his ex is from Chicago," James said. "Isn't she?"

"That's where he met her." Dan nodded his head and checked either end of the alley again. "He left when they split up."

"That would have been a long visit. I think the timing's off," William said. "According to Amanda she divorced Royce three years ago and moved here. According to what we have learned, he left California for Chicago almost ten years ago. He moved to California from North Carolina."

"He told me he moved from North Carolina to Chicago," Dan replied. "He said he moved from Chicago to California because of his ex."

"Did he tell you anything about his military service?"

"He said he couldn't get into the service. That he tried. He said it was something to do with his brother being over there and they wouldn't let them both enlist at the same time."

"Then how did he get a military ID," James asked.

"How did he make deliveries on base without getting caught?" William asked.

"I had the military ID," Dan said. "Not Royce. We'd go to the enlisted men's club. That let the guys know he had the goods. After a couple of beers, I'd get a room at the barracks, if they had a room available and I'd leave and he'd stay. The guys would pick it up there. If they didn't have a room, he'd call and I'd meet him at the front gate. Fort Douglas, we didn't worry about. He'd go by the commissary and drop a couple of hints and they'd meet us at Lilly's or The Dead Goat."

"He has been seen on post without you. Does he have a fake?"

Dan shook his head. "We used my ID. He didn't have one."

"He has a valid military ID," James said.

Dan's eyes narrowed as he stared at James then he looked

away, suspicion and confusion evident.

"What about when he lived in California?" William asked. "Did he tell you why he moved? Why did he come to Utah?"

"He said some girl he dated accused him of raping her," Dan replied. "He said he was given a choice to leave and not go back, or be arrested. I know how things can happen so I believed him."

William leaned back and watched Dan, his mind going over what Jeremy had told them. "Where did Royce move from California? Did he tell you?"

"Just Stockton. It was Utah or Oregon and he got a job offer from Utah first so here he is. Let me guess, that wasn't what you guys heard."

"You're right about Stockton, but he made a stop or two before Stockton. He wasn't approached by the cops, either, but there were several women who filed complaints about an intruder. All those complaints came in during the same time frame Royce was in those cities."

Dan sat back, lit another cigarette and checked each end of the alley one more time before looking back at them. Dan paused for a minute then he stood.

"Look, I gotta go. I don't want to get caught talkin' to you. George knows I helped Royce and I really don't want to tangle with one of George's goons or be accused of helping the cops. No offense."

"Do you want us to give you a ride?" William asked.

"No, I rode a bus. Didn't want them to see my car. I'll just take a different bus and make a few extra changes. I got my pass."

"Are you sure? We can get you home safe and get you some protection."

"Nah, I got it. Thanks, though. If you see Royce before I do, tell him thanks for the bullshit!"

"Dan," William pushed. "What about the statement? We need your testimony."

"You got my number. Call me when you're ready."

They watched Dan stride angrily up the alley thinking about what Dan had said.

"Royce was the assailant in California." James said. "He left California because he was running, not because they cut him a break."

"We know he sold on base now, too," William said. "I hoped Dan wouldn't pull my bluff."

As Dan turned east toward Main Street they sat a half a block south, debating the wisdom of tailing him, neither of them feeling at ease.

Dan climbed on the bus, taking one of the front seats, but they weren't comfortable, so they shadowed the bus north on Main until Dan hopped off walking toward a bus stop on State Street, weaving his way between parked cars. He approached the stop south of one of the many bars along this stretch of State Street, one of the men leaning on the bus bench pushing himself off to meet him. Dan nodded and pulled out his cigarettes.

They broke off surveillance temporarily, turning right a half a block north and driving toward State Street. This would put them behind the bus when it pulled out. When they reached the bus, the bus was departing, and the stop was empty. William pulled in behind, tracking the vehicle but they didn't see Dan. James shot William an alarmed glance, both men on alert. They continued to shadow the bus to Forty-Five Hundred South, Dan never getting off. Something was wrong.

William swung around the bus and sped to the next stop. James got out, examining each seat and passenger as the bus pulled to a stop and disgorged its cargo. No Dan. They would go back to William's and call him. William had his phone number.

A call went across the portables at eleven p.m. about a body dump behind a fast food restaurant on State Street and Twenty-One Hundred South. They hadn't been able to contact Dan, so William called James. James agreed, but they didn't want to be obvious. William laughed. Salt and pepper team and they were trying to be inconspicuous.

Too many bodies were piling up James joked as they pulled into the parking lot. They climbed out of William's car and recognized Dan then remembered the man bumming the cigarette.

"Damn it!" William exclaimed. "We offered him a ride and protection. He refused."

They approached the officer in charge who summarily brushed them off. William gave him Jeremy's number and an eyebrow raised.

"We need to know everything you can tell us," William said. "If not, our reports will say the Salt Lake City Police refused to co-operate in a criminal investigation and, for you, things will only go downhill from there."

The officer keyed his mike, requesting clearance. It wasn't guaranteed they would get the co-operation, but it would give them some time to investigate on their own.

While they waited for the officer's call back, they inspected the body and made note of the wound in his arm. It had been staged to look like an overdose, but the mark was too visible.

By the time Dan's body was loaded into the coroners van it was almost two a.m. and the officer still had not received a reply. That was fine. William let him off the hook and told him Jeremy would deal with Chief Vanders and Captain Ohlmet.

"We should have recorded that conversation," William said. "We needed the witness, the testimony."

"Aw, but we did, buddy. I got my party toy's remember?"

32

Friday night William was performing so James staked out Royce's apartment solo. They had no doubt Royce held the key to discovering George's involvement in Amanda's abduction, and Dan had given them the address. When they checked with the management office they were told he had moved, but James poked around and found the car Royce had driven when they fleeced him. Not a word had been heard from the chief or the captain. He hated not being able to run a plate or do a background check.

At nine p.m., Royce pulled out of the complex heading east, but he didn't go as far as State Street; instead he turned left on Main Street. James followed as Royce drove north, stopping in front of Pearl's on Main. James parked a half a block south and trotted across the street to a pay phone. Would Eddie be kind enough to let him in the emergency exit, please? Jogging to the rear of the building, light flooded up the narrow stairwell and into the side street as James hurried down.

"I'm not here," James whispered.

Eddie simply nodded. No questions would be asked.

James got comfortable at the end of the bar closest to the restrooms, and noticed Royce didn't join George. Dan had hit that one, too, they were a divided camp. William tilted his chin up slightly indicating he had seen the same thing. George sat at a table near the back; one of his men talking to him. Evidently George didn't like what he was being told, either. His body language projected his anger. The backup performer returned for the second set, and George stormed up the steps, James changing targets. He would reacquire Royce tomorrow. He wanted George to lead them to Amanda. He slipped off the barstool and nodded at Eddie as he trotted down the hall.

James pulled into traffic a couple of cars behind George, maintaining a loose tail. George made a quick stop at a building that was under renovation then the limo was on the move again, stopping in front of one of many old hotels turned flop houses. One of those George had slated for demolition. James parked his car in the alley and surveyed the area, making note of the cars parked behind the buildings. He climbed out and walked around the run down structure. The rotting clapboard siding was peeling and falling off, gutters dangling below the tops of the parapet. Two fire escapes hung haphazardly from the roof. One on the north side and one off the alley above a window, with a light on, on the second floor.

After he'd climbed the fire escape on the north side of the building, James did a crouching run across the roof to the fire escape above the window then took a look at the rusting ladder below. Better than nothing. He took a moment to scan the area, for anything out of place, thinking about his decision. If a sniper was in the shadows, he would be a wide open target.

James climbed down then balanced with one foot on a corner of the window sill; his arm wrapped around the bottom of the metal frame, and peered inside. Amanda was sitting on the bed, her back to him. Priorities had just changed.

A man opened the door and stepped inside wearing the same suit George had. Part way into the room the man stopped, facing the door, his back to James. He glanced over his shoulder at Amanda then said something to someone out of view in the hall, but kept his back to the window, preventing James from recognizing him. One more glance at Amanda and he walked out.

James tapped lightly on the window, finding it hard to control the urge to shatter the glass when she ran toward him. He wanted her out of here, but Jeremy's words echoed in his mind. *'We have to make sure when this lady is pulled out, it is done safely.'*

"Can you hear me?" James asked.

She nodded, a smile lighting up her face.

"Good. Don't say a word. Just nod your head yes or no."

She nodded again.

"Are there guards on your door? Does this window open?"

Another nod then she shook her head, acting like she was hitting something.

"It's nailed shut," he said to himself than raised his voice so she could hear him. "Don't go anywhere."

He shook his head when she laughed. That wasn't the most intelligent statement. James reached for the rung above him at the same time a bullet lodged in the window frame, spider webbing the glass and the report from a high-powered rifle rang out. He ducked to the side, dangling from the fire escape then pulled himself back up as he perused the area.

"Cover yourself with those blankets." He pointed to the bed behind her. Things had changed, again.

Balancing with one hand on the fire escape above and his foot on the lip of the window, James pushed the glass in along the frame with his other foot, forcing the pieces out along the lines of the cracks and avoiding being sliced. He called Amanda over and she draped a thick fold of the blanket over the bottom sash then he helped her squeeze through the narrow opening.

"You have no idea how good it is to see you," Amanda said.

"Come on," he said. "There's a dude in the alley. We gotta hurry. Once on the roof stay down so no one sees you, okay?"

She nodded, grabbing the rungs and going hand over hand, James steadying her until she could get a foot on a bar. "Royce said he made a deal with George," she told him, explaining what Royce had said. "George planted the camera on my desk at work, too."

"Good girl," James said. They had George now. That was trafficking.

A quick peek to check for anyone who might be following them and James climbed over the parapet after her. There was the brittle crack as a bullet embedded itself in the building then James ducked. A shot rang out with a half second delay then he led Amanda across the roof, stopping above the northern fire escape. He hesitated a second. Both of those shots should have hit. In tight quarters like this, the person shouldn't have missed. Were they being herded?

"Follow me. I'll catch you." Being given few options, James swung himself over the edge, disappearing down the side of the building. He dropped silently onto the pavement below and took a step back. "Come on. The car's right here."

"Okay," she said under her breath. Half way down, she stopped. "James, I can't move! JAMES! I'm caught, I can't move! Crap!"

"Hold on." He climbed back up to unhook the fabric. "Can you tear it? Never mind. Slip out of it. I'll give you my shirt."

"It's too tight!" she said jerking on the top. The harder she tugged the more frantic she grew. She closed her eyes and exhaled loudly in an attempt to calm herself, then started yanking on the fabric again. "Where's the damn hook?"

Footsteps slowed on the roof above them and they glanced up

expecting to see a guard with a pistol aimed at them. No one was in view, but a shadow came visible on the side of the neighboring building.

James skimmed the alley once more, a shadow faded into a crevice between the buildings across from them and the reality hit him. They had been herded.

"James, go. I don't want him shooting you! GO!"

"I didn't get this close to lose you," James replied. "The one time I can't get the damn clothes off a woman!"

"NO!" Amanda shoved James away with her foot, a dull thud sounded beside them and a hole appeared in the clapboard siding two inches from the ladder. The shot echoed in the alley with its customary delay, James freefalling in the darkness below then Amanda looked up a guard peeking over the parapet.

The guard aimed the pistol at James and Amanda climbed to the rung above, straining against the thin fabric, trying to grab the guard's wrist then her top ripped.

"Oh, of course," she snapped.

James landed on his back on the pavement, the breath forced from his lungs, pain radiating into every muscle. He rolled to his side, gulping for air. A swimmy image of Amanda jerking on the man's arm came into view. He struggled to stand falling into the neighboring building then flattened himself against the wall. He drew his pistol and a loud crack echoed in the manmade canyon of brick, wood and steel then the back window in his car shattered. He ducked and did another sweep of the area, but saw no one. The spaces between buildings provided the perfect cover for a sniper.

James turned to check on Amanda, the only thing remaining was her blanket and her top, the guard carrying her across the roof. That had to be the man who had carried her out of the club.

"AMANDA!" James yelled, the realization dawning on him. She was why he hadn't been hit. Now that Amanda had been reacquired, it was open season on him.

James dove toward the alley, a round screaming past, burying itself in the wall where he had sat. Another went through the trunk of his car. James peeked over the fender, a rifle barrel poking out between buildings as a man readjusted his track. He vaulted for a dumpster, wanting a little more metal between him and that bullet. One more shot echoed between the buildings then his thigh was on fire. If he hadn't jumped when he did, that would have been his head.

He keyed the mike, acting on nine years of automatic responses. "Shots fired!" he said, giving dispatch the location then he released the mike. "For monitoring purposes only," he muttered sarcastically. And keyed the mike again. "Repeat, shots fired! Assailant has a woman in custody!" He repeated the address and released the mike.

This would be fun to explain. Being involved in a gun fight and he was on leave. And Captain Ohlmet would hear about it. He forced himself to stand, holding in a scream, as a car peeled out of the alley. A scan of the vehicles in the alley and he noticed an empty space. He pulled his t-shirt off to wrap his leg then hobbled for the front of the building, cringing with every step. A car sped away and he slowed, using the wall to keep himself upright. So damn close!

James made it to the front corner of the building as two squad cars squealed to a stop and emptied of their patrolman then he recognized William and Captain Ohlmet climb out of their cars. He rolled around the corner and slid into a sitting position on the sidewalk, angry because he had been so close and failed. Angry because he had been stupid enough to get shot. And he was still angry because he had allowed her to get taken to begin with. The officer's approached with guns drawn, his head beginning to spin as he fought to keep from passing out. He had to stay awake. He couldn't let Amanda down again.

William noticed the blood on James pant leg and the t-shirt, tapping the captain on the arm.

Captain Ohlmet ordered them to release James while William took James weapon and inspected it then gave it to the captain. No burnt gun powder and when the slide was pulled, a cartridge clicked into the chamber. It hadn't even been loaded. The captain nodded to where James had been sitting and William stepped to the side, leaning nonchalantly against the wall blocking the patrolmen's view of the portable.

James' car would be impounded as evidence and the captain wanted them in his office at o nine hundred tomorrow morning. Military jargon. Captain Ohlmet was pissed.

When the excitement was over, William drove James to the hospital, pulling under the emergency canopy and helped James inside, flipping their badges as they rushed through the doors. With James in an exam room, William stood off to the side out of the nurses' way.

"William," James called, waving an arm and beckoning him closer with a finger. "I gotta question for you."

"Shoot, my man."

"What is the one thing you see most of the time with the homeless people? Other than their clothes are dirty and they sleep on the street."

"I can name a number of things," William answered. "Why?"

"Shopping carts," James said. Then he laughed, giving a drawn out sigh. "I think the pain meds are kicking in. They put all of their belongings in those shopping carts and take the shit with them everywhere they go." James laughed again and lay back on the pillow. "I'm sorry, William. This is some goood shit."

"You may have something." William laughed along with his

partner now. "Where'd you come up with that idea. About the homeless people, I mean? Was it Royce?"

"Kind of. His comment just opened a door and then we go to that flop house…." James was quiet for a minute before he picked up the narrative once more. "The hotel just made me think. Homeless come and go, but they use those flop houses and no one bothers the homeless. We avoid them at all costs. We may have found out how George gets his deliveries. Also…." He didn't complete the sentence.

William let it hang for a minute. "Also?"

"Yeah." James laughed again. "They didn't try to shoot me until they had Amanda back. It was like we were being herded to the fire escape. Pulling her out of that window, I was a big ass target hanging there, but they missed."

"I get the feeling you don't want to tell the Cap, either."

"Not a rainbow's chance in hell. I want to talk to Jeremy again first. And I want to know where the Cap and the chief stand."

James grew quiet as the meds kicked in and they lapsed into a comfortable silence, the same silence they had adopted when sorting things out on a call. Then James laughed again.

"That's why Royce knew what we meant when we asked about George getting deliveries in South Salt Lake. William, I don't like this all of a sudden."

"You aren't the only one," William replied

33

William rose early the next morning to call Jeremy and go over James' ideas. Neither was more than a hunch, but they wouldn't quit nagging at him. After he'd explained them Jeremy agreed they might be onto something and the more they talked, the more certain Jeremy became that the men were correct. On both counts. When James found Amanda, George had been forced to – not only move her – but move part of his operation as well. Now they needed to find George's distribution point.

William then told Jeremy the police had taken every publicity shot of Amanda Eddie had, a heavy sigh audible across the phone line. William asked if any more had been learned about the tape of Captain Jakes call and Jeremy told him nothing had been mentioned in any of the reports by Captain Ohlmet or Chief Vanders, and that was concerning. He would handle that aspect without their aid so as not to involve them further. William hung up undecided about whether they had made the right move. Neither he nor James liked relying on others to do their work for them.

When William pulled up outside the hospital he could read

James' frustration. He walked around to open the passenger door and James tried to stand but the nurse pushed him back into the wheelchair. William laughed, knowing if the tables were turned, he'd be going through the same thing. He was then given a tongue lashing for not allowing James to remain in the hospital. James had just undergone surgery and should not be up and about yet. William nodded respectfully and promised to keep a close eye on him.

Once off the hospital grounds James let out a sigh and leaned back in the seat. "I hate this. I can't drive and Brunhilda wouldn't even let me stand up."

William laughed.

"Did you call Jeremy?"

"Yes," William answered, explaining what he and Jeremy had gone over as they drove to the station.

The two walked through the doors a few minutes after eleven. They were late, but the captain would have to deal with it. It takes more than Chief Vanders to move hospital red tape. William held the door for James while Captain Ohlmet and Chief Vanders waited, the captain eyeing them disapprovingly. Neither man liked the look on his face, but James had been involved in a shooting. While he was on leave.

Once in the captain's office, Captain Ohlmet leaned back in his chair, folding his hands in his lap. He flicked his eyes between the two then leaned forward, elbows and hands on his desk.

"Okay, James, I want to know what happened. I didn't expect to be called out to keep your ass out of jail. We went over it real quick last night, but I didn't want you bleeding to death. I want the full story today."

At least they weren't getting their butts chewed for being late.

"We hoped they had found the guy," William said.

"Not yet," Chief Vanders answered. "We need more than huge and over six feet. You're over six foot."

William shrugged and kept his mouth shut. That wouldn't last long, but he had to make an attempt.

"I followed Royce to the club," James said. "When Royce arrived, George disappeared. Since we all think George is in on this, I decided to follow him. I figured I could always reacquire Royce today. So much for that." James explained the rest of the episode omitting his idea about the gunman and the homeless people. He was more comfortable waiting for Jeremy. "And it shouldn't have escalated to the point of calling you," James continued. "I have my concealed carry permit and – as you and William figured out – my weapon hadn't been fired. There wasn't even a cartridge in the chamber. I wasn't prepared to use it last night. Trust me that will change."

"That doesn't change the fact you are on leave and you were involved in a gunfight. Do you have any idea what the media can do with this? And you used the damn portable!"

"What the hell else was I supposed to do? Say, excuse me dudes while I find a pay phone and call the cops. I was trying to free a kidnap victim…."

"Enough!" Chief Vanders said, cutting them off. "Will you both just calm down, please? James, do you think it was George?"

"The dude was wearing a suit exactly like George's, but I didn't see his face. Amanda told me George paid Royce twenty grand and unlimited evenings with her for his help nabbing her. I guarantee George has already moved her again but Royce will know where they took her. How else will he enjoy those evenings?"

"Unless George plans on screwing Royce out of that part of the deal," the chief said. "Anything else?"

"We didn't get a chance to talk," James answered, puzzled over the last comment. "I was just trying to get her out of there without either of us getting shot, which wasn't a complete success."

"Have you talked to Jeremy, yet?"

"I called him this morning," William answered. "He said he'll let us know if he finds out anything."

"Well, we did get some good news," Captain Ohlmet said. "Search warrants were signed at o seven hundred this morning for said flop house. Officers are on sight now and they found three slugs in the building. One in the window frame, one close to the roof where James said they would be, and one by the fire escape. They also dug one out of the building next door. We have those slugs out and we have the ones from James' leg and his car. They appear to be from the same high-powered rifle. Also, we received a report this morning from the Morgan County Sheriff's Office. They found a car someone tried to run into East Canyon Reservoir. Fortunately the water wasn't deep enough for the car to sink. The tires match the tracks we have for the suspect vehicle. They found strands of hair and saliva on the car's rear seat."

"Who's the car registered to?" James asked, expecting to hear it was on a stolen vehicle report somewhere. If that was the case, they were at another dead end.

"Julie Barron. She sold it to our victim in the Great Salt Lake," the captain replied. "Any questions?"

"Julie?"William asked.

"Yeah," James said. "Who put the bugs on our badges? If it was one of you, I might not come back to the department. We trust you and you're screwing us over?"

"It wasn't us," Chief Vanders replied. "It was probably Jakes."

"Thank you, sir," James said, taken by surprise. That had been a quick a comeback. Just blame it all on the late Captain Jakes.

"I want to know why you still haven't dropped the charges against us," William added. "You have proof Jakes was being blackmailed and two of his officers were supposed to be arrested. We're the only men on the force who have been brought in on any charges. What gives?"

"We don't anyone to know we have that recording," Captain Ohlmet answered. "We want it to look like we're still unaware of what's going on."

"So, Jakes wasn't the only man on the force involved?"

The chief shook his head and stared at Captain Ohlmet. The captain dropped his gaze and shrugged.

"You're still not back on duty," Captain Ohlmet said, "but the men know to cooperate with you better in the future. Anything else, Chief?"

William glanced between his superiors. Nice sidestep. Now it felt like they were being railroaded, but not by the bad guys.

"Jeremy contacted me this morning," Chief Vanders said. "He has officially started working for Mr. Bonner so he will no longer be as available. With what Amanda told James we could arrest George, except George has moved again and now we have to find him, and she is gone so we have no witness. The disc we turned over to Jeremy – the names have all been confirmed as low level men in the Reno syndicate. Captain Jakes stepped in way over his head, but without what he did, we wouldn't have learned what we have."

William and James left, baffled by their superiors' last move, and the last two answers. One of them was hiding something.

James stared across seat at William. "We need to do some digging, buddy," James said. "You're right. Some of these Domino's are way out of place. What the hell are they doing? Do they think we're stupid?"

34

The door opened and Amanda came up fighting. She reached for the lamp, but her wrist was twisted behind her back then a strap snapped over her mouth. She gasped, as two huge arms encircled her waist pinning her arms to her sides, then she was lifted off the bed and carried toward the hall. She splayed her feet, bracing one on either side of the door frame and pushed. He wavered and she shoved harder. He lost his balance and she started kicking and squirming. He went over backwards, striking the footboard on the bed, and released her then she bolted for the living room, yanking the gag off her mouth as she dropped to the floor. She pulled the pistol from behind the stereo speaker and pressed her back against the wall, flipping the safety off. Slowing her breathing and closing her eyes, she listened to his footsteps. She could focus on sounds better if she kept her eyes closed and tonight that was working to her advantage.

He was on the opposite side of the wall now and she peeked around the corner. Only three feet away. She moved back against the wall, took a deep breath then waited until he started around the corner. His shoulder rubbed the wall as he moved and she stepped out, aiming the pistol at his head. His hands flew up in an automatic response and he took a step back. She took one more step away from the wall and hoped she wouldn't go to jail for murder. This was self-defense. She was shooting an assailant. And this wasn't the first time someone had come into her home. There had been numerous calls to her previous address. At the last minute, she moved the muzzle to the right and fired. The bullet flew past his head and into the darkness.

"One more step," she said between clenched teeth, "and you are mine. I won't miss next time. I promise."

She moved the gun back so it was aimed at him once again and took a step back, but he lunged forward and slapped the weapon out of her hand.

Her body jerked back and hit something solid. A quick glance to the side, nothing, and she looked back to the front, he was gone. Another look to her right and everything was dark. She opened her mouth to scream, but nothing came out. She tried to run, but she was standing on a ladder. A ladder to nowhere. Only black. She didn't know if she was awake or asleep. Panic started to set in, her heart racing. She attempted to jump backwards again but, his beefy arms still held her.

Her eyes fluttered open then closed, she finally opened them, fully awake to see strange surroundings. She glanced at the blanket she clutched to her body, felt the heavy leather of the sofa behind her, looked down, her top was missing, but the bottom half was still clothed. If you considered under things being clothed. She sat up, her head spun. No headache, they hadn't given her as heavy a dose. A shadow appeared in her periphery, the guard from the previous evening now standing in the door to the kitchen.

It started coming back. The big man carrying her, the ladder – fire escape – in the darkness, James trying to rescue her.

The huge man ducked out and returned with a cup of coffee

and two pieces of toast. He went back to the kitchen and came back with a spoon and a jar of jam.

"I'm not a cook," he said. "This'll have to do. As soon as you're finished we're leaving. If you promise not to fight I won't drug you this time."

Amanda sat up and clasped the blanket tighter over her chest. "Do you have some clothes I can put on? I'd rather not go outside dressed like this.'

"I'll steal something from Mr. Bonner." He walked down a hall and returned, tossing a t-shirt and a pair of sweatpants onto the sofa beside her. "I won't put a gag on you, either, if you promise not to yell. You scream and I'll double the dose this time. Deal?"

Amanda nodded and he went back to the kitchen. When she'd finished dressing and ate, he returned and took her cup then dishes clattered when he cleaned up. He came back, blindfolded her then pulled her to her feet. Once she was standing he pulled her hands forward and slapped a pair of handcuffs on her then lifted the shirt and fondled her breasts.

"You know," he whispered. "It was real hard staying in that bedroom last night with a pretty little thing like you just laying out here waiting for me. Especially as nice as those are."

He laughed and stepped back, nudging her toward the door.

Amanda grabbed a handful of denim in passing, bunching it tightly in her fist, the fabric giving grudgingly. She recognized more than jeans in her hand and squeezed even harder, pulling down as she did. The man bellowed and sucked in a lungful of air.

"I told you I wouldn't yell or fight," she said. "But I didn't tell you I wouldn't defend myself if given a reason, or the chance. I guess David's little pep talk didn't mean much."

A beefy hand slapped her and her head snapped back then she landed on the floor. The slap hadn't drawn blood, but the surprise had caused her to emit a small yelp.

"If I didn't have my orders," he hissed. His breathing was heavy, the man panting to catch his breath "You would be mine, right now. Now, GET UP!"

Amanda pushed herself to her knees and he jerked her the rest of the way to her feet, leading her outside and shoving her into a waiting car. The car reversed quickly, horns blaring as he shot into traffic then they were flying forward, the momentum plastering her against the seat back. When the car stopped, the guard removed her blindfold and a door rose in front of them revealing a cavernous space with another car inside. A dark colored pick-up and a limo were parked off to one side. George's headquarters, she presumed.

He half dragged her up the stairs to the top floor and opened a door at the end of the hall, where he removed the cuffs then he ordered her to give him the clothes and pushed her inside. The lock clicked and she glanced around her new surroundings. This one was furnished even sparser than the last one. An obligatory bed and night table with a lamp, a small table by the door and a mirror on the wall above it. A camera had been positioned above the mirror and she could see one in each corner of the room. No chair in the corner this time and no knob on the bathroom door.

That afternoon the guard returned and threw a nightgown at her.

"Get dressed. You have company coming."

Amanda stared at the gown and slipped it on. At least she was wearing more than a pair of panties.

In the bathroom Amanda bumped into the sink, the pedestal scraping across the cracked tile revealing a hole in the floor. She peeked inside the tiny opening and found a packet. George had hid packs of these pills in the other room, too. Only they had used the mirror there.

A guard had come in one time, ostensibly to inspect the room, and when he left, the bottom of the frame had been loose. It showed a gap. Being nosy, she had dropped the wood slat and out came the packets. Twenty-five pills per baggy, a marked value of a hundred bucks per. She had appropriated almost every packet, not wanting George to get too suspicious. She checked the frame following every room inspection after that.

And since she was under surveillance, no one bothered to check her. Her attire usually had a front piece that hung over the front so she secreted them in her panties until she could hide them under the mattress.

Until James had tried to liberate her and the guard had dragged her to George's. While James kicked out the window, she'd relieved the mattress of its cargo. Once here, she rolled the bags in the legs when she removed the baggy pants and slipped them under the nightstand. Lying on the bed, she had counted her ill-gotten booty before they brought her the new gown.

She pulled this pack out, tossing them in the air, catching them absently then stuffed the pills in the bra.

An hour later a mild mannered dude wearing a three-piece suit walked into the room. He took his coat off and laid it over the table by the door and she realized he wasn't as little as he appeared. Under the tailored shirt and tie, he was quite muscular. He excused himself and strode into the bathroom. When the door closed she pulled herself up and leaned on the wall, preparing herself for what was to come. It only took a few seconds and, as expected, he emerged angry.

"You know I paid extra for that stuff," he said, staring at her coldly. "A lot of extra money." He attempted to grab her, but Amanda lunged off the bed avoiding his grasp.

Now on the opposite side of the bed, she only had one escape route – except for the way she had just come – and that was around the foot. He planted himself, arms crossed, legs spread, where he could reach her no matter which direction she moved, and glared.

"I guess we have a standoff," she said.

Amanda leaned into the wall and studied his stance, debating her next move. He would try to stop her no matter which way she moved, but if she could dodge to her left, throw him off his game she might make it around the end of the bed. If she was fast enough. Or that was her theory. She wasn't entirely confident it would work. Or, she could try and make it across the bed and use the lamp base against his skull.

"I can be patient, too," he said. "Especially since, I've already paid George."

Amanda smirked and shrugged one shoulder.

"What? Did you just change the hiding place?" He took a step closer.

"You might say that," she replied. "I have an idea. Since you paid George lots of money, and you feel like you've been cheated, but you're not the only jackass he's sent in I've discovered more than you paid for. What do you think; maybe we can do a little trade?"

"Maybe." He took another step toward her.

This wasn't the way this was supposed to go.

Amanda jumped, rolling over the bed and reaching for the lamp. The bed bounced as he followed, seizing her before she could reach the lamp. She jerked her knee up, striking him a glancing blow just beneath the ribs. He rolled, grabbing her wrists and twisting her arms behind her back.

"You don't seem to be doing too well," he said. "That could work to my advantage."

"Things are not always as they appear." She reached inside her bra and pulled out the pack of pills. He lunged attempting to grab it and she wrenched her arm above her head. "This is only one packet. I have several more of these stashed. How much is this packet worth to you, lover boy?"

"That depends," he said. He maintained his hold stretching to reach the drugs. "How much are you willing to relinquish?"

She bucked, using her legs like pistons, throwing him off balance, and rolling the opposite way. Now closer to the bathroom door, she stood and dangled the packet in front of him.

"May I?" she asked.

"It looks like you won this round," he said. "What do you propose?"

Amanda shrugged. "I know you pay a hundred a pop for each packet of happy pills...."

"The happy pills, as you call them, aren't the only thing I'll lose money on," he said interrupting her. "I pay a hefty price for the pleasure of your company."

"News flash Romeo, I don't share my body with just anybody. How much are you out?"

"You are correct. Each packet of pills costs me a hundred bucks. You, however, are three hundred a pop. Tonight with you and one packet of happiness is four hundred dollars. How many of those little packets do you have in your possession?"

Amanda walked up the side of the bed, her eyes glued on him, and reached under the stand, pulling out five packets of pills. "Here are six packets," she told him. "We make a deal. I give you these and when you leave I give you four more. That's a thousand dollars worth of happy for a four hundred dollar tab."

"That is tempting. And if I don't follow the rules?"

"There are a lot of ways to get even. One packet of these and they would only find your body in the morning."

"Is that a veiled threat?" he asked. "How would you pull that off?"

"I thought it was stated fairly plainly," she retorted. "I have my ways. I'm now getting tired of your games. Decision time!" She moved toward the bathroom and stopped in the doorway. "I can flush them just as easily. I don't much care."

"If I agree," he continued.

"You walk out a lot happier."

"And if I don't?" He walked over and took the pills in one hand, wrapping his other arm around her and pulling her close.

"Dream on." Jerking her knee up, she caught him full in the groin and spun to the left, driving her foot into him again.

"Fucking bitch," he squawked, doubling over with a groan as the air blasted out of his lungs.

"You want to walk out of here with the happy pills, or do you want me to work that last maneuver again. I can make it hurt real good, asshole."

He pulled himself up and leaned against the wall. "Give me the rest of my payment."

"It's been a pleasure." She pulled out four more packs and handed them to him.

"Next time it will be on my terms," he said. A single rap on the door and he hobbled out.

Amanda waited until the door had closed, then sighed. "There won't be a next time," she said to the empty room.

35

Amanda laid on the bed, surveying the room in greater detail. She had to know every inch of this place to get out of here. She had to remember to look for fire escapes, find out what floor she was on, and how to break that window without alerting the guard. She had to work this just like she did her singing.

The guard returned an hour later and gave Amanda a gift box, nodding as he backed out. Amanda opened it to find a satin nightgown folded neatly and wrapped in tissue paper, a bottle of perfume nestled in the center. Removing the perfume and the exquisite gown, she stared at the Ivory satin with its fancy beadwork and matching duster, envisioning how much this had set George back. Something slid inside the box when she went to set it down and she removed the tissue paper and peeked underneath.

There was a smaller box tied with ribbon and a bag containing make-up. Amanda opened the box and discovered a Ruby pendant and earrings. Once she'd showered and dressed, she surveyed her reflection in the mirror, gingerly touching the reddened area where the guard had slapped her, curious if the man earlier had noticed it. The thought flitted away, her mind settling on George's plans. George never did anything unless there was something in it for him. What was he planning now?

"You clean up nice," George said from the doorway. "I knew I hadn't wasted my money on you."

"I wouldn't be so sure," she retorted. "It doesn't matter what I wear, I'm not going to stoop to your demands."

George grabbed her by the back of the neck and shoved her face into the mirror.

"I would suggest you watch your mouth. This," he said, "is how I expect you to maintain yourself once you're out of here. The gentlemen I set you up with will expect a lady on their arm. One who will not embarrass them or be a smart mouth. And since you are not the one forking out the cash to pay for the clothing, or the housing, it will be in your best interest to at least tolerate me when I'm present. And that doesn't matter what I am requesting. Do I make myself clear?"

"Excuse me," someone said. "I hope I'm not interrupting."

"No, please come in," George replied. "We were just having a discussion about her attitude."

Amanda snickered and George shot her a warning glare before backing away.

"So I heard," the gentleman replied, eyeing Amanda. "You're sure this is the young woman you want me to train? I question that because of our previous encounter."

"Yes, sir," George answered. Then he stuffed his hands in his pockets. "This is Amanda. She's a bit stubborn, as you know."

Amanda gaped, surprised. Why did he intimidate George?

"If you don't mind, sir," the gentleman said. "Amanda and I are going to have a little talk."

"Of course," George replied.

"And, George," he continued, "I would appreciate it if you and your men stay away for a while. It is hard to hold a decent conversation with a prospective student when their pimp is hovering about. If you don't mind, of course."

"Of course," George repeated.

Once George had disappeared the gentleman made a visual sweep of the room, his eyes coming to rest on each of the cameras before he scanned the perimeter. He looked back at Amanda, bewildered, and she stifled a giggle.

"From what I see," he said, "you seem to take great pride in agitating Mr. Bonner. Is there a reason for that?" He paused, checking the room once more. "I apologize, but they haven't given us anything to sit on in here."

"I think the no seating part has to do with my new station in life. As a whore I'm only supposed to lie down."

"Please," he said, waving his hand on a dismissive manner. "I am here to go through a short interview session with you, nothing more. After your performance with me the other night and hearing George's side of things, I would like to know, which is the true Amanda?"

"What business is that of yours?" she asked.

Then a frown appeared.

"I think I understand why he has asked me to begin your training early," he continued with a sigh. "I would still appreciate an answer to my question."

"I don't know," she answered with a shrug.

"Sit down up there," he said. He pointed to the head of the bed and watched her as she stared at him thoughtfully, then he sat on the foot. "I will sit here. Now, back to my original question. Why do you enjoy angering Mr. Bonner so much?"

"I don't know how to deal with all this," she finally said.

"With all what?" he asked. "A woman as gorgeous as you should be used to men desiring them. Why is this so different?"

"I don't know," she repeated. Reminding herself he had no

idea what had happened. "As you said, I take great pleasure in making George angry."

"Some say that is a subliminal form of foreplay. A form of seduction. Control. Push the other person's buttons. Invite them in by pushing them away. Mr. Bonner is a good looking man. Could that be your game?"

"Oh, hell no!" she blurted, a look of disgust crossing her face. "George is a pompous ass, and him or no man controls me!"

"I believe I understand," he answered. 'Well, that answered that.' "I doubt he would be my cup of tea if I was a woman. Now, let's get to the real reason I am here. I would like you to curtsy for me, please. Come on," he said, when she looked confused. "Please, do not tell me you don't know what a curtsy is?"

"You mean I actually have to curtsy before I lay down and spread my legs?"

"No, you do not have to curtsy before you spread your legs," he said in a mocking tone. She had to control that mouth. "I need to gauge your presence in a social setting. If you go to an opera, or a play, you will be expected to show some manners. You may even need to curtsy. Now, can I get some cooperation, please?"

"And afterwards?" she asked.

"That depends upon the services the gentleman has paid for," he replied. "As an escort you don't need to worry about being roughed up. The clientele are much more refined."

"That's a real comforting thought," she retorted.

He sighed and eyed her. She was going to be trouble. He could see it already.

They remainder of the evening was used going over what Amanda considered nonsense. She wanted nothing to do with this; the manners were out-dated and stuffy. Jeremy noticed this, but that was his job, after all. Teach the girls what they would need to rub elbows with the rich. Once he had concluded the session, he walked to where she sat and leaned over, taking hold of her hand.

"Follow me, please," he whispered.

"And if I don't…."

"Just do it," he said firmly.

Amanda heard the tone and followed him to the door.

"Thank you," he said. "I told you before I would not take advantage of you. I will not. Please, trust me for just a moment."

She nodded.

"I am getting the feeling you do not wish to be here. How soon do you want out?"

"About two weeks ago would be perfect," she replied.

"I'll see what I can do. I would appreciate it if you learn to be patient. You might be the golden girl right now, but push it and Mr. Bonner will dispose of you. Play the game. Now, I will see you in a few days." A single tap on the door and he faced her once more. "You don't think you're not playing now?"

A puzzled expression crossed her face. Did he know about the drugs? If he knew would he tell George? Then he smiled.

"You are biding your time, waiting for the perfect opportunity, are you not?"

She nodded again, more of a nervous bob than a real nod.

"You are playing."

36

William picked James up the next morning and the first thing James asked was if anything new had been uncovered during the search of the flop house. William called the station as soon as they returned to his apartment, putting the phone on speaker for James benefit, and was told nothing new had been learned. They found no clothes, no trash, no sign anyone had been there. Flop houses were usually used heavily by drug addicts and the homeless and, with no city services; it should have been littered with trash and feces. They knew Amanda and any traces of her would have been removed, but they hadn't expected George to sanitize the entire building. William thought about his conversation with Jeremy and – in that light – with the possibility of George sending men in to see her, it made sense. All city services would have had to be working. And James said there had been electricity. Like George's other buildings that were slotted for demolition, it had been one more front.

"However, we do have some good news," Captain Ohlmet said. "The last time they went through the lady's apartment they lifted several more sets of prints and, except for yours, they all belong to the same person."

"Anyway to connect them to Royce?" William asked, thinking about what the captain had said. *Several more sets of prints.* It sounded like they had lifted prints before. "We have no proof, but he did admit to being in her apartment. And she told James that George paid Royce to help grab her."

"We still need his prints," Captain Ohlmet said. "We contacted Fort Douglas and Tooele and we're waiting for them to reply to our request for information. So far neither request has worked its way through the proper number of channels. Jeremy's superior is trying to push it through from his side. As soon as I hear something, I'll let you know. It looks like you gentlemen were right. We have two separate cases involving one woman."

"Is that why we weren't told about the prints?" William asked.

Captain Ohlmet hesitated like he was choosing his words before he answered. "Yes, it is. I was told to keep it close."

'Close my ass,' William thought. He and James were being kept out of the loop and they were running out of patience and time.

"We need a favor captain," James said. "We need to know if George goes into the bar tonight. With this on my leg I'll be obvious, but we want to flush him out. Grab his attention. Officer Johnson volunteered to camp out on this one so if George is there we want a page from the plain clothes inside with three 7's. And we might need to use the portable. We'll only use them to request backup, though. Just an FYI, sir."

"I'll let them know. Don't use the portable."

"Cap…"

"Just don't, James. Leave it there."

William hung up and James shook his head.

It was eight p.m. before they received their page and picked up Timothy. James went in while William and Timothy waited outside. James had his party toy, and William had the recorder and the monitoring device. Timothy was in the backseat with his portable waiting to find out where he would be planted. He would be their homeless man, but they didn't know where he would hang out. That was the reason for tonight.

James spotted George at his usual table, his eyes narrowing at the sight of James' leg. George had put things together. James leaned one of his crutches on a chair by the table and hobbled to the bar, ordering a beer. It had only been a couple of days, but he was getting good at this one crutch crap. Seating himself and taking a drink, he watched the guys playing pool. He wanted this to appear as normal as possible. He could see George beyond the pool tables walking his direction and acted like he didn't notice. George sat down across from him and nodded at his leg.

"It looks like you met with a slight accident," George said.

"You might say that," James said. "Had to have surgery. I just wanted to let you know we'll be collecting tomorrow."

"You're sure you're up to that?"

"Yeah. That's why I came in tonight," James replied. "I didn't want you to think I was M-I-A or anything. I'll probably finish this one and head out. I'm not supposed to be driving yet. I took a bus," James added.

William listened to the conversation then moved his car to the end of the block.

James looked up when the hinges on the back door screeched and Royce walked in. George jumped from the chair and headed for the rear of the bar, shaking his head. One of the bouncer's met Royce, shoving him back outside. Just like at the club, Royce was still around, but he was no longer welcome with George.

James turned so he faced the window.

"Call for a tail," he said. "We need a car on Royce. He has been escorted out."

"Timothy's already on it," William answered.

The back door squawked and George left, and James notified William. William backed down the street as close to the bar as possible and waited. James hurried out the front giving up on the crutches as he hop-skipped for the car.

"What the hell, dude?" James asked.

"You told George you took the bus," William answered. "I didn't want him or his men to see us sitting out here."

"Good call."

James turned with his back to the passenger window, keeping watch on the corners of Eighth South and Ninth South on State Street. He wanted a good view of both intersections. He didn't want to miss George.

Three minutes later George's limo appeared at the intersection of Eighth South and State Street, James nodded.

The limo crossed State Street going west, William following. It took a left on Third West, driving south finally pulling through the double doors of the rundown building James had seen George inspect previously.

"That the building?" Timothy asked as they drove by.

James nodded. "We need as much info as you can get. We have no idea where they moved her, but we hope you'll hear a few tidbits hanging out here. The accommodations aren't so nice, but you know how it is."

"No problem. Goes with the territory. If I need anything, I'll call." He dropped a piece of paper over the seat back between them.

William pulled around the corner and parked while Timothy climbed out, pulling the blanket closer about his shoulders.

William opened the note.

Brown and Roberta, south of Thirteen Hundred South.

William looked up, Timothy already jogging up the alley,

diverting between structures shuffling west. William drove around the block while James read the note. They rounded the corner and Timothy was sitting with his back to the building. James saluted, Timothy returned the salute, then lay down and rolled over.

"How are we supposed to work this if our phones are tapped?"

"I guess he'll think of something," William answered.

William took one more look in the rear view mirror pegging Timothy where he laid huddled against the wall. A half a block behind them a car he had seen outside the bar pulled away from the curb, easing up behind another vehicle. It wasn't an unmarked and it wasn't one of the department's undercover cars. He took a left at the next intersection, dousing the lights and turning south into an alley. Spying an empty parking pad between two empty buildings, William inched forward then backed into the space until the rear of the car kissed the porch, shoving it into park. William slumped down where he wouldn't be seen behind the door post, but he could still see out the windows, James following suit. A few minutes later the car William had spotted drove by the mouth of the alley. As it crept by, the brake lights came on then it backed up. William turned the light switch as far to the left as he could, killing the interior lights, and opened the door just enough he could slide out.

"You stay here," he ordered, pointing at James. "Do not leave this car unless you absolutely have to."

"I think that's a mute point," James answered dryly as he lifted his leg a half an inch.

"Nothing is a mute point with you," William retorted. "I've worked with you eight years."

William crept to the edge of the building and slid a piece of fencing that leaned against one of the buildings across the parking pad to conceal his car. The car started down the alley, its lights off, crawling past where they were hidden stopping at the end of the alley. It sat there for several minutes before turning in the direction of Third West. William raced for the street the taillights coming on a block north.

Rushing back to the car, William moved the fence back to where he had found it and pulled out. When he drove out of the alley, he left the lights off until he was confident they were clear. His mind now raced back to Timothy. The man was wide open and unarmed. Driving past the building, Timothy was gone.

"That wasn't one of George's hired men," James said.

"Are you sure?"

"Yeah. I've seen the car at the station."

Back at William's they walked in and found a message on the answering machine.

"Yo, just letting you know Mr. Brown is fine. I'm headin' back to the crib. Oh, wait. I think I got the wrong number."

"I ain't driving you home tonight," William told James. "Use the guest room."

37

Arguing in the hall woke Amanda and she sat up then all fell quiet followed by a soft tap on the window. She turned on the lamp and Royce waved through the window, a piece of paper pressed against the glass with one hand that read, *'5 minutes'*. He pointed to the door and held his other arm tight against his side and she wondered if he'd been hurt in a fight. Amanda shrugged, and held out her arms. Royce grinned broadly, opened his coat revealing an extra t-shirt and pair of pants then disappeared. How had he got here? There was running in the hall then keys turned in the lock. Royce flung the door open, handing her the clothes.

"Come on, we gotta go," Royce said. "I locked the guards on a balcony down here."

She slipped on the clothes and followed him, wondering if it was really a balcony or just a small stoop with stairs leading to a narrow walkway between buildings. She had seen that many times in Chicago and here in Salt Lake City.

"Where are we going?"

"Don't worry about it. I didn't want George finding us, so I thought it best if we laid low for a day or two."

'He had avoided that one nicely.'

She smelled alcohol and debated if this had been such a good idea.

They neared a small alcove and Amanda slowed. If the guards had keys – which she suspected they did – they would hide here. Royce hadn't thought this all the way through. Nothing new there.

Movement to her left stopped her and Amanda backed up, flattening herself against the wall. A shadowy hulk appeared to her left and Amanda ducked away, but it only took one giant step for him to grab her, jerking her into the alcove. Gripping her tightly, he stepped back into the hall and brought the muzzle of his gun to bear on Royce. Amanda took the heel of her stiletto and ground it into the man's arch. The guard did a half growl half roar and lifted her off her feet like a doll. Footsteps faded down the stairs then the guard laughed, sliding the pistol back in its holster.

A door slammed below then a second door closed and Amanda dropped her head. Could she please catch a break? Just one.

"Nice try," the guard said. "Mr. Bonner is waiting."

They stepped into the hall just as George topped the stairs.

"Did Royce really think I would have cameras in the rooms and not around the perimeter or in the halls?" George asked. "I applaud him for his effort, but I can't allow anyone to get in or out without my knowledge. Come, my princess."

Amanda eyed the guard's gun debating if she should attempt to steal it, but between George and The Incredible Hulk, the odds were not in her favor.

George put an arm around her and kissed her softly on the top of the head then escorted her back to her room. At the door he took the clothing and ushered her in, his eyes flitting from corner to corner. The guard followed and her mind raced. She had covered the cameras and she wondered what George would do, or if he had even noticed. He had to. He wouldn't have a feed from them.

"I've given you a lot more leeway than the other girls," George said. "I've even allowed you to play your little game. Now you need to start cooperating. Anyone else would have been disposed of already."

He put one hand behind her head and pulled her in for a kiss.

"Put your arms around me. Men like to feel your bodies respond to ours. We like to feel like we're desirable. Cold doesn't cut it."

Amanda eyed the guard over George's shoulder and dropped her gaze to the holster then ran her arms around George's waist. All she had to do was reach that gun, before he closed the door, and she would be out of here. She leaned her body into George and returned the kiss.

"That's better," George said.

George leaned in for a second kiss, Amanda pushed with her legs, knocking him off balance, and he took a step back, flinging his arms wildly before stumbling into the guard. Amanda pushed harder, reaching behind George to grab the edge of the door. At the same time she grasped the guard's pistol with her free hand, pulling it from the holster. The guard's arms waved frantically as he fumbled for the door, Amanda swinging it out of his reach. She stepped back, George and the guard landing in a tangle on the floor. She aimed the pistol at them and motioned up with the muzzle, both men holding their hands out then George stood. Amanda pointed to the guard with her chin and flipped her head in the direction of the bathroom.

"Lock him in there," she instructed George. "Take his belt and fasten it to the door. Fasten yours to the bed then hook the belts together."

Amanda waved George in. George nodded and walked into the room, keeping his eyes glued to the pistol.

"NOW! Put him in the bathroom."

"Amanda…."

"SHUT UP!" she yelled. "DO it!"

George beckoned the guard to stand, taking his own belt off as the man removed his. He looped one belt through the hole in the bathroom door then pushed the man in before he fastened his to the bed frame. George's hands then began an upward arc in her direction. Amanda flipped the gun and slammed the grip into the side of his head, the bone cracked and blood sprayed and George collapsed.

"PULL HIM IN!" she yelled at the guard.

The guard stared at the muzzle of the gun, temporarily frozen. Amanda took a step forward then he dragged George's prone figure in with him. Amanda pulled the door closed, fastened the belts together and tightened them. When she had finished, she bolted for the hall, scooping up the clothes as she ran, the guard yelling in the background. She should have cold-cocked him, too.

Stopping at the top of the stairs, she checked for visitors then slipped into the clothes. Once she'd dressed, she aimed the barrel in front of her, sweeping the area as she moved. On the main floor, she checked both directions and studied the stairs above her then raced for the door. She yanked the door open, peered outside, dodging to her left and collided with one of George's men. He grabbed her wrist then slammed her against the wall. Her back screamed and her lungs froze as the guard forced her hands above her head, one of his knees between hers, pinning her body against the wall with his. There was an asthmatic screech then she was drawing air in again.

'Just one break.'

"Yo, Frank! I got her!" the man called. "I need some help here man!"

There was a flash to her right and someone grabbed the gun, flipped the safety on with his thumb and dropped the magazine all in the same fluid move, then footsteps ran toward them, stopping to her left. The stranger backed away, vanishing into the night.

They returned Amanda to her room, another guard having released George and his roommate. George was standing at the foot of the bed, a washcloth over the knot on his head. He beckoned with his fingers for the clothing once again.

"You know, if you had hit me any harder I could be dead," George said.

"Couldn't happen to a nicer guy," she retorted, handing George the clothing.

George nodded to one of the men and strode for the door. The guard punched her and there was a squeak from somewhere then she was gasping for air and flying backwards. The wall hit her back and she crumpled to the floor, her breath coming in a screeching wheeze. George stopped in the doorway and stared at where she lay.

"I told you," George said. "I'm the one who owns you. You will not do this again. You have one more chance, and that's it. You are on borrowed time." George flicked his chin at the cameras and she looked up. He had removed the washcloths.

Amanda lay where she was willing the pain and the tears to subside, remaining motionless, not even having the strength to yell. She faded in and out until the sun broke over the rooftops then pulled herself off the floor and onto the bed. She was trying so hard to be strong, but she felt like a failure.

She had just drifted off when keys jingled in the lock and David entered. He closed the door as she struggled to stand, and then he was standing beside the bed, guiding her back onto the mattress.

She wasn't up to dealing with him now.

"No, precious. I won't take advantage of you when you're hurt if that's what you're thinking." He sat beside her, rubbing her back softly, his voice gentle. "I told you not to push it, didn't I?"

She nodded and closed her eyes.

"I hate to see a beautiful woman go through what you are. It would be so much easier if you would just quit fighting." As he spoke, he pulled the covers back and checked where she'd been struck.

"What do you care?" she asked, her voice a hoarse whisper. "And how do you know what happened?"

"Cameras. George has them working again, remember. And I really don't like hurting women."

"That's why you tried to slap me?" she retorted.

"No. George watches me quite closely. I have to make it look good."

"What's George going to say when he sees you in here? Aren't you afraid of George?"

"I set the system to back up, he won't know I'm here. And no, I'm not. George can't hurt me and he knows it. It's called playing the game."

Amanda nodded again, confused.

"I'll return tomorrow and check on you. Okay?" David gave her a kiss on the cheek and walked out, hesitating in the doorway. "You need to start playing."

Amanda awoke the next morning and checked her abdomen in the mirror, noticing the angry purple bruise covering most of her abdomen and her ribs. It still hurt like hell to breath. One of the guards opened the door and laid some clothes on the table along with her breakfast then said she was leaving. She stared, dumbfounded. David said he'd be back today. Why that crossed her mind, she had no idea.

The guard returned and led her outside; Amanda closed her eyes and tipped her face up, relishing the suns warmth. A homeless man approached and she opened them, alarmed at first. Then she remembered the stranger who had tried to help her the night before. The man touched her nose with his finger and smiled.

She returned the gesture, searching his eyes then recognition struck. This was Timothy. She'd met him at the club. He smelled of alcohol and perspiration this time, but that would make it easier for him to play. Being a black homeless man allowed him to blend into the scenery on the busy streets. He curled up on the sidewalk like he was asleep and nobody bothered him. The perfect cover. George's man pulled her forward then Timothy winked and let them pass.

"Which park are we meeting George at?" she asked.

"He said Park City," the guard answered.

The guard closed the limo door and she felt the drugs taking effect. The damned breakfast!

"I'm sorry," she said. "I got confused."

38

William and James were counting the last of the previous evening's pick-up for George when the phone rang. Expecting it to be Jeremy or Captain Ohlmet, William answered with his usual greeting.

"Yo, what's up?"

"Hey, dude," someone said. "I gotta problem with my wheels. Can you pick me up at Roberta's on California Avenue? Sorry, this is Mr. Brown. I'd appreciate it if you could hurry."

William hung up and grabbed his keys as he ran for the door.

"We gotta go, my man," he said.

"What's happening?" James asked. "Slow down! I can't run as fast you."

"Mr. Brown just called," William answered.

They pulled up at the intersection of Roberta Street and Browning Avenue, a car with California license plates flashed its lights and pulled out, driving east on Browning before pulling into an alley on the north side of the street. A couple of hundred yards in, the car pulled under a carport and Timothy stepped out, pointing to a parking space concealed by a tree and several overgrown Lilac bushes. Once they were hidden inside the foliage, Timothy walked over and squatted by the car.

James climbed out and limped around, leaning on the left front fender.

"What's up?" William asked.

"I found Amanda," Timothy said. "She was in that building you guys had me staking out."

"Are you positive?" William asked.

"I'm positive. After I went back the other night a man in a limo arrived. He looked like money. And then that dude, Royce, got into an argument with the guards. He left and five minutes later he came back and headed inside. I'm not sure how he got in unless he unlocked the door earlier, but five minutes after he went in the second time he came flying out the door and raced north, two of George's goons following him. My guess is he was trying to spring her because Amanda came flying out the same door shortly afterwards, gun in hand and ran head on into one of those men. He pinned her against the wall and called for back-up. I tried to help, but his help arrived too fast so now I had a gun pointing at my head and I'm unarmed."

"Don't sweat it. You did the right thing," James replied. "No one wants you getting hurt."

"Back to square one," William said, as he leaned his head on the headrest. "When are we going to catch a break?"

"Don't know. But they left this morning," Timothy added.

"Yes!" William exclaimed under his breath.

During the last conversation with Captain Ohlmet they had gone over the possible places George would move Amanda to and one of them was his home outside Cascade Springs. If their hunch was correct, once they had confirmation Georges' group was at Cascade Springs they would be on their way. They had run the routes and numbers a hundred times. It shouldn't take more than an hour and a half.

"Not so fast, bro," Timothy said. "Amanda asked which park they would meet George in. The dude said he thought they were going to Park City."

"Park City?" James said surprised. "Damn it!"

"Never mind," William said. "So, why the hell are we meeting here?"

"Captain Ohlmet already pulled the men back from Cascade Springs and called Park City," Timothy told them. "They are on the lookout for George's group now. Park City is only about a forty minute drive, so they should have arrived by now, if that's where they went. I'm going to play a hunch and go back tonight. See if I can find anything new."

William glared out the windshield. "The Cap had no intentions of letting us help with this shit, did he?"

"No," Timothy answered. "Sorry, dudes. When I found out, I had to say something. I was originally told you were helping them. Here's my code." He handed William a note. "This'll get you in the station. Maybe you can get one of the guys from vice to give you some info on the sly." Timothy stood and gave the two a high five. "Hang in there. I know this is tough, but FYI, the Cap was right. You two are the best. I gotta go in case they're tailin' me." Then he pointed to the note. "If asked, I'll have to deny I gave you that, though."

"Understood," William said. "We appreciate this."

Redemption felt good. Even if it was only partial.

"You ready to spend the night at the police station?"

"Absolutely," James said.

Thirty minutes later they pulled into the rear of a parking lot across the street from the station and William trotted to the back door. He waited until James joined him then punched in Timothy's code.

"You know they're going to recognize us on the security

footage," James said.

"Timothy's code shouldn't draw any alarms," William replied. Even so, he perused the building for any sign of Chief Vanders or the captain before he continued inside. "They asked us to help them with this shit, and clear our records, and now they push us out."

James nodded and they headed for the bank of desks in vice. They had questions they wanted answers for.

Two more hours and they were in the break room making coffee. They sat at one of the tables and went over the information they had been given, trying to piece things together. They were still coming up a few pieces short. William glanced up at the clock and thought about the captain's comment about possibly having more than one person on the inside, then dropped his cup in the trash.

"I think we need to go," William said. "We have to try and stay out of trouble."

"You think that's possible?" James asked, laughing.

39

Chief Vanders arrived the next morning and pulled up the security scans from the night before. He watched the screen and frowned then picked up the phone, dialing Captain Ohlmet's extension. He had had concerns about William and James trying to bypass security, and had been checking the footage religiously every morning. Now he had to find out if they had help, or if they had worked out a way to trick the system. Picking up the phone, he told Captain Ohlmet what he'd seen, and that the captain would have to handle them, they were his responsibility. Captain Ohlmet hung up, dialing William's number and told him to pick James up and be at the station in ten minutes, hanging up before he could get an argument.

Captain Ohlmet was waiting outside his office when they entered the main lobby and he waved them in. Once they were seated, he sat down and stared at them across the desk.

"Still no news, I take it?"

"Not that we've heard," William said. This was uncomfortable all of a sudden. "We talked to vice last night. Made a few more inquiries. Any news?" He didn't like the scowl on the captain's face.

"How'd you get in?"

Both men stared at the captain then he turned his computer screen so they could see themselves coming through the rear door.

"We followed Timothy in?" James said, dropping his head when he realized he'd phrased it as a question. "He told us he had to check on something."

"Check on something," Captain Ohlmet repeated. "He didn't happen to tell you what that something was did he?"

"No, sir," James answered. He glanced over at William, working on what he should say. "I guess it was something about George. He's the department focus right now."

Captain Ohlmet nodded, but they were getting the distinct impression he didn't believe them. He turned the monitor so it was facing him again and studied the screen.

"Well, Timothy called this morning," Captain Ohlmet said, watching them. "He went back and stayed outside George's again last night. When he checked the building it was wide open. He hasn't been inside. I didn't want him going in alone. The judge should be signing the search warrant sometime this morning. Once it is in my hot little hands officers are going to go in and check the place out."

"And we're sidelined for this one, too," William said.

"Yes. You're still on suspension."

"Captain, you wanted us to help with this investigation, and that's what we're trying to do. Now, you're not letting us in on it. What the hell gives?"

"This is part of what gives," Captain Ohlmet replied as he pointed angrily at the screen. "You aren't supposed to be in here, but I receive a phone call from Chief Vanders about you two letting yourself in, and now you lie about how you got in. That show's you punching in someone's code to enter the building."

He jabbed angrily at the screen again. "Coincidentally, Officer Johnson's code was used at the same time, but Officer Johnson happened to be sleeping on a sidewalk. These are time stamped, gentlemen." His voice had raised a decibel and they checked to see if anyone had noticed, but no one was watching. "Will you, please, explain that to me?"

Neither man spoke. They weren't going to out Timothy.

"I didn't think so. I need your pagers, the portables and your badges. I'll let Jeremy know we've removed you from this operation."

They laid everything on the captain's desk then looked him in the eye.

"William…"

"Don't bother, Cap," William said angrily. "You said you wanted us to help you, but now you cut us out of the pattern. You have a recording that proves we are innocent of the charges leveled against us, and you are doing nothing. Someone has placed bugs on our badges, our phones and apartments are bugged, and there are the times I have been tailed. What kind of game are you playing?" He was almost yelling now.

Captain Ohlmet raised his hands in a hands-off gesture and nodded toward the door.

"I'll have officer's escort you out."

"Don't fuckin' bother," James snapped sarcastically.

At William's car James leaned back in the seat and sighed. "What the hell is going on, William? How are we going to find Amanda, and clear our names now? Obviously they aren't in a hurry to get us reinstated."

"Don't know. Want to check out an abandoned building?"

"Absolutely! Think we got time?"

"Don't know that, either, but what's he gonna do? Fire us?"

"No, arrest us," James replied.

It was only fifteen minutes until William and James stood in front of the run down building George had last used as his headquarters. Examining the grimy exterior, William couldn't imagine the inside being too much better than the outside and wondered what it had been like for Amanda.

They had brought their Polaroid, and were going to document every square inch of the place for Jeremy. They needed to find the physical proof that George had paid for Royce's help. So far, all they had was Amanda's word – and she was M-I-A again.

Moving from room to room, they found tantalizing clues about George's involvement in trafficking, but no evidence. Nothing that could be used in a courtroom. When they reached the second floor, it looked like it had been used as an apartment, complete with a child's bedroom and a large walk-in closet. A few items of clothing still hung on hangers allowing them a brief glimpse into the lives of the people who had once occupied this space. They had to admit George had gone to great lengths to make sure the interior didn't match the rest of the building. They headed toward the stairs then William walked back to the child's room and stared inside. None of the information the department had, mentioned George having children.

A door banged in the alley behind them causing William to jump and James to laugh at his partner's reaction. Nothing like being paranoid when doing a search. As they continued their inspection of the deserted structure, William was beginning to think this might be another dead end, just another transfer point. James stopped when they reached the fourth floor. This was the last place to look. So far, they had lots of pictures, but had found nothing to point them to Amanda.

James took a quick breath when he opened the last door and stepped inside. William followed and understood James reaction. He could smell her perfume. It was Amanda! Once inside William's eyes were drawn to the only furniture in the space. A bed sat on the wall facing the door, a nightstand with a lamp sat beside it and a small table sat next to the door, a mirror hung on the wall above that. They could see the telltale hole where a camera had been positioned above the mirror. William stared at the bed for a minute then forced himself to look away. That's when he noticed the imprint in the wall. He hoped that wasn't from her.

Scanning the walls, William found where other cameras had been positioned in the corners near the ceiling. George was making more money off these girls than they knew. He moved on to the tiny bathroom and noticed the hole where the knob should have been, then glanced down finding the scratch on the floor. He bumped the sink with his hip and the pedestal moved. Sliding it to the side he found the hole. It was empty, but he had a suspicion what it had been used for. James appeared at the door and he noticed his partner was taking this hard. Maybe he had stepped into the middle of something without knowing it. Then he reminded himself they had to keep moving. They were running out of time.

"You going to be alright?" William asked once they'd finished the walk through.

"Yeah," James answered. "Just thinking about that wall. Now, let's get out of here before the boys in uniform show. We have to talk to Jeremy again."

They walked outside and William watched a dark-colored pick-up pull away from the curb across the street. He observed it for a minute then climbed into the car.

"I…uh….if you and Amanda had something going and I screwed it up. I'm sorry. I didn't know you…. No one said anything."

"Nope. You're good." James said. He looked across the car and smiled. "We didn't have anything going. It really was just like I said."

"I've never known you to lie, but every man on the force thinks you bed every woman you meet."

"Yeah, well, you can't believe everything you hear. And I wouldn't lie to you. You're my partner, my brother. You watch my six and I watch yours. If you ever need anything, ask. I'm proud to have you as my partner, on or off the force."

"Back at ya, my man." William chuckled and play punched James' shoulder. The best partner the department could have given him. The best friend he could have.

"Besides, without Amanda, I wouldn't have met Karen."

William pulled into traffic, his mind still on the truck.

He checked his rear view mirror and glimpsed an unmarked pull up in front of the building followed by two black and whites. Then he glanced down at the stack of Polaroid's and wondered how much of this the department would try to keep to themselves. If they were all on the same team, why the disparity, the exclusion? He shook his head and wondered about this job he loved so much.

"You thinking the same thing I am?" James asked.

"Probably," William answered.

40

William paged Jeremy, receiving the call back in less than ten minutes, and Jeremy was pissed. Captain Ohlmet had informed him of the department pulling the two.

"They threatened to pull my organization also," Jeremy said. I informed them neither of them have the clout to pull that off and threatened to turn them over to federal authorities for perpetrating the scam against you. So, this is what we'll do. I have already sent you an information package...."

"We just received it," William said. "Sorry, I didn't mean to cut you off."

"You're fine. There is a small manila envelope inside which contains ten or fifteen cards that resemble business cards. I was only sending them in case you ran into someone better connected than your chief, or captain, but you will use them as your means for getting what you need from now on. Those cards will get you farther than your badge and do it easier. Anyone you talk to can key in the number printed on them and you are in. They won't have to confirm a thing."

William opened the envelope and pulled out the cards. They

looked like any other business card, except they had a seven digit number and were significantly heavier.

"They're here," William said. "They're heavy."

"Because they have a tracking device built in. If anything happens, I can find you. Also, I told Captain Ohlmet you will be working solely under my guidance from now on. That means you will start receiving information via fax. Men should be there sometime this afternoon to set it up. It also means anytime they request a warrant and it is signed by the judge, you will know. You will also know where this search will be conducted, and they won't be able to block your access. The officer who helped you, do you think you can count on him to keep you abreast of things inside the department?"

"I'll call him," William said.

"Remember your phones are tapped," Jeremy reminded him. "I have ways to block that on my end, but you don't."

"I'll use the payphone across the street. Any word as to why the Cap and the chief decided to pull us? How are we supposed to find out who started this shit?"

"They are saying it's because you gentlemen refuse to follow orders, but you are not on duty so you have no orders to follow. Not from them. Someone is definitely covering something up, gentlemen. That's why I've ordered the fax. Just keep working with Mr. Bonner and let me know what you find, or if you need anything. Now, I need to get things ready for the upcoming job with Mr. Bonner."

They hung up and waited a few minutes before speaking. Both men sorting out their own thoughts.

"What do you think?" William asked. "We were told to do whatever we needed to and now we're pulled for not following orders. What orders?"

"I don't like it," James answered. "But I'm glad we talked to

Jeremy."

William made a fresh pot of coffee and turned the stereo on, just in case the place had been bugged, then they sat down at the table and started going through the information Jeremy had sent. Part way through, they decided if what they were reading was true, Jeremy was right, something was being covered up. William looked up from the papers at James.

"Part of this we already knew," William said. "But, here's something new. This shows a child named Sarah, born in 1969 to a Julie Barron and a Royce Warden."

"Is it the same Julie Barron who fills in at the club?" James asked.

"Good question," William answered. "Before that there is no record of a Julie Barron. She never existed. And, according to Royce's military records, he was involved with a nurse in Vietnam named Julia Howard. They returned stateside around the same time and then it shows them going their separate ways in late 1968. Julia Howard disappears and in 1969 Julie Barron arrives on the scene and files paternity papers saying she has Royce's kid."

"Julie has a daughter named Sarah," James said. "That building we just went through had a child's bedroom."

"I noticed the kid's room," William answered. "I wonder if George knew about Royce."

"I would think he did. But I thought they pulled Royce back early and put him in a psyche unit?"

"This says he was brought stateside for medical reasons," William replied, "but he wasn't discharged. He was released shortly after Julia slash Julie got home. She didn't pull her full enlistment, either. It shows them using the same address for several months then they were discharged and went their separate ways."

"Now Amanda moves here and Royce magically appears and a

man tries to rape her when he's having a nightmare."

"Not to mention Julie's here. Makes you wonder if he knew her and Sarah lived in Salt Lake City," William said.

James shrugged.

"Amanda said he thought she was Viet Cong," William continued. "I've heard stories about what the North Vietnamese women did to our service men. I don't know firsthand since I was stationed stateside, but I'll bet the man is having some problems in that area. He was pulled back early. End of some secret op and that means we weren't being given the run around by the military brass. He was in Nam, but not in the Army. He was involved with the political arm of the venture. The psyche unit could have been a cover for pulling him back once he completed his assignment. And the psyche eval would have been part of the scam for pulling him back."

"That would explain this Julia Howard's disappearance," James said. "She was in on that op. Julia Howard disappears, Julie Barron shows up stateside and she and Royce shack up together for a while...."

"Until the paperwork is completed," William said, finishing James thought. "She was his cover."

"You know," James said. He dropped the papers he was reading and looked up. "I just thought of something. George is having that compound renovated in Reno. I wonder if that compound is ready. If it is they might be taking Amanda there."

"You mean instead of Park City?"

James nodded and went back to his reading. "Just a thought, buddy."

They were going over the last of the information when Captain Ohlmet called. He wanted to meet them at D.B. Cooper's as soon as he got off.

"Afraid to talk because of the taps?" William asked.

"Your phones are no longer tapped," the captain answered. "Just be there." He hung up before William could respond.

At five minutes after five they were leaning on William's car, the captain pulling in behind them. He opened the door and directed them inside.

"What's up?" William asked. "I thought we weren't in on this."

"Technically you're not," Captain Ohlmet answered. "But I talked to Jeremy and he said he needs you inside. The chief isn't happy about it, but there's nothing I can do."

"And what about you, Cap?" Williams asked.

There was long silence while the hostess seated them.

"I'm caught in the middle," he replied. "I just need you back on duty."

"You have a funny way of showing it," William answered.

Captain Ohlmet leaned back abruptly and sighed, staring back at William. "Have you learned anything new about Royce?"

William returned the gaze for a second. They needed inside. It was time to quit pushing. "We went by his place of employment and his apartment. He hasn't been at work in a week and the management office said he hasn't paid his rent this month or the last half of his deposit."

"We knew that. Anything else?"

"He's following Amanda," James said quietly. He looked Captain Ohlmet in the eyes and debated saying more, ultimately making the same decision as William. They needed inside, but he would skirt the new info until they knew where the captain and the chief stood. "I know, we have no proof, but she moved here from Chicago and he moves here. She disappears and now Royce disappears. Walked out on his job, his apartment, everything. And he has a car and a driver's license now. Thank you very much for that bit of information, Cap," James said sarcastically. "The man is following Amanda. I guarantee it."

"Okay. I'll bite. Why would he follow her?" Captain Ohlmet asked ignoring James jab. "You said they were married once. Anything to do with that?"

"Were," James replied. "Amanda showed me the papers. And we have his friend come to us and he dies," James said. He didn't finish the sentence; instead he looked at the captain and noticed the captain looked guilty. "You heard anymore about that, Cap? Still have Cause of Death as a drug overdose?"

"We're still looking into it," Captain Ohlmet asked. "Why would you think anything different?"

"What about George?" William asked. "Is he in Park City?"

"Well, you could be right about Royce, so we need to find him," Captain Ohlmet said. "Have you talked to Jeremy lately?"

"Yeah," William said. "He's pretty pissed at your antics."

The captain glanced between the two and knew they weren't going to tell him anything further. They were playing the same hand he was.

"Gentlemen," Captain Ohlmet said, "you're free to go. Just watch your ass. Remember, you are not officially on duty."

Both men nodded and stood. Time to find their wayward little boy, Royce Warden. But they weren't doing it for the department. This was for Amanda and their jobs. With Amanda gone, the assaults had stopped, but it was an uneasy quiet. No one knew when, or even if, they would start again. There were still too many questions. They were working on a hunch and they were getting tired of being led around by the nose.

"The Cap wanted us here to go over this?" William asked once they were outside. "We could have talked to him when he called."

"You got me, buddy," James answered. "But I'm getting the feeling we're stuck between the good guys and the good guys. I am starting to get seriously paranoid."

William parked in front of his apartment and watched one of

the department's undercover cars pull in across the street.

"We've been conned," William said. "And I'll bet I was right when I blew up at Captain Ohlmet. Our phones aren't the only thing being bugged."

"I thought the Cap said they weren't tapped?"

"And I'm Egyptian royalty," William replied. "One of the department's street cars just pulled in across the street."

"Well, you got the complexion," James said. He laughed for a second then sighed, being nailed by William's glare. "Never mind. Wait here."

James slipped out of the passenger door, using other cars as a blind until he reached the end of the parking lot then he crossed the side street north of William's apartment. Once across the main drag, James doubled back south until he reached the parking lot, made a circle to the west around other vehicles, stopping one row behind the suspect car. James kept his body low and peeked over another vehicle, his leg straight, willing the throbbing to subside. He had to remember to be careful with this shit. When he had the pain under control, James returned the way he had come, confirming William's suspicion.

"Now, I want to know if my phone really is tapped," William started to say, "because if mine is…."

"Mine is," James said finishing the thought.

"And we need to check our apartments for bugs again."

James stopped on the landing and looked up at William.

"Damn, are you sure?"

41

Amanda opened her eyes and gazed around the huge bedroom expecting to wake up and discover it was a dream. After the cramped and filthy room she had been in this was a mansion, but it was just a fancier cage. She climbed out of bed and dressed, walking cautiously down the hall. She neared the dining room being teased by the aroma of coffee and waffles. Real homemade waffles? A man was setting the table, making sure all was perfect, her eyes widening in surprise. It was the man from Salt Lake City.

Unconsciously looking him over, she noticed the Brocade vest and slacks didn't match the athletic build and expressive eyes. Eyes that saw everything. She hadn't noticed that before.

"Good morning," he said. "Breakfast will be ready momentarily then you may finish your morning routine." He smiled as he looked her over then turned away, pulling himself back to the duties at hand.

Amanda sat down, but continued to examine the surroundings, expecting George to materialize at any given moment. After breakfast, she began an investigation of the new place, peering into the nooks and crannies looking for cameras. She found several, all tucked away in innocuous little places that afforded whoever was watching the best view of the goings on. Obviously, the ones that bothered her the most were the ones in the shower and the bedroom. She was relieved there were none near the commode. At least she could pee in peace.

"Would you care to see the view?" the gentleman asked.

"You mean I can go outside here?" Amanda asked. She had always enjoyed her morning cup of coffee outside.

He nodded and directed her to the balcony then went back inside. She surveyed the area, noticing the mountains and the trees. Then her thoughts reverted to how long it would take for someone to find her. Park City wasn't big, but there was plenty of real estate to cover when you were looking for one person. A person who had nothing someone could trace them by.

She went back inside and learned her chaperone was here to teach her the rules of proper etiquette. If she was to hobnob with the people George wanted her to, she had to know how to handle herself like a lady.

He refilled her coffee, and told her he was running to the store. She got comfortable on the balcony thinking about the easiest way to get out of here. She was leaving, but she had to learn a few things first. The screen slid open surprising her and Amanda looked up to see George standing in the sliding glass door.

"Enjoying the view?" George asked. "You seem to be deep in thought."

"Yes, I was," Amanda said. "You've provided me a very nice place to live, but I want to go home. I miss being around people who care."

"You haven't given me a chance, princess," George said. He reached out to stroke her cheek with the back of his hand, but she recoiled from his touch. "You insist on fighting me. Why?"

"I'm not your princess," she said. "I'm not a piece of property to be bought and sold."

"Aw, but you are," he answered. He grabbed the back of her neck and squeezed as he pulled her to her feet. White hot fingers of pain shot into Amanda's head and down her back at the same time. 'How could one simple move hurt so much?'

"Let's move inside to finish this. I hope you're going to learn a lesson today." He held one arm in a crushing grip, as he steered her through the living room and down the hall. "Smile for the cameras," George instructed as he maneuvered her past the foot of her bed and into the dressing room.

They stopped in front of a padded bench, and he reached behind him with his foot to close the door, but he had to remove one hand on her to lock it. When he turned to push the lock, Amanda swung, losing her balance and forcing them both into the door, splintering the wood with their combined weight. Writhing in a continued effort to free herself, she punched George in the throat and tripped over the bench. She twisted to catch her fall and sprawled face first onto the carpet. George choked and attempted to grab one of her ankles, but she continued kicking wildly then pulled herself to her knees and crawled to the other side of the bench. She picked it up, striking him along side of the head. George stumbled then she unlocked the door and bolted for the living area.

She raced to the front door, searching desperately for the lock. Not seeing the usual, she struck one solid blow on the door, exasperated. A frantic look away, attempting to find a place to run, but only saw the balcony. Another glance down the hall and George was sprinting toward her. She darted through the sliding door and closed it with one hand, wedging a patio chair between the handle and the stationary panel with the other. George grabbed the handle and shook the door violently then the sheets of glass shuddered as a door closed somewhere behind him. Amanda backed away and climbed over the rail, debating her next move.

Someone yelled behind her, but she didn't dare take her eyes off George in case that table slipped. Then her tutor appeared and grabbed George's shoulder, jerking him back, George landing on the floor.

"NO!" he yelled. "Open the door, Amanda!"

Amanda stared at the ground below, and then shifted her gaze to the neighboring balcony. It was only six feet away. She could reach that. Another look through the glass as she inched her way toward the far balcony and George picked himself up, moving toward the front door. Once George was gone, Amanda climbed back onto the balcony and pulled the chair away from the door, allowing it to slide open.

"My word," her tutor said. "What in the world happened?"

She could only shake her head. He put his arms around her to comfort her then the tears started.

After dinner Jeremy straightened the kitchen and sat down at his desk, trying to work out how to handle this. He had taken this position to get closer to the syndicate, and take George down while doing it, but he hadn't expected to catch the man attacking one of his students. His thoughts reverted to the lady William and James had been attempting to keep safe and he was more positive than ever this was that Amanda.

He labeled the surveillance tapes of George dragging Amanda down the hall and the ensuing fight, and decided from now on she wouldn't be left alone. She was his responsibility, his charge. He had been hired to train her and keep her safe from anyone who might get too rough and, as far as he was concerned, that included Mr. Bonner. The contract he had signed with George had just been cancelled.

Jeremy watched Amanda where she sat, beckoning her to join him when she glanced up. She looked terrified. He patted the chair next to his when she walked over and he hesitated again, unsure as to how to do this.

"Miss Amanda," he said. "May I bother you for a moment?"

"Of course," she said. "Is there a problem?"

"Perhaps. Mr. Bonner's visit today ….." He stopped, seeing the tears when she averted her eyes. "Please. I wanted to apologize. I didn't know Mr. Bonner would be here or I would not have left you by yourself. If you ever need anything, don't hesitate to tell me. Do you understand?"

"Yes," she answered. "Thank you."

"I am not sure you do," he replied. "I mean *anything*."

The tears escaped again and now that they had started, they were proving difficult to control. She only nodded, more of a nervous tic than a nod and kept her eyes averted.

"Oh, dear, come here," he said. "I wasn't trying to make you cry."

He held her until she composed herself and lifted her head.

"Do you feel better now?"

She did a tiny hike of her left shoulder and sniffled. "I'm sorry. Please, forgive me."

"There is nothing to forgive you for. After what I saw, I don't blame you. But I meant what I said about talking to me about anything. *Anything*," he stressed again. "Are you going to be alright?"

"Yes," she said. "I appreciate your concern."

"We will talk again later," he told her. "I told you on my last visit I would get you out. That still stands. I will help you."

She wiped the tears from her cheeks and hurried to her room. That had been strange. She wasn't sure what he had meant by 'perhaps'. This man was a hard one to gauge.

42

Amanda awoke the next morning to a gentle tapping then her tutor poked his head around the edge of her door. She had nicknamed him, Mr. Tudor because of the way he carried himself. Mr. Prim and Proper. It was all about the decorum.

"Excuse me, Miss Amanda," he said, "I apologize for waking you, but there's a gentleman here to see you. I'll set the coffee on the balcony. Would you like me to set you out something to wear?"

"I got it," she replied. "Tell him I'll be there in a minute."

"Yes, madam."

This was awkward. She got out of bed and dressed quickly, then applied her make-up and pulled her hair back with a barrette, curious as to whom this visitor was. She walked into the living room and a man stood on the balcony, his back to the sliding door. Mr. Tudor shrugged, shaking his head as she raised a questioning eyebrow, indicating he didn't know the gentleman.

"There is coffee on the table, madam," he said. He spoke just loud enough to be heard outside.

"Thank you." She stifled a laugh, feeling like she had just been transported back to the 1800's.

Amanda was slightly taken aback when her visitor turned to face her. He was actually quite good looking. He had a nice smile, easy and comfortable. Salt and pepper hair, nice muscular build, average height. She had learned to assess her surroundings and everyone who was in them.

"Sorry to keep you waiting. I wasn't expecting visitors." She directed him to one of the chairs and seated herself so she was facing the sliding doors. It would be impossible for someone to surprise her again.

"My apologies," he replied. "I wasn't trying to disturb you."

"You're fine," she said. "What brings you over?"

"It was a last minute decision," he said, sizing her up. The police training never left one, he guessed.

He sat down opposite her while she poured their coffee. Loved the hair. Not too much make-up. She was keeping it natural. Hypnotizing eyes, perfect smile and body. Well endowed in just the right places. The single male on the prowl never left, either, he admonished himself silently.

"Sorry, the name's Mark Willis. I'm new to the area and, well, I thought maybe you could show me around. I live across the way." Nothing like stammering like a school boy.

He pointed to a condo straight across from hers and thought about broaching the previous day's events then decided to keep his questions to himself.

"I'm sorry," she answered. "I'm new to the area, too. I would have no clue where to take you, Mr. Willis. I'm flattered, though."

Somebody was actually trying to pick her up. George hadn't taken human nature into consideration when setting this up.

"Perhaps, we could explore our new home together," he said. "I would love to take you to lunch or dinner."

"Thank you," she said. She smiled self-consciously as she

blushed. Had it been that long since she had been given an honest compliment? "I'll leave the offer open, if you don't mind."

"Not at all," he said. "Are you sure I can't talk you into lunch, or a simple dinner downtown?"

"Excuse me, Miss Amanda," Jeremy said. "I apologize for interrupting your conversation and I don't wish to bother you; however, I was thinking you might enjoy getting out of the condo and socializing some. I also realize it is last minute."

"I would love that," Mark said. He glanced between the two and grinned broadly. "What time should I pick you up?"

"Well…Actually that sounds nice," she answered. "I guess." Nothing like being railroaded into a date, but this might be that opportunity she'd been waiting for.

"How about one?" Jeremy asked.

"I'll be here," Mark said excitedly. "Amanda, right?"

Amanda nodded and Mark rushed out the door.

Jeremy shrugged and grinned impishly when she nailed him with her eyes.

Mark returned promptly at one, beaming like a boy on his first date. He was glad she had changed her mind, he said. Amanda smiled and scanned the area, memorizing as much as she could while Mark opened the car door for her. As he drove he noticed she took in every detail, like she was planning her escape, but an escape from what? Maybe the gentleman who had been there yesterday.

Mark took her to one of the better cafés in town and asked for a table by a window and noticed she scrutinized the area here just as closely. After lunch, they sat around longer than was normal laughing and telling stories. He finally decided it was time to go. The waitress was looking a little perturbed. They had tied up the table for more than two hours. She didn't make any money that way. He paid the bill and gave her a larger than customary tip to make up for the inconvenience and saw the smile when she nodded her thanks.

"If you'd like we can go for a walk," Mark said. "There's supposed to be some pretty nice shopping around here."

"Actually, I'm not much of a shopper," she told him. "Is there something else we can do?"

"Want to go back to your place? We can watch some TV."

"No, I'm fine," she answered a little too quickly. "I like it outside."

"How about a gondola ride?" he asked.

"That sounds fun," she said. "I've never been on one."

"Gondola ride it is. I know you said you're not much of a shopper, but I heard there's a cool little gift shop at the top. I can get you something as a souvenir of our first date."

"I would like that."

The rest of the afternoon was spent browsing the gift shop, taking in the views from the trails and enjoying the quiet, Amanda taking the opportunity to get a better visual on the direction she needed to reach the interstate. It was only a ten or fifteen minute walk from the condo to downtown, the interstate a short twenty or thirty minute jog from there. Unless she caught a ride before she reached the main road. By six-thirty they were both hungry again so they ate dinner at the restaurant at the top and watched the lights come on below.

Mark dropped Amanda off that evening and noticed the men, one off to each side and thought about her situation again. Memories of the man dragging her off the balcony intruded and Mark wondered if there was a relationship. He didn't see any rings. He leaned in for a kiss; she hesitated then returned the kiss. No relationship, he decided.

"Thank you, Mark. I enjoyed it very much. Call me in a couple of days. Maybe we can do this again. And thank you for the beautiful bracelet. I love it."

"Maybe we can do dinner and a movie next time."

"Maybe dinner at your place," she said already feeling guilty for stringing the man along, but they said to play and George wasn't going to touch her again. "I'll even cook."

Mr. Tudor opened the door and Amanda thanked him then reached inside after he'd walked away. Finding the slide to unlock the door, she turned the outer knob, making sure it was unlocked. She had watched Mr. Tudor and learned how things worked.

Once inside her mind quickly moved to what she would need. Evenings in the mountains were cool so she might need a jacket. She didn't know how long before she would catch a ride. Maybe a heavier shirt or a sweater.

Amanda waited until Mr. Tudor was busy at his desk then stole quietly up the hall, her coat tucked tightly under the arm away from him. She dropped her coat on the chair by the door and pulled a movie off a shelf, acting like she was interested, placing it back on the shelf and then walking to the balcony. Daylight had faded and she took in the lights glittering around them, waiting until she was confident Mr. Tudor was busy. She then crept to the door and picked up her jacket. There was a soft 'bing' when she opened it and she froze. Grabbing a video again, acting like she was going through them, she saw Mr. Tudor stick his head out. He smiled, and looked puzzled, then disappeared back into his office, and Amanda exhaled. Too close.

Dodging the guards, she tiptoed down the stairs and jogged to the rear of the building, pulling on her jacket. Another look over her shoulder and she trotted across a vacant lot. Next stop – Salt Lake City. Half way to the street an arm wrapped around her shoulders and someone gave her a peck on the top of the head. It had to be Mr. Tudor. Luck really was running out much too quick.

"You are not being a good girl tonight, Miss Amanda," Mr. Tudor said. "Here I was trying to be nice and you pull this. What do you suggest I do? I don't want to tell Mr. Bonner."

"I don't know," she said. "After his visit, what am I supposed to do?"

"That is why I said, if you needed anything to let me know." He had turned her around, guiding her back to the condo. "Do you want to talk about what happened?"

"No," Amanda said. "I want to slice the man open like a ripe watermelon."

"I believe I understand that," Jeremy answered. He opened the door and pushed her gently back inside. "From now on, I will double check this door to see that it is locked. A few words of caution. Do you think, if you did pull off this disappearing act, that Mr. Bonner would just forget about it and let the police come after him?" Not getting a reply, he continued. "You didn't think that far, did you? I am also curious. I told you I would help you so why do you feel the need to escape in such a manner?"

Amanda shrugged and walked to her room, admitting he was right. George would not allow himself to be arrested without a fight.

Jeremy shook his head when the door slammed behind her. She really was a stubborn one.

Once Amanda was sleeping, Jeremy started going through information he'd received. He quickly dismissed the first seventy-five percent of the women. She wasn't black, Latina, or an escaped convict. He continued to sort through the pages, finally coming to a newspaper article about the missing woman from Salt Lake City.

A Miss Amanda Granger disappeared during a fire in the club in which she sang and was presumed to have been abducted. Police believe that, in the confusion, Miss Granger was spirited to an unknown location inside the building. The alarm on the emergency exit had been disabled and once the fire was out, she was taken out the rear door. According to sources, the police believed the fire was a decoy used to draw people out of the club. A spokesman for the department said they were currently looking for two suspects in her disappearance, but had been unable to locate them.

A publicity shot of her performing graced the top of the column. That left no doubt that this was her.

His hunt for the syndicate brass just took a detour.

A second article caught his attention.

The bodies of two teens wanted in connection to a fire in a downtown Salt Lake City club which resulted in the subsequent disappearance of a Miss Amanda Granger were found at separate locations in the Salt Lake valley. One of the boys was found in the Great Salt Lake. His body had been found wedged against a wall of the partially submerged Great Saltair Pavilion. The suspect's cause of death has not been confirmed.

The second boy's body was found by a night watchman at Kennecott Copper in Magna, Utah. He was floating in one of the mines tailings ponds. Police are asking the public for any information regarding his death and the disappearance of Miss Granger.

It continued with a recap of the article detailing Amanda's abduction. Pictures of both teens had been included with this article as well. It was the boys from the security video.

"Well, Amanda," he said. "We have officially met."

43

William and James pulled in front of the bar prepared for another evening at George's. Instead of the usual bombardment from the hookers, the ladies crinkled up their noses and drifted away, a homeless man strolling up to William's car. The man asked them to meet him at Dee's on North Temple. Be there in an hour. William nodded, acting like he was shooing him away, the man shuffling across the street then the car they had seen on Browning Avenue turned left off Ninth South heading north on State Street.

They pulled into the restaurant's parking lot, Timothy leaning on the trunk of his car. He'd cleaned up and changed clothes. They parked across from him and he pushed himself off the car and ambled inside. As they walked toward the doors, they saw the host pull out a menu and Timothy raised three fingers signifying three guests and followed the man to the rear dining area.

"We may have something," Timothy said once they'd been seated. "Park City thinks they found Amanda."

"Yes!" William exclaimed.

"I overheard Captain Ohlmet talking to a couple of detectives and he said Park City had a new officer go in for his first day of duty this morning. It seems this officer lives right across the parking lot from a lady who resembles Amanda. And her name is Amanda. The captain said the guy told his captain he took her to lunch Saturday. He also said George Bonner roughed her up once. Supposedly George showed up again this morning, but was only there a few minutes before he left, then a car pulled up and two men escorted Amanda out followed closely by her butler carrying a small suitcase. The officer called his Cap and told him they were moving her and that's when Park City called us."

"This morning?" William said. "How long ago?"

"From the conversation I overheard it was only about an hour ago. The officer tried to follow them, but called back fifteen minutes later and said he lost them in traffic. He had a partial license number and it's from Nevada. Park City's doing a search now with what he got."

"When do we go get her?"

"It's not going to be that easy," Timothy said. "The Cap also told them – and he was very specific – that you and James are not on the force. If they happen to run into you they aren't to tell you anything. You are supposed to sit this one out."

"The captain?" William said, surprised. "We're not on the force?"

"We gotta contact Jeremy," William said. He stared out the window, thinking out loud more than talking.

"I'm sorry I gave you guy's bad news again," Timothy said. "I know that isn't what you wanted to hear."

"Detectives are probably in Park City by now," James said.

"Cap said they have to wait for Park City to get the warrants," Timothy told them. "They might not go in until tomorrow morning."

"This is bullshit," William said. He saw James expression and knew – just like him – his partner was fighting the desire to choke the crap out of the chief and Captain Ohlmet. "When do you want to go to Park City?"

"Let's page Jeremy," James answered. "Find out when he's leaving. We'll be in trouble with the department, but Jeremy said his rules bend more than the departments."

"We're already in trouble with the department," William replied. "And Jeremy said they can't keep us out with those cards."

William pulled into a parking space at his apartment building and paged Jeremy. When Jeremy called he confirmed what Timothy had told them. He was in the company of the missing Amanda Granger. He also told them he would be joining her in Reno and would be out of the condo before eight p.m. If they wanted to gain admittance they had to be there before he left. They asked about the captain and he told them he had not talked to Captain Ohlmet yet, but the captain had paged him so he would have to return the call.

They walked out of the apartment at five p.m. hoping to beat the detectives. They arrived in Park City and parked in front of the condo at the same time the moving van pulled out. They walked through the door and the place had already been wiped clean. Jeremy met them and led them to a small office off the kitchen, showing them a video on the counter and told them it was of Amanda's mad dash up the hall followed by George. He explained the police would be here and he had wanted to leave them something, hence the tape. That was his contribution for now. He had told her he would help her, but he felt like he had failed. That was also where his guilt lay. He had more time to gather evidence against George and the syndicate now, but he didn't want this happening to anyone else. Then he excused himself and disappeared.

They stared at the tape, William slipping a glove on to put the tape into the player then he stopped. As much as they wanted to watch it now, it would be wiser to let Park City find it. Technically they weren't here.

Ten minutes after Jeremy's departure, Officer Willis and the detectives from Park City drove up. One of the detectives pulled a piece of paper out of his pocket. They had their warrant. Park City officers walked in and James and William flashed one of the cards Jeremy had sent them, explaining they had found the door open when they arrived then continued their walk through of the now empty space.

"I feel like I'm responsible for this," Mark said from behind them.

Both men stopped and waited for Mark to catch up.

"How so?" James asked.

"A guy was here that I've seen before. The first time he was here he hurt her," Mark said, explaining how she had barricaded herself outside and climbed the rail. "He was here this morning and I didn't want to see her get hurt again so I grabbed a beer and sat down on the balcony. When I did, I waved."

"That's okay," William answered. "You were only trying to help. We would have done the same thing."

Park City found the tape Jeremy had left and called them into the office. The tape clearly showed Amanda bolting through the broken door of the dressing room then the angle changed and she was racing up the hall with George behind her. It was the precursor to the story Mark had just told them. William walked onto the balcony trying to feature the kind of man who would do this. James joined William a couple of minutes later.

"You ready to head back to Salt Lake?"James asked. "I don't want to push our luck and be here when the detectives arrive."

They climbed into William's car, heading for the interstate. As they merged into traffic, they recognized an unmarked car exiting, one of the detectives from Salt Lake City driving. They'd dodged one again. An hour later they were walking through the door at William's, the phone ringing.

"William," the captain snapped. "I talked to the detectives I sent to Park City. They said they were the second set of officers to show up. Park City P.D. said the prior team was already in the condo when they arrived. One of them happened to be on crutches. You wouldn't care to explain that, would you?"

"From Salt Lake City?" William hoped he sounded innocent.

"They didn't say Salt Lake City specifically," he replied. "But who else would be there?"

"Ain't got a clue," William answered. They knew the captain wouldn't buy it, James was on crutches. "We just went to get something to eat. And the last we heard we weren't on the force. We don't have badges; we aren't officers so why call us? What did they find?"

The captain remained quiet for a few seconds. "I think you're full of shit," he finally responded. "But I'm going to ignore that. I wanted to let you know George and Julie are in Salt Lake City for Sarah's surgery. Sarah is Julie's daughter. We have men posted outside all entrances to the hospital, and on the floor where the little girl's recuperating. We hope we can catch them once the girl's released and George is back at work. Now, you wouldn't care to let me in on what was found in that condo, would you? I know you're lying William, I started out as a patrolman, too."

William glanced over at James and saw his partner shrug. He stayed quiet debating how much he should say. He could be setting them up.

"The taps are off your phones," the captain added, reading William's mind. "If that's your concern."

"One of them," William admitted. "You have our badges so how could anyone say officers were there? Who told you?"

He waited the captain out, not wanting to divulge anything.

The detectives would tell the captain what Park City found and they couldn't afford to incriminate themselves further.

"You guys are bucking for that termination, aren't you?"

"No, sir," William answered. "We're just trying to do a job. A job we were volunteered for, by you, under someone else's guidance. It was that or not find out who framed us. Now, we've been dragged into this other mess and you're not allowing us to work anything. Plus, you have evidence that proves we're not guilty and you're sitting back and doing nothing. You aren't giving us many options, Captain."

"Just don't do it again."

"Yes, sir."

William hung up knowing, if they were in this position again, it would happen again. He stared out the window and tapped the receiver absently with his index finger, then gave an unconscious shrug.

"What's on your mind?" James asked.

William jerked his head in the direction of the door and they went outside.

"You think they were trying to get us to cop to being there? If so the shit just might start flying."

"Possibly. But we got Jeremy's magic cards," James replied. "We weren't there for the department."

44

Amanda covered her head with her pillow barring the light from blinding her. Movement behind her caused her to roll over and squint to open her eyes. Finally dragging them open, Mr. Tudor was industriously organizing her things. As he put the last of her belongings away she noticed something she hadn't seen in Park City. Under his stiff upper lip Brocade vest, Mr. Tudor was armed.

"Good morning, Miss Amanda," he said. "How are we doing?"

"Ugh," she groaned, screwing her nose up and drawing the pillow back over her face. "Morning? What in the world do they use in those shots? They're brutal!"

"Headache?"

"Horrendous."

"I'll make you a good strong pot of coffee, and then I'll make your breakfast. Oh, I set some clothes out for you, too," he called over his shoulder.

When Amanda hadn't made her appearance in forty minutes, Jeremy returned and observed her from the door. He wished they wouldn't use drugs on these girls. Some of the men used too heavy a dose and it could take days for them to wear off. He had attempted to intercept it yesterday, but the man had done it many times before. The guard had inserted the needle and pushed the plunger down, injecting the drug before he could stop him. This made him even more curious about George's involvement in trafficking. Women and children didn't necessarily have to be shipped overseas for it to be called trafficking. Jeremy helped Amanda to her feet then steadied her until they reached the bathroom door.

"I think I've got it," she said, grasping the doorframe firmly.

"I'll wait here for you," he said.

She decided to forego the makeup this morning. She wasn't confident she had enough strength to stand that long. She opened the door and found Mr. Tudor had indeed waited. He helped her to the dressing room and once she'd finished dressing, she found him waiting patiently outside that door, as well. Taking his arm, she allowed him to aid her as they walked up the hall.

"So, how long have you been doing this?" she asked. "How many girls have you trained?"

"I've been doing this about fifteen years," he replied, acting as if it was the most natural thing in the world to train women for this line of work. "I've trained about thirty to thirty-five young ladies," he continued. "But this is my first year with Mr. Bonner."

"What's your name? I nicknamed you Mr. Tudor."

"That will do. I have been called a lot worse."

She liked his smile. It was provocative with a hint of mystery. Maybe it was the eyes, they danced. They laughed when he smiled.

"Exactly what kind of work do you do?" Was he a butler, or a tutor? He was armed so maybe he was a bodyguard.

The hall opened up into the living room and she surveyed the room, attempting to locate any cameras that might be hidden here. She found them, mounted in the usual places. They had tried to camouflage them, but she had learned where to look.

"The same as Park City," he replied. "I'm here as your tutor. I am supposed to teach you the finer nuances of being a lady."

"I mean your real job," she said, her voice firmer. "Tutors aren't normally armed, are they?"

"You are very observant." She really did notice everything. He had also noticed the change in tone. She was more than just curious. "I have to admit you are not the type of woman I would typically expect to be doing this kind of work."

"You're very good at side-stepping questions, too."

"I have had a lot of practice. Now, let's get you some coffee. I'm going to forego the training for today. They gave you a larger dose of sedative than usual. I guess Mr. Bonner was afraid you would wake up on the drive over."

"Over? Where are we?"

"Reno," he answered. "There is a pool on the other side of the house. If you would like we can go for a swim."

"Actually that sounds fun. I don't really swim, but I enjoy playing around in the water."

"Well, maybe I can help with that. You are making me feel like a bit of failure. I'll put you out a suit."

He just wanted to get a better feel for Amanda.

She finished eating and admitted he had been right. She felt much better. She returned to her room and picked up the suit he had set out, inspecting the tiny thing. Which was front and which was back? The tag was almost as big as the bottoms. She shrugged and decided it probably didn't matter. Neither side covered much, but one side wouldn't cover anything. She slipped it on and surveyed her reflection in the mirror. This was not a swimsuit. It covered even less than that first outfit in Salt Lake City sans the fishnets and stilettos. She wouldn't make it to the pool until she had finished some very necessary alterations. The most important one being a front piece that concealed the bruise from George's goon.

It was almost thirty minutes before she made her appearance.

"I don't remember that being the suit I laid out for you," Jeremy said. "Actually, I don't remember you having a suit like that."

"I had to make a couple of modifications. You won't catch me wearing that skimpy little thing."

"Miss Amanda, you are going to have to get used to that if you work for Mr. Bonner. That is what the gentlemen expect. You have to show them your assets. Flaunt them or you will not get requested. If you are not requested, you won't make any money, and if you are not making money, Mr. Bonner isn't making money and he will not be able to keep you employed."

"I don't plan on working for Mr. Bonner," she snapped vehemently. "My assets are mine and nobody else's. And I don't plan on flaunting them, either. No one owns me, and I'll do whatever I have to, to get out of here. With, or without, your help."

"I fear I may have stated that wrong. Let me try this again." He leaned forward and lowered his voice. "Remember I told you that you would need to play along to an extent?"

She nodded.

"For the guards benefit, please do so. They report to Mr. Bonner daily. Now," he said bringing his voice back to a normal tone, "when gentlemen hire you to escort them around town to some of these events, they are going to want to see what they are paying for. They do not want to see you in a gunny sack, or looking like good housewife material. I am not talking about to their bedrooms. You are not advertising that at this stage. I am talking about a date."

Amanda started to say something, but Jeremy held his finger up and grabbed her arm, pulling her to him. She looked in his eyes and saw the anger.

"No," he said forcefully. "Play. At the rate you are going, you are only going to get yourself killed. Do..You…Understand?"

Amanda nodded, surprised. He let her go and she backed up, rubbing her arm as she slipped into the warm water.

Jeremy sat on the concrete pool surround watching Amanda, and understood why George felt he had to have her. She was beautiful, sexy, unpresuming, almost to the point of innocence. Those same qualities would draw men to her, which would give George repeat clients for her services. Plus, she had an underlying confidence a lot of women didn't possess. She was comfortable with herself. And she wanted nothing to do with George Bonner. A man like George couldn't handle that. He wouldn't be satisfied until he had conquered her and that would destroy her, and then George would simply throw her away.

A couple of hours of playing around in the pool and Jeremy returned to the house to fix dinner. Once inside, he pulled out his pager and keyed in the last two addresses where he had seen Amanda, requesting copies of any videos in someone's system in the last thirty days. He wasn't comfortable searching from here so the experts inside could do it for him. Once he had confirmation that they had received his request, he sent another message giving them the address in Reno. He wanted the tapes sent here.

The fax started howling and he looked over to see information from his commander coming across the line. Going through the pages, he realized he needed to call William, but he had to keep it short. He only had a brief period of time before any trace or recording would override his safeguards. Before he picked up the phone he received another page. They showed videos of a woman matching Amanda's description at several locations. They would send him copies of them as well. Jeremy shredded the fax sheets, and dialed William's number.

William answered on the third ring and he sounded angry.

"Good evening, William," he said. "I only have a short time in case this line has been tapped, but I have something I wanted to let you know. In regards to your thoughts on the homeless people, it seems your hunch was correct. The organization has intercepted two cars this last week alone, both with Nevada plates. The men dropped bags into seemingly random trash receptacles. Homeless men and women then picked them up. When those people were stopped, said bags were found in their shopping carts and they contained drugs and the address for that apartment hotel in South Salt Lake. We stopped the cars and the men had more drugs and large amounts of cash. We know how Mr. Bonner is doing it now so we will continue to intercept his deliveries until he catches on. If you need to, contact Captain Ohlmet or Chief Vanders for guidance."

"That's not going to happen," William retorted.

"What has happened, sir?"

William then quickly went over the last meeting with Timothy and the conversation with Captain Ohlmet after their visit to Park City. Jeremy sighed and told them to page him from now on. The organization was faxing information to them anyway.

"I will call again in a few days," Jeremy said. He hung up thinking about this new twist.

"Who was that?" James asked.

"Jeremy. He said we were right. They have already intercepted a few of our destitute individuals with the goods. They also picked up the delivery boys with the cash, and more contraband. He'll call again in a few days. And Amanda has been relocated to Reno. I don't know about you, but I'm ready to head out. We're still officially working on our own."

"I think I like your idea," James said. "Do you want to wait until Jeremy calls back? We don't even know where she's at."

"No, but George was working on that compound over there."

"And if it isn't finished?" James asked. "Reno's bigger than Park City."

"You're right."

A couple of minutes later, Mr. Brown called and wanted to know if they would come get him again. Same place as before. Ten minutes later they were parked under the cover of the Lilacs. Timothy climbed out of his car and scanned the area, before approaching them.

"Park City called the Cap again this morning," Timothy told them. "They got a hit on that partial plate from Park City. It came back registered to Julie Barron-Warden in Winnemucca, Nevada. But, it doesn't look like Ms Barron has been using the Nevada property. That property is currently leased."

"Are they checking on Julie?" William asked.

"I ran a search on my own," Timothy answered. "It shows Ms Julie Barron living in a duplex on the west side, but she has not renewed that lease. All utilities have been disconnected as well. Her DL is still showing the same address, but DMV shows she has a new car."

"Nevada address?" William asked.

"Nevada address," Timothy repeated as confirmation.

"That explains George working on that compound in Reno," James said. "It'd be easy to say he was heading to Winnemucca on business and detour to Reno."

"I wonder how long he's been doing business in Reno?" William continued.

"I called Reno, too," Timothy said. "Property records show a Mrs. J.B. Bonner purchased a fairly large estate about a mile from the interstate."

"Mrs. J.B. Bonner?" William asked, surprised. "As in Julie Barron-Bonner."

Timothy shrugged, giving him a high-five. "Reno said there's no sign that George is there," Timothy added.

"George wouldn't be there," James answered. "Amanda and her butler or housekeeper would be the only people living there. George would only drop in from time to time. That's her home. I ran a check on the services boards and George hasn't made any announcements in Reno yet, so he's probably not ready to show Amanda off."

"What if Captain Ohlmet finds out about your search?" William asked. "How you covering that? We don't want you to get in trouble."

"I used Captain Jakes info," Timothy answered. "I didn't want them going to the Cap and having it come back on you, or me. And I don't like you guys being hung out to dry."

"You know they'll blame us anyway," William responded. "We appreciate the thought, though."

"Maybe not. I went in the round-about way. Captain Jakes security clearance hasn't been deactivated yet, and I used the chief's to get it, and voile!"

"I like you better all the time," James said with a laugh.

45

Jeremy sat across the table from Amanda and thought about the conversation with William. He had been having concerns about the reports, but he didn't want to think Chief Vanders and Captain Ohlmet were behind a cover up. Unless they were trying to make the insider tip their hand. If that was the case, they should have notified the parties involved. Especially their own men. The phone rang and he excused himself, hoping it wasn't Mr. Bonner. It was.

"Amanda has an engagement Thursday evening," George said. "Also, I plan on driving over in a few days and she needs to be prepared to spend her nights with me."

"Yes, sir," Jeremy replied.

While George continued in the background, Jeremy debated how far he should push. If George had no contract with Amanda, George would simply refuse to provide one. A telltale gambit Jeremy had seen before.

"I would like to see a copy of Amanda's contract," Jeremy said. "There seems to be some confusion on her part about what her duties will include. I would like to clarify that for her."

"I don't have to provide you with proof of anything," George replied. "Having her ready for her appointments and her debut is your only responsibility."

The receiver slammed and Jeremy returned to the pool. That had been a more intense reaction than he had anticipated, but it gave him his answer. Now, to verify it with her.

"Miss Amanda. We seem to have a slight problem. Mr. Bonner has set you up with an appointment and if he receives an acceptable report from this gentleman, he will work more in, but I am going to help you. We will do a mock date tonight and tomorrow I will see about taking you on a real date. Now, I need to start dinner and set your clothes out."

Amanda's shoulders drooped and she heaved a heavy sigh as the tears started.

"Are you going to be alright?"

"Mr. Tudor, why do I have to be here?" she asked. "I'm tired of him sending men in to try and do as they wish with me for an hour of their time. I'm tired of beating myself up keeping them off of me. I'm tired of his men beating me."

"His men beating you?"

Amanda nodded and lifted the front piece on the swimsuit, revealing the fading discoloration. Jeremy's sharp intake of air told her he had not been aware of how George corrected his women.

"I suppose if I hadn't cold-cocked George with a pistol I might not have been hit," she continued, "but it was almost worth it to see George hit the floor."

"Well, I imagine that would have contributed to it," Jeremy replied. "He still should not have had this done. Are you going to behave if I leave you for a short time? No climbing the walls?"

She nodded, shook her head and pulled herself out of the pool.

"Yes or no?"

She nodded.

"Good, I'm going to leave you now and start dinner."

Jeremy disappeared into the house, diverting in the direction of her room.

Amanda watched. He would be setting her out something to wear. This dressing for the occasion was absurd, but it might be a good idea to pay attention. She wasn't going to be a part of Georges' harem, but if she wanted out of here these 'dates' could be the key. And to get out of here, she had to get out of here. Coming to this conclusion Amanda took extra time with her hair and make-up. Mr. Tudor had said she needed to play.

When she made her appearance, Jeremy smiled appreciatively.

"You look lovely, Miss Amanda." He did a quick twist of his wrist, directing her back the way she had come. "This will begin your formal training, madam. When you have a gentleman caller you will not come this way. These are the personal quarters."

At the end of the hall Amanda was greeted with a dining area, dance floor and seating area, cameras strategically placed here as well. Music floated in the background and a larger courtyard begged for her to investigate. The walls were fronted by cactus and other native plants and stood approximately seven feet tall. If she had to, she could climb. Amanda giggled, remembering Jeremy's question about climbing walls. She brought her attention back to Mr. Tudor and noticed he looked much different when he was 'dressed', as he called it.

"This is where the entertaining will take place," he was saying. "Even if the gentleman has paid for other favors, he will not be taken into the private spaces of the home. Mr. Bonner has not set you up with any appointments of that kind, yet."

"Yet," she said with a sigh.

"Normally, I will bring your caller in through those doors," he said, shooting her questioning glance as he pointed to a set of double doors on the far side of the dining area. He then directed her gaze to two chairs on the opposite side of the room. "If he is only looking you over, this is when the gentleman will decide if he feels you are worth paying the extra money for the honor of being seen with you in public."

"For the honor of being seen with me in public," she repeated. "Kind of like an audition for the bedroom?"

He heard the tone and thought about George's decision once again.

"It is a bit of a game, but none of the gentlemen with money want their peers to think they have to resort to hookers for something as simple as dinner and a dance so we find girls of higher caliber to escort them to events when they're in town. Anything further than that will be set up in advance and the lady – in this case, you – will be informed and can pack a bag with the appropriate attire."

The last stop on his guided tour of the entertainment wing was the safe room at the end of a short hall, and a bedroom bathroom suite. He opened the door to a king size bed on the wall facing the door, a night table and lamp flanking it on each side and a settee at the foot of the bed. A dresser with a mirror sat on the wall beside the door, the wall to the right had two doors. One went to the bath, he told her, and the second was to a walk in closet. He opened that door and she was greeted by a large array of silk and satin gowns and matching dusters. She lifted her eyes, sweeping the walls and ceiling, searching for cameras and noticed the mirrored tiles above the bed. She sighed and hung her head, fighting the tears. This had not been a good day.

"I am sorry, Miss Amanda, but you have to know everything about this end of the home, in case you are here and Mr. Bonner, or anyone else, gets too rough."

"What if I'm not here?"

"There will be the times you are not," he answered. "We are going to try and get you out of here before that happens. And you will not go to some sleazy motel. Remember, you are an escort not a hooker."

Amanda nodded and followed him back to the dining area trying to disseminate this new piece of information. To her they were one and the same. One just cost more.

Once she was seated Jeremy changed the subject.

"It has been a long time since I had a date with such a beautiful lady," he said, noting the puzzled look. "You look confused."

"I am confused, but…I don't know. So, how do you manage to keep yourself pulled together? I need to learn that art."

"Some days are harder than others," he answered. "You really have no clue what an escort does, do you?"

She shook her head and hiked her left shoulder.

"This is the largest extent of you duties. Manners and lots of them. Most of the men who fork out the kind of money these men do, are not going to want a lady in the bedroom who acts like a hooker on the dance floor." He hesitated a moment then set his fork down and looked across the table at her. "Amanda, what kind of contract did you sign with Mr. Bonner?"

"None. One minute I was standing on the stairs at the club with the piano player and the next I woke up in a room with no way out. My ex came in and told me George paid him twenty grand for his help grabbing me. Mr. Tudor, I want to go home."

"I am working on that. You have to trust me."

"I know," she said trying to smile.

After several dances and a couple of glasses of wine, he reached across the table and patted her hand softly.

"Shall we?" he asked. "It really has gotten late so, let's pretend the hall is the driveway and your bedroom door is the door into the house. Okay?"

She took his hand and followed him until he stopped at her door, then he tipped her chin up to face him.

"You need to remember we are being watched so play just a tad. And if push comes to shove. Keeping yourself alive is not the same as being a hooker. Understand?

"Yes," she said.

"Please trust me."

She did a jerky nod, making her decision. If he was going to help her, she had to help him, help her. She would play, as long as he was running interference.

"Play," he whispered. Then he cupped her face in his hands and kissed her.

"I do hope we gave them a good enough show," she said, placing her hand on her diaphragm.

"I do believe we did. Are you alright?" he asked.

"Butterflies," she said with a giggle.

"Butterflies?" He gave her another kiss and wondered what 'butterflies' meant.

46

Amanda closed the door and listened to Jeremy's fading footfalls in the hall, then changed her clothes and peered out the window. Something didn't feel right tonight. She climbed into bed and felt along the edge of the stand, then ran her fingers up the back of the headboard until she had found both emergency buttons. Jeremy told her to push one of those if she needed help. The one on the nightstand would alert him and the one on the headboard would alert the police along with him. Ten minutes filtered by as she watched the clock and the shadows on the wall. A thud at the front of the house disrupted the silence and she peered out, the guards watching the shadows by the front of the wall. A barely discernible silhouette crept along the wall on the west side of the property, partially hidden in the landscaping. A glance toward the guard house, and only one man remained. She turned back to where the shadow had been, but it was gone. The guard returned, shaking his head as he lit a cigarette.

She snuggled under the blankets dozing in and out until she startled awake at two a.m. She listened intently, the gate by the pool squawked and she peered out of the window again. Both guards were gone. She tiptoed to the living area as an outline dropped out of sight behind the lounge chairs, melting into the shadows. A guard walked past and nodded in her direction. If they found anything they would notify Mr. Tudor. A few minutes later the door to the room next to hers opened then clicked shut. Then something scraped the wall, moving toward her room. Her door opened a crack and she pushed the button on the night table. The person stood silhouetted in the door, glancing from one side of the room to the other, then slipped inside. A couple of minutes later her door was flung open, flooding the room with light from the hall.

"Mr. Tudor," Amanda said. "Is that you?"

Not waiting for an answer, she turned the lamp on and darted for the door, her body being thrust against the hallway wall. She looked up, realized she was holding her breath and recognized Mr. Tudor. She really did need to learn this man's name. He put his finger to his lips and she nodded, pressing her body tighter against the wall.

"Head for my room, please," he whispered, prodding her gently toward the end of the hall. "Push the button by the door. That will alert the guards."

Amanda ran to Jeremy's room, flipped the light on and pushed the button then started back toward her room, stopping in the doorway. What could she do? Kiss the man to death? She didn't even have a weapon. Most men had a back-up piece if they worked security, or law enforcement. He was technically her bodyguard.

She opened the drawer in the stand beside the bed, nothing. She then moved to the dresser and went through the drawers in it, but was met with the same. Glancing around the room, a shoulder holster hung behind the door, empty. That would be the one he was carrying. She exhaled slowly and forced herself to slow her inspection, spotting the second drawer on his night table. It was locked. Damn it! How could she help if she couldn't find his back-up piece?

One more sweep of the room and her eyes stopped on the bed. Amanda knelt, sweeping her hand over the floor but came up with nothing. She then looked under it and, with nothing visible, turned her head to look under the nightstand finding a leather holster attached to the bottom of the stand. She pulled the gun and dropped the magazine. It was missing one. That would be the one in the chamber. She slid the magazine back in and flipped the safety off.

Five feet from her bedroom door the light went out then there was a faint click as the door closed. She pressed herself against the wall, gliding silently until she stood beside the doorway. A deep breath and she turned so her chest was against the wall then pushed the door open, allowing what light was in the hall to penetrate the darkened room.

"Mr. Tudor," she said. "I got your six."

Amanda remained still for a few seconds; eyes closed, her forehead resting on the drywall, trying to catch any sound from within. She reached around the doorframe and swept her hand up the wall, turning the overhead light on. A quick back step so her back was tight against the wall and she shimmied the few inches to the door, clutching the pistol in front of her. Another slow, deep breath to calm herself and Amanda pivoted around the door frame and into the room, locking her elbows as she swept the space, following the barrel with her eyes.

Jeremy nodded as he reached behind the headboard, activating the signal for the police. There was a muffled scraping and Amanda glanced toward the door, curious about where the guards were. She quickly returned her focus to the room just as someone lunged toward her. She planted the end of the barrel against a man's forehead, giving a slight push so he would step back.

"FREEZE!" Jeremy ordered.

"I would suggest you back up," Amanda said calmly. "I'm not a good little girl when holding one of these."

The man stepped back and held his hands out, smiling hesitantly. He looked familiar, but she couldn't place him. He was covered in greasepaint.

"Back up," Jeremy snapped. "Slowly."

The man took a step backwards then bolted toward Amanda, grabbing the pistol and jerking it to his right as he moved. The muzzle dropped and, with her finger on the trigger, fired. There was a deafening explosion then the intruder stumbled backwards, blood oozing from a wound in his side.

"STUPID!" she yelled, almost screaming.

Sirens howled in the distance and footsteps rushed up the hall as Jeremy nudged her out of the room. He turned her over to the guards, returning to her room, but the man was gone. They hadn't heard a sound. Intermittent splatters of blood led to the front courtyard, where the intruder had vanished into the night. The police could handle it from here.

Jeremy returned to patrolmen in the hall, weapons trained on Amanda. They were erring on the side of caution, having no idea what she might do. She held the gun in front of her and down, feet braced, still grasping it firmly. Jeremy reached down and took hold of the pistol, setting the safety as he did.

"You handled yourself admirably," Jeremy said calmly. "I'm proud of you, my lady. Let go of the gun, please. The officers need to talk to you and they can't do it if you're armed. Do you understand?"

"I know," she said, releasing the weapon, her hands out to the side so the officer's could see them.

Jeremy handed one of the patrolmen a card then dropped the magazine and cleared the chamber. The officer read it and slid it into his pocket then made a call on his portable. Four hours later the excitement was over and detectives had allowed Jeremy to move Amanda's clothing to the neighboring bedroom. Hers was a crime scene now.

Jeremy walked Amanda to her new room and she leaned against him, her body trembling. He pulled her close, and closed the door behind them. She wanted comfort, reassurance, he recognized the fear when she tipped her face up to his, but they were dangerously close to that boundary they should not cross.

'She is only my charge,' he told himself. 'One does not get involved with ones charge.'

He watched her eyes close as he cradled her face in his hands, a single tear tracing its way down her cheek then they kissed and all manly resolve dissipated. He awoke later, Amanda lying peacefully beside him and thought about how he would explain this then remembered he had not brought the cameras up. A single slash of moonlight cut across her face and her eyes flitted open, startling him.

"Are you alright?" Amanda whispered.

"Never better," Jeremy answered. 'Definitely not working this assignment right,' he thought, as he kissed her and pulled her close.

Amanda awoke to the aroma of fresh coffee and Jeremy's soft kisses.

"Good morning, Miss Amanda. I trust you had a good night's sleep."

"And you?"

He noticed she had avoided the question.

"I haven't slept that well in ages, madam. I have coffee and juice waiting for you. Breakfast will be ready momentarily."

"Thank you," she answered. "Did Mr. Tudor sleep late this morning?"

"Yes, madam," he answered. "Are you alright?"

She offered a tentative smile and nodded.

"Get dressed, please."

"What about the cameras?"

"Mr. Bonner has already called. I knew he would. I alerted the authorities and they notified him. Come now. I have to finish breakfast."

She noticed he had avoided a direct answer.

Amanda walked into the dining room and watched Jeremy. His mannerisms gave nothing away, but he had a deeper furrow on his brow than she had seen before.

"You said George called. What did he want?"

"One of the guards told him about us. He is not happy with me for sampling the merchandise so my employment with Mr. Bonner has been terminated…"

"Oh, no, Mr. Tudor!

"It is quite alright, Miss Amanda. He was trying to force me to leave today, but I told him if he allowed me the privilege of staying for a standard two week notice, I would not testify against him, if he went to trial."

"But what am I going to do when you're gone?"

"I will not leave you here alone," Jeremy said. "You are my number one priority." As he talked, she turned away and stared outside. "Miss Amanda, it is obvious you are not alright. Is it because of last night?"

She dropped her gaze and he sat her coffee on the table then kneeled in front of her.

"Listen to me, please." He recognized the slightest of nods then she turned away again. He reached up and turned her face back toward his. "Look at me, please."

She looked at him and he saw the barely controlled tears.

"I'm sorry, Mr. Tudor."

"Don't apologize," he said. "Last night was just one of those things that happen sometimes. That really bothers you, doesn't it?" He searched her face, but she only gave a weak smile and a nervous half shrug. "Mr. Bonner should never have brought you here," he said with a sigh. "You aren't accustomed to doing this, are you?"

"Not really," she answered. Then she laughed. "God, I feel stupid. I mean, I'm no puritan and this is the eighties, but I don't usually go to bed with some man just because he happens to be there."

"That's why you have been so worried about your duties." He recognized another tiny nod. "Some women – like you – just don't feel comfortable making love to everybody and that's fine. I promise I will try to control myself better. For what it's worth, I don't sleep with just any woman who happens to be there, either. And you are the only woman I have ever lost a job over."

"Was it worth it?" she asked. Then she leaned her head back and laughed loudly. "I'm so sorry."

"No need to be sorry. It is good to hear you laugh, though. Now, breakfast is served, madam. Once I have everything worked out, we will be heading out across Nevada."

47

William and James met at Sambo's. Their new office they had joked once. No matter what Captain Ohlmet said, their phones were tapped and their apartment's were probably bugged. They had conducted a search on their own and found nothing, but neither man was confident they hadn't missed something. They wanted to go over plans for their next visit to the bar without anyone eavesdropping. And they damn well didn't want the chief hearing them talk about their collecting for George.

When they had finished going over the new information, and pulled to the exit, William glanced to his left. A car matching the description of Julie's new car, complete with Nevada plates, was coming up fast. No one had seen George or Julie but they had read an announcement in the paper about her daughter, Sarah, passing away. With the little girl's funeral tomorrow William debated if he should follow. They decided he could always, tuck in behind it and, if it wasn't Julie, abort the tail.

Three blocks north the car pulled in at a thrift store. They followed, parking a row over where they could still keep a visual on it. Julie walked inside then came back out with a cart. They did a quick scan of the parking lot looking for anyone who might work for George before approaching her. Julie should recognize them from the club and hoped that would make her more comfortable talking to them.

"I'll meet you guys inside," James said. "With these crutches I'm obviously not an employee."

William agreed as James peeled off, heading inside.

"Julie?" William said.

She jumped and William looked at the pavement hiding his discomfort.

"Didn't mean to scare you. Here, let me help." He started piling boxes into the cart. "How are you? We heard about Sarah. Sorry about your loss." Even as he said the words, they sounded hollow. Losing a child must be the worst pain in the world.

"Thank you," Julie answered forcing herself to smile. "I'm fine, I guess. Just bringing some things to the thrift store. I had to get out of the apartment."

"We'd like to talk to you for a minute if you feel up to it," William continued. He placed the last of the boxes in the cart and hoped he looked like an employee.

"That'll be fine." She hiked a shoulder and did another visual sweep of the parking area. "We can talk inside. If that's alright."

"You look nervous. Is George having you watched?"

"I think so. You know George. He doesn't trust anybody." She followed William inside and once she'd completed the donation process, started going through the racks of clothing.

"See anyone who works for George?" James asked from the opposite side of the rack. "The last thing we want is to get you in trouble."

"No," she said. She glanced between the two men then went back to perusing the clothes. "I know why you want to talk to me. It's about George and that missing lady, isn't it?"

"Yes," William answered. "Do you know anything about it?"

"Not directly. I was going through sympathy cards and I found one from a man named Jeremy Hamilton. He included the name Amanda on the inside. I wondered if that was her."

William stared at Julie, perplexed. She knew Amanda. She had performed with her. Was she that afraid of George?

"Is there anything else you can tell us? Did the card have an address on it?"

"I think you'll find her here," Julie replied. She slid the card to William between shirts and surveyed the store and parking lot once more. "I was going to call the cops today anyway."

William read the card then slipped it into his hip pocket.

"We appreciate that," James said. "Any idea how George pulled this off? Has he talked to anybody?"

"I hear him talking to people about stuff all the time. I've learned not to pay attention to it. I didn't want to get in trouble. I had Sarah to worry about. Now it's not so important. I can always just skip town and sleep in the car. I know he was real thick with Royce for a while. They used to talk about the military bases a lot. Once they got into an argument about a woman and I assumed Royce was trying to talk George into a free night with one of the hookers. George wouldn't have liked that. She'd keep the whole hundred on the next john."

"How long before Amanda's disappearance was that?" James asked.

"About a week, I think. Maybe ten days. George spent a lot of time with his security staff after that. Then the lady disappeared."

"But you never heard him mention any names? Nothing that might point us somewhere?"

"No." She looked up and shook her head then went back to the shirts. "I remember he came home one night and he could barely walk." She laughed at the memory then glanced outside again. "I asked him what happened and he said he fell. I wonder now if that was from her. It was the day after that fire."

"Is there anything else you can remember? Has he left town recently for any overnight stays?"

"No." She shook her head again. "With Sarah's surgery he's been staying home more."

"Thank you," William said. He reached into his pocket and handed her a business card. "We really don't want you to get hurt so if you need anything, or think of anything, give us a call. My home number's on the back."

Julie nodded and took the card.

William picked up the car and met James at the door, trying not to draw too much attention to the crutches. They stayed quiet until they were away from the building.

"That was interesting," William said. "Julie acted like she didn't know who Amanda was, but they performed together."

"You read that, too," James said. "At least we know where Amanda's at now. Man, I hope Jeremy calls soon."

"I know that," William answered. "It feels like it's been a month and it's only been a day. I feel like we need to be doing something. Think we should page him?"

"Don't know, buddy," James replied. "Your call."

48

William's phone rang at seven a.m. the next morning. Captain Ohlmet wanted both of them at William's apartment by o eight-thirty for a conference call. Military jargon again. he called James, and headed over to pick him up. While William waited for James, he opened the glove box and took out the tiny ring box. It wasn't the normal wedding set. Amanda had told him once she liked Buttercups, so he had ordered a set with Diamonds and Citrine. He would be happy with a simple band, but he wanted hers to be as special as she was. The passenger door opened and he looked up as James plopped onto the seat.

"I know you're about tired of picking me up all the time," James said as he heaved a sigh. "I know I'm tired of not being able to drive."

"No problem," William answered, closing the box. "Any word on when you can start driving?"

"Next week," James said. "Beautiful rings." He hadn't seen that coming. "She's going to love them."

"If I ever get to propose," William said. The best partner the department could have given him.

"Did the captain say what they wanted?" James asked.

"Nope. Makes me wonder what they're up to, though."

The phone was already ringing when they arrived at William's. Captain Ohlmet must be getting his butt chewed, James joked as William ran to answer it.

"Gentlemen," the captain said. "Park City P.D. called…"

"And why are you calling us now?" William asked, cutting him off. "You wanted nothing to do with us a few days ago. We aren't officers, remember."

"Look, I just got my ass chewed by Assistant Chief Robinson because Jeremy went above him and the chief, so I am making sure you guys are in the loop now, okay? I told you before; I'm stuck in the middle on this shit. Now, Park City found a sale bag of cocaine. It's the same stuff that killed the girl in Liberty Park. And we've had a citizen come forward who said they saw both of the murdered women behind George's establishment with George. He also said it was common practice for Mr. Bonner to entertain company in the back of the limo. If you know what I mean. We have requested more search warrants and we're going to go through the bar with a fine tooth comb. We don't expect to find much, but I thought you two might like to be involved so I have a couple of tuxes with your names on them." The captain's standing joke for the vest with the words *'Police'* emblazoned across the back was a tux. "We have also learned George is still here in Salt Lake City. We just have to find him."

"We talked to Julie yesterday," William said. He instantly regretted the comment and noticed James' grimace. He shouldn't have said anything and now debated how much he should divulge.

"Did she tell you anything?" the captain asked.

"She said she received a sympathy card from Jeremy. We gave her our condolences."

"Did she give you the address off the card?"

He glanced at James and saw the shrug then James frowned and made the sign for a phone call. James was reminding him of the tap.

"No," William said. He rolled his eyes and cringed when he spoke. Technically he hadn't lied. She hadn't given him the address; she had given him the card.

"Have either of you seen the news this morning?"

"No, sir," William answered. "You woke us up. We've been doing that undercover thing at night."

"What's goin' down?" James asked.

"We received a call from Green River, Utah this morning. One of the Emery County deputies' pulled a car over with two of George's men in it. It was registered to Julie Barron-Warden of Winnemucca, Nevada and had expired plates. That's why they pulled it over. One of the men pulled a gun on the deputy. The deputy's partner returned the favor. Obviously, they are under arrest.

"When they searched the car they found a body bag in the trunk. They opened it and Julie was inside. Her hair was still wet and there was soap residue on her. Her throat had been cut so there is no doubt about her cause of death. But, because of the nature of the crime and her connection to George Bonner they did the autopsy first thing this morning. The M-E said she'd had intercourse prior to her death. And, just like the women at Liberty Park and Silver Lake, her ankles were tied with a pair of panties. They think the killer is doing that just for fun. His way of taunting us. Are you alright?" he asked when he heard their sudden intakes of air.

"Fine, Captain," William answered.

"Please tell us we can nail George now," James said. "We can include the ones from a couple of years ago, too, can't we?"

"That's what we're looking at. The DA thinks we need something a little more solid, but we're still going to push it.

We're trying to tighten a couple of loose ends in that area. With the citizen's statement about seeing both girls with George, and three women killed under the same set of circumstances and in similar manners, and Julie being George's girlfriend, we used that for the search warrants. Obviously, the panties and the pose are going to help us. George got stupid. We hope to find what we need to tighten the noose when we do the search."

"Have the men called an attorney?" William asked. "Was it George's?"

"Yes, but so far no one has come forward to claim them. We hope it stays that way. Park City called again and said one of the residents in those condos called the police about a lady walking away from the grounds very briskly. A man caught up to her and took her back to one of the units. She just thought it was strange."

"It's strange alright," William said. "Why didn't she call sooner?" William shook his head. Was she well meaning, or feeling guilty?

"When are you going into the bar to do the search?"James asked.

"O eight hundred tomorrow morning. I guess this means you guys are in?"

"Absolutely," James answered. "We'll meet you at the party."

"And you say he moved?" William asked.

"We hope to discover where when we search the bar. We have one warrant that is open for just that purpose."

The two sat at the table after the captain hung up and stared at each other for a few seconds before saying anything.

"You thinkin' what I'm thinkin', buddy?" James asked.

"Definitely," William answered. "George killed Julie. He killed those other two girls, too."

"He's also our perp for the murders from two years ago," James said. "I notice the Cap didn't officially agree or disagree."

"Maybe he doesn't want to jinx the investigation by giving out too much information too soon. I wonder how much trouble it would cause if we head to Reno? We are still working on our own, right?"

"That's what I heard. Should we let Jeremy know what we're doing and where we are in case he needs to contact us?"

William nodded. "I'm for heading out as soon as we get done with that search but – if we find George's new address – that will take most of the day. How about the day after?"

"Count me in," James said.

"I'll page Jeremy."

49

Jeremy watched Amanda walk up the hall at the same time his pager vibrated. She was gorgeous, even in blue jeans and a t-shirt. She smiled and he remembered the feel of her skin under his hand, soft, warm, silky. Her skin against his. Her lips when she kissed him. The freckles across her cheeks. Her brunette hair, tinged red by the kiss of the sun. Perfect. His pager did a reminder buzz, pulling himself away from his thoughts and he checked the screen. She sat across from him and he told her he would finish breakfast as soon as he finished with this call.

"William," he said when William answered. "Any problems?"

"We just talked to the Cap and he invited us to the search of George's bar and possibly his apartment. He said he's stuck in the middle and only called because you went over his head. Sounds like he's trying to straddle the fence to me. Any news?"

"I haven't called him since Park City," Jeremy replied. "Who told him I called?"

William's thoughts went to the assistant chief's warnings. Assistant Chief Robinson was covering their backs. "I don't know. He said Assistant Chief Robinson nailed his ass."

"Thank the assistant chief for me. If it wasn't him, when you know more, let me in on it. Either way, I'm glad someone had a talk with them. Just so you know, I am working on pulling Amanda out the beginning of the week. That's four days. I have a few details to take care of first. If we are discovered, George would order both our executions, so I want to pull her out without George's knowledge. I am also in possession of some information that will help your case immensely. What was your reason for paging me?"

"James and I are thinking about heading that way."

"If you do, page me when you arrive. I need to know where you are staying. If I don't hear anything from you, I will call you back in two days."

"Sounds good. James and I talked to Julie and she gave us a card with an address in Reno."

"That is it," Jeremy said. "I sent her the card. Remember to page me if you come this way. I have to go now."

"Thanks, Jeremy."

Jeremy walked back to the kitchen and thought about the conversation with William. The line had been full of static. Their phones were still tapped. But he was glad the assistant chief had stepped up for them. He poured another cup of coffee, then the phone rang and he hoped it wasn't Mr. Bonner again. It was and Jeremy caught himself cursing silently. George had called to give Jeremy an update on Amanda's itinerary.

"What are the plans?" Amanda asked when Jeremy returned. She didn't like that look.

"That was Mr. Bonner. He has set you up with an appointment for tonight."

"What kind of appointment?"

"He has decided you are ready to begin all aspects of your duties. He thinks if you can roll over for the hired help you can rollover for the paying gentlemen. All I know as of now is the gentleman will be here at seven p.m. Mr. Bonner also said he expects you to be more obliging when he comes to visit, if you get the meaning."

"What are we going to do?"

"I have been thinking about that. We can drug the gentleman tonight. Mr. Bonner, I'm not sure about."

"Mr. Tudor!" Her face showed equal parts revulsion and fear.

Jeremy laughed softly at her expression. "I am sorry, Miss Amanda. I couldn't resist. I will figure something out."

The fax machine began its incessant squealing and Jeremy left to check it, and Amanda hoped this was a mistake. George hadn't set her up with any appointments of that nature. Jeremy returned and laid the man's picture on the table in front of her.

"Evidently George took him into the club in Salt Lake City while you were performing. It seems this gentleman was quite taken with you. When he found out about your position, he called and requested two hours of your time as soon as it could be arranged. Nothing outrageous, just the standard duties associated with your station as a lady for hire so, I am afraid, there is nothing I can do unless he gets too rough. If he does anything to harm you, I will be there."

"And how will you know that?" she asked.

"I will not be watching your activities," Jeremy reassured her, seeing the wide-eyed stare. "Remember the safe room. When you open the door, I will hear a buzzer in my room. If you are unable to get out of the bedroom, there are the emergency buzzer's just like with our intruder."

"I thought you said...?" She halted the question, as she glared at the picture. "Never mind. So, George was shopping me around before he even kidnapped me?"

"It appears that way, madam."

"Okay, my 'station as a lady for hire'..." She didn't' finish that sentence, either, already knowing the answer.

"Yes, my lady. The same thing my employment has been terminated over. Sexually gratifying activities between two consenting adults. We inadvertently screwed things up."

"That's what I was afraid of."

By six p.m. all preparations had been completed and Jeremy had set Amanda's ensemble out. It was time for them to get dressed.

"Do not let him push you into anything too soon," Jeremy said. "When it is time I will come get you, and I will push that as far as I dare. It is all fairly well scripted."

"That sounds reassuring," she retorted. "Do you change my clothes for me, too?"

"Being a tad testy tonight, are we?"

"Just a tad. I haven't been this scared since Park City."

"It will be alright," Jeremy said. "You need to relax, please. Go make yourself presentable. I still need to put the wine on ice and get dressed. I promise to be right beside you."

Five minutes before seven Amanda met Jeremy in the hall.

"What do you think?" she asked. "Is he here?"

"You look ravishing," he answered with a smile. "He hasn't arrived yet."

"Did he cancel?" she asked excitedly. "Could I be that lucky?"

"If he did, he didn't call." Jeremy chuckled when he saw her excitement.

"Mr. Tudor, you don't look happy."

"This is highly unusual. Normally when a man forks over six hundred bucks he's going to be there to collect what he paid for. Let me call Mr. Bonner."

Jeremy returned and told her as far as they knew the night was still a go. He put dinner in the warming tray and did a visual on the gate one more time. No man skipped an appointment of this nature. Not when they had paid that much, in advance.

By eight-thirty they still hadn't seen him. Jeremy and Amanda enjoyed the meal and got some practice in on the dance floor. By nine-thirty he still hadn't made his appearance and Jeremy was growing concerned. At ten p.m. a limo pulled through the gates and a tall, portly man stepped out, surveying the grounds before he nodded. He wasn't the man from the photo. Three more men climbed out, one of them Jeremy recognized from the fax. The other two headed to the guardhouse while Amanda's caller walked toward the main doors.

"I already know this isn't normal," Amanda said from beside him. "What's going on?"

"I believe this gentleman is here to collect you for the syndicate," Jeremy answered. "Those men probably have orders to dispose of ours. Mr. Bonner screwed up." He wanted to get closer to the inner sanctum of the syndicate, but this wasn't how he had envisioned doing it.

"Crap! I can't even work as a hooker and do it right!"

Jeremy chuckled then grabbed her arm and propelled her toward the safe room as the men approached the door. Stopping in the guest room on their way by, Jeremy took a pistol out of the drawer in the night table then shoved her the last few feet to the safe room. He closed the door behind them and handed her the gun.

"Stay here," he said. "Do not leave this room unless you have to. I am going to check on our guards and locate his men. I've seen you handle one of those. Use it if you need to."

Jeremy darted through the door into the private space and made a dash for the patio. The double doors in the front of the house kicked open as he let himself out the sliding glass doors moving silently past the pool, entering the guard shack through the rear door. Their men were in the corner, bound and gagged. Jeremy put his finger to his lips for them to stay quiet, and then instructed them to stay down until they heard from him. They bobbed their heads while he undid their gags, then he stuffed the fabric into his pocket, borrowing a cigarette lighter. He scanned the surrounding area, noticing a second limo parked across the street.

Jeremy did a crouching run toward the rear of the limo in the driveway, keeping out of sight as he slid under it. A quick peek from under the huge car and he pulled the fabric out then loosened the plug on the gas tank, winding a corner of the fabric around the plug and tightening it again. One more check of the grounds and he set the soaked rags on fire then scooted from under the limo. He returned to the guard house and told the men to remain where they were. Before he reached the gate by the pool he was knocked to the ground by the explosion, the windows shattering. Footsteps raced toward the front of the house while Jeremy picked himself up, stumbling into the house and trying to focus. Two shots rang out as he raced for the door to the safe room then it was flung open and Amanda bolted into the room.

"MY ROOM," Jeremy yelled. "LOCK THE DOOR." Still dazed from the blast, he tripped over the sofa, catching himself on the coffee table, the fog finally beginning to lift.

Amanda recognized the glazed stare and took a half step then stopped and raised the pistol, bracing for the shot. Jeremy continued in her direction, his vision clearing slowly then raised his weapon, aiming for the mouth of the hall, the same as hers. Amanda glanced behind her at Jeremy and nodded, locking eyes with him as she mouthed 'Fire when I drop'. Jeremy returned the nod.

Two men appeared, instantly back pedaling. Amanda fired and dropped, Jeremy firing next. One of the men clasped his hand to his shoulder and fell into the wall, his partner lunging to the floor. Amanda started to pull herself up, Jeremy grabbed her and dived behind the breakfast bar, dragging her with him. The men staggered back the way they had come, while Jeremy picked himself up and followed. He halted his chase when the waiting limo sped away, what was left of the first limo still burning in the driveway.

The explosion had activated the fire sprinklers and Jeremy turned them off then leaned into the wall for a second before he ran back to Amanda.

"Are you alright, Jeremy?" she asked.

"I should be fine. The limo went off sooner than I expected. In the meantime, the police should be arriving momentarily. I'm proud of you, my lady." Tonight had not been good, but she had pulled through like a pro once again.

The shrill sound of the telephone startled them both, the police driving through the gate at the same time. He would let the men deal with the officers. He answered the phone and disconnected the cameras.

"What the hell happened?" George barked.

"You almost lost your prize concubine. You didn't check Miss Amanda's appointment carefully enough, sir. I believe he was with the syndicate. You should have let me screen him. Now, if you don't mind there are several officers here I need to speak with."

"Keep her safe," George ordered. "I'll be there Tuesday."

"I will endeavor to do so," Jeremy answered.

Jeremy talked to the officer's then called to have the windows covered and strode up the hall to the safe room. Two bullets had struck the wall by the lock, but the mechanism was undamaged. The police had already removed them and a tow truck was backing in to remove the charred remains of the limo. Jeremy pulled his gaze back to the interior of the house, surveying the damage. This looked nice didn't it? She had an engagement tomorrow night and the place was a mess!

50

William picked James up at seven-thirty the next morning and they headed for George's establishment.

"Did you talk to the captain yet?" James asked.

"Nope. I figured we'd talk to him this morning."

Twenty minutes later they were outside George's bar talking to Captain Ohlmet, Chief Vanders hovering beside him. It was more unnerving talking to him in person, but they had made their decision. Especially after his informational two-step.

Chief Vanders attempted to step up and bar their involvement, but William slapped one of Jeremy's cards in his hand. The chief scowled while Captain Ohlmet's countenance showed surprise, and William forced himself not to gloat.

"First of all, Captain Ohlmet invited us to this party," William said. "Second, Jeremy is with Amanda in Reno and Bonner is involved. We need to move."

"Let Captain Ohlmet call Park City," the chief said, recovering some of his bluster. "Captain Ohlmet said Officer Willis has volunteered to go with you guys and keep you out of trouble. That makes me more comfortable since neither of you have a badge but, I think, Officer Willis is tied up on a drug case right now."

"Why are you involving Officer Willis?"

"He's the one who located her in Park City, and you two don't have badges," the chief answered. "If you're representing this city, you need an active badge. Jeremy's cards won't cut through that as far as I'm concerned, and the last I heard, I was in charge of this department not you, Jeremy, or Captain Ohlmet."

"And if we aren't representing the city?" William countered.

James read William's expression and jumped in. "Jeremy wants us to page him if we head to Reno so he knows where we'll be. And before you argue, you said we were working on our own. Just keep it legal."

"Two days?" Captain Ohlmet questioned. He held a hand up at his side signaling the chief to back down. "That's Friday."

"Maybe," William answered and hiked his shoulders. "We don't need Officer Willis to drive over. We'll use Reno's help to grab George."

"William…" Captain Ohlmet began.

"Look," James interjected. "We've been lucky so far, but we can't guarantee that luck will hold. We know where she's at, Jeremy's there and we can use Reno's help. You guys told us to get it done, let us. And Jeremy's cards carry more clout than you do, anyway."

Captain Ohlmet's eyes widened for a second then he walked away, the chief nodded with a smug smile and followed.

James tapped William on the shoulder.

"So…Where'd he get two days or Friday?" James asked.

"Don't know, but I think that answers our questions about the phone."

Eight a.m. the next morning Jeremy received another page from William. He excused himself and told Amanda he would cook breakfast when he returned.

"Good morning, William," Jeremy said. "In case you are unaware, your phones are still being tapped, but I have taken the necessary precautions on my end. Is James there this morning?"

"He is," William answered.

There was a second click then James' familiar greeting floated across the line. "Hey, buddy!"

"Has a decision been made about your trip?"

"We are heading that way this morning," William said. "As soon as we get off the phone."

"It will be good to see you. Page me when you get here."

"You said you're working on a plan. Can we help you when we get there?"

"I still plan on leaving Monday evening under cover of darkness. That way Mr. Bonner will be unaware of what we're doing. He is supposed to be here Tuesday. That is how you can help. You bring George Bonner down. You are running under the auspices of my organization; take advantage of it. I will let you know when we leave and where you can find her. Anything else?"

"We were invited to participate in the search of Bonner's bar yesterday and – other than Chief Vanders doesn't think your cards are worth squat – the search turned up everything we need to press charges against George for drugs and reinforce the info we gathered. Plus we found George's address. When we went by his apartment he wasn't home so we had his security staff let us in. George was stupid and called the station threatening to sue us. I was told his attorney followed up on the threat and felt pretty stupid when he found out we had a search warrant. That gave us legal right to be there. We uncovered new evidence there, too, including blood in the shower drain, but we kept that to ourselves. We don't want George running. The Cap is going back to the judge for the arrest warrant. George can't say anything then."

"Good. I'll handle the issue with the cards, but that answers the question I had for you. I had assumed Captain Ohlmet and Chief Vanders were continuing to give you mixed signals."

"Yeah, you could say that. I don't know what's going on, but it smells of political bull."

"It is. They are close to finding out who their turncoat is. Mr. Portman was working for some heavy weight people, but he is willing to take the fall to cover them. If the chief or the captain threatens you in any way, let me know. My organization will cover you there, as well. Now, I am dangerously close to running out of time. Page me when you get to town."

When Jeremy returned to the kitchen Amanda was finishing breakfast. Surprised, he wasn't sure what to do, that was his job. It was kind of nice, though. Almost like being given a day off.

"Are you up to tonight's appointment?" Jeremy asked, moving up and kissing her neck. He had promised to control himself, and he had been, but she was just too beautiful this morning. "You know, you really shouldn't tease a man like you do."

"What have I done?"

"All you have to do is breath, my lady." He moved down, kissing her shoulder. "What do you think? Another night of unbridled….communication?"

"Mr. Tudor! I thought I had an engagement tonight?"

"You do, but it will only be a simple dinner for two here at the house." He continued nuzzling her neck. "Mr. Bonner has made no mention of anything special, so I assume the gentleman is only going to look you over."

"Will they be finished with the entertainment area by then?" She could hear the men working, as she put their food on the plates.

"They are almost finished with the windows and the floors now. Once that is done, they will bring in the new furniture."

"I'm not thrilled about doing another appointment at all.

Especially after last night."

"I will be right here beside you again. You two will only be alone when I leave to bring dinner. His name is Layton. Mr. Travis Layton.

"Mr. Tudor, will you stop?"

"And ruin a perfectly good make-out session?"

"You are the only one involved in this make-out session."

"Turn around and I'll invite you to the party."

"And if I don't want to join the party?" She turned and faced him as he kissed her slow and gentle. "You are not playing fair," she breathed. "And breakfast is ready."

He let out a sigh and backed away, picking up the plates as he did. "So what has turned you so against making love?"

"It isn't making love I'm against. I just don't want to share my body with every single man I meet."

"And you are not here under the best of circumstances," he admitted. "So what can I do to change that stubborn mind of yours?"

"What about George and the cameras?"

"Now you're not playing fair," Jeremy replied. He set the plates down and turned back to her, cupping her face in his hands and kissed her again, her body melting into his. "That's more like it. But…"

"But?"

"You're right. About George that is. Now, let's eat so the food doesn't turn cold."

51

By four p.m. William and James were ensconced in a hotel in Reno, waiting for a reply from Jeremy. While they waited, William called the captain and gave him their number at the hotel. He listened to the captain's angry rant for ten minutes, finally making an excuse and hanging up. Then they took the street map they'd purchased and began searching the address. They wanted to know where they were going if Jeremy needed them.

"I have to make another phone call," Jeremy told Amanda.

"Good afternoon," William said. "We were beginning to wonder if you'd call."

"The phone in your room was tied up the first time I called. Did you bring those cards with you?" Jeremy asked.

"Yeah, we got 'em."

"Good. I am going to call the Reno Police Department and give them your names. Since you two will be working with them, I want to make sure, if anything happens, you will not be left out of the loop so they will need to call and verify who you are. Page me again when you hear from them."

Jeremy hung up and called the Reno Police Department. Thirty minutes later, he received another page and debated calling from the compound again, but caution dictated otherwise. He may have made too many calls as it was. Instead, he headed for the payphone at the convenience store on the corner. If asked, it was a routine run for a bag of chips or six pack of beer. He called the hotel and was told everything was set. They had received their call from Reno P.D.

He returned to the compound with the beer and the chips for appearances sake, setting the chips on the breakfast bar, he put the beer in the refrigerator and sat down on the sofa. Amanda walked over and sat beside him, pulling one of his arms over her shoulders and the other in front of her, holding them with her hands.

"Are you trying to make Mr. Bonner jealous?" he asked.

"No. Just getting scared. It's almost time to leave."

"Yes, it is. Don't be scared. Just continue to trust me. Are you ready for dinner?"

"I'm starving. I trust you completely."

"I'm glad to hear that." There was that trust he had been working toward. Finally.

Jeremy had Amanda and dinner ready and waiting when the gentleman arrived. As the evening progressed he handled himself like a gentleman and didn't even care to dance. He was less concerned about her abilities in that area than he was her abilities to handle herself like a true lady. After the allotted time, he excused himself. He hadn't even broached the subject of the bedroom. Jeremy was surprised, but Amanda was elated. She didn't want to see him again. He was nice, but this whole acting like a lady thing was growing tedious. She wanted to kick back in her jeans and relax. And the thought of the bedroom with a stranger – no thank you. Especially a man as old as him.

Once the gentleman had left, Jeremy lit the fireplace and turned out the lights. Grabbing them each a beer he sat down on the sofa beside Amanda. There was something relaxing about the flames as they danced along the tops of the logs. She snuggled up close, Jeremy content to hold her. Not knowing Amanda, he had screwed that up once and he didn't want to do it again.

"I think you would like camping," he said, his voice hushed. It was quiet. Serene. He didn't want to break the spell.

"I love camping! When I was about seven or so dad and I used to go ice fishing and it was the best fun. We went hunting once in a while, too. I wasn't as good at that as he would have liked, though."

"Couldn't kill the poor things?"

"I have no problem shooting them. It's the skinning part. I hate the blood. It smells funny, and your fingers get sticky. Yuck!"

"Have you seen Lake Tahoe?" he asked, still staring at the flames. "I have a hunting cabin there. That is where I go now and then between training sessions. It helps me unwind and leave this world behind."

"You aren't Mr. Tudor, are you?" Amanda asked. The stress and the games probably took their toll. That would help reverse those effects.

"No," he answered. "It's a persona I use to keep myself sane. I hate what they do to the girls, so I do what I can to help them gain the strength they need to hang on."

"Have you ever thought about getting them out?" she asked, curious about this other man she was being introduced to. "I mean, like you are me?"

"I get part of them out," he answered, breaking away from his musings. "The ones who want out, anyway. Usually I can spirit them away and they disappear into the night. It is not uncommon for girls to decide to go back home. None like this, though. I have never had one who was there due to abduction. You are a rare case, Miss Amanda."

"Don't they get suspicious?"

"The men? No. It's normal for the girls to play the game long enough to realize they aren't going anywhere then they save up enough to go home to a real job and their families. Some of the women discover it sooner and simply walk away. There have been a few who worked their way into the hearts of one of their gentleman callers and ended up married. That is a rare occurrence, too. Some of the less reputable men just get the girls hooked on drugs. If they don't perform as they need to on the escort side, the men shift them to the street. Anything to turn money on them. If the women still don't perform as desired, they turn them loose and the girls usually end up as a coke whore, OD'ing and dying on the street."

"You don't like that, do you? You really do care about all of your charges, don't you?"

"That is why I do it," he answered. He would tell her the rest later.

52

Jeremy went to wake Amanda the next morning with the usual tap on the door, but she was already up, opening the door before he could knock. He gazed down at her and stepped into the doorway, beckoning her to join him with his finger. She stepped up and he cupped her face in his hands, kissing her, her breath leaving her in a low moan.

"Do you know hard it was not to join you last night?"

"Huh-uh," she answered, her hands sliding up his back.

"If we keep this up, I will show you."

Amanda leaned back and laughed softly. "Then we need to move, because you aren't playing fair again. And George is liable to do more than fire you."

"That's why we're kissing here. The cameras can't see through the door." He laughed and patted her rear, shooing her to the dining area.

The rest of the day flew by, Jeremy pushing her harder about manners and acting like a lady for George's benefit. Soon it was time to play dress up again. But this time it wasn't for some man's entertainment.

Amanda walked into her room and saw where Jeremy had lain out a form fitting jade green number. She showered, fixed her hair and make-up then slipped into the dress, inspecting her reflection in the mirror. As she stared at the woman in front of her, Amanda took in every detail of the mermaid cut bodice and how it flowed from the pearl encrusted medallion at the waist, to the floor. Just tight enough to cling suggestively, but loose enough to move easily. She bent her left knee and rocked her leg on the toe of her shoe showing off a mid-thigh slit. Just enough to tease. A slight twist to check the derriere and she spotted the diamond necklace and earring set on the dressing table. Money definitely had its advantages. She caressed the stones gingerly before putting them on. One last look in the mirror and she smoothed the dress over her hips. Tonight, she would play that game.

She strolled into the living room, put her hands on her hips and struck a pose.

"Amanda, you take my breath away," Jeremy said.

"What's the occasion?" she asked. "This dress is gorgeous! And the necklace...Mr. Tudor, this is too much."

"Tonight I have the pleasure of being your escort," he said. "This will be your coming out party. You are making your debut tonight."

"Coming out party?"

"Tonight will announce to the city that there is a new player at the table, and there will be no doubt as to who that person is. You are raising the bar and challenging the status quo. You will be the one every escort will attempt to outdo."

"You can't be serious. That makes it sound so official."

"It is my dear. Temporarily, anyway. We are still playing the game, remember. Now, I must dress."

Jeremy hoped she would think about what he had just said. The way she looked tonight, she would leave an indelible mark on the world of high-class. She might even get away with the sass.

He had discovered he liked it.

When he joined her he gave her a kiss on the cheek.

"We cannot talk here," he said. "You do look ravishing, Miss Amanda."

"Why, thank you. You like that word ravishing don't you?"

"It has a certain ring to it, I think."

He opened the limo door and guided her in, then moved around, sitting beside her. He laid his hand on her leg and patted it gently. Not sure what she should do, Amanda rested her hand on his. She didn't know what would happen tonight, but her heart was pounding.

When they arrived at the restaurant a valet scurried over and Jeremy leaned toward her.

"Remember two things," he whispered. "If you are unsure about anything, defer to me. I am your gentleman caller. And, as I told you in Park City, if you need anything – ask."

Jeremy helped her out of the limo, and then winked as he kissed her hand, chuckling when she smiled. The most beautiful woman he had ever seen.

"Have you been here before?" she asked. Then she realized the absurdity of that question. He had been training escorts for fifteen years. Thirty to thirty-five girls he had said.

"A couple of times."

"Jeremy!" the maître d exclaimed, shaking Jeremy's hand vigorously. "It's good to see you again my friend. It has been a long time. And who is this exquisite creature?"

Amanda smiled noting the emphasis on every word of the last sentence.

"This is Amanda," Jeremy answered. "It is good to see you again, too."

"Amanda," the man repeated as he eyed her. "I expect we'll see a lot of Amanda. Why am I not surprised? Only the best ever graced your arm."

He hurried away and whispered instructions to the waiters as he pointed in her and Jeremy's direction. Then he rushed back and assured them they would be seated momentarily. They couldn't keep someone as important as Jeremy waiting. Amanda was amazed at how fast things were done when one was perceived as 'important'.

It was only two or three minutes and they were guided into a huge room filled with round tables draped in white linen, maroon squares accenting the tops. Lights were dimmed, giving it an air of elegance she had never seen before. Candles and single roses floated in glass bowls in the center of each setting. Waiters and waitresses were dressed in matching black silk slacks with white tops. Grey Brocade vests and thin black ties finished the look.

Other diners laughed stupidly, reminding her of a scene from one of those Hollywood movies, as they hugged furs and dripped with jewels. A thief's paradise if they could get in. She smiled hoping she didn't look like she was casing the joint.

"Are you alright, my lady?" Jeremy asked.

"Yes." She giggled and looked up at him. "Just doing a mental calculation on the haul if someone was to rob this place."

Jeremy smiled and his eyes danced and she was floating into warm blue pools. She looked away quickly, breaking the spell, still feeling the warmth of his hand on her back and thinking about his new name. Jeremy. She liked that name. Now, she wondered who the real Jeremy was.

"So, what is it you want to discuss? I know I'm scared half to death."

"There is no reason to be scared," Jeremy answered. "You just need to relax when in new situations and settings. And we need to discuss your current…circumstances, shall we call them. But first, let's enjoy an expensive meal on Mr. Bonner. Would you like me to order for you?"

"Yes, please," she answered with a sigh.

"Relax, my lady," he said. "Are you an adventurous eater? Do you like to try new things?"

"It depends upon those new things."

"We won't be quite so adventurous tonight then."

After he had ordered he pointed out the powder room and reminded her which utensils to use with what, and how to sip ones wine like a lady. Amanda rolled her eyes and watched his eyes dance, dropping her gaze quickly. Her breath caught for a second and she looked up to see him smiling across the table, her mind going back to that morning and the way he kissed.

The waiter returned and refilled their wine glasses, Amanda exhaling softly and hoping he hadn't noticed her reaction.

The meal was heavenly and they were waited on like royalty, and between courses and the waiter, she came to the conclusion Jeremy was meant to be the person who made all the decisions. This made her curious. She wanted to know about Jeremy before he started working with the escort services. He was good, but he didn't have the air of a servant.

"Jeremy, you are an enigma. One minute you're the stiff upper lip dude dressed in his Brocade vest and the next you're the perfect date. Who is the real Jeremy?"

"I have learned to separate work from pleasure. Most of the time."

"So, is tonight work or pleasure?"

"Tonight is definitely pleasure, my lady."

"What did you do before you started working with the escort services? You don't seem like a person who takes orders well. You are more like the person who should be giving the orders."

"I was at one time. But that was in another world a long time ago."

"Tell me about it, Jeremy." She leaned forward expectantly,

like a school girl getting ready to hear the biggest, baddest secret her best friend could ever tell her. "I want to know everything about you."

"No, you don't," he answered. "The less we know about each other, the easier the parting will be." 'That was laughable,' he thought as he glanced down and chastised himself quietly, hoping she hadn't noticed the move.

That last remark was curious to Amanda. She had never thought about how much more personal our lives become when we know more about the other. That was why divorce from a partner of twenty or thirty years was so much harder than leaving someone who had only shared five or ten years with you. The weave of the web became tighter with each passing year.

Once the meal was over, Jeremy pulled a card from his pocket and the waiter appeared, scurrying away and reappearing within seconds.

"Do you like to dance?"

"Why, yes!" she answered, her eyes lighting up.

"Waltz, two-step, fox trot?"

"I have no clue. I just try to follow my partners lead."

"Music?" he continued. "Country, rock, jazz, blue grass, blues, Lawrence Welk?"

"Oh, most definitely jazz or blues. But don't expect me to stay quiet."

"Really? I think I know the perfect place."

The limo stopped in front of the club and Jeremy leaned forward, speaking quietly to the driver, then he slid the partition closed. After Amanda was safely out of the limo, the driver sped away.

Amanda discovered Jeremy was well known here as well. He even had his own table next to the dance floor.

"You must have some clout!"

"I just call ahead and make reservations."

"And they magically know your name and which table is yours the minute you walk in. I didn't hear you tell anyone you had a reservation at either establishment. I think you're fibbing."

"You might be right. Just continue to trust me and follow my lead. We must make Mr. Bonner think you are being a good girl, okay?"

She nodded, even more curious now.

Part way through the evening they announced amateur night for anyone interested. Jeremy raised his and the emcee moved to their table, Jeremy pointed to Amanda. The emcee raised an eyebrow then Amanda took the microphone and walked on stage. Her jitters quickly faded and she was in her world. A few notes and the audience were believers, moving with the rhythm, some of them even singing along. This was what every singer wanted, acknowledgement and acceptance, and Amanda quickly got lost in the performance.

"So, what else did you want to talk about?" she asked once she'd returned to the table. "And what does our evening out have to do with my new profession?"

"Tonight is exactly what you were being trained to do. You are a super expensive date, with lots of outdated manners and a few added benefits. But now, with us leaving, we have to play the game from a different angle. I told you, I will get you out of here, but you have to help me. No more fighting, no more arguing. Do you understand?"

"Anything! I know you said you would help, but it's so hard to know who to trust."

"That I understand," he said. "I am looking at pulling you out of here Monday evening. That's only three days."

"Jeremy, you work out the details and I'll do whatever you think is best."

They were returning from another spin on the dance floor

when Jeremy did his usual scan of the room, noticing two men eyeing them closely. Jeremy paused and raised her hand, presenting her one more time, allowing him to get a better view, instantly recognizing James and William. They had their back-up.

Amanda took a quick gulp of air and clutched Jeremy's arm tighter when he seated her, staring wide-eyed, the question plain, and Jeremy nodded. She covered her mouth, her hands trembling. She was really going home!

"We need to talk to them, my lady," Jeremy whispered. "Can you arrange that?"

She bobbed her head a little too quickly and smiled.

Right on cue a waiter brought them a drink – courtesy of the gentlemen at the table in front of the stage – and the emcee invited her to sing one more song. She walked on stage and asked if they knew a specific song, a song she could perform while mixing and mingling with the audience.

As the band and the singers started their intro, Amanda made her way off stage. She arrived with Jeremy so she started with Jeremy, working her way through the audience to the table with William and James. Deciding to pick on James first, she noticed him wince and the brace, raising an eyebrow, he shrugged. She smiled, playing with his hair before leaning over and kissing him gently then winking at William. She sat on William's lap, and laid her head on his, keeping the microphone far enough away it didn't pick up her voice.

"Jeremy wants to talk. Follow us when we leave."

William kissed her, doing an exaggerated dip as he bent her over his lap. Amanda blushed and the audience erupted with laughter.

53

James eyes followed Jeremy and Amanda as they danced and he thought about the information they had been given through the taskforce. Jeremy was the best escort trainer out there. Jeremy had even admitted he was a trainer. Plus he had said he was training Amanda, but they had been introduced to Jeremy as a member of law enforcement. So, who was the real Jeremy?

"Makes you curious, doesn't it?" William asked, reading James mind.

"Yep. The best trainer the escort business has, and he works for law enforcement. There is definitely more to him than meets the eye. Only had a couple of girls in fifteen years he deemed inappropriate for what they were trying to train them for. What would it be like to have a job like that?"

"I thought he said he's been under for years, but he doesn't have a handler. He works on his own. Unless his handler is this 'Commander' he talked about."

James shrugged and continued watching them thoughtfully.

"He's introducing Amanda," James said. "This is her debut. Her introduction to gentlemen who are looking for only the best.

He has got to be cutting this one close to the wire. To go this far and then pull her, if he screws this up, he could get shot."

"I hope he knows what he's doing," William said. "Maybe I should introduce myself."

"Maybe. It might be considered a little country roadhouse chic, but it might get you a dance. We are just playing." James nudged William under the table and laughed. "They're returning to their table."

William scanned the room and attempted to gauge if someone was watching them. From all the information they had been given, the possibility was there George, or the syndicate, would have someone on her and Jeremy. That made him nervous. He wanted to grab Amanda and run, but they had to do it safely. And they had to grab George.

"Good evening," William said. "The name's William. William Harrison."

"Please, sit down." Jeremy shook William's hand and nodded to the chair beside Amanda. "We don't stand on formalities."

"Thank you." William felt uneasy all of a sudden. "My friend and I are visiting and thought we'd stop for a minute or two. I love jazz and blues so this was the logical place." He scanned the room once again, bringing his gaze back to the table with James, waving for him to join them. His sweep had only garnered views of men ogling Amanda. Any of them could be the mole.

Amanda ran her hand softly up the inside of William's leg. She then removed it and sat back so the men could talk. That was what ladies did, she had learned.

'If she does that again, we will be finding a motel,' William thought. Then he returned the gesture, hearing Amanda's breath catch. 'Touché!'

Jeremy noticed the exchange and chuckled softly.

Between visits from the cocktail waitress, they learned more about Jeremy's plan to pull Amanda out. He also noticed Jeremy was very guarded about what he said and how he said it. He also didn't go into great detail.

"Amanda said to follow you when you leave," William said.

"Perhaps you and the lady would care to dance," Jeremy said. He nodded in the direction of the dance floor and his eyes did another quick scan of the club. "We will talk more later."

"I would love to," William answered. Jeremy was obviously changing the course of that conversation.

They returned to the table and Jeremy whispered something to Amanda. When the next slow dance began she walked over to James. James hesitated, but she smiled and helped him to stand.

"We are being watched," Jeremy told William. "Nothing more will be said here."

William took another drink, dipping his chin to acknowledge Jeremy's statement. Another skim of the faces, noting the security personnel and one police officer exiting the side door, but no one stood out.

James and Amanda returned and Jeremy suggested an all night diner where they could get a booth and nobody would listen in on their conversation. With everyone in agreement Jeremy had the club call a taxi.

By the time they arrived at the restaurant, William had noticed, Jeremy only nudged Amanda's arm to guide her in any direction he desired for her to go. He helped her in and out of the taxi, the seat in the restaurant and he poured her coffee, ordered for her, and was generally overly attentive.

"Is this normal?" William asked when Jeremy left the table. "I mean you don't have to do much of anything."

"Basically," she answered. "It's not a bad life if you don't mind strange men pawing you. It's kind of like strangers setting your dates up for you. Except for the added benefits."

William blinked, surprised and leaned back.

"We haven't made it that far. So you don't have to worry. Everyone is still alive and no murder charges have been filed."

"However, if Miss Amanda stays here much longer that may happen," Jeremy said, overhearing them when he returned. "She is a very stubborn young woman."

"That is something I already know," William said, "So, other than what we have already discussed is there anything we need to be aware of?"

"Once we are out of here, my plans are to take her back to my retreat in Utah," Jeremy explained. "There, she will be safe until after Mr. Bonner's trial. I also have copies of a few tapes from her time with George. I thought they would help with your case against him. I had them sent to me at the compound so you can take them with you tonight if you wish."

"Is one of them the one you left at the condo?"

"No, sir," Jeremy answered. "One of them is the precursor to that. It is a tape of him attempting to accost her in the dressing room. The one I left was only a small portion of that afternoon's entertainment. It is not a pretty scene, but Miss Amanda is a fighter so he wasn't successful." Jeremy continued, explaining about her being punched by the guard and her encounter with a few prospective johns, along with Royce. "Those were all before I started training her," Jeremy finished, "but Mr. Bonner should be in prison. I have agreed not to testify against George, if he goes to trial, so I thought I would provide your department with the tapes."

"Amanda," James said, "we noticed in the last room he had you in there was a large imprint in the wall. Is that the one Jeremy is talking about?"

"Yes," she answered.

William remembered the indentation in the wall and looked away. He had hoped that hadn't been from her. Now that he knew different he could feel the anger, but he had to control it.

She then explained that hitting George with the butt of a pistol had initiated that incident, and she continued telling them about working trades with several of the johns.

"Damn! I'm proud of you girl!" James said.

Jeremy's pager beeped and he looked down at the screen.

"Excuse me, please. I need to use the phone."

They watched Jeremy walk away and William turned back to Amanda. "How are you holding up?"

"Much better," she answered. "You don't know how good it is to see you guys."

William gave her a kiss and pulled her close. "No, but I know how good it feels to see you."

When Jeremy rejoined them he looked confused.

"We seem to have a bit of a problem," he said. "Police are at the compound. Mr. Bonner says the power is out, as well, but we aren't sure why the officer's are there. We don't know if it was a break in or vandalism. It could be the owner of a rival stable warning Mr. Bonner. If that is the case, they are letting him know they are not happy with you for disrupting their business. It is already out on the grapevine, you are the premier lady in Nevada. That will justify the three hundred dollars an hour he is asking for your services." Jeremy stopped hearing William choke. "Are you alright, sir?"

William nodded, swallowing hard.

"You should probably arrive a few minutes after we do," Jeremy continued

"We can do that. Thanks to you, Reno knows we're here," James said, laughing at William's expression.

"That will work fine, then. Mr. Bonner was supposed to pay us a visit Tuesday, it may be sooner now, but Amanda and I need to get back to the compound."

"You didn't tell me he was coming," she said. "Why didn't

you tell me?"

"And ruin a perfectly good date?" Jeremy waved for the waitress, and paid the bill then asked her to call a taxi for them.

While they waited, Jeremy pulled out his pager and keyed in a message then slid it back onto its case. A taxi drove up, Jeremy gave the driver the address and they were gone.

"I think George Bonner will be behind bars for many, many years," James said, watching the cab drive away.

"Makes me feel a whole lot better knowing he's with her," William said. "Three hundred bucks an hour? We might be in the wrong business."

James laughed again. "I don't think Amanda would agree."

It took twenty minutes for the taxi carrying Jeremy and Amanda to pull up to the scene. Jeremy was then given the short version of the events. Neighbors called in a disturbance at this address and told them there had been a power outage. Officers arrived and found no one on the premises. No guards, no lights, nothing.

William and James pulled up, Amanda looked beyond them as they approached, noticing an officer in uniform with a cast on his right hand. They locked eyes and he nodded and walked away, fading into the crowd. David. Why was David here? Why was David wearing a police uniform?

54

After they'd talked to the officers, Jeremy escorted Amanda onto the grounds, opening a locked panel on the pool house where he flipped one of two switches. The second switch reactivated the cameras and George didn't need to know the officers from Utah were here. Then he did a visual inventory.

Light flooded the grounds and the interior of the house and Amanda gasped. It was breathtaking. The privilege of money was on full display for all to see. Jeremy led Amanda into the house then returned to allow William and James entrance and let the officers from Reno know nothing was missing.

"Miss Amanda is changing out of her evening attire. She will join us shortly," Jeremy told them.

"I notice the compound is entirely walled," James said, his gaze following the perimeter looking for cameras. He knew they would be here. This type of a set up was always monitored.

"Yes, sir," Jeremy replied. "We are very concerned about the privacy and security of the lady of the house. Especially since most people do not understand the difference between an escort and a hooker. If you will excuse me. I will retrieve Amanda."

Jeremy returned, Amanda bouncing excitedly beside him. He leaned and whispered in her ear, to which she glanced around the room at several locations the men assumed held cameras. Jeremy smiled and shook his head, and all decorum vanished as she hurtled towards the men, hugging and kissing them excitedly.

Jeremy turned, directing them down a hall.

"Shall we?" he asked. "Would anyone care for coffee? I have some ready."

"Yes, thank you," James said.

"This is one hell of a house," William said. He gazed around the room as they emerged from the hall and thought about the cost to maintain a set up like this. George definitely had more money than the department was aware of. "Is this set up specifically for this type of business?"

"Not really," Jeremy answered. He had returned, handing them each a cup. "It is designed for entertaining. People who do more parties than intimate entertaining would have a larger dining area and a much larger dance floor."

"I see you're armed. How far would you go to keep Amanda safe?"

"My life is not as dear as hers. That is part of my job. That is why I get paid the amount of money I do. Had I been aware of what Mr. Bonner was capable of, I would not have left her alone in Park City."

The power came back on and Jeremy rushed to unhook the cameras, and call George to let him know all had been brought back on line, except the security system. As soon as the police left, he would bring the cameras back up. Jeremy hung up, removing a box from the locked drawer in his nightstand and returned to the group, giving it to William.

"These are the tapes I mentioned earlier. I will warn you again, they are not pretty, but I think you will be proud of her. Now, how do you gentlemen want to handle the rest of this? I can keep her here, or I can play like there are still issues with the system. Obviously, if she is here it will be easier to grab George."

"Which is going to be the safest for Amanda?" William asked.

"Why would it make a difference if I'm here?" Amanda asked. She glanced between the men unsure of this now.

"With you here Mr. Bonner will have no idea what we have planned," Jeremy answered. "If you leave tonight and I have to maintain the system in a down situation he will start asking questions. We do not want him showing up unexpectedly. We want everything set so we can bring Mr. Bonner to justice with the least amount of surprises. As things set, he may come this way early anyway."

"I want to see George arrested, too. I would really like to see him dead."

"Those are strong words, Miss Amanda. You may want to rethink what you wish for."

"I can't take that back after what he's done to me, and whoever else. I know I'm not the only one."

"I do understand," Jeremy said. "Now you have a decision to make. Do you want to stay here, or leave with the gentlemen?"

"I need to know how you're really doing, Amanda," William said, thinking about Julie. Murdered to save George. "You've been through more hell than I could imagine. Like Jeremy said, though, we want George behind bars for the rest of his life."

Amanda shrugged and stared at the floor. She looked up and glanced between the three men then looked back at the floor and sighed. This was hard. She didn't want George behind bars. She wanted the man dead. How could she explain that to them?

"Why don't we get some rest and talk in the morning?" Jeremy said. "I believe this should be left up to her and we aren't getting anywhere now. I promise to contact you as soon as she has made her decision."

Amanda nodded and William and James gave her a kiss on the forehead before leaving. It was her game now. Jeremy made sure the cameras were working, then refilled their cups and sat down across from her.

"We need to have a serious discussion in the morning," Jeremy told her. "If you decide you don't want to wait for Mr. Bonner, I'll call William and have him pick you up. But you need to make that decision before noon." He checked his watch. "Our scheduled departure is day after tomorrow now."

Jeremy's pager vibrated and he pulled it out. The guards were safe and in custody, but they had been on the syndicate's payroll. That explained why they had not been killed when the syndicate attempted to take Amanda, and how the men had known about the safe room. Tonight had been planned to make them vulnerable. He needed to be more aware of their surroundings for a short time.

"What will you do, Jeremy? How will you handle George?"

"I won't be here, either," he answered. "But as long as you are still in this house, George will show up. I hate doing that, but you are the perfect bait. Now, let us sleep on it and we'll talk in the morning. Cameras are up and watching us once again."

"In that case," she said, "I'll see you in the morning." She flipped the camera a bird then bounded down the hall.

Jeremy shook his head. If they weren't so close to getting her out of here, she would definitely get them in trouble.

55

Voices in the private space woke Jeremy. Even without guards, no one should have gotten in. Not without it sounding an alarm. Suddenly alert, he wondered if it was Amanda and jumped out of bed and slipped on his clothes, moving silently to the door. The buzzer in her room sounded followed by the one for the safe room. Grabbing his pistol Jeremy peeked around the doorframe, footsteps moving away from him toward the entertainment wing. Creeping to Amanda's room, she was gone. He picked her clothing up off the settee, entering the safe room from the private area. He handed Amanda her clothes and raised a finger to signal for quiet. She dressed quickly and awaited further instructions while he listened for further sound.

"Did they see you?" he whispered.

"I don't think so," she answered.

"Stay here."

Jeremy opened the door and glided down the hall into the entertainment wing, following the men outside where they squeezed between the gates, climbing into a waiting pickup. Jeremy slipped into the shadows by the wall and pulled out his pager, keying in the license number while the truck sped away. Once it had disappeared he went back inside and instructed Amanda to grab an extra set of clothes then he went to his room.

He pulled up the security screen and saw where they had disabled the alarm. Easily done if one knew enough about these set-ups, and the former guards knew the system almost as well he did. He grabbed his back-up pistol, strapped his shoulder holster on and slipped his pistol into it, grabbed the extra magazine for each weapon and a box of ammo then put everything into a backpack. If whoever had been here was playing hardball he had to be able to retaliate in kind.

Stopping at the closet, he grabbed two t-shirts and a pair of jeans and stuffed them into the pack with the ammo and the pistol, set the cameras to back-up then hurried to the kitchen. Jeremy opened one of the drawers, took the contents out then lifted the bottom, revealing a large amount of cash. He removed the money, replaced everything in the drawer and returned to Amanda's room. This wasn't how he had planned to get her out of here, but they were leaving.

"Are you ready?" Jeremy asked.

"Yes," Amanda answered. No instructions had been given; she simply shrugged on a windbreaker and waited.

Jeremy pulled his back-up pistol and the extra magazine out and handed it to Amanda then folded her clothes into the pack. She slid the pistol under her belt, dropping the magazine in her pocket, and they moved carefully through the darkened house, Jeremy checking that Amanda was keeping up.

At the main entrance he peered cautiously outside before leading her toward the rear of the property, following the wall until they reached the pool house. One more check for unwelcome guests and he took out a flashlight, giving it to Amanda then pushed her ahead of him into the narrow space between the pool house and the wall.

When they reached the corner Jeremy pointed out the dimples between stones and climbed to the top, surveying the area once more. Satisfied it was clear; he helped Amanda scale the wall then dropped silently onto the opposite side, steadying her as she slid down. They were standing on a steep hill above a narrow road. Jeremy continued to guide her, helping her navigate the slope to the street then led her to the convenience store, hiding her in the shadows then he walked quickly to the payphones at the front of the building.

William picked up on the third ring, his voice groggy from sleep.

"Lucy is moving," Jeremy said.

He hung up, slung the pack over his shoulder and noticed a truck parked forty feet back from the corner, three men crowding the bench seat. It looked like the truck that had driven away from the compound. He drifted around the corner of the store and the truck moved closer, stopping before it reached the intersection. Jeremy walked to the rear of the building, taking Amanda by the hand and started up the street.

"Are you doing okay?"

"Yes," she said. She held his hand firmly with both of hers keeping in stride. "I trust you completely. Are you okay?"

He exhaled slowly, realizing he wasn't. She picked up on everything. "I am glad you have chosen to trust me. I am just not sure that we are in the clear. Once we pick up the vehicle, we will be on our way. I called William to let them know things have changed. Scared?"

"A little bit, but I know you'll take care of me."

They turned a lazy corner and Amanda slowed, pulling Jeremy toward her.

"Is there something wrong?"

"I thought I heard footsteps," she answered. "Behind us, to our right."

"I heard it, too, madam. Just stay with me, okay?"

Amanda grasped his hand tighter, taking a surreptitious look to her right.

Jeremy noticed her move and pulled her closer, putting his arm around her shoulder.

"I saw them," he whispered. "See that tree about forty feet to your right...."

"Someone's behind it," she said. "There's another man on the street behind us and a truck following him."

"You're very good at this." He caught himself admiring her.

Amanda raised a finger to her lips and did a tentative nod to her right and saw the dip of his chin.

Forty yards ahead an old garage loomed out of the darkness. The hushed crunch of dead grass could still be heard behind them and Amanda tugged on his sleeve, nodding to her right again. Jeremy raised an eyebrow and she winked, the move barely noticeable under the street light.

"Just act like you're disgusted," she whispered.

On the far side of the building, Amanda peeled off to her right, Jeremy throwing his hands up in mock disdain as she slipped into the shadows, Jeremy acting like he was trying to keep up. Footsteps approached on the asphalt, a second set at the rear of the building.

Amanda crept around the back corner of the rickety old structure, holding her breath. Exhaling slowly, she made out the figure creeping behind the building moving lightly on the balls of his feet. She dropped silently to her knees and pulled the pistol out of her waistband, waiting for him to pass. He was still six feet from the corner, but if he reached it, Jeremy would be wide open. She raised the weapon, sighting down the barrel and waited another second. The instant he poked his head around the back of the garage his hands swung up, the silhouette of a gun gripped firmly in them, and Amanda pulled the trigger.

There was a distinctive 'thub' of the silencer and his body twisted, falling as he turned. She bolted forward, sliding her gun into her waist once more and took his gun then raced toward the street. Amanda emerged from the shadows, and the truck did a nosedive, its brakes screeching when the driver hit them and lifted his weapon. Amanda stopped, raised the other man's pistol and fired through the rolled down passenger window. The driver looked surprised and a dark dot appeared on his forward, blood running into his eyes as the truck careened across the road its nose falling into a ditch. She glided toward Jeremy as noiselessly as a ghost and peered around the corner; the man staring straight at her. He had taken his eyes off Jeremy when he heard the commotion.

Jeremy caught a glimpse of movement when the man darted off the street in his direction; a low rumble could be heard from the truck as it drew closer then tires screeched. Watching the man in his periphery the man braced and lifted his pistol then jerked his head to his right. Jeremy was holding his pistol against his thigh and twisted to his right, lifted the nose an inch and pulled the trigger. At this distance that 's all he needed for the perfect body shot. The man dropped then Amanda raced around the front of the building.

"What are you doing out there?" Jeremy asked.

"Sorry," she answered. She was talking breathlessly, nervous. "I nailed the dude behind the garage and the driver of the truck wanted to play target practice. I didn't give him a chance."

Jeremy surveyed the street to verify they had no further tails then they dragged the men across the street, rolling them into the ditch in front of the truck.

A hundred yards farther north sat another dilapidated garage. Fifty yards before they reached it Jeremy pushed her behind a tall row of shrubs, out of view of anyone on the streets and led her to the back of that building. He unlocked a side door revealing an older Toyota Land Cruiser. Once he'd closed the door and flipped on the lights he moved to the rear of the vehicle and tossed the backpack in.

"If I remember, you used to go hunting with your father," he said, lifting the seat on an old bench. "That means you know how to handle a rifle."

"Kind of."

"I think you're fibbing. The way you handle that pistol says more than 'kind of'. Your father taught you well. There's a sleeve between the seat on the passenger side and the center hump, slide this in it. Here are a couple of extra magazines."

Amanda smiled and stowed the rifle and ammo. Jeremy did the same on his side and grabbed two sleeping bags, tossing them into saddlebags in the back of the vehicle then he motioned for her to climb in.

"Let's go. Feel good to get out of there?"

"Yes."

Jeremy turned the key in the ignition and the engine roared to life, and Amanda smiled again. It might not look like much, but it sounded like it wanted to run. He pushed a button on the dash, the garage doors swinging open. Amanda glanced behind them as the rickety old doors closed. Another chapter in her life gone. One she didn't want to repeat.

"I know how to use a compass, too," Amanda said. She closed her eyes and leaned back in the seat. "In case you need to know."

"Miss Amanda, you really are the perfect woman."

"I doubt that. I just hate shopping, playing dress up, and going to tea parties. We're heading south now, aren't we?"

"As I said. The perfect woman."

56

Jeremy and Amanda were quiet as they sped east, turning off the interstate onto Highway 50. She had opened her eyes and was gazing into the darkness beyond the headlights. The moon was hanging high in the sky, the barren hills like silent sentinels in the distance. The ground was a ghostly gray as she tried to discern sand from sagebrush, but only found darker patches of gray to distinguish between the two. An occasional flash of moonlight reflected off the shards of glass sparkling on the roadside. Every now and then a hulk, like some primordial entity, loomed off the desert floor, revealing itself as a rusted out truck body. Joshua Trees poked up every few miles as well.

She tilted her head back and let the wind blow through her hair. She had no idea what was happening and she didn't care. As long as she wasn't in some mans stable. It felt good. She felt free for the first time in weeks. She only hoped this wasn't a dream. She didn't ever want to wake up back where she had been.

"How much longer before we get to where we're going?"

"About six hours. Getting tired?"

"A little. Are you okay? You're driving."

"I should be fine. I promise to pull off if I need to."

Jeremy was keenly aware that, once George discovered she was missing, they would only have a short respite, if any. With the guard's disappearance, George may have already started toward Reno not knowing Amanda wasn't there. Either way, Jeremy was taking her to his private retreat outside of Cedar City, and Delta would be a nice convenience stop. He needed some rest and she could use more than she had been allowed, but Cedar City and the relative safety of his retreat was only a couple of hours from there. They would be fine with something to eat.

Amanda awoke as Jeremy pulled the vehicle off the highway onto a side road, scanning the horizon and saw the sun up and bright. She looked at the dash clock and it read seven a.m.

"How much farther?" she asked.

"About three hours," he answered. "Can you drive a stick?"

"Like I'm part of it."

She wound her hair into a make shift pony tail and exchanged places with Jeremy, then dropped the Land Cruiser into gear and continued east toward Utah.

The slowing of the Land Cruiser woke Jeremy and he glanced around familiarizing himself with where they were. They had reached Delta.

"Hungry?" Jeremy asked.

"Famished," Amanda replied.

"Good, pull in up here and we'll grab some breakfast."

They decided to forego the comfort of a booth for one of the tables, but it still didn't take long for Jeremy to realize how tired he was, even after his short nap. They ordered and he watched Amanda across the table. Things were weighing on her, too. She was strong, but she was human.

"Feeling better?" he asked after they'd eaten.

"Yes," she said wearily. "But I guess I'm more exhausted than I thought. This body doesn't want to move."

"Me too, but we need to go. If Mr. Bonner is looking for us his men will be getting close."

Jeremy pulled out onto the highway, heading west. There was a small road a mile or two outside of town. He didn't want to use the interstate in case George's men were looking for them. He turned off the highway and checked the rear view mirror for any sign they were being tailed. The road looked clear and he stopped and put the canvas top up. The least this vehicle resembled the one that had just left Delta, the better.

They pulled through the gates of Jeremy's retreat just before eleven.

"Jeremy, you have excellent taste. This is beautiful," Amanda said. "I'm amazed someone hasn't snatched you up already."

"I would have thought you figured that out already. Or, are you saying that because I have impeccable taste in clothing? Well, maybe because I'm an excellent cook." There was a slight frown and he smiled. "Thank you, my lady."

He left Amanda on the porch, and took the backpack out of the Land Cruiser, pulling it into the garage and backing a car into the driveway. Then they went inside and he called William.

"Lucy is delivered," Jeremy said.

"Any problems?" William asked.

Jeremy thought about the men they had left in Reno and quickly dismissed them. "No, sir. All went smooth. We're going to get some rest now."

Jeremy then led Amanda down the hall showing her, her room.

"This is a full guest suite," he told her. "You will have plenty of privacy here."

"Thank you again, Jeremy," Amanda said. "I don't know what I would have done."

"That is part of my job and you helped immensely. Now, I don't know about you, but I am exhausted."

"Can I ask a favor?"

"Of course. If I can, I will."

"Can we cuddle?"

She didn't know why, but today she was the little girl who needed someone to hold her. She wasn't a little girl anymore, but she still needed hugs.

"We can cuddle," he answered.

Jeremy had to admit sometimes he needed cuddles, too. Men weren't supposed to, though, were they? Lying down beside her he was content to hold her. She had been through so much, but she kept powering through. He pulled the bedspread up to cover them, her soft breathing telling him she had fallen asleep.

"Sweet dreams, my lady," he whispered, then he passed out beside her.

57

Since plans had changed, William and James drove by the compound. Jeremy and Amanda were gone, but they needed to find a safe place to hide while they waited for George. Jeremy had stressed the location of a safe room and it sounded perfect. Jeremy had given them the security code so William parked facing the gate and keyed it in rolling the heavy metal entrance open. He automatically raised his eyes scanning the area and following the perimeter of the wall, spotting the cameras.

"Pull it in," he called as he raced for the house.

He ran to Jeremy's room, unplugging the system and yanking the tape out of the deck. The last thing they needed was George recognizing them. He joined James and they did a walk through, stopping outside the safe room. They pressed the nail, the door popped open and inspected the walk-in closet size space; this would be the best place. They could come back tonight to insure they were in position, and George wouldn't even know they were here.

When they arrived back at their hotel the message light was blinking. William called the front desk and was told Captain

Ohlmet from Salt Lake City, Utah had attempted to contact them. They returned the captain's call and learned they were being ordered back to Salt Lake City. They had been reinstated and were back on duty effective immediately. The department found their leak and, with Captain Jakes blackmail tape, all charges had been dropped.

The evidence recovered during the search of the bar, and at George's apartment, gave the department everything it needed to obtain the warrant for George's arrest for sales and distribution, prostitution, the murder of Julie Barron, plus it tied him to the previous murders. Captain Ohlmet wanted them in town before the department moved, they needed the tapes Jeremy had given them to bolster those charges. Captain Ohlmet thought they would like to be there for the party, too. He had their tuxes waiting. Everybody was meeting at the station at o seven hundred tomorrow morning. He was rolling on this one, as well.

They threw their clothes into their bags and checked out, anxious to arrest George. The only loose end remaining was Royce. The department was still actively looking for him, but so far had had no luck locating him. Royce's time in the jungle had taught him how to go to ground and stay low.

Six o'clock the next morning they were at the station eager to get this over with. They wanted George behind bars and were happy to be back at work. When they arrived, Captain Ohlmet waved them into his office.

"William, James," he said. "I need to talk to you guys. Let me call the chief and Captain Kirby in."

"No problem," William answered.

The captain was already on the phone. He hadn't waited for their reply.

Captain Kirby walked in followed by Assistant Chief Robinson. William and James glanced into the hall, confused, looking for Chief Vanders then recognized the four star insignia of the Police Chief on Assistant Chief Robinson's uniform.

"It's alright," Chief Robinson said. "There's a lot you're not aware of."

"So…." William said, hesitantly. "What happened to Chief Vanders?"

"Vanders retired," Chief Robinson answered.

William started to say something and Captain Ohlmet dropped his head and shook it. William remembered the department had found their insider, but he didn't want to believe it had been the chief.

"Let's just say Vander's no longer had the best interests of the department in mind," Chief Robinson said. "No more will be said. Do you understand?"

Both men nodded, understanding the warning.

"Good. Captain Ohlmet. I believe the rest of this is your baby."

"Men," Captain Ohlmet said. "First, I want to apologize for some of my actions. At the time they seemed necessary, in hindsight I feel like I left you hanging in the wind. That was not my intentions."

William and James nodded.

"Have you two thought about applying for a detective slot?"

"No, sir," William said.

"Well, it's not all desk duty so start thinking about it. We want you and James to stay on these taskforces. You can't do that out of a black and white. It seems you also have a couple of fans in the form of Lloyd Farmer and Captain Kirby. Kirby here has already approached me. He thinks you're too good to put back in a squad. You're two of my best men and I hate to lose you, but Chief Robinson and I think he's right. Report to the detective bureau first thing Monday morning. Captain Kirby is expecting you at eight a.m. On the flip side of that coin," he said, his voicing softening, "I'm going to miss working with you guys. Now get out of here. Have a great day."

"I thought you were rolling with us?" James said.

"Changed my mind. Have fun and congratulations."

They pulled up to George's as a limo sped north toward town immediately thinking they'd missed him. One of the SWAT teams reported over the radio that George was still onsite. William and James jumped out of their squad, surveying the surrounding area. Two other members of the SWAT team were in position on the fire escape. One of them back handed his partner in the chest and pointed inside. When they rushed the security desk one of George's guards made a run for it.

"POLICE!" three voices yelled in unison. "FREEZE!"

An officer stood in front of him, arms braced, weapon ready.

The guard stopped and held his hands where they could be seen.

William patted the man down then moved to the second man and once he had been cuffed William patted the third man down, cuffing him to one of the drawers on the desk, reading the men their rights.

"You get to answer the phones, my man," William told the man at the desk. "Now, who left in that limo?"

"I don't know," the guy answered. "He didn't give me his name and I didn't ask. There were two men here when we got here. An old dude and two other men got off the elevator and left in the limo."

"Isn't this desk normally manned twenty-four hours a day?" William asked. "Where are the night men? Were the two men who left with the old dude the night guards?"

"No, sir," the guard answered. "The night crew wasn't here when we got here this morning."

William grabbed one of the other men and started outside. It was time to call their bluff.

"You and I, we're going to go out here and have a little

discussion. See, out here nobody can hear us."

"You can't do shit," the man said, as he laughed.

"I can do whatever I want to," William answered. "It's going to be your word against mine. Besides, technically, I'm not a patrolman anymore. Now you can answer my questions or I get to have some fun on my last day in this uniform."

They started out the door and the phone rang. James smacked the man at the desk on the shoulder and told him to answer the phone. He hesitated and James put it on speaker, holding his weapon where the man could see it.

"My last day in this uniform, too," James whispered.

It was George asking about the security team from the night shift.

After George hung up, James unhooked the cuffs from the desk, locking them behind the man's back and handing the three off to patrolmen with instructions to take them to the station and make sure they were comfortable, laughing at the last part. He ordered another team of officers to search the area for possible bodies. There were two, maybe three, men unaccounted for. They called for back up to aid in the search then posted two men at the desk. Four members of the SWAT team accompanied William and James upstairs; the remaining officers beginning a floor by floor search.

Outside George's apartment William and James stationed themselves on either side of the door, a member of the SWAT team behind each of them and two farther down the hall. Receiving the go ahead from James, William pounded on the door.

"POLICE! OPEN UP!"

The chain lock slid out of its slot and the deadbolt disengaged, George stepping back as the door opened allowing them entry. William took point, cuffing George and reading him his rights.

For once, William allowed himself to gloat and nodded with a smile and a salute as they led George outside. 'Now who's won,' he thought as George was taken away.

William gave the rest of the men their instructions then he and James continued inside, moving to the room the SWAT team had pointed to. They closed their eyes and turned away at the sight of the girl's body, William calling for techs.

After completing the search of George's apartment, they took turns hammering away at George and his thugs. George refused to answer any questions about the girl, except to say she was already dead when he was awakened by a man he had never met.

An hour into the interrogations, they received word the night shift guards had been found in a dumpster a half a mile south of George's building. Single shot to the back of the head. Execution style.

"Well, even without George's cooperation, it has been a good day," William said, watching James over the roof of his car. "He will be behind bars for a very long time and Amanda is safe."

58

The aroma of coffee and breakfast beckoned Amanda. 'Some things should never change,' she thought as she padded up the hall. Jeremy stood in the kitchen, but there was no Brocade vest. A simple long sleeve t-shirt was molded to his torso, a pair of blue jeans hugged his hips. As if sensing she was there, he turned and smiled.

"Good morning. How did you sleep?"

"Wonderfully."

She sat at the breakfast bar and took the offered coffee gratefully. He made the best coffee!

"What are the plans for today?"

He walked around and sat on the stool next to her. "I thought you might like to relax for a change and I need to run into town."

"As usual, you are right," she said.

"You should be fine for a while. Just make yourself comfortable. And we do have television."

"Perfect," she replied.

When they finished their meal, Jeremy picked up his keys and grabbed a windbreaker, then gave her a kiss and walked out.

Closing the door behind him, Jeremy laughed, realizing what he had just done.

Amanda showered and dressed then got comfortable on the sofa and turned the television on. She skimmed through the channels, one of the local news broadcasts catching her attention.

A Mr. George Bonner of Salt Lake City, Utah was under arrest and being charged with the murder of Julie Barron-Warden along with numerous other charges, including the abduction and attempted rape of Amanda Granger.

It continued detailing the charges for prostitution, sales and distribution of a controlled substance and the murders of the girl found in Liberty Park and the woman at Silver Lake, along with several murders from two years prior, a body that had been dumped behind a fast food joint on State Street, and a hooker whose body had been discovered in his apartment.

Amanda gaped as she listened. Her mind racing in circles. After all she'd gone through it had been relegated to a three minute spiel on one of the local news broadcasts. But he was under arrest. George had been caught. And she wanted to know about Julie. Why would George kill Julie? She wanted to know how long before she went home.

Then she thought about Jeremy. His calm demeanor and easy smile had become her new normal.

"Jeremy!" she said under her breath.

Jeremy overheard two men talking while he was at the grocery store. He needed to call William. He wanted to make sure George really had been arrested. The conversation he heard said George had been arrested in Salt Lake City not Reno. Jeremy dropped the coins in the phone, reflecting on what he would do after this was over. Amanda's wide open honesty had become his new normal. He was going to miss her terribly. He was amazed at how much it hurt. And they had only spent one night together.

William answered on the second ring, all business and Jeremy noticed the use of 'Detective' not 'Officer'. He realized he was going to miss working with the men as well. What an intricate web we weave.

"George has been arrested," William answered when Jeremy asked. "Captain Ohlmet called the hotel and left a message pulling us back to Salt Lake City. When we got here, they already had everything set. The judge set bail at one million dollars, but George was out by noon. If you don't mind, I think we'll all feel safer if you keep Amanda with you for a while."

"No problem," Jeremy replied.

"How is Amanda?" William asked. "I know she's a tough little lady, but this whole ordeal must be wearing on her."

"She is an extraordinary lady, but she has her moments. I think the not knowing is probably the hardest for her."

"I understand. We appreciate all you've done for her." William hesitated, staring across the desk at James. "I have a question for you."

"Go ahead."

"We were told the department found their insider."

"Yes, sir."

"How much do you know? We came in yesterday and were told Chief Vanders retired and Assistant Chief Robinson is the new chief."

"That is correct, sir," Jeremy answered. He paused, debating how much he should reveal. "There is nothing out there to explain exactly what transpired. The latest information says Chief of Police Luther Vanders retired, voluntarily forfeiting his retirement package, and Assistant Chief Anthony Robinson was appointed as his replacement. Obviously there was some legal maneuvering, but I will let you know if I learn more. I feel I owe you that much. My Commander is also sending you a token of his appreciation in the form of compensation. His way of saying 'Thank You' for all your help."

"Thank you, Jeremy. We appreciate that."

After he hung up, Jeremy's thoughts switched to Amanda. He didn't know if she had heard the news, or how she would feel if she had.

Walking through the door the look on her face told him everything.

"Jeremy, have you heard?"

"I heard at the grocery store. Here, help me with these, please. I'll get the rest of the things. Then we can talk."

He handed her the bags then started back to the car.

"And?" she asked once he'd returned.

"And, I called William to verify what I heard. Mr. Bonner has been arrested, but he is already out on bond."

"So... Where does that leave me? Am I going home?"

"Not yet," Jeremy replied. While he put the groceries away, he explained what he had overheard along with what William and him had discussed. "Now, shall we eat? I picked us up a sandwich for lunch."

They ate their meal in silence, neither of them knowing exactly what would happen next, or how far George would go to get the charges dropped. No one trusted George.

"I made a stop before I went to the grocery store," he said breaking the silence. "I didn't think two pair of jeans and two t-shirts would suffice when we didn't know how long you would be here. I put your new things in your room. I think you need to put them away."

A few minutes later, he heard her exclamation of delight when she found the surprise he had hidden in one of the bags.

"JEREMY!" she said, as she ran up the hall. "Oh, my God, it's gorgeous! I'll cherish this forever!"

She opened the box and stared down at the ring, its diamonds and emeralds, shining up from their setting.

"Make sure it fits," Jeremy said. "Try it on."

"But, why'd you buy me this?"

"Think of it as a souvenir. A reminder that if you are ever in need of anything, at anytime, you are to call. Wear it on your right hand as a symbol of our friendship. I hope our memories will be strong enough for you to remember me."

"I will never forget you Jeremy." She gave him a kiss then he slid it on her finger as she thought about what he had meant. "It fits perfect. How do you do it?"

"A practiced eye. Now, I want to remember you just as you are. Happy, smiling, and beautiful. I'm trying very hard to get us back to a sense of normalcy."

"You mean we had a normal somewhere in all of this?"

"You do have a point there, madam." He shooed her down the hall to finish putting her things away. "Tomorrow we start more training," he called after her.

59

Amanda woke and rolled over facing the clock. Five a.m. She listened intently for any sounds that might have disturbed her, but all was quiet. She pulled her robe on and walked to the breakfast bar. A shadow moved on the deck and she immediately feared the worse, George had found her. She moved up close to the glass and peered outside but saw nothing then moved to the sliders and pinched a tiny section of the curtain to the side. The pool surround was up, moonlight reflecting off the water, steam rising invitingly from its surface. But nothing was out of place. Had it been an animal? They were in the country. She padded quietly to Jeremy's room and hoped she didn't sound paranoid.

When she sat on the bed he opened his eyes, lids heavy from sleep. He had kept to his word about the training and they were both exhausted by the time evening came.

"Miss Amanda," Jeremy said. "What are you doing in here?"

"I woke up and couldn't get back to sleep. I saw something outside. I don't know if it was an animal or what, but it was in the back by the deck."

"I'll check for you."

"Do you mind? Something doesn't feel right."

"I'll be back in a few minutes."

There was the slightest of nods as Jeremy slipped on his jeans then moved silently through the house checking that all doors and windows were secure, before moving to the grounds. He found nothing, deciding to check again in the morning.

He returned to his room and found Amanda asleep on top of the covers. Jeremy pulled the bedspread up and slid in beside her feeling her snuggle up close then he kissed her forehead. She giggled and draped her arm over his side. He closed his eyes and breathed in the scent of Amanda.

Amanda awoke once again to the aroma of fresh coffee. Jeremy was already up. He was always up before her. Sliding from under the bedspread, she shrugged on her robe and picked up her nightclothes then padded to the breakfast bar.

"Good morning, my lady. How did you sleep last night?" Then the frown appeared. "It's alright, my lady. We are not the only people who have done this."

"I know. It's just." She hesitated. "Uncomfortable, I guess. I feel so stupid."

"Just being curious now," he said, pouring her coffee. "But how many men have you known – in this manner?"

"Counting you and my ex?" she asked as she blushed. "Three."

"I think I understand now. But just so you know, you are far from being considered a whore. Okay?"

"Okay, but what if we don't see each other again?"

"Then we don't," he stated matter-of-factly. She nodded and he chuckled. "Let's try this again. How did you sleep?"

"Heavenly, how did you sleep?" Amanda took the proffered cup as the grin broadened. "What are you smiling about? You look like you have something on your mind."

"Heavenly. I always have something on my mind when I see a

beautiful woman first thing in the morning."

She dropped her head. "I assume you found nothing last night."

"Not on the grounds, but I found a nice surprise sleeping in my bed." He laughed when she looked away. "I checked things again this morning and I found footprints, but I don't know if they were made by the guards or if someone was here. I will keep a closer on eye things."

"So it wasn't my imagination. Sometimes I feel like I'm going loony."

"Rest assured you are not going loony."

"What are our plans?" Amanda asked "Where do we go from here?"

"We continue to wait. If they want you to testify, William will let us know and we will go to Salt Lake City."

"Why? They have the tapes. They have our statements. I don't want to see that man again, ever!"

"That's between the judge and the attorney's," Jeremy replied. "Currently, the DA is trying to get them to allow the statement, citing duress on your part if you are forced to face Mr. Bonner again."

"Can we do one night of nothing? Order a pizza?"

"Of course. I thought you might like an afternoon to relax anyway. What would you like to do?"

"You decide."

"I have the perfect idea."

They spent the day hiking in a small valley and riding the three-wheeler. On their way back, Jeremy checked a tree branch hanging precariously low on the fence. It wouldn't be long before it was resting on the fence. He couldn't have that. The security line ran along that section of fenceline and if it was damaged it would compromise the system. They got back to the house and he notified the guards then ordered the pizza. It had been nice to wander without any particular agenda. They had done nothing important, but it had been a satisfying day.

"I'll clean up and see you in a few," he said.

"I suppose that means I should, too."

They started toward their rooms when the sounds of people scuffling echoed up the hall, stopping Jeremy in his tracks.

"JEREMY!" Amanda yelled. "DAMN YOU! JEREMY!"

He bolted from his room as a man dragged Amanda toward the deck. Jeremy raced after them trying to figure out how the man had gotten in. Outside Jeremy scanned to the south toward the fence and located the intruder wrestling Amanda toward the valley. Jeremy vaulted over the deck railing when something dropped to the ground. He automatically checked his pistol, it was still holstered. The person stopped and stared at him, holding Amanda to his right, his eyes narrowing as Jeremy reached for his pager. It wasn't there. Jeremy crouched and groped along the ground, keeping his eyes focused on the man and Amanda. Finding the pager, Jeremy keyed in 9-1-1 then continued his pursuit. The man was charging through the underbrush once more, Amanda's struggling slowing them down.

60

Jeremy's guards received the 9-1-1 alert as well and three minutes into the run his men approached along the fenceline, one from either direction. Jeremy pulled his pistol, holding it behind his leg, continuing to inch closer. The man stopped again, growing anxious which made Jeremy nervous. They could be like caged animals if pushed too far.

"Are you alright, Amanda?" Jeremy asked.

"Yes," she said.

"What's the matter?" the man asked. "You afraid you're going to lose your new source of income? You going to use her like George wanted to?"

"She is only here until George goes to prison," Jeremy replied.

"BULLSHIT!" he bellowed. "You're just like all the others. You only see dollar signs. You want to see what happens to your whores when we find them?"

The sudden change in the conversation confused Jeremy.

"That's what she is, isn't she? Just another whore sent to maim an American GI. I'm not stupid; I've been in country longer than a week."

"No. It's not like that. Release her and we can talk about this."

A twig snapped behind him and the man spun around, grasping Amanda with one hand, brandishing the knife with the other. He turned back to face Jeremy, his eyes panicked, the knife held against Amanda's throat. Jeremy slipped his gun into the back of his waist, holding both hands up.

The guard to Jeremy's left moved out of cover, placing himself in front of Amanda and her assailant, then leaned his rifle against the fence, holding his hands up and out. The man waved him away from the rifle with the knife. The second guard took a step forward and the assailant spun to look at him. He had lowered his weapon, holding his hands up as well. The man looked back at Jeremy, the rear guard silently picking his rifle up once again.

Jeremy crept closer, putting himself in a better position, then the man grabbed Amanda's throat with one hand and dropped his knife blade. He leaned forward and whispered in her ear; Amanda nodded, but didn't complete the move. Instead she held her hands near her waist, coiled and waiting. The man shifted the knife to his left hand holding her with his forearm the blade close to her throat, then he started to unbutton his clothing.

"I'm going to have some fun before I slice your precious whore," the man called. "See, I don't mind audiences."

Amanda moved swiftly, taking the man by surprise as she raised her arms. Grabbed the arm holding the knife she thrust it away from her, while she twisted and ducked, elbowing him in the side during the move. He dropped the knife then she jumped forward, turning and striking him in the throat. His eyes opened wide and he choked, surprised by what had just occurred.

Amanda reached to his right, wrestling a pistol out of his waist. The guard in front of them picked up his rifle and aimed at the intruder, Amanda took a step back, keeping the pistol aimed at his forehead. Jeremy raised his weapon and started forward.

"What in the hell are you doing?" Amanda asked.

Jeremy hesitated, puzzled, as the man shrugged.

"I have gone through all of this hell because of you!" She dropped her gaze and her eyes narrowed. "You were the jackass in Reno? What the hell? I should have let George's goon shoot you in Salt Lake City."

Jeremy dropped his eyes and glimpsed the blood on the man's shirt. Her strike had reopened the wound. Then he remembered the photo he had given James and William. This was Royce Warden. In Reno he had been covered in grease paint.

Royce glanced down for a second and Jeremy moved in.

"AMANDA, DROP!" Jeremy yelled.

Royce lunged forward toward Amanda then there was the 'thub' of a silencer and Amanda obeyed, blood running down Royce's face. She had fired. She hadn't faltered. Jeremy raced forward; his only thoughts of reaching her. She stumbled toward him, Royce's body falling in the same direction. The rear guard grabbed Royce's shirt and used Royce's momentum to fling him toward the fence, the front guard grabbing Amanda then he pushed her toward Jeremy. Jeremy caught her, holding her.

Police sped through the gate, lights flashing and sirens screaming. Amanda clung to Jeremy as they went over the attack and her suspicions about the occurrences in Salt Lake City. Before the officers left, Jeremy asked that they lift a set of prints off the deceased man and send them to the Salt Lake City Police Department.

After the officers had left, Jeremy sat on the sofa beside her and stared out the sliding glass doors. A part of his normally safe retreat had become a crime scene.

"I need to talk to my men. Will you be alright for a short time?"

Amanda nodded.

Jeremy stopped in his office first and sent a memo through Salt

Lake City's system letting them know about the fingerprints. When he had finished he went outside to talk to his men.

The absence of any notification bothered Jeremy. There should have been an alert when Royce entered the house. Then he remembered the shadow the night before. He inspected the door onto the deck and found a thin magnetic strip wire hooked to the alarm with alligator clips. Royce had disabled the alarm here and in Reno. Reports had told them Royce's assignment in Vietnam involved more than time in the jungle, this confirmed it.

Jeremy was finishing up the reset on the security system when his phone rang. It was William. They were in the office going over a few last minute details when the memo came through the system. They wanted to know what had happened. And they couldn't wait to receive the prints for comparison.

Jeremy explained, including some of the things Amanda had told the officer's. They all agreed with her summations, but were surprised. The police had been scouring Salt Lake City and Royce had followed her to Reno and Cedar City.

Jeremy joined Amanda, creating an impromptu dance floor in the living room, took a bottle of wine out of the wine cooler and put the pizza in the center of a small table, and then he seated her and started the music. They had paper plates, napkins and plenty to drink. He just wanted her to relax.

"Would you care to dance?"

She smiled and he offered her his hand. While they danced he thought about how much he loved the feel of her body as it moved with his, and the way it had felt the time they had snuggled up in front of the fireplace. He found himself amazed at how one person could have such a profound effect on others. She didn't even try. She just walked into the room.

Jeremy lay down beside Amanda that night, pulling her close and starting the dance again. A dance he would never grow tired of, her body moving in complete unison with his once again. How could something feel so perfect when he had allowed it to get totally out of control?

Waking later, Jeremy brushed the hair off Amanda's cheek and thought about how he would continue his work. He couldn't do this job in the same manner any longer. Amanda had changed that. She had made him realize how much more was at stake for some of the women these men were using. He still wanted to help them, but he had to find a new avenue for giving the women that aid. He reached over and kissed her softly on the cheek, and she ran her hand up his back. The most exciting dance of his life. He really had screwed up this assignment.

"You okay?" she mumbled.

"Never better," he replied.

61

Amanda finally received the news she had been waiting for. George Bonner was on his way to prison, and she could go home, bringing the ordeal to a close. And she wouldn't have to face the man in court. The tapes Jeremy gave them, along with their statements and the recording of their meeting with Dan, had clinched the deal. It took jurors less than one day to come to a verdict, and even less time to sentence him. A few charges for prostitution had been dropped, but those didn't count in the grander scheme of things. George's attorney would file appeals which could take years. Amanda didn't care. It was the end of September and she could have her job back at Berringer & Hardy. And Eddie was waiting with open arms when she wanted to return to singing.

"And you live in a new apartment," William told her during one of their phone conversations.

She covered the phone with her hand and looked up at Jeremy.

"I live in a new apartment," she said. "How did I manage that?"

"Don't know, my lady, but I imagine we'll find out."

A week later, William was giving her the grand tour. Jeremy and James stayed in the background while William walked her through.

"Originally I wanted to have it all decorated and everything put away," William said. "But I'm not as good at that as you are so I decided to wait. I just thought you might not want all the bad memories associated with the old apartment. Anyway, this is about the same as the one you had and we pitched in and paid the first three months rent for you. That should give you time to get things going at work and everything. I'm babbling aren't I?" he said.

"Something like that. Are you alright, William? And who are 'we'?"

"Timothy, James, the girls from Berringer & Hardy and me. We didn't want you worrying about anything. Oh, and look at the closet in this bedroom." He took her by the hand and led her back up the hall. "I know how women like their closet space so… You know… What do you think?"

"I think it's perfect. Why are you so nervous?"

"I was so afraid I would never see you again…. I should shut up, shouldn't I?"

"I understand," she replied. "I missed you, too."

"Okay. I didn't know how you would feel. So… Um… This is hard. How do you feel?"

"Well….Since I just got home from going through hell, and I still feel completely overwhelmed, I really don't know. Maybe we should take the time to relax and be real people instead of cop and victim. I hope I said that right. I care for you very much and I can't imagine not seeing you, but I want to meet me again."

"That I understand. Are you ready to join everybody then?"

"Let me change clothes and freshen up," she said. "I'll only be a minute." She had led him back to the living room.

"I want to stop and change, too," he said. That wasn't exactly the answer he wanted to hear, but she hadn't completely blocked the pass. She'd just deflected it.

"I have an idea," Jeremy said. "Let's do dinner and celebrate Miss Amanda's homecoming. Tonight is my treat. Where is a good place eat?"

"Bourbon Street," James replied. "Everyone planned on meeting there anyway."

"Sounds perfect," Jeremy said.

"Is everybody ready?" William asked. "I know I am."

Amanda glanced across the living room at Jeremy. Something was bothering him.

"William, Jeremy and I will meet you after I change. I promise to hurry and that will give you time to change. Go ahead." After James and William left Amanda walked over and took Jeremy's hands in hers. "You look uncomfortable. Is there something I should know?"

"Just a tad," Jeremy answered. "I'm not sure I should say anything, but I don't want to stop seeing you, my lady." He could train a woman to be the perfect arm candy, but couldn't tell the perfect woman how he felt.

"I don't want to stop seeing you either, Jeremy. Maybe I'll be able to visit before the snow flies."

"That is all I need to hear. And you still have my promise." He held her right hand up, showing off the ring. "I will always be here if you need me. I will probably get myself a room tonight, though."

"As you wish," she said. "Just so you know. William and I are going to try and get past the cop and victim thing first. Does that make sense?"

"Actually, it makes perfect sense. And we still have a date at Lake Tahoe."

"Can we wait until spring?"

"We can wait until spring. Now, shall we celebrate your homecoming?"

They had only been at Bourbon Street a couple of hours before Amanda grew uncomfortable. Everyone sensed it and made the decision to end the party early. Jeremy was first to leave. He thought William wanted to spend time with Amanda. William and Amanda left next. She was feeling anxious. William just wanted to hold Amanda. Back at her apartment, he flipped the deadbolt and put his arms around her.

"Amanda, you act like you're frightened."

She glanced around at the bare walls.

"There aren't any cameras here," William said, noticing the move.

"I know." Then she laughed. "I used to hang a washcloth over the camera in the shower. I always took two with me. One to wash with and one to cover the camera. I guess this episode has had more of an effect on me than I thought. It's nice to be home."

"I was going to ask if you'd like a guest for the evening" he whispered. "But I don't know how you feel."

She shrugged.

"I'll be perfectly happy just holding you," he added. "That isn't the only reason I missed you."

She nodded and held on tight. She had missed her caramel colored eyes and skin like velvet. She felt safe when he held her.

"You get to make omelets in the morning."

"I haven't been to the store yet," William answered. "It looks like we get to order omelets to go."

"Damn the bad luck."

62

Jeremy drove back to Cedar City the next morning considering this new dilemma. He had finally found a woman he wanted to stay with but didn't know if he should pursue her. Maybe he should allow her to have that normal life she said she wanted, give her and William time to work things out. That might be the best. Maybe it wasn't. Why was this so difficult all of a sudden?

He pulled through the gates and sat in the Beast for a few minutes feeling the silence. The place already felt empty. At least he had two weeks with her at Lake Tahoe in the spring.

As he entered the house, he keyed in 'Downtime' on his pager, and hit enter then walked to the room she had used. He closed his eyes, still smelled her perfume, saw her body under the covers, heard her laughter at the breakfast bar, and opened them again, gazing around the room. He could count the nights he had spent with her on one hand, but they had been the best nights of his life. She had wormed her way under his skin without even trying.

Once again, he debated staying in this line of work. But what else would he do. There wasn't much call for an unemployed undercover law enforcement operative with no ties to anyone.

Fax tones drew Jeremy away from his thoughts and he hurried to the office to retrieve the sheets it was spewing forth. The top sheet was his confirmation along with a short message.

Thank you for your hard work. We have an up and comer to monitor. The information net says George is still active from the inside and his nephew, Jonathan, is being groomed to take over. Pull a four person team together as soon as you're able. We are growing. Next stop – the syndicate.

He already knew the people he wanted on that team, and he would see Amanda again.